THE

By Harriet Smart

The Butchered Man: Northminster Mystery 1
The Dead Songbird: Northminster Mystery 2
The Shadowcutter: Northminster Mystery 3
The Hanging Cage: Northminster Mystery 4
The Ghosts of Ardenthwaite: Northminster Mystery 5
The Echo at Rooke Court: Northminster Mystery 6
The Fatal Engine: Northminster Mystery 7
The Witches of Pitfeldry: Northminster Mystery 8
Moonshine and Mercury: Northminster Mystery 9
Tarleton's Coffer: Northminster Mystery 10
The Wounded Oak: Northminster Mystery 11
Mummer's Night: A Northminster Novella
Carswell's First Case: A Northminster Novella
Emma Vernon's Northminster Ghost Stories
The Dolls at Heron's Reach
The True Value of Pearls
The Daughters of Blane
Green Grow the Rushes
The Wild Garden
The Lark Ascending
Reckless Griselda
A Tempting Proposal

THE HANGING CAGE

by

Harriet Smart

Published by Anthemion

Fourth Edition

ISBN 978-1-907873-57-7

Made with Jutoh

Chapter One

A hotel ballroom was an incongruous resting place for a corpse, Felix Carswell thought.

However, the room did not appear in any guise of gaiety. In the dull grey light of a stormy day in November, a little before noon, it was hard to imagine dancing or music, let alone flirtation.

It was just as well, given the grim circumstances. The previous afternoon, an inquest had been summoned there, after an unfortunate young woman had been found dead in her bed. The coroner had at once adjourned the inquest and sent for Major Vernon to come from Northminster to The Falcon Hotel in Whithorne, a market town to the south east of the county.

"She poisoned herself, gentlemen," Dr Fellowes said to Felix and Major Vernon, as soon as they came in. "And really I do not see why there is any need for your being here, let alone for a post-mortem. The girl seems to have drunk a noxious skin tonic. The servant said she saw it sitting on the dressing table the evening before – the bottle quite full. It was empty the next morning. Perhaps she even meant to destroy herself."

"And what makes you think that?" Major Vernon said.

"She was somewhat skittish. Hysterical, even."

"Miss Barker was your patient?" Felix said.

"No, but she was an acquaintance. She was friends, of sorts, with my younger daughter – not a great intimate, we did not wish to encourage that – but they are of similar ages and she has – she had – been the novelty of the town for the last four months."

"And why was that?" Major Vernon asked.

"She was supposedly worth upwards of fifty thousand. Or so her guardian has put about. What the truth of it is, I don't know."

"That would be Mr Ampner?" said Major Vernon. Dr Fellowes nodded.

"I wonder where the money goes now," Dr Fellowes went on. "Or if there even is any."

"You think Mr Ampner may have exaggerated her circumstances?" Major Vernon said.

"It wouldn't be the first time," Fellowes said. "My own fool of a brother nearly came to grief in such circumstances in Leeds some thirty years ago – he was sure she had a fortune." Fellowes sighed at the memory of it.

"And you think Mr Ampner capable of such sleight of hand?" the Major said.

"He would want her married," Fellowes said. "Miss Barker wasn't exactly marriageable, if you want my frank opinion."

"Why do you think that?" said Major Vernon.

"See for yourselves, gentlemen," said Dr Fellowes, and climbed onto the dais on which the body was lying on a trestle table, covered by a sheet. He turned back the sheet to uncover her face.

Felix climbed up to join him and could not help but frown at what he saw.

Miss Barker was calm in death. Her serene expression combined with her youth and her beautiful coffee-coloured complexion were striking. He bent over her, wondering if he could detect a faint scent of bitter almonds, and then peered at her skin. Was there a bluish tint to it, indicating that prussic acid might have been at work? It was hard to see in the grey light.

"Poor child," murmured Major Vernon.

Fellowes went on: "Quadroon, I should say. Handsome of course, yes, but..." He covered her face again.

"I need to take her back to Northminster for the post-mortem," Felix said. Major Vernon nodded. "As soon as possible."

If prussic acid was involved there was no time to be lost, for it was a volatile substance.

"As you wish," said Dr Fellowes. "Though what you hope to achieve, I don't know. I strongly recommended a verdict of death by misadventure – there is charity in that – but young Master Johnny Earle was very insistent on adjourning the inquest and sending for you. When his father was coroner, we would not have had any of this business, but then we did not have silly young women with more money than sense, running rings around their guardians. If you ask me, Johnny Earle had his eye on her, like all the young bucks about here, and it's clouded his judgement."

The door at the far end of the room opened and a young man, tall but rather stoop-shouldered, came briskly in, taking off his rain-soaked overcoat.

"Major Vernon, my apologies, I was called away," he said, throwing the coat over a chair. He came up to them, hand extended. "John Earle, at your service."

"A pleasure, sir," said Major Vernon. "This is my colleague, Mr Carswell. He is a medical man."

"Dr Fellowes has outlined the matter to you?" Earle said, shaking Felix's hand.

"Yes," said Felix, though he would have liked to say that his outline was ill-considered and prejudicial.

"Thank you for coming so promptly," Earle went on. "I hope your journey was not too arduous. This weather and that road are not good companions."

"We made good time, all things considered," Major Vernon said.

The carriage had, in fact, got stuck twice on the way, as the road had turned to mud as they approached Whithorne. They had left at a little after six and travelled all morning – a laborious eighteen miles, even in Major Vernon's new carriage.

"You must excuse me now, gentlemen. I have living souls to see to," Dr Fellowes said. "If that is all, Earle?"

"Yes, thank you, sir," said Earle.

Fellowes left, and Felix could not help wondering, from his girth and his flushed complexion, if he would not make a detour to the coffee room for a glass or two of port before continuing on his rounds.

Mr Earle now stood looking down at the covered corpse, a melancholy expression on his face.

"I understand you knew Miss Barker?" Major Vernon said.

"Yes," he said. "I only danced with her the other night – here. She was in the highest of spirits that night – the night before she died." He turned away and said, "I must be plain with you, sir. I was attracted to her. I cannot deny it, and I wasn't the only man in the town to feel it. She had a quality – she was certainly sought after. But she and I, well, we had formed an understanding, at least I think we had. I told her that night that she had engaged my feelings, and that I was willing to marry, if..."

He stopped and climbed down from the dais, and then walked a few paces down the room, attempting to compose himself.

"My mother was not entirely happy," Mr Earle said. "Of course, I do not need consent from anyone – but when a man marries, he brings a new daughter into the house and it matters that the women should not be at... well, I shall not say loggerheads, for that would be disrespectful both to my mother and to Miss Barker. I am certain they would have moved heaven and earth to avoid such things, but I wished to spare them the effort. I wanted the matter entirely smooth before I went further, and I explained this to Miss Barker, who of course, understood perfectly..." He broke off again. "I fear I could not be impartial in the matter, so I adjourned the inquest. It seemed the only thing to do. There are too many questions to which I could not find answers. As I said, she was in high spirits – our conversation had pleased her, and when we parted, well, we were both full of hope. That this..."

He gestured back towards where her body lay. "I cannot believe it, although I have seen the evidence with my own eyes."

"Are you prepared to allow me to undertake a post-mortem, sir?" Felix said after a moment. "I would like to do it back in Northminster. There are some complex tests that will have to be made, given that poison may have been involved."

The thought of the post-mortem clearly distressed Earle. After a moment he said, "Yes, of course. You will need my signature."

He walked down the room to the table where the papers from the inquest had been laid out, sat down and wrote out the necessary permission. He blotted it dry and handed it to Felix.

"Thank you for your candour, Mr Earle," Major Vernon said. "Now, this is a mere formality, you will understand, but in the light of what you have told me, I must ask it. What did you do after Miss Barker had left the ball, which you say was a little after eleven?"

"I would have gone home, but my mother and my sisters were with me, and my sisters would not have been at all pleased with me if I'd made them leave before the final dance. I did dance again with Miss Thriplow and then with Agnes, my sister, and then we went home after that, when the party broke up."

"And you were at home for the rest of the night?"

"Yes, naturally. We walked home – we live not far away. I sat up doing some work until one or so in the morning, and then I went to bed, as usual."

"And a servant or perhaps one of your family could testify to that?"

"No," he said. "I am always the last to go to bed." He got up from the table. "I had better go and make arrangements for her removal, if you will excuse me."

And they were at last alone with the corpse.

Felix, who had only been allowed the most cursory glance by Dr Fellowes, drew back the sheet and looked at her with more care. Major Vernon joined him.

"A love-struck coroner and possible poisoning," said Major Vernon.

"And lots of money, apparently," said Felix, taking out his hand lens.

"Not to mention her exotic ancestry," said Major Vernon. "One hopes she wasn't made to suffer because of it. That might be a reason for self-destruction, of course. Not easy to have such a heritage, even if she was so handsome. What was it Dr Fellowes said: 'the novelty of the town'? He did not spare her his contempt, even in death. That wouldn't be easy to deal with, and she was so very young. Even Mr Earle's declaration of love, sincere though I'm sure it was, was damning with faint praise."

"And the high spirits a façade?" Felix said.

"Perhaps," said Major Vernon. "Perhaps she had learnt to put on the most pleasing appearance for all of them. And then that grew too much for her to bear."

"It is more likely to be that than anything," said Felix. "When poison is involved, it is most commonly linked to self-destruction – the statistics bear that out, year after year. And her age and sex count against her in that matter. But one can never be certain until we have more facts. Unlike Dr Fellowes, I don't think that the circumstances alone indicate it."

"Then we will call on Mr Ampner, and see those circumstances for ourselves."

"With luck they have preserved some evidence," said Felix. "I want to see that bottle of tonic, for a start."

Leaving the ballroom, they found a man waiting to speak

to them.

"I am Hawkins, the undertaker here, sir," he said. "Mr Earle said you want her taken to Northminster. Are you sure?"

"A necessary inconvenience, I'm afraid," said Major Vernon. "To the Constabulary Headquarters at The Unicorn."

"Normally there would be no difficulty, sir," said Mr Hawkins, "but now, with this rain... you will have seen the state of the road this morning. It will be impassable now. To be frank, sir, it might be better to wait until tomorrow, or even the day after."

"It was half-flooded already," Major Vernon said. "Mr Carswell, can it wait?"

"No later than tomorrow," Felix said, "if at all possible. Otherwise I shall have to do it here."

"I shall do my best as soon as I can, sir," said Hawkins. "We're like an island here in Whithorne, when the rain comes and the river swells. Spring and autumn, you can never be sure of anything." He shrugged. "Sometimes, I wonder how they are going to get that railway in over Yardley's Marsh. They've been working away at it long enough."

They left him to his work and went to the private parlour that Mr Earle had arranged for them at the hotel. Here they found a cheerful fire, sherry, coffee and sandwiches.

"I wish they had finished the railway already," said Felix, going to the window and looking out at the sodden and deserted street. The rain was now lashing the window as the wind got up. "That road was diabolical."

"We will certainly not be going home today," Major Vernon said, from the fireside. "Fortunately, this seems a comfortable enough place."

"Unlike the rest of this town," said Felix, shivering and joining Major Vernon by the hearth, "if Dr Fellowes is typical. I should not trust him to treat a dog."

Major Vernon smiled, and poured the coffee. Felix sat down by the fire and stared into it, a beef and mustard sandwich in his hand. He ate and attempted to be philosophical. He had not really expected to get back to Northminster that day – Major Vernon had already warned they might be away for at least a night, given the remoteness of the town, and he had packed accordingly. But the necessary absence now tugged at him. He had been obliged to leave in a great hurry and he felt he had parted from Sukey badly.

They had begun a conversation the night before which had not ended well, and he knew from her manner that he had given offence. She had said he was forgiven, yet he had not felt it. She had rolled away from him and gone to sleep. So he had left her bed and gone upstairs to his own room, a miserable procedure at the best of times, and particularly wretched in these circumstances.

He had thought of leaving her a note, but could not think what to write, and had fallen asleep having failed at the task, and when the morning came there had been no time.

She had been in the hall to see them off, but Major Vernon had also been there. There had not been a moment to say anything of use and he had not even been able to kiss her goodbye. Now he was eighteen miles away, marooned in this strange town, for how long he could not imagine.

There was a knock at the door and the waiter came in, enquiring, "Excuse me, gentlemen, I am right in this – one of you is a doctor?"

"Yes," said Felix, with his mouth full of bread and butter. "I am."

"I've a woman here needs your help. She's come from her mistress. Will you see her? She's expecting – her mistress, that is. It's Mrs Yardley up at the castle."

"Yes, of course, send her in," Felix said.

The servant followed the waiter into the room, her clothes showing all the signs of the continuing downpour.

"I've been looking all over for Dr Fellowes but I can't find him," she said. "They said at his house he was here, but he ain't. Will you come to her, sir? She's bleeding, bleeding like nothing else."

"Of course," Felix said, getting up and draining his coffee cup.

The woman glanced skywards, as if to thank God for the providence.

"This way, sir," she said, going to the door, as he pulled on his overcoat. Major Vernon held out his medical bag and hat, like a well-trained footman.

"There is a short cut through the back here," the woman said, already halfway down the passageway.

"When did the bleeding start?" he said, as he followed her.

"A little yesterday before she went to bed, and then it stopped. But this morning, about two hours ago, it began again. It's shocking to see it."

"And how close is she to term?"

"Eight and a half months," said the woman.

"First labour?"

"Yes," said the servant. "But she's miscarried a few times since."

"How old is she?"

"Just twenty, sir. She was nearly a child when she married," and then added darkly, "too young."

"Were you her nurse?" Felix asked.

"Yes, sir," she said.

He followed her out of the hotel into a paved court, and then through a gate which led to a twisting lane, bounded on both sides with high walls. Another gate led to a steep and treacherous path, down which the rain was running in torrents.

At last, they reached a substantial stone gateway, the shelter of which provided momentary relief from the downpour. Felix wanted to catch his breath for a moment, but the servant went swiftly on and he had to follow her across a great courtyard to the imposing grey stone edifice that loomed up in front of them. On a bright day it might have looked picturesque. In such disgusting weather, it looked like a prison.

This impression was not dispelled as they entered the house. They crossed a cheerless great hall, bristling with a panoply of dangerous-looking weapons. Felix thought he saw, hanging from the rafters, one of those notorious cages in which it had once been the barbaric custom to place the bodies of executed criminals.

He followed the woman up a great staircase hung with threadbare tapestries, and through a succession of large apartments. These rooms might have been luxurious and impressive had they not been so ill-lit and crammed with ugly old furniture.

At last, after the ascent of another set of stairs, this time set into a tower, they reached the young mother.

Her room was a little better than those they had passed through: there was a fire in the great fireplace, numerous oil lamps had been lit, and the ancient bed had been hung with bright, modern chintz. Yet the same profusion of ancient knick-knacks covered all the other surfaces, and the window had panes of coloured glass further obscuring the light.

His patient was not in her bed, but on a low chair. This might have been comfortable and practical for a woman in her advanced condition, had it not had a ludicrously high back, formed into a crocketed arch. It would have suited a sturdy bishop in a cathedral, but not a fragile girl.

Mrs Yardley was little more than a girl, and very small and slight. The great distension of her belly only added to the idea that her maid had suggested earlier: that she was not formed to bear children.

As he approached her, Felix fixed his expression into what he hoped was a polite, encouraging smile, and reminded himself that such appearances were often deceptive. Women had a strength and courage in these matters that could carry them through the most arduous and unpromising conditions.

At the same time he noticed that the pail sitting nearby was full of heavily bloodied napkins.

She stared up at him, her face pale from blood loss.

"Who is this, Grace? Where is Dr Fellowes?" She spoke very softly. She was clearly already very tired.

"This is Dr Carswell, ma'am," said Grace. "I found him at The Falcon. Dr Fellowes was not to be found, but providence sent this gentleman."

"I am from Northminster, ma'am," Felix said.

"But you are a Scotsman," said Mrs Yardley.

"Yes, ma'am."

"My mama always liked Scotch doctors," she said, and managed a wan smile, which was encouraging.

"That is what I thought, ma'am," said Grace. "The moment he opened his mouth, I knew he was heaven-sent!"

"Will you let me help you, ma'am?" he said.

Mrs Yardley nodded, and Felix hoped he would not disappoint her. There was no knowing what complications he was about to be faced with.

"When did you last have a contraction?" he asked, crouching down beside her.

"Not for an hour or so – is that not right, Ellen?" she said, consulting the other servant in the room.

"That's right, ma'am."

Felix knew then he would have to work fast. These were not promising signs. There was a chance that the child was already dead. He pulled off his coat and rolled up his sleeves.

"Perhaps if you could manage to get onto the bed?"

She assented, and with Grace's help, staggered the few steps across the room. They then arranged her on the edge of the bed, which was fortunately well raised from the ground, with a pile of pillows to support her, and kneeling on the floor, he was able to make a proper examination.

The bleeding was still worryingly profuse and the cause clear enough: the placenta had detached itself and was presenting itself, blocking the os uteri and the safe passage of the child. Another difficulty was that the child appeared to be lying in the breech, in which case he would first have to turn the child and then deliver it. He would probably have to use forceps: a useful instrument, but a risky one.

Chapter Two

"Who is Mrs Yardley?" Giles asked the waiter.

"The Squire's lady. Lives at the castle. Up the lane behind here, sir," said the waiter, gathering the dirty crockery onto his tray.

"And he's the principal gentleman in the town?"

"Yes, sir, in town. But then there is Lord Milburne's place, Woodville Park. That's a much bigger house, and very handsome. I was thinking of going for a place there. There's been talk of the new young Lord taking on a lot of new people. He's been throwing money around, they say. Thought he might pay well."

Giles smiled. "He's only recently come into the property, then?"

"Yes, sir, very recently. Saw him at church the other Sunday. Quite the swell, he is. Looks the part. The story is that he only got it by chance. He never thought he was going to get it, but there were all these deaths in the family, and he gets a letter saying it's all his now, and the title. Imagine the luck of that! Ah, it's all right for some."

"A large fortune, then?"

"So they say. Mrs White, that's the mistress here, she likes to reckon things up. She says he must be worth forty thousand pounds a year." The waiter shook his head. "And he had scarcely nowt before. Quite a tale, isn't it?"

~

The guardians of the late Miss Barker, Mr and Mrs Frederick

Ampner, lived in some style, in a large, modern house on the edge of the town, with its own small park. It would have been an easy walk in good weather, but as the rain persisted Giles was glad he could travel there in a closed carriage.

Mr Ampner, an attorney in late middle age, was as substantial in his figure as in his property and received Giles in a well-appointed study. He seemed genuinely affected by the circumstances.

"Fellowes seemed certain she took her own life," he said. "But I pray that is not the case. I am glad Mr Earle sent for you to not let that verdict prevail – at least not without some investigation. Yet, I do keep thinking, given the bottle we found in her room, that it's not beyond the bounds of possibility. But why – that is the great question. Neither my wife nor I can think of any reason why Annabella would..." He stopped, his distress evident enough. "Mrs Ampner is not well," he went on after a moment. "This business has utterly prostrated her. I have sent for Dr Fellowes to come and see to her, but he is taking his time."

"He seems to have been in demand today," Giles said. "My colleague, Mr Carswell, who is a medical man, was called away to the castle to attend to Mrs Yardley because Dr Fellowes could not be found."

"It would not be the first time," said Ampner. "Dr Fellowes, well – I do not like to gossip, Major Vernon, but he is believed to be intemperate, and he is certainly unreliable. That is why Johnny Earle sent for you. He feels, and with some reason, that Dr Fellowes' judgement cannot entirely be trusted. But we are all at his mercy, given there is no other doctor in the town, and the apothecary is too wretched a specimen to have any confidence in. Mrs Yardley is fortunate to have secured your colleague's services. Perhaps he might call on Mrs Ampner later?"

"Certainly," Giles said. "He needs to collect various specimens from here, you will understand. I'm asked to enquire how much evidence has been preserved."

"Oh, it is all there, just as it was found yesterday morning. Johnny Earle told us to close the door on it, when she was taken away. We knew of course that you gentlemen would need to see it all."

"Perhaps you could give me the sequence of events as they happened yesterday?" Giles said, taking out his notebook. "At what time was Miss Barker's death discovered?"

"A little after eleven. I wasn't here. I was at my office. Annabella's maid Susan discovered what had happened. She had been told not to wake her before eleven, because of the ball the night before. In fact, both Mrs Ampner and Annabella, and indeed Mrs Ampner's brother, were all still abed."

"Mrs Ampner's brother? His name, sir?"

"George Gosforth."

"He lives here with you?"

"He's on a long visit," said Ampner with a pained expression.

"So Susan went in and found her mistress insensible?"

"Yes, and went at once to my wife. And my wife sent for Dr Fellowes, who I think came just after noon, about when I came back home, for Mrs Ampner sent for me too; and then quite by chance, just as Dr Fellowes was coming downstairs, Johnny Earle walks in. Poor man. He had called to pursue his suit, not find her dead."

"You knew that he hoped to marry her?"

"Yes, he has been frank with me from the start. I told him, 'yes, of course', for he is an excellent fellow, and clearly had the best intentions towards Annabella. But I told him that he must win her fair and square. That the choice would be hers, not mine. Because Annabella was not the sort of girl one could tell to do anything. She was not wilful, sir, don't misunderstand me, but she knew her mind. I liked that in her, and that is why I trusted her to say yea or nay to all those suitors. And that is why I think Johnny is quite right to have sent for you. It cannot be suicide. She was not such a fool, nor so wicked. She was a good girl, a proper Christian."

"And quite a few men wished to marry her?"

"Yes. And not just for her money, but for her character. Which pleased me, for there are some people who would consider her beneath them, because of her mother's people, but I have never held with that sort of nonsense, and I know that is why her father trusted her to my care. He knew..." And then he fell into silence, glancing away from Giles. "My care," he said, quietly, struggling to control his tone. "And now she is dead – dead under my own roof, where she was put to be cared for. I have failed her, and that is the plain truth of it."

There was a tap at the door and a woman's voice said, "May I come in?"

"Of course, my dear," said Ampner, getting up and opening the door. Giles rose and saw a handsome woman in her early thirties, dressed in a striking silk dressing gown.

"Oh, I did not know you had company," she said, seeing Giles and shrinking back a little. "I should go up and dress."

"This is Major Vernon, my dear," Ampner said, taking her hand and leading her into the room. "Major Vernon, this is my wife. I think he will have some questions for you, Mary."

"Only if you are feeling well enough, ma'am," Giles said, making his bow.

"Are you feeling better?" Ampner said.

"Yes, a little," she said.

"I am sorry to say, my dear, that there is no sign of Dr Fellowes."

"I don't think I shall need him after all," said Mrs Ampner. "I am feeling much better now. What I was wondering, though, is where Georgie is. No one seems to have seen him."

"George?" said Mr Ampner. "I have no notion. He will be back for dinner, I am sure."

"I'm worried about him," she said. "He was so distressed last night. He was very fond of her. It has been terrible for him."

"It has been terrible for us all," said Mr Ampner. "And notwithstanding George's distress, I'm disappointed he has not stayed at home to look to you, my dear."

"But he knows I have you to do that," said Mrs Ampner.

"Yes, but a true brother in such circumstances..." Ampner broke off. "Come and sit by the fire, my dear. I do not like you standing in that draught."

She obeyed him, and sat twisting the folds of her dressing gown in her hands.

"He did not even leave a note," she said to her husband.

"And has he ever left a note before?" said Ampner.

"No, no, I suppose not."

"He will be home for dinner," Ampner said, patting her shoulder.

"I hope you do not mind me being so direct, Mrs Ampner," Giles said, "but when you say your brother was fond of Miss Barker, do you mean he had intentions towards her?"

"Oh, goodness no! Georgie would not have presumed. He would not have dared!" said Mrs Ampner. "Of course not. No, it was simply that they were fond of each other. Like brother and sister." She spoke emphatically with an appraising glance at her husband. "We live such a quiet life here," she went on. "And Georgie has been such a comfort. He has been reading to us while we do our work. He reads very well. My late mother always thought he could have gone on the stage."

"And what is your brother's profession?"

"He hasn't quite decided," Mrs Ampner went on. "He's still very young."

"He's one and twenty," said Mr Ampner. "Not so young."

"And you are quite certain there was no romantic

attachment?" Giles said.

"No, no!" she said. "He would not have kept that from me, nor from Mr Ampner. I should not have allowed him to stay if he had said something of that sort." Giles nodded. "Besides, Georgie is in love with quite another young lady – Miss Earle. Perhaps that is where he is now, declaring himself!" She finished with a nervous laugh.

"Lucy Earle?" said Mr Ampner. "Surely not. That's the first I've heard of it. She'll never have him. He has no money to speak of, Major Vernon."

Mrs Ampner looked rather mortified at this and rose from her seat.

"Of course he would not confide in you, my dear," she said after a moment. "Why would he, when you are always so unkind? It's hardly his fault –"

"Unkind?" said Ampner getting up. "And as to the question of fault, well, a man must try to get on, that is the way it is, my dear, and George needs to face that fact, sooner rather than later. He wasn't born to be a gentleman of leisure. He has to work like the rest of us. It may seem cruel, but it isn't." Mrs Ampner stared at him, as if she were about to dissolve into tears. He again rested his hand on her shoulder. "And I am sorry to bring up such a tender subject in front of a stranger, but Annabella is dead, and I can't be pretending at such a time."

His voice broke at the end of this speech and he turned away from them both. Mrs Ampner was staring into the fire and Giles could see there were tears rolling down her face.

"Please excuse me, I shall go and look at Miss Barker's room," said Giles, going to the door. "I shall ask one of the servants the way."

He climbed the stairs, hoping he would not hear the sound of raised voices through the solid door to Mr Ampner's study. He wondered if he would be able to do a brief search of the infamous George's room. He was not entirely convinced by his sister's declaration of a lack of romantic interest. A young man with apparently few prospects and little inclination to work, faced with a beautiful young heiress living in his sister's house, would surely find it hard to resist the opportunity of advancing himself by such means. His unexplained absence and his sister's distress at it only made Giles more interested in speaking to him. He would have to be found and interviewed, even if it was just to eliminate him from any taint of suspicion.

A housemaid, coming out of a bedroom with a basket of dirty linen, was happy to show him to Miss Barker's room, and also to point out the rooms of the other members of the household.

Annabella Barker's room must have been one of the best bedrooms in the house. It was large, with a bay window overlooking the gardens, and no expense had been spared on its decoration. It was the room of a girl who led a comfortable, unfettered existence, with plenty of pin money and a guardian who had great affection for her. There was evidence of the usual pursuits of respectable young women: a satin-wood work-box, a table set up for flower painting, an embroidery hoop on a stand and a guitar lying on the window seat. There were a few books on a fretwork shelf: light, unremarkable works of popular poetry. On the table by the bed lay a well-thumbed Bible and a prayer book. There were ribbons in both, marking the appropriate collects and readings for the time of year, and he noted that she had put the ribbons ready for the next morning's portion of scripture. Would she have done that if she had intended to take her own life?

He turned his attention to the dressing table. Here he found the empty tonic bottle, a piece of evidence that was entirely circumstantial until further tests had been done. Giles wondered why the doctor had been so eager to ascribe the death to this particular tonic, even when a natural cause of death had not yet been ruled out.

The bottle was of a common sort, made with clear glass, but the label pasted on it was not. It had been decorated with painted flowers, and written in fancy script were the words: 'Precious Dew'. The neck of the bottle was embellished with a length of pink silk ribbon, tied in a bow.

Giles removed the stopper and sniffed it. It smelled of rose water.

Also on the dressing table were two lidded baskets, which contained more bottles and pots, a mixture of the medicinal and cosmetic, many with the same carefully decorated labels and different coloured ribbons dangling from their necks. They also had fanciful names. There was another full bottle of 'Precious Dew', but also a flask of 'The Crystal Elixir', pots of 'Crème de Perle' and 'Crème de l'Alabaste', and even a little tin box containing 'Rouge d'Amour'.

Surprisingly, given the care lavished on the labels and the extravagance of the ribbons, the name of the supplier was nowhere to be seen. Perhaps it was discretion on the part of the maker, or Miss Barker had amused herself making up her own concoctions and decorating the containers. But why would Fellowes at once suspect an apparently harmless-looking tonic?

Whatever the case was, Carswell would no doubt wish to test them all.

~

"And you are certain it was this bottle that was full when you left Miss Barker?" Giles asked Susan, Miss Barker's maid. He had asked her to come up to the bedroom.

"Yes, sir."

"And did she say anything to you about it, what it was for?"

"No, sir."

"But you saw it there and saw it was full?"

"Yes, sir."

"Was it there when you were helping Miss Barker to dress for the ball?"

"I think so, sir," said Susan.

"Did you tidy up the dressing table after she had left?"

"Yes, as I always do, sir."

"Were there pots and bottles all over the table?" said Giles, indicating the contents of the baskets.

"I don't really know, sir. I suppose so."

"But you are certain the bottle was there when Miss Barker was getting ready for bed?"

"Are you saying I didn't see what I saw, sir?"

"No, I just want to get it straight for myself. How many candles were lit?"

"I can't remember, sir," she said, with anxious despair in her voice. "I just know what I saw: that the bottle was full that night and in the morning it wasn't. And that my mistress was..."

"Yes?"

She hesitated and glanced away.

"Nervy," she said at last. "Definitely."

"But not melancholy or crying?"

"No, no. Worried, maybe. Not that she said anything about such things to me. She was a good mistress, but not that sort. I wish I could tell you more, sir. She told me to go to my bed after I'd unlaced her, and that she could manage the rest. She told me to remember to say my prayers. And so I went, and that was that." She sighed.

"Were you with your mistress when Dr Fellowes came in?"

"Yes. I didn't want to leave her, sir."

"And when did he first ask you about the bottle on the dressing table? Or did you point it out to him?"

"I did. I told him that it had been full and now it was

empty. I was thinking all sorts, that she – well, she was so..." She made a pantomime of agitation. "I didn't know what was in that stuff. I mean people don't just die, do they, not without a breath of sickness first?"

"You don't know where she got any of these things from, I suppose?" he said, holding up one of the beribboned bottles.

"No."

"She didn't make any of these up herself?" He held it out to her and she took it and stared at it.

"No, no, I don't think so."

"You said she did not confide in you, Susan, but from your observations of her, would you expect that she would take her life?"

"No, sir," she said, emphatically. "That is what I can't understand – why are they all saying that, sir? She was very good, always reading her Bible and telling me to do the same. She knew it was a terrible sin. I can't imagine she'd do it. You mustn't think that she would, sir, I beg you. She was very kind and such a good mistress to me."

~

Giles questioned the other servants, all of whom confirmed Susan's account of things. There was a sense of incredulity at her death, as well as considerable and perhaps uncommon respect for the late Miss Barker. Her virtue was never doubted and her piety much spoken of. Yet intimate with the servants she had not been. They apparently knew nothing.

When he was done, he asked his driver Jack Smith whether anything had been said about Miss Barker that was less complimentary, when he had been drinking his tea in the kitchen. Smith shook his head. He was a good driver, and had an excellent way with horses, but he was taciturn and lacking in curiosity about his fellow men. It would have been better to bring Holt with him on such an expedition, but Holt was taking a week's holiday, visiting his sisters and various other relatives in the north of the county.

Although it was still raining when he had finished his business at the Ampner residence, Giles sent Smith with the carriage and the evidence back to The Falcon without him. He wanted to walk alone. He felt the need of some exercise to start his mind working on the various problems that Miss Barker's death had thrown up.

The rain had eased up a little as he set off, although it was still not by any means enjoyable to walk through.

Giles tried to distract himself with the puzzle that the situation presented, but he could not help but feel as if the cold, dank hand of Death himself was leading him along the deserted streets of Whithorne. He could not forget the youth, beauty and apparent virtue of a woman who now lay in her coffin at the undertakers, her mortal remains awaiting the violation of a post-mortem. He hoped her spirit had found some kind of rest; that her piety had not been in vain and that there was some kind of deliverance for her.

Chapter Three

An hour or so later, Felix was beginning to feel some despair. Kneeling on the floor, stripped down to his shirt sleeves, he had with difficulty managed to turn the child. As a result, there had been a passage when the contractions had begun again, and he had hoped that Nature would assist with the delivery of the child. But they had been feeble and not prolonged, and the child remained stubbornly in vitro. Neither was the feeble state of Mrs Yardley at all encouraging. She was managing to sip a little brandy and at least remained conscious, but Felix was now wondering how much time they had left for a successful outcome.

He would have to resort to the forceps, that was clear enough, and do the job as quickly as he could. He did not even have his preferred set with him. He had lent them to Peterson, the new police surgeon at Northminster, who had more work in the accoucheur's line – not least with Mrs Lazenby, the wife of the new Chief Constable, who was expecting twins. He had only a short pair with him, and he was not sure the head had yet descended far enough.

However, he went and warmed them by the fire, and gave directions to one of the maids to ready a bath of warm water.

"We ought to fetch Mr Yardley," he said to Grace.

"He won't be any use," she said.

"I am not sure I should go on without his –"

"Just do what you must, sir," Grace said, "and the master can wait."

So he went back and set to work, attempting to achieve that delicate balance between gentleness and force necessary for the procedure, and after some long, laborious minutes, he managed to dislodge the child from the womb.

He fell back on his heels, a little surprised that he had achieved it. He had the child, a boy of reasonable size, in his arms now, and he was able to cut the cord. Although the child was breathing, it was shallow and laboured. He was, in short, struggling. Felix turned and placed him into the bath of water, unsure that it would do any good, but without recourse to anything else. For a long moment he was certain that all was quite lost, but the warmth of the water worked some reviving magic on the child. He began to scream quite lustily, even with a sense of outrage at this treatment. Grace, who had been crouching down beside Felix, took charge of him, smiling broadly at this sudden show of life.

Felix staggered to his feet and went to see to Mrs Yardley. These moments were as critical for the mother as the child. He was pleased to find she was comfortable, although now quite exhausted.

Grace said, "It's a boy, ma'am, a handsome boy!"

"Thank God!" Mrs Yardley managed to say.

"Yes, he's going to be quite a handful," said Grace, as the screaming continued.

"And he's hungry," said Ellen, the other maid.

Felix busied himself with the delivery of the placenta, which naturally caused Mrs Yardley some further distress, but she seemed to gain heart and fortitude from the sound of her screaming child.

"Will you nurse him, ma'am?" he said, when she was finally settled back in bed, and able to take him into her arms for the first time. "It may be a struggle for you when you have lost so much blood, but with care it could be managed. It is always better if a mother can."

"Yes, yes," she said, gazing down at the child. "Oh, what a darling. Thank you," she said, glancing up at Felix, her eyes wet with tears. "I thought he was quite lost. I felt sure of it, and yet – oh, thank you!"

Felix turned away, for Grace now wished to get the child latched onto the nipple. He could only hope that fatigue did not overwhelm Mrs Yardley completely and that her determination to feed her child would pull her through the next few hours. She would be in a precarious condition for some time, and would need to be watched carefully, but the signs, although weak, were hopeful enough.

He discovered he was in a shocking state after his work, his bare arms and shirt front covered with blood. He was also tired and hungry. He gathered up his instruments and Ellen took him into the adjoining dressing room where there were cans of hot water and towels. Here he was able to make himself a little more respectable, although he could do nothing about his shirt. His waistcoat covered most of the damage but it was stained irrevocably. It was a little irksome to have spoilt it, for it was the first Sukey had made for him. She had even embroidered, in red silk, a heart containing the intertwined letters 'F' and 'S' in the corner of the tail.

It had been sacrificed to a good cause, he told himself, as he retied his cravat.

"He's sucking well now, Doctor," Grace said, coming into the dressing room. "And plenty of milk by the look of it."

"Good," Felix said, getting his coat on. "I must go and speak to Mr Yardley. If he is at home?"

"I wouldn't know about that, sir," said Grace and departed.

There was another door in the dressing room, left slightly ajar. Taking up a candle, Felix could not resist the temptation to glance in. He saw a large, gloomy room containing a huge bed constructed from dark wood, every surface of which was covered with carving. Was this Mr Yardley's room, he wondered, a little shocked by the paintings on the walls: they were ancient, clumsy pictures of saints and martyrs meeting various horrible ends, with spurts of blood flowing out of them in a physiologically incorrect manner. An odd choice for a bedroom, he thought, and supposed Mr Yardley must either be unnaturally pious or have a morbid temperament.

It was a relief to return to Mrs Yardley in her brightly lit bedroom. Mother and child were doing as well as could be expected given the circumstances. Mrs Yardley's natural excitement at the event had given her face a pleasant colour, and she was sitting up in bed taking some broth. The smell of this was delicious and made Felix feel even more hungry. He was on the verge of asking Grace if he might have a cup as well, when the door was flung open and a gentleman came striding in.

From the manner of his entrance, Felix surmised this could only be Mr Yardley.

The new father was dressed in a fur-trimmed, red velvet dressing gown and on his head was a flat cap, also of velvet, with a tassel dangling from it. This outfit, combined with his neatly trimmed red beard, made him look as if he had stepped down from one of the family portraits. Felix expected him to be wearing doublet and hose beneath his gown, but instead he wore a gaudy silk waistcoat and a skin-tight pair of inexpressibles.

"Deo gratias!" Yardley exclaimed. "What wonderful news! And I was cursing this weather for keeping me from the chase! But it was meant to be – otherwise I should have missed this most auspicious event! My dear Julia, you have surpassed yourself!" He went over to the bed and seized her hand rather roughly, and kissed it extravagantly. Then he abruptly let go of her hand, as if he was casting away a glove, and turned away from her with a flamboyant swish of his gown. "Let me see him!"

The boy, now washed, neatly capped and gowned, and carefully swaddled, was handed to him and at once began to bawl at the top of his lungs. The noise for Felix was a reassuring one – the child was doing well and he could not help smiling at it and at the comical expression on the father's face, as he dealt with this ungracious greeting.

"Is that anyway to speak to your father, sir?" said Mr Yardley, who did not look comfortable with a child in his arms. "What a fine noise, though! Very fine! And he has the look of a Yardley. Quite pronounced, I should say."

"He was nearly lost," Mrs Yardley said. "If Dr Carswell had not been here – how shall I ever thank you, sir?" She sounded tearful.

"He needs feeding again, ma'am," said Grace, taking the now red-faced and furious child from Mr Yardley who was all too glad to relinquish him.

"Yes, yes," said Yardley, now heading to the door. "Let us leave the women to their business. We must go and drink a toast, sir!" he added, with a sweep of his arm to indicate that Felix was to go with him. "Ah yes, a bumper is in order!"

"Fetch me at once if there is any change," said Felix to Ellen. He was a little uneasy about quitting her so soon. "The slightest weakening or discomfort, yes?" The maid nodded. "You only have to call, ma'am," he said to Mrs Yardley. Mr Yardley was already gone, leaving the door open and a great draught behind him. She gave him a nod and a slight wave to dismiss him.

Yardley was now running down the stairs, and so Felix followed.

Then Yardley stopped in his tracks, turned and pointed up at Felix, his hand formed into the shape of pistol.

"Carswell!" he said. "Yes, yes, of course! The master of Ardenthwaite, am I correct?"

"Yes," said Felix, slightly irritated he had made this connection so quickly.

"What a most excellent thing for the birth of my boy! We are fortunate indeed," he said with a slight bow. "It is rarely that one can say one's medical attendant is nearly one's equal!" he added with a laugh, then carried on down the stairs, at the same speed as before.

Felix wondered whether he was supposed to be insulted or flattered by this. He was too tired and thirsty to care much, and too anxious about the state of his patients upstairs.

"Fellowes, now," Yardley went on. "Fellowes. Well, what can one say about such a rogue? I suppose he sent you here?"

"No. It was quite by chance. Your servant Grace came and asked for me when she could not find him. I'm putting up at The Falcon. I'm here on some other business entirely. It was lucky I was here, all in all."

Felix followed Mr Yardley into a library. Here again was the same profusion of clutter: weapons, armour, skulls, taxidermy as well as heaps of books of every size and age. A stuffed bear on its hind legs loomed over the table where the footman was laying out the punchbowl. An antique gold goblet had been placed in its claw.

Seeing Felix staring at it, Yardley gave the bear an affectionate pat, and said, "Do you like my drinking companion? He is a fine fellow, isn't he? I am very lucky to have him. He killed three people!"

"He did?"

"In a little place in Germany. He came out of the forest and went to dine in a village." Yardley rubbed and patted the bear again. "Excellent company he is – and he never takes a drop!"

The manservant left, and Felix hoped he might return with something more substantial than the plate of biscuits which lay on the table. Mr Yardley now proceeded to pare lemons and crush lump sugar into the punchbowl.

"I always prepare this myself," he said. "There is a knack to the mixing of it. When I was up at the University" – he gave a little chuckle – "even the fellows of my college attempted to purloin my recipe and my method. They sent a scout to spy upon me at my alchemy but he did not succeed in learning it! No, of course he did not! I could not allow that." He gave another little chuckle, and he stirred the punch with a flamboyant gesture. "Could I?" He took from his pocket a silver box and from it scattered a few crumbs of some unknown substance. "A touch of ambergris," he said. "Most essential. And of course, freshly grated nutmeg. Also Batavian arrack. Very hard to get, but necessary. And brandy – French for preference – and of course champagne!"

Felix eyed this concoction with some suspicion. He would have preferred to be sent below stairs to the housekeeper's room for a glass of bad sherry and some bread and cheese. But he could not offend his host, so he had to accept the silver tankard that was offered.

"No, no, do not sip it like a woman!" Yardley said. "Drain it, sir! You will not got the full effect."

Felix hesitated, watching Yardley down his bumper, and then took courage, despite his empty stomach, and drank deep. It was delicious, very sweet and aromatic, but he doubted how much of it he could manage to consume.

"To Mrs and Master Yardley," he managed to say, making a vague toast.

"Yes, yes, indeed!"

"I think they will both do well," Felix said.

There was an awkward pause.

"Was there much blood?" Yardley asked suddenly. It was not said soberly, but with a touch of ghoulish curiosity.

For a moment Felix could not think what to say. He took another sip of the toddy and said, "Mrs Yardley did have severe flooding, yes. But her strong maternal feelings carried her through the worst of it. She was determined. That is always a great advantage."

"She is from good stock, of course," Yardley said. "The daughter of Baron de Warke – they trace their lineage back to Charlemagne himself! You can see that in her cheekbones, I think. You see?" He indicated a portrait of Mrs Yardley that was hanging on the wall. It was rather a stiff image, Felix thought, with the lady dressed in odd medieval-style garb.

"A wedding portrait?" he said, not being able to think of anything complimentary to say. He put down his tankard and reached for a biscuit, determined to get a little ballast inside him.

"Yes," said Yardley. "I had her sit to Axelmann in Germany on our wedding journey. The costume and pose was my suggestion – Axelmann was pleased with it! In fact so pleased, he wished to keep it for himself. I let him take a copy, of course." Yardley refilled Felix's tankard and his own. "Are you married, sir?"

Felix shook his head.

"Thinking of it, though?" Yardley said. "You will need to beget some heirs of your own. Have you a dam in mind? I would imagine your noble sire has quite –"

"I think, sir, you may be misinformed about my connections," Felix cut in. "Perhaps I should go and see to Mrs Yardley. The post-partum period can be extremely dangerous, especially after such a traumatic labour."

He started towards the door.

Yardley started to laugh, in rather an unpleasant fashion.

"You cannot lay claim to Ardenthwaite, and deny him, surely?" he said, in the same disturbing, jocund fashion. "How unfeeling of you, sir, when I have heard so much about the noble Marquess' devotion. It is the talk of the county, of course."

Felix was on the verge of turning back, trying desperately to think of some suitable remark to deal with this impertinence. He felt it as keenly as if Yardley had poked him in the stomach with one of his antique swords.

But at that moment the door opened and a lady entered. She had a pronounced limp and used a staff to support her. But her figure was so handsome and elegantly turned out, that the staff seemed to be more like an instrument of great office. She walked straight past Felix, as if he were invisible, and went up to Yardley.

"Here you are, Briggs, of course!" she said, a disapproving expression on her face. "With your blessed punchbowl!"

"We have much to celebrate!" said Yardley. "You have been up to see him?"

"I have been up to see them both," she said, with some emphasis on the 'both'. "Both seem comfortable, thank God, but I only heard by the merest chance. Why, pray, was I not informed at the earliest instant of the crisis?"

"My dear sister, I have no idea. I was as much in the dark as you," said Yardley. "I didn't hear a thing until that wretched Grace, who evidently thinks she is the mistress here, bothered to send a girl to tell me we had an heir! We ought to let her go, do you not agree, Amelia?"

"No, indeed," said the lady. "Mrs Yardley would only go with her and we cannot have that sort of scandal. You cause enough trouble as it is, brother."

"I believe Grace was only thinking of her mistress," Felix ventured. "She is an excellent woman as far as I could judge, and if she had not acted as promptly as she did then there might have been little to celebrate."

Now the lady turned her attention to him.

"You are the Scotch doctor? Grace said she found you at The Falcon."

"This is Carswell of Ardenthwaite, Amelia, no less and no more," said Yardley. "Lord Rothborough's own –"

"Enough, Briggs, enough!" said Miss Yardley. "We shall not stoop to gossip when this man has done our family such a service. Dr Carswell, thank you. I believe we owe you the life of both mother and child." She put out her hand. "I am Amelia Yardley."

Felix took it and made his bow.

"We are fortunate you were at hand," she said. "What brings you to Whithorne?"

"Police business," Felix said. "Mr Earle, the coroner,

asked my employer Major Vernon and myself to come and investigate an unexplained death. A young lady called Miss Barker. Perhaps you knew her?"

"The mulatto girl?" said Yardley.

"She's dead?" said Miss Yardley. "Oh, dear Lord! How terrible. And the coroner and the police involved!"

"Shocking," said Yardley.

"It cannot be murder, surely?" Miss Yardley said.

"We don't know," Felix said. "When I have done the post-mortem, things will be clearer, but apparently the road is flooded, and we will not be able to get back to Northminster until the day after tomorrow."

"It cannot be done here?" said Yardley.

"I would prefer not to, but it may come to it, if the weather does not improve."

"It is not set to," said Miss Yardley. "And even if the weather does change, the Northminster road is always the last to drain."

"Then it must be done here," said Yardley. "Indeed, we have the very place, Dr Carswell, under this ancient roof! The old kitchen here would be most suitable, from what I have read of these things. Justice need not be inconvenienced by the weather."

"Poor, poor girl," said Miss Yardley. "It is the worst of fates for her."

"I really should go and see Mrs Yardley," Felix said, going to the door. "Perhaps a servant might show me the way?"

"I will take you there myself, Mr Carswell," said Miss Yardley. "I cannot resist another sight of my handsome young nephew. Briggs, will you come?"

"Later," said Mr Yardley, giving his punchbowl a stir. "Later."

Chapter Four

Giles continued his sodden walk back to The Falcon, looking forward to the fire and some coffee, when he turned a corner and saw two boys fighting.

As he ran towards them, he saw their schoolbooks and caps had been thrown to the ground and an unpleasant fracas was in progress. This was not a mere schoolboy scrap – the boy on top was holding a knife to the neck of the other. Giles dragged him off, the result of which was that the knife went flying from the assailant's hand and lay glinting on the slippery cobbles. The boy struggled so hard to evade Giles' grasp that it needed two hands to keep hold of him, such was his state of animal fury. As a result the other boy leapt to his feet and ran off without a backward glance.

"Stop!" Giles called out. "Stop!"

But the boy had no intention of obeying him. Giles could not give chase for risk of losing the other, who was still putting up a fierce show of resistance. The fugitive could be dealt with later, Giles decided, certain there were not so many places in Whithorne where a respectable lad could hide. He turned his attention to the knife-wielding terror who was squirming in his arms.

Giles finally got him under control by means of a pair of handcuffs. He was a little worried that the boy's slender wrists would easily escape them, but the boy seemed genuinely frightened by the sight of them, and gave up his fight at last.

"What's your name?"

"Rivers, sir," stuttered the boy, unable to look Giles in the eye.

"How old are you?"

"Thirteen."

"And those are your books on the ground there?"

"Yes, sir, some of them. Some of them are Latimer's."

"That was the other boy?" The boy nodded. "You're at school together?"

"Yes. At the Abbey." He gestured up the lane, behind him.

"And, that," said Giles, moving the knife on the ground a little with his foot. "That is yours?"

There was no answer.

"Is that your knife?" Giles said again, tightening his grip a little.

"Might be," he said at last.

"I hope you know how serious that is, to put a knife to another fellow's neck."

"I had to," the boy burst out. "I had to!"

"And why?"

He fell into silence again.

"I am going to take you straight to the Bridewell, Master Rivers. Since you are determined to behave like a common hoodlum, you will have to be treated as one."

"Oh God, sir, no!"

"Then where do you live? Your father can deal with you."

"My father's dead."

"Then I am sure your mother –"

"It was because of her, sir, that – that –" he blurted out. "Her and my sister. He insulted them! He said they were – he insulted them!"

"What did he say?"

"I don't like to say it," the boy said. "It was too – you understand, you must, sir, you're a gentleman! I couldn't let him say such a thing and get away with it, could I?"

Giles repressed a sigh at this sorry tale. He did not yet know if he was dealing with a habitual liar attempting to put his actions into an acceptable light, or if this was genuine outrage. He reached down and retrieved the knife, putting it into his pocket.

"Where do you live, Master Rivers?" he said.

"St John's Lane."

"Then I think we had better go and speak to your mother."

At least then they would be out of the rain, although it was not going to be pleasant telling a hapless widow about her errant child.

The house was a modest one, in a modest street. The widow Rivers and her family were clearly not in good circumstances.

A girl holding a ginger cat opened the door to them. She was a smaller, female, drier version of Master Rivers and she gasped at the sight of her brother in the company of a strange man.

"Oh, Mama," she said, turning abruptly. "I think you'd better..."

The front door opened directly into the front parlour. The room was not squalid, but it was by no means luxurious. There were two old chairs sitting ceremoniously on either side of the fireplace, but no fire. On the mantelpiece was a pair of handsome silver candlesticks that stood out as the only symbols of gentility in this frugal environment.

Mrs Rivers emerged from the back of the house. She wore a blue and white striped apron over a black dress, and had wrapped a scarf of the same stuff about her lustrous hair. On another woman this might have looked like a mark of servitude and poverty, but it had been arranged so well that she looked as if she were about to sit for her portrait. Even in the dull light of an undistinguished room, it was evident that she had the sort of beauty and composure that would have been remarkable in the most exalted circles.

"Yes?" she said. "What is going on?"

"Shall I speak or shall you?" said Giles to the boy.

The boy was frozen in terror now at the sight of his mother.

"I... I..." he began but could manage no more.

"Forgive my intrusion and interference, ma'am," Giles said. "I found your son attacking another boy – Latimer – in the street. Your son had a knife to his neck. Naturally I had to intervene."

Mrs Rivers took stock for a moment and said, "Naturally." Then she added, "And you, sir, are...?"

"Major Giles Vernon at your service, ma'am," he said. "I should add, I am a police officer."

"Latimer, you say?" she said.

"Yes, ma'am."

"Johnny, what do you have to say for yourself?" she said, advancing a little towards her son, who stood looking pointedly away. "John, look at me." He managed to do so. "Is that what happened?"

At length the boy nodded.

She pressed her hands together and then to her lips for a moment, composing herself.

"Latimer," she said again. "Oh Johnny, Johnny –"

"He insulted you!" Johnny burst out. "He insulted you and Louisa! He called you whores! He said that he'd have Louisa just as his pater had you! For money!"

There was a miserable silence as Mrs Rivers absorbed this information. Then quietly she said, "Go into the kitchen and get dry, Johnny. We will talk about this later. I must speak to Major Vernon alone."

Giles released him from the cuffs and the boy left the room quickly, as if glad to be out of his sight.

"I am sorry I cannot offer you a fire here, sir," Mrs Rivers said, sitting down. "Our circumstances are not as I would wish. I'm sorry as well that my son's conduct has brought you here. My apologies, and my thanks. I cannot even offer you a glass of wine by way of thanks."

"Has he ever been involved in anything like this before?"

"No, at least not that I know of. He has always been very good, very obedient. A great support to me. This is not how he usually is. It is distressing."

"The other boy – I wonder if you should speak to him and his parents to establish the degree of provocation involved, before you deal with him."

"You are merciful," she said, with a slight smile. "From your appearance, and your profession, I would expect you to recommend that I flog him."

"That rarely does any good," Giles said. "At least in my experience. I was a vile boy, and my father a great traditionalist, but it didn't seem to reform me. It only made me resentful."

"So what did reform you?" she said.

"My mother had a clever way with words. Her ill-opinion was far more terrifying to me than any number of punishments from my father."

She smiled again at that, and he was once more confounded by her great beauty. It was hard not to be affected by it.

He was reminded of a conversation he had had long ago with another young officer. They had been talking about famous courtesans, and how they must differ from ordinary whores, and that their beauty and manners must be of a superior order to command such ridiculous prices. "I suppose," his companion had said, "that they can make a man sick with longing just with a smile or the wag of a finger."

It was a strange thing to find a woman like that in an overlooked corner of a town that had no claims to anything but obscurity. It would be difficult for Mrs Rivers, he imagined, living that cheese-paring sort of life. As a respectable widow and mother of children, the allure of a courtesan would be an inconvenience rather than an asset. It would give rise to gossip.

He could not help wonder for a moment if there was not some truth in Latimer's insult – not that Mrs Rivers was a whore, but that she was perhaps involved with his father. Perhaps the father had made some careless mention of her desirability and the boy had spun a fantasy about it, which in turn he had used to torment an enemy. Giles disliked this train of thought. It was not pleasant to doubt her virtue.

"But I should at least confiscate his knife," Giles added, taking it from his pocket and holding it out to her. "And tell him that no gentleman fights in such a fashion."

"That advice would be far better coming from you, sir," she said. She took the knife and turned it in her hands. "This was his father's. He is not supposed to have it. He must have taken it from my things." She shook her head and then rose and laid it on the mantelpiece. "There is no difficulty with the law in this, is there?" she said after a moment. "You did say you were a police officer, sir?"

Giles nodded and said, "It might be counted a case of common assault if the boy's family wished to press charges and there was evidence of injury. But if they do not complain, then... I assume you know the family?"

"Yes."

"They will likely be as embarrassed by this as you must be," he said. "What the boy said was... perhaps your son's offence is more understandable in the light of that."

"I shall have to speak to Mr Latimer, certainly," she said, with a sigh. "What a wretched business! Wretched weather and more wretched news."

"Might I ask you something?" Giles asked, wondering at her downcast manner. "You did not know the late Miss Barker?"

"Yes," said Mrs Rivers. "Is that why you are in Whithorne, Major? You are certainly not in the common pattern of policemen. I heard there was going to be an inquest and that usually means dreadful things –" She broke off, with a shake of her head. "Poor Bel. I can't quite believe it. It breaks my heart to think I shall never see her again."

"You were friends?"

"After a fashion. Mr and Mrs Ampner are hospitable and are kind enough to ask me to their evenings now and then. I do not expect it of them, although Mr Ampner and my late husband were friends as boys. I am not exactly an ornament to their society – I have no illusions. But when Bel came to live with them, we did establish a sort of friendship. She was in need of friends, and perhaps those of us on the margins, for whatever reason, find ourselves drawn together. And my daughter, Louisa, who is just sixteen, adored her. She is so unhappy. She can't begin to understand it. She has been crying out her heart. Have you any idea yet what happened?"

"Not yet, I'm afraid. But we shall do our best to find out as soon as we can, if that is any comfort for your daughter. And it would help me if I could talk to you both about Miss Barker. Perhaps I might call again tomorrow morning?"

"Yes, certainly," she said.

"You must know Mr Gosforth as well, then?" he said, going towards the door.

"Mrs Ampner's brother? Only a little."

"What do you make of him?"

"A civil young man, handsome, yes, but a little lacking in direction. And perhaps a touch foolish. Certainly liable to get himself into scrapes. Mrs Ampner is always worried about him. She dotes on him, of course, but I think she feels he is going to disgrace himself at any moment. Why do you ask?"

"He has taken himself off somewhere, and Mrs Ampner seemed inclined to be worried about it. Does he have any particular friends or haunts that you know of?"

"Lord Milburne has taken him up, that I do know. They have been fooling about pretending to be medieval knights or some such. Learning to joust, I believe. And Lord Milburne has promised us all a fancy ball – no, I beg his Lordship's pardon – a medieval revelry." Her amusement died on her lips, and she sighed. "Oh poor Bel, she was looking forward to that!" She paused for a moment, composing herself. "Mr Gosforth might have gone out to Woodville Park, that is Lord Milburne's place. That would explain why he has not come home. The road will be impassable. We have a curious geography here, sir, you may have gathered. We are an island at such times!"

Giles took his leave, and made his way back to The Falcon. It was about five o'clock and the gloom of the rain combined with the dusk to create a miserable atmosphere, as if the town itself was swathing itself in crêpe.

Chapter Five

At six o'clock, Felix judged it safe to leave Mrs Yardley and her son, having given instructions that he was to be fetched at once if there was any deterioration. He was anxious to be away before he was asked to stay for dinner.

Returning to The Falcon, he found Major Vernon installed in the private parlour between their bedrooms. He was sitting in an uncharacteristic state of repose, his bare feet resting on the fender, a coffee cup in his hand and gazing into the fire. But there was plenty of evidence that he had been hard at work. There were papers and a plan of the town spread across the table, while on a chest stood a host of fancy cosmetic bottles, to all of which white evidence tags had been added.

"Did the day go well?" asked Major Vernon.

Felix sat down by the fire and pulled off his wet boots.

"I think so," he said. "It was touch and go for a while. But a healthy little boy in the end, and the mother bearing up as well as can be expected in the circumstances. I shall have to go back later and check on them." He hauled himself up from the chair in order to take off his coat. "I need a clean shirt."

"Your bag is next door," Major Vernon said. "There should be a fire in there. I ordered one for you."

Felix went through and found he had a comfortable bedroom at his disposal, warm and with a generous bed. It made him remember he would be alone that night. He took off his shirt and stood gazing down at the little embroidered heart on the tail. He pressed it to his lips for a moment, wishing desperately he could kiss her instead. He then looked at the bloodstains and began thinking of the various tests he had been attempting to formulate to identify different types of bloodstains on textiles. The shirt, although ruined, might make a useful sample.

"What are all these?" Felix said, returning to the parlour, stuffing the tail of his clean shirt into his trousers.

"The contents of Miss Barker's dressing table. And that one on the left is the alleged bottle –"

"That was full and then empty," said Felix, picking it up and examining it.

"I spoke to the servant," said Major Vernon, getting up. "She is quite convinced of what she saw, and she may well be right, but that doesn't prove that Miss Barker drank the contents, does it? There was a full bottle there as well, in these baskets. One might easily have been substituted for the other. Imagine – you have a full bottle to hand and then realise that there is a little left in the previous bottle. So you put the full one away in the basket and leave the other, now empty, on the dressing table. I am assuming, of course, that the contents of both were perfectly harmless. I do not want this full or empty bottle business to colour our thinking of what may have caused death. It disturbs me that Dr Fellowes pointed that out so eagerly. It is disingenuous, to say the least."

Felix nodded.

"He is either stupid or wilful," Felix said.

"Or attempting to misdirect us?" said Giles.

"Then he is a fool," said Felix.

"The Ampners seemed to think little of him. That he is unreliable and given to tippling."

"That was what Miss Yardley said," Felix said. "There was nothing else in the room that seemed suspicious, other than these? The chamber pot? Any dirty basins?"

"Nothing. Earle told them to leave the room untouched, which they assured me they had, but I only have their word for it. The chamber pot and the wash basin were gone. Whether that was deliberate or not, I don't know."

"I need to do the post-mortem tomorrow," Felix said. "The sooner we have the cause of death, the better."

"Yes. But where? I have been to the Bridewell and it is not suitable."

"Mr Yardley has offered me the use of the old kitchen at the castle," said Felix. "I am not sure how suitable that would be either."

"Is that the father of the newborn?"

"Yes, Squire Yardley," Felix said. "He's a trifle odd, to say the least. The house is full of old weapons and instruments of torture and goodness knows what. I think he has a ghoulish temperament. He seemed to derive pleasure from the thought of my performing a post-mortem under his roof. Never mind the state of his wife and child." He sighed. "But it might be just the thing. And I need to get on with it."

"The sort of man who enjoys an execution?" Major Vernon said.

"Exactly," said Felix.

"Go and see the undertaker first," said Major Vernon. "He may be able to accommodate you."

"I hope so," said Felix. "I want as little to do with Yardley as possible. He knew who I was, of course, and made all sorts of unpleasant insinuations."

"Shall we go and get some dinner?" said Major Vernon, putting on his coat.

"Yes, and a good bottle of something," said Felix, picking up his own coat. At that moment the rain hurled itself against the window and rattled the sashes. "If this rain carries on we will all be driven up the hill and forced to beg him for shelter," he remarked.

"Let's hope it doesn't come to that," said Major Vernon.

Chapter Six

An early call at the Ampners revealed that George Gosforth had not come home the night before. Mrs Ampner's anxiety was now bordering on the hysterical – far beyond what might be expected in such circumstances.

"It was suggested to me," said Giles, "that he might be at Lord Milburne's house – that the weather trapped him there?"

Mr Ampner thought this likely.

"He's been spending enough time there," he said. "They are friends after a fashion, though I don't imagine that will last. Indeed I hope it won't, for it gives the boy notions, being taken up like that."

"Did he say anything about going there to you, ma'am?" Giles said.

She shook her head.

"He did not even say he was going out," she said. "Not a word. That is what I cannot understand. He was here when Dr Fellowes and Mr Earle were here – he was such a comfort – and then I looked for him, and he'd gone! And now..."

"I think it most likely he is at the Park, my dear," said Mr Ampner. "He was fond of her, that's true enough, and perhaps he wanted to take comfort with his friend. It is likely no more than that."

Mrs Ampner seemed to struggle to accept this, but at length she did. Yet Giles wondered if her concern was that he had taken flight out of fear of being implicated in Miss Barker's death. Why she might assume this was another question.

"Do you have his picture, ma'am?" said Giles.

She did, in a locket around her neck.

"It was only done this summer," she said. "It is a good likeness."

It showed a slender, fashionably-dressed young man, handsome, and with carefully curled dark hair.

"And you are absolutely certain that there was no sentimental history between Miss Barker and your brother?" he asked, handing back the locket.

"Quite sure," she said.

"And you, sir, you have not seen anything that made you think that there might be?"

Ampner considered for a moment and then shook his head.

"Please let me know if he does come back. You can send any message to me at The Falcon, or the Bridewell if that is more convenient."

"Of course," said Mr Ampner, showing him to the door. "Is that all today, sir?"

"Yes, thank you. Do you think the roads will clear today?" he asked. The rain had stopped, and the skies looked set fair.

"We can only hope so," said Ampner.

Whithorne was drying itself slowly under the influence of weak sunshine, and presented a slightly more cheerful aspect, though it was still cool and damp, with a brisk wind ruffling the surfaces of the many puddles.

At the little house in St John's Lane, Giles followed Mrs Rivers upstairs to a room that was well placed to catch what sun there was, with a long, old-fashioned latticed window. Louisa Rivers was sitting beneath it with a piece of sewing, but she got to her feet when they came in. Like her mother she was a great beauty, but at the same time she looked alarmingly pale, with violet shadows under her red-rimmed eyes. Her hair was the same deep chestnut shade as her mother's, and equally thick and wavy, but in her case it hung about her shoulders in an unkempt tangle, instead of being elegantly constrained.

"This is Major Vernon," said Mrs Rivers. "He is trying to find out what happened to Bel. He wants to speak to you about her."

"If you don't mind, Miss Rivers?" Giles said.

"Do I have to?" she said in a whisper to her mother.

"Yes, I'm afraid so," said Mrs Rivers.

"It will help us greatly if you can bear to," Giles said. "And you want to know what happened, I am sure."

She did not answer, but stood turning her work in her hands, looking pointedly away from him.

"Must I?" she said again to her mother.

"It will only be for a little while," said Giles, but he hoped that the conversation might be longer than that. Her reticence hinted that she might be concealing something important.

"Please, won't you both sit down?" he said, taking the other chair and putting it next to the one where she had been sitting. He would have to content himself with a stool, such were the sparse furnishings. "Then we can be at our ease."

"Yes," said Mrs Rivers, sitting down and patting the space beside her. Giles took his own place, and then at length Miss Rivers sat down too.

"Thank you," said Giles. "I know this must be painful for you. To lose a friend in such circumstances is a horrible thing."

"How do you know?" she said, with sudden vehemence.

"I lost a school friend when I was about your age. He died suddenly of a fever. It was..." He was surprised for a moment by the stab of pain that this remembrance brought him. "At the time – unimaginable."

"What was his name?" she asked.

"Hal," Giles said. "So I understand a little – but it must be worse for you. I had the comfort of knowing why he had to be taken. But for you, there is no answer to that question yet. But that is why I am here, to find that answer for you."

"What was he like?" the girl asked.

Giles considered for a moment. Hal had been obsessed

with two things: the greatness of the Duke of Wellington and how soon he could contrive to lose his virginity. As these had been Giles' own obsessions, they had got on pleasantly.

"He understood me," he said, "as no one else seemed to do." He watched her reaction. "Was that the case with Miss Barker?"

She looked out of the window for a long moment, clearly preparing an answer.

"We were just friends," she said. "That's all."

"I know it isn't all," he said. "Help me, Miss Rivers, please?" She pursed her lips. "I know, let us start with something simple. Tell me what you did together. When you went to call on her, or she came here. That did happen, yes?"

"Yes, I suppose," said Miss Rivers.

"So she would call on you and come here?"

"Yes."

"And you would sit and talk?"

"Yes, of course."

"About what?"

"Things."

"Yes?"

"Private things," she said. "Very private." She got up from her chair and walked across the room, so that she stood with her back to the far wall. "And I don't see why you need to know them, sir! What difference can it make? And perhaps she's just dead because she's dead! People do die, just like that, all the time. Your friend did!"

"He had a fever. Miss Barker seems to have been in perfect health, dancing the night before at a ball. That she was found dead in her bed the next morning for no apparent reason means that something may be awry."

"I don't want to talk about this," she said to her mother. "I don't. I can't! Please will you just let me alone?" she begged, with a great sob.

Mrs Rivers rose and went to her, laying a kind hand on

her shoulder.

"Louisa, darling –" she began, but the girl bridled at her touch.

"Just leave me alone!" she exclaimed and threw herself face down on the bed in the corner, and began to sob into the counterpane.

Mrs Rivers looked helplessly over at Giles, who put up his hands to suggest that there was no point continuing. He left the room at once and went down the narrow stairs to the sitting room where he had talked with Mrs Rivers the night before.

Mrs Rivers joined him a few moments later.

"I am sorry. I cannot account for her reluctance."

"It doesn't matter," Giles said. "Perhaps you can tell me something of their friendship – their habits. Did she come here often or was Louisa much at the Ampners?"

"About half and half. They were close, despite the fact that Bel was a little older. I wondered at it sometimes, but they seemed to take to each other. It was good for them both."

"And what did they talk about?"

"I don't know exactly. I left them to their own devices – they would rather sit upstairs without a fire than be downstairs in the kitchen with the rest of us. Girls do like their secrets. I remember that myself. My sisters and I would keep fearful secrets from my mother. I suppose that I should not flatter myself that my daughter is any different."

"My sisters were like that, and then they seemed to grow out of it and become confidential with my mother once more."

"You're right. One does grow out of it. But we are in the thick of it here, and it is not helpful to you, sir, for which I apologise. My elder children are being great thorns in your side. I shall have to make sure the others behave themselves," she said glancing at the door to the kitchen. "In fact, will you excuse me a minute?" she said, going to the door and opening it.

"I do not object to a kitchen," said Giles, "if there is a fire in it."

He was not particularly cold, but he wished to see the rest of the house and talk with her a little longer, to see if he could glean anything more about Annabella from her. Neither was it unpleasant to be in her company. She was as warm as a good fire herself, and he found himself wondering why on earth she had not remarried. Her children were as pretty as she – a responsibility, yes, but not an objectionable one.

"Yes, yes, of course," she smiled. "So silly of me. You must be cold."

They went into the kitchen where two small girls were engaged in some complicated game on the floor, using wooden spoons and handkerchiefs as dolls. They only had one real doll, dressed in red silk.

"Bel gave them that doll," said Mrs Rivers rather quietly. "She was very kind to them. They will feel her loss too, though differently from Louisa. She would bring cakes and sweets, all those little treats that I cannot afford, alas."

"Are those your youngest?"

"Yes, Sophie is seven, and Frances eight. Then there is Richard who is twelve and at school with John, whom of course you know already. Regrettably." She sighed and went to the fireside. "Here it is, such as it is. Please, sir, sit down and get warm."

"Do you have any help here?"

"A girl comes in three mornings a week. She does the roughest work for me, and I send out the laundry. And Louisa is very good. That was why it was such a pleasure that Bel and she became friends. It let her have some relief from this rather wretched life of ours. Would you like some tea? I will have some, and I should take a cup up to Louisa by and by."

She went and filled the kettle and set it on the hob, while Giles did as he was bid, and took his ease by the fire. It was not at all unpleasant to sit there and watch her make the tea, and listen to the quiet chatter of the two girls in the corner. His mind wandered idly from the business in hand into a vague fancy where he was the father of five such children, and Mrs Rivers his wife. When he found himself imagining that latter part in lascivious detail, he was forced to get back to the point, which was not easy when she smiled so appealingly as she handed him a cup of tea.

"So Miss Barker and your daughter, did they go about together?"

"Yes. Miss Barker was asked everywhere and Louisa went with her. To Mrs Yardley at the castle, for example. She often had them to tea. She is not much older – she was something of a child bride."

"Tell me more about George Gosforth. Have you heard any gossip about him?"

"Gossip?" she said, pulling her chair a little nearer the fire. "Does gossip help your business?"

"Always. There is often a lot in it. You never heard Louisa and Bel talking about him, for example?"

She considered for a moment.

"Sometimes. I don't think they had much respect for him. He may be handsome but he lacks – oh, how does one put it? He lacks substance. He is young and one hopes he will acquire some, but then, some people never do, do they? Their characters remain slight. Pleasant but slight. A little like Lord Milburne."

"Ah, so you know him too?"

"Only a little. And I'm not being fair to him. He does have a little more about him than Mr Gosforth, and I think he will grow into his position quite nicely. But at the moment..." She could not help smiling. "He is somewhat interested in fancy dress and medieval notions. His mother, who is the most sensible, forthright woman you can imagine, is at her wits' end – not that she lacks wit. She is one of the most amusing people

I have met. He was prancing up and down in armour, and a plumed helmet, and she said, 'Clearly I should not have read Ivanhoe three times when I was carrying him. It had a pernicious effect on the child in my womb'." Giles smiled at this, and she said, "Is that not quality gossip for you?"

"Definitely," he said.

"Good. Now I will take some tea up to Louisa and see if she is any more willing to talk. I shan't be long."

He was left alone with the girls and their chatter. One was saying, "No, no, I don't think that's at all a nice thing to do, Miss Brown," to the doll in red silk, when there was a loud, impatient knocking at the front door, and a man's voice called out, "Alice? Alice, are you there?"

Rising from his seat, Giles heard the door open. He went to the kitchen door and saw an elegantly-dressed, middle-aged gentleman standing in the parlour.

"Who the devil are you?" he said to Giles.

Mrs Rivers came running down the stairs.

"Mr Latimer," she said. "What a surprise."

"You don't know, do you? You don't know what that wretch of yours has been up to. Threatening Ned with a knife! A knife! The poor lad was too afraid to go to school today, and he was up all night, sick with fear!"

"I do know, yes," Mrs Rivers said, in a calm, careful voice. "In fact, you have this gentleman to thank that this situation is not a hundredfold worse. Major Vernon broke up their fight, and brought John home."

"Their fight?" said Latimer. "Ned was pinned to the ground, with a knife to his throat, absolutely unable to defend himself. I hardly call that a fight!" He turned to Giles. "He did mention you, sir, that you pulled John off him, and he was able to get away. For which I'm grateful. And I'm sure you will agree, it was not a fight but an out-and-out attack upon my son's person!"

"At that point, yes, that was how it seemed," Giles said.

"But John said that there had been a strong insult, to which he was responding."

"You only have his word on that," said Latimer.

"Yes, of course. But it seemed to me that he might be speaking the truth. The insult was an extremely specific and unpleasant one, and I suspect John would have to be a quick-witted liar to come up with such a line to defend himself to me and his mother. It had the ring of truth about it. Of course, I don't know the boy or his previous character, but I have some experience in these matters professionally."

"Which is?" said Latimer.

"Forgive me, I should present myself, sir," Giles said. "I am Major Vernon, Superintendent of the Northern Counties Criminal Investigation Office. I was formerly Chief Constable of Northminster."

Latimer digested this information.

"Of course," he said. "Earle mentioned you were about. Well, professional considerations aside, I would like to assure you that my son is not in the habit of bandying about such insults that make other boys leap upon him and put a knife to his throat. He is a gentleman's son and I have raised him accordingly!"

"And of course you cannot entertain for a moment that he might have lied to you!" burst out Mrs Rivers. "No, it all has to be John's fault! Of course!"

"Don't seek to excuse him," said Latimer. "I knew this would be the case. I knew it!"

"I do not!" said Mrs Rivers. "What he did was very bad, and I have made that clear to him. But what Ned said – it was utterly foul, and one would need a strong character to let such a remark pass. You would have horsewhipped anyone who said such a thing to you, I'm certain."

"So what was it, then?" Latimer said.

"I can hardly bear to repeat it," said Mrs Rivers, walking across the room to avoid Latimer's fierce regard. "It was so unpleasant –"

"Just say it, for the Lord's sake!" exclaimed Latimer.

Mrs Rivers closed the kitchen door, then swallowed hard and said, "He called Louisa and me whores and said that he would have Louisa for money just as you had had me."

Latimer shook his head.

"I cannot believe that. I cannot believe that he would say such a thing."

"John swears that he did. He was scared half to death that Major Vernon would carry him off to the Bridewell if he did not tell the truth. He was defending my honour and that of his sister, and that is the truth of it, even if he went about it in entirely the wrong way. I cannot ignore that," Mrs Rivers said. "Can I?" she added, with a look of appeal at Giles.

Giles wondered how much honour Mrs Rivers had left to defend. Ned Latimer's insult, ugly though it was, possibly revealed an important truth about the nature of the relationship between his father and Mrs Rivers. They were certainly far more than acquaintances. Latimer had betrayed himself with his use of Mrs Rivers' Christian name. Was she his mistress? But then why was her situation so wretched? Latimer looked extremely prosperous and could easily have made her life a great deal more comfortable.

He glanced again at Mrs Rivers, who was standing, in all her glorious beauty, in a patch of sunlight on the floor, her back straight, her features formed into a mask of fierce dignity. Perhaps she had chosen to resist him and take the consequences. That was a brave choice given the circumstances, and perhaps a heartbreaking one, for there had been a great deal of passion in their angry exchanges. Was he looking here at the wreckage of an illicit love affair, which had wounded their children as much as themselves? Ned Latimer's insult sounded as if it were born of shame and disgust at his father's actions, as much as from youthful lust and profound confusion about how he was supposed to behave.

"I cannot accept that," said Latimer. "He would not have said that."

"Perhaps you might speak with their schoolmaster?" Giles said. "Or, better still some of the other boys, who may have seen the whole thing develop. Then you will be able to get to the truth of the matter. If that is what you want, of course."

"What do you mean by that, sir?" said Latimer. "That I might not hear what I want to hear?"

"That is always a possibility," Giles said. "And Mrs Rivers has every right to investigate further. She admits her son's conduct was not what it ought to be. It would help her to know exactly how it came to pass so that he can be correctly steered in future."

"Yes, exactly, sir!" said Mrs Rivers.

Giles knew he was putting the cat squarely amongst the pigeons, but it struck him that Latimer needed at least to acknowledge the possibility that his son could be just as unruly as Johnny Rivers.

The threat of questioning others would seem as good a way to accomplish this as any, for any investigation of this nature would be likely to lay Mr Latimer's own conduct squarely in the line of judgement. His scowl showed that he understood that well. He could not defend his own son without admitting his own fault.

"I will speak to him," said Latimer, after a long, uncomfortable moment. "Though what good it will do any of us..." He gave a sigh. "If he has lied to me and said this thing, then..." He shook his head and put out his hand vaguely in the direction of Mrs Rivers, as if attempting to make a conciliatory gesture.

Giles decided this was the moment to take his leave. They were, no doubt, glad to see him go.

He walked away, ruminating on the problem of Louisa Rivers' reluctance to speak. Perhaps, once she was beyond the first shock of her friend's death, she might be more willing to talk. He felt certain that her reticence was significant – but he wondered if he were the right person to gain her confidence. A woman might be better suited to such a task. Someone like Sukey Connolly, perhaps.

He turned into the main square and saw the Northminster Mail Coach heading towards The Falcon. The road must be clear again, he thought with some relief, and letters could be sent.

Chapter Seven

"Mr Yardley has taken the body?" Felix asked again, scarcely understanding what Hawkins the undertaker had just told him.

"Yes, sir," said Mr Hawkins. "He said he'd spoken to Mr Earle about it, and that they'd decided the best thing was that she was to go up to the castle and you could do your business there."

"But he did not have a letter of authorisation or some such?"

"No, sir. But he is on the bench with Mr Earle. And he is the Squire. I wasn't going to argue with him. He's not the sort of gentleman that you can argue with. It doesn't do for a fellow like me to get on the wrong side of a gentleman like that, sir."

"He will find the same applies to me!" exclaimed Felix. "He had no right to do this, no right at all."

Felix made his way up to the castle, wondering how he was going to deal with Yardley's actions. He supposed he would have to accept the situation, for it was more important to get the post-mortem done quickly. There could be no progress until they had a cause of death.

When he had paid his call on Mrs Yardley after dinner last night, the Squire had not been in attendance on his wife. Miss Yardley had been there, and had apologised for her brother's absence. He was, she said, casting horoscopes; Felix had wondered if this was not some kind of euphemism for being in his cups. If yesterday's punchbowl had been in any way characteristic of his drinking habits, this seemed likely.

Proudfoot the butler opened the door to him, and he asked to be taken straight up again to Mrs Yardley.

"Yes, sir, of course, but the master asked me to bring you to him as soon as you called."

"I will go to your mistress first," Felix said. "Will you show me up?"

"I must take you to the master first," Proudfoot said. "I have my orders, sir."

Felix hesitated for a moment. He was annoyed at this but he decided he must acquiesce. He did not want to cause any difficulty for the man, who was only trying to do as he was bid.

"Very well."

He imagined they would go up to his library, but instead Proudfoot took him outside again and across a court, into what seemed to be the most ancient part of the castle. A heavy door opened onto a flagged passage, which led in turn to a pillared chamber, well-lit but noticeably chilly. Here the coffin had been set on trestles. This was presumably the old kitchen that Yardley had spoken of. It was in many respects suitable for the purpose. There was even a pump set above a stone sink.

But despite these advantages, Felix's heart sank. For at the far end, sitting in an X-frame chair, wearing a black, fur-trimmed velvet gown, was Yardley.

"Well, Doctor, do you like my arrangements?" Yardley said, leaping up. "It should suit you well. I have had them put out basins and towels, and so forth. Basins are necessary, I understand, for placing the removed organs, yes?" Felix could not answer for a moment. Yardley's excitement was worrying. "And here, we have a fine bottle of serçial," Yardley went on, "in case we require a stirrup cup."

That 'we' confirmed Felix's fears. How on earth was he going to dismiss Yardley without causing offence? The thought of reproaching him for commandeering the body seemed ridiculous now. The important thing was to get rid of him. He glanced around, wondering if he could secure the doors from the inside.

"Thank you, sir," he said. "It all looks much in order. I would like to begin as soon as I may – if you would be so kind as to take your leave now."

"Take my leave?" Yardley said.

"Yes, sir," said Felix. "This is no sight for a layman."

"Yes, yes, of course," said Yardley. "Indeed. But I am an avid student of the sciences. You cannot object to having a witness to this important process, surely?"

"I am afraid I must," Felix said, wondering if Yardley was so deluded that he believed the study of astrology made him a student of science.

"That is hardly what I would have expected of you, Carswell. Surely all progress in your profession comes from the sharing of knowledge in an open and generous manner."

"That may be so, but this is not a place for a layman," Felix said. "This is a police investigation."

"Then it is surely a place for a Justice of the Peace? We Justices are still your masters, Doctor, if I understand the legislation correctly. You cannot act at all without our say-so. And I say it is entirely proper for me to remain and watch you conduct this procedure."

"I might make an exception for the coroner," Felix said, "but I am afraid I must ask you to leave. Your assistance is much appreciated but I cannot let you stay here." He walked towards the door as if to show him out, hoping he would at last concede.

Instead, Yardley said, "But I could assist you. And it would be such a privilege."

"It would really not be proper, sir," said Felix, feeling more and more exasperated. "You have already bent the law to your own will, so to speak, by bringing the body here without adequate authorisation, albeit in an attempt to assist me, and I must take care not to do anything else that might prejudice the case in hand."

"And how, pray, might my being here do that?" said

Yardley.

"I cannot say. We know so little at this stage. For all I know, you may have some connection with this poor woman's death and want to know what I discover to see how safe your position might be."

"Well, well, there is a suggestion," Yardley said with a smile, which made Felix wonder if his argument might not be so ridiculous. "Am I a suspect? How fascinating."

"No, sir, of course not. But you might be. My point is that at this early stage one never can tell. And that is why you must leave, or I shall be obliged to leave myself, and come back with two constables and Mr Earle and insist that she is taken away from here, which would cause a regrettable delay. If you have any interest in justice, which I am sure you do, then you will let me work in peace."

A moment passed, and Yardley laughed and made a low, rather theatrical bow.

"Very well, very well, Master Sawbones, I shall let you to your grisly work. Your oratory does you credit. I cannot resist such arguments!"

"Your assistance in providing this place is much appreciated," Felix said, relief pounding in his chest. Yardley swept past him and out of the door. Felix hoped he was not the sort of man given to the long nursing of grudges, but he rather feared he was.

The door had a bolt. It looked both heavy and noisy and Felix thought it politic not to lock it until Yardley had got some distance away from the door. He did not wish it to look as if he had immediately locked out his host.

My host, he thought, turning back into the room and the covered coffin. It was strange hospitality indeed.

~

After nearly two hours of work, the cold of the room had begun to gnaw at him. His fingers were working less nimbly, and he covered up his work and decided to take a brief respite, before moving to the next stage. He ran about the room a few times to get warm and then took a small glass of the serçial that Yardley had provided. He was a little loath to take any of it, but he was shivering.

He had just taken a first, warming sip when there was a knock at the door. With some trepidation, he went to the door, telling himself that it was a servant, for surely Yardley would never knock in his own house – he would have tried the handle first.

"Yes?" he asked.

"Mr Carswell?" It was Major Vernon.

"Are you alone, sir?" said Felix.

"Yes."

With some relief Felix drew the bolt and admitted the Major.

"How did you manage that?" said Felix in some astonishment. "I practically had to push that wretch Yardley out of the door. He would not leave me alone. He was relentless. Did you bribe the butler?"

"Not quite. The two constables I had with me had a salutatory effect on him and I think Mr Yardley has gone out."

"You spoke to Hawkins, then?"

"Yes. How far have you got on? The road is clear again. Mr Hawkins has his hearse ready. You can travel back with them, if you like. It won't be comfortable, but needs must."

"I will do that. I'm not inclined to let her out of my sight. Fortunately, I'm only at the preliminary stages – but what we have so far is interesting."

"So?"

"Cause of death was most likely poison," Felix said. "Fellowes was right about that, if nothing else. Cyanide in some form or other – prussic acid, perhaps." He drew back the sheet that covered her. "You will observe the lividity has a pinkish tinge," he went on. "That is a well-established indication of the presence of cyanide. Now look at the blood – how bright the colour is, cherry-red – and the organs all have a similar reddish tinge. Those are strong indications." Major Vernon nodded. "In addition, on first opening the body, I smelled bitter almonds. It was faint, as you would expect, for it is over forty-eight hours since she died, and cyanide is extremely volatile, but it was there, clear enough. Of course, there is much more work to be done, testing the organs for the presence of cyanide, especially the liver and the stomach. But that cyanide is the agent behind this seems more than likely."

"And these?" Major Vernon said, pointing to the curious pattern of marks on her thighs. "They look like burns."

"They are," Felix said. "And they are puzzling."

"Did she drop hot wax on herself?"

"The burns are too deep and regular. And they are in different stages of healing. They look to me deliberate, as if someone has pressed a heated metal object, perhaps the handle of a fork or some such against her bare skin. Do you see what I mean?"

"Yes. That is odd, to say the least. Some of these look quite fresh." Major Vernon winced as he spoke. "Some kind of punishment? If she was being treated cruelly then it makes an impulse to self-murder understandable."

"Quite," said Felix. "Which brings us to the next question. How and why did she take the stuff? Did she mistake it for something else, or was it deliberate?"

"Accidental poisoning is common enough," said Major Vernon. "How much would she need to have taken?"

"Very little. Two or three grains dissolved in a solution is enough to cause a fatal asphyxia."

"And apart from the scent of almonds, does it taste of anything?"

"It also tastes of almonds. In fact it can be used, in a weak solution, as almond flavouring – if you are foolhardy, that is. I have read of deaths caused by a cook being too heavy-handed and the original distillate being unexpectedly strong. A stupid thing to have in a kitchen!"

"So that is a possible source? Perhaps the tonic that she is supposed to have drunk was flavoured with it?"

"I didn't smell almonds there," said Felix. "But it is volatile – it may have dispersed. There may be some residue in the bottle, though."

"I shall have to find out the source of those bottles, and give the Ampner's kitchen a search," said Major Vernon. "Another thing that concerns me is that they all swear that no one went into her room between midnight and eleven the next morning. I find that too convenient. I wonder if some evidence has not been removed. Perhaps the poison was in another bottle altogether which has now been spirited away, for some reason or other. Mrs Ampner is certainly not telling me the whole truth. She is unnaturally concerned about the unexplained absence of her brother."

"He has not turned up yet?"

"No, unfortunately," said Major Vernon. "I should very much like to talk to him. Now, how shall we proceed? Shall I fetch Hawkins? You should be on your way as soon as possible."

Felix nodded.

"Did you say Mr Yardley has gone out, sir?"

"Yes."

"Then when I have finished here, I had better go and check on his wife. I hate to leave without at least seeing all is well. I meant to go earlier, but..." He gave a shrug.

"I will tell Hawkins not to leave Whithorne without you," said Major Vernon, going to the door.

Chapter Eight

In the end, Carswell did not join Mr Hawkins on the box seat of his hearse but decided to go back with Smith in the carriage, along with the contents of Miss Barker's dressing table, carefully labelled and packed up.

"And all was well with Mrs Yardley and her son?" Giles enquired, just before he climbed into the carriage.

"Mercifully, yes," said Carswell. "And she is being well looked after. Do you have any letters for me?"

"How did you guess?" said Giles, smiling and taking them from his pocket. "This one, I hesitate to give you, though. It is for –"

"Mrs Connolly," said Carswell reading the inscription. "Sir?"

"I have asked her to come here. I would like her to do something for me – for the investigation, that is. She is particularly well-suited to it, but of course, if you have any objections to my employing her in such a fashion, then nothing more need be said about it."

Carswell put the letter with the others.

"She would never forgive me if I did object," he said after a moment. "She's already made it clear enough that I shouldn't allow myself to presume anything of that nature." He said it rather bitterly.

"Have you quarrelled?" Giles asked.

"Just before we came here," Carswell said. "It was about those damned Germans! I told her that it was quite unnecessary for her to give them rooms, indeed that I didn't want them in the house at all. Well, you do not either, sir, I think. But of course, she insisted that it was her business to decide what is what, and certainly not mine! So no, I should not dare attempt a veto!" He climbed into the carriage.

"Go back and make peace," said Giles, closing the door and speaking to him through the lowered window. "She has probably changed her mind about it; she won't want to offend you, as you don't want to offend her."

"I hope so!" said Carswell.

Giles watched the carriage depart, hoping he would not be the cause of more trouble between them. He had written the letter asking for her assistance and then, seeing Carswell, felt it best to ask his permission to approach her on the matter. If she had been Mrs Carswell, and not Mrs Connolly, he would not have hesitated to consult him. It would have been offensive not to ask him. However, she was not Carswell's wife, and nor was she subject to her lord – facts which she obviously wished Carswell to remember. Letting those rooms to the Germans against his express wishes was a clear sign.

Giles, in truth, would have preferred that she had not let the rooms to these people. He had no wish for the house to be invaded by strangers, but she was only doing what she had set out to do and balance her books. He consoled himself with the thought that it was a large house and they would perhaps not be irksome. But for Carswell, who was both a husband and not a husband, it would be not so easy to swallow his pride and agree to it.

~

Woodville Park, the country seat of the Earl of Milburne, lay a pleasant two-mile ride from Whithorne, as Giles discovered later that day when he hired a hack and went to see if George Gosforth had taken refuge there. The house itself was an impressive structure, built a hundred or so years ago with all the careful regularity of that era, but it had an impoverished, neglected look, as did the grounds in which it was set.

As Giles dismounted and tethered his horse, a tall woman in middle age, dressed plainly, whom he supposed to be the housekeeper, emerged from a door under the steps and gave him an enquiring glance.

"Is his Lordship at home?" he asked.

"He is, indeed, sir. And who may I say is calling?"

"Major Vernon," said Giles, "from the County Constabulary."

She looked at him rather carefully, and in a fashion that had she been the housekeeper, he would have found a touch insolent, but her manner of address and the fine timbre of her voice had made him realise that she could not possibly be that.

"Forgive me, sir, but did you once serve with the Thirty-third?" she said after a moment.

"Yes, ma'am, I did," he said, surprised by this. He now studied her features with more care, trying to place her in the faces of that period in his life. She was remarkably familiar, now he thought of it, but was that just because she had strong and interesting features? "Are we acquaintances?"

"I believe we are," she said.

Then he recognised her, and he could not help smiling. He remembered her, heavy with child, sitting with Mrs Herries, the Colonel's wife, watching the horse-racing. She had gone away shortly after that for the birth of her child, and her husband, a brevet Major, had not been with them much longer. He had scraped together the purchase money for the Lieutenant-Colonelcy in the Sixteenth. He had grumbled about the shocking cost of it and Giles had himself been shocked at the time, knowing his family resources would never allow him to attain such heights.

"Mrs Maitland," he said, putting out his hand. "What a great pleasure."

"It seems age has not touched us at all," she said, shaking his hand. "Twenty years and we recognise each other as if it were last week. What magic elixir have we been consuming?"

"In my case, I think it is because I never looked young," he said.

"Nonsense," she said. "You looked extremely youthful. You had that great crop of flaxen hair, so carefully curled at the sides, and swept forward." She passed her hand over her forehead. "Thus!" Giles started to laugh, remembering now all the brief but pleasant moments he had spent in her company. As the wife of a superior officer, he had not dared to admire her, but he had liked her. She had always been diverting. "Mrs Herries and I were always fascinated by your hair and that of Mr Wilson. We were certain you were competing to be named the regimental dandy."

"That's entirely possible," said Giles, with a dismissive gesture.

"Tell me the truth, sir – I beg you," she said. "It was a deadly rivalry, surely? You and Wilson..." and now she began to laugh. "Oh, forgive me," she said, attempting to stifle it and failing.

"Wilson always had the edge on me," Giles said. "I never took it seriously enough. I drew the line at the rose-scented pomade."

She shook her head vigorously at that, her hand over her mouth, still attempting not to laugh. She turned away in order to compose herself.

"Forgive me," she said a moment later, turning back to him. "I am behaving like a schoolgirl. Well, I was little more than that, then, and you were not much older. That was such a delightful year! I was sorry to leave the Thirty-third."

"We were sorry to lose you – and your husband, of course," Giles said. "I trust he prospered with the Sixteenth. It was the Sixteenth, I think?"

"Yes," she said, and then sighed. "And we ought never to have done it. It ruined him – his health and what fortune he had. His health broke down entirely within a year of the birth of our son and he had to sell out. That broke his heart, and he died six months later." She gave a shrug. "A sorry tale. I hope life has treated you more kindly, Major Vernon," she added with the emphasis on 'Major'.

"I'm sorry to hear that. He was a fine man and an admirable officer," Giles said. "I learnt a great deal from him."

"Thank you. He always spoke of you as having great promise. I could not see past your hair, of course, and he told me I was a hoyden for laughing at you. I am sure you have fulfilled all his prophecies. Constabulary, did you say? So you are a policeman now?" He nodded. "How extraordinary. The wheel of fortune turns about in the oddest way, does it not?"

"Yes, but we make our own destinies too. I chose this business."

"Ideally we do," she said. "But sometimes destiny is thrust upon us. That is the case with my son, and all this!" She gestured around her.

"Your son," he said. "Of course. That would be Lord Milburne? I had heard he came unexpectedly into the title."

"It has been the strangest business," Mrs Maitland said. "My husband belonged to the most remote, cadet branch, and there had never been any expectations. They certainly did nothing to help my husband when he was in greatest need. I wrote to them – against all my principles, let me tell you – to ask for charity in such a fashion, but matters had got to such a state that I was willing to try anything. So I wrote to the Lord Milburne of the time – I am not sure which one it was, for there have been three in the last twenty years – and he did not even answer me. And now everything is in my boy's lap! What a great change! And you have come looking for him – why, might I ask?"

"I wanted to talk to him about George Gosforth. I understand they are friends."

"Regrettably, yes," said Mrs Maitland.

"Regrettably?"

"He is a vacuous ninny and not at all a suitable companion for my son," she said. "And I do not apologise for such a damning assessment of his character. Neither am I terribly surprised to find a policeman enquiring about him. I have half-expected something of the sort." And before Giles had a chance to ask her why she felt this so strongly, she went on. "You will wish to know why, of course. Perhaps we should go inside and find a fire and some refreshment? I will just go and get someone to deal with your horse. You cannot leave her standing out here. It is going to rain again, I can feel it."

"I hope to God not," he said, looking up at the glowering sky. "Thank you, but I am not sure if I have time to spare at present, ma'am, though I should like nothing better, I assure you. What I need to know at this moment is whether Mr Gosforth is likely to be with your son, and if so, where I might find them."

"I very much hope he is not," she said. "I have told my son that he must end his association with Gosforth and that I will not admit him to the house. He may have defied me and sought him out – it is possible – but he will not be under this roof, I trust."

"When did you last see Gosforth?"

"He was here a week ago, and that was the reason I have laid down the law. It became intolerable."

The glowering sky now began to hurl rain down upon them.

"You really should come inside," she said, gesturing towards the door. "I have not seen Charles since breakfast, but I do not think he has gone anywhere this morning. We shall find him somewhere. Please?"

"Of course," said Giles. It would not delay him much, he decided, and he certainly needed to know what Gosforth had done to provoke such a dire sanction from Mrs Maitland.

She took him inside, throwing out directions to the various servants who met them, and then led him upstairs.

The house might have been large but it was bleak. It had none of the comfortable refinements of a great house – just vast, sparsely furnished rooms, formal in style, but now badly distressed and neglected, the treasures all dispersed.

"I considered quartering myself in the housekeeper's room downstairs," she said, opening the door to a room that had signs of having been made habitable, with a bright fire burning. "For that is a far more comfortable affair than this. But although we do not have a housekeeper at present, and I do all the work of one, and a great deal more, I thought I had better keep my distance, for the sake of my authority – such that it is, over so few servants. This was the boudoir of the countess before last, so it is appropriate enough for me, given our present conditions. I am definitely given to sulking."

"The house seems..." he began, searching for a circumlocution.

"You don't need to be polite about it, Major. This house is a horror in need of a substantial fortune to make it bearable. And then another fortune on top of that. My boy will have to marry two heiresses. Or else I shall insure the place and burn it to the ground. I have thought of that quite seriously on several occasions, particularly in this rain. The roof – dear Lord, the state of it is beyond imagining! But then you would have to arrest me, would you not?" she added.

"I should do it kindly," Giles said. "And I think, given this awful damp season, you would not be successful. So there would be no charge to answer."

"The hand of Providence at work!" she said with a laugh. "Making my roof leak so that I am tempted into crime and then prevented from it!" A middle-aged maid came in with a tea tray. "Thank you, Patton," she said.

"Raining again, ma'am," said Patton. "Would you credit it?"

"Patton, is his Lordship at home?" Mrs Maitland asked.

"I believe so, ma'am. Shall I send Mr Imbury for him? I

think I saw him going out to the riding school after breakfast."

"Yes, Patton, if you would," said Mrs Maitland. "Tell Imbury to tell him that there is a gentleman here to see him. Do not let him mention me, or his Lordship will never come!"

Patton sighed at that and said, "He will if he knows what is good for him, ma'am. Silly lad. I'd box his ears, ma'am, that's what I would do!" She departed and Mrs Maitland seated herself at the tea table.

"Will you take some tea?" she said. "I have brandy to put in it, if you despise it female fashion."

"Female fashion is entirely to my taste," he said, sitting down on the sofa opposite. "Patton has been with you a while, I take it?"

"She nursed my son. Well, we nursed him between us, so to speak. He was a hungry boy. Now speaking of milk," she added with a smile, "how do you like your tea?"

"Black, no sugar, if you please," said Giles, unable to prevent himself smiling back.

"Most austere," she said, handing him his cup and studying him as she did so. "Are you very austere these days? You have that look of the monastery about you – no, there is something of the Jesuit about you – a soldier priest from the cinquecento. Or have I muddled my dates – when did the Jesuits begin?"

Giles sipped his tea. There was certainly no need of sugar, brandy or cream in her stimulating company.

"A Jesuit?" he said. "No one has ever compared me to that before. Do I look so hard and zealous?"

"You might, if you rid yourself of the bad habit of smiling," she said. "That spoils it. But you are so thin, Major Vernon. I do not remember you so thin. Can I persuade you to a piece of Patton's seed cake? No, I insist."

"I was ill this last summer, and lost some weight," he said. "So I will happily accept that."

"Good."

"Now, if I might be Jesuitical for a moment," he said, "and quiz you a little about Mr Gosforth. Why did you ban him from the house? How did he offend you?"

"It was not one particular thing. It was an accumulation of offences. I tried to tolerate them both for as long as I could – after all, Charles has little to divert him here, and a man must have leisure as well as work – I am not so unkind as that; but when Gosforth was here, it was as if any sensible thought he might have had in his head was entirely dismissed, and replaced by spun sugar."

"Is this to do with the medieval revelry?"

"Had you heard about that?"

"I was speaking to Mrs Rivers."

"How interesting. Now, what did you make of her? I should love to know. Is she not the most beautiful thing you ever saw? If I were a man I am sure I should be utterly enslaved."

"She called you the most amusing woman she had ever met."

"Whithorne is such a dull place! A fool like me can sustain a reputation for wit simply by speaking in complete sentences. So she told you about my son's ridiculous ambitions?"

"She did."

"We are in no position to be throwing fancy balls. In fact we would be hard pressed to host a dinner," she said, getting up. "This is my difficulty." She went to her writing desk and picked up a pile of papers. "These."

She dropped them down on the tea table.

"Bills," said Giles. "I see."

"I thank God for the rain for keeping the bailiffs from our door!" she said. "Gosforth has encouraged him in his folly. They have been playing at knights together. I could forgive it if they were ten, but they are nearly twenty!" She sat down beside him on the sofa and began to sort through the bills, handing them to him in considerable agitation. "Look at this one, sir, look at it! Fifty guineas for a velvet damask surcoat trimmed with gold braid! And this – rose pink silk hose! Or this one – a jewelled garter. But this one – this is the worst of all – antiquities: three suits of armour – five hundred guineas. Five hundred guineas! I don't know whether to laugh or cry, truly I do not! The absolute folly of it! Oh yes, and here we have the bill for the engraved cards to go out and invite the entire county and his wife and his mother-in-law!"

Giles looked through the bills, aware of her anxious eyes upon him. They painted a picture of reckless expenditure that was breathtaking and deeply troubling.

"Perhaps you could scare some sense into him," she said. "It is beyond me. I have failed utterly. I am a disgrace to have let it come to this. Too little too late in banishing that idiot Gosforth, you will all say. The weak son of a weak mother, no doubt! Witty but weak!" She got up from her place and walked away to the fireside, staring down into the flames. "Forgive me, sir. I have not been able to speak freely about this to anyone. I am taking advantage of an old acquaintanceship. Forgive me."

"You mustn't blame yourself," he said. "A man of twenty is responsible for his own actions. His mother is not."

"Very gallant," she said. "But the world will not see it that way, and I agree with them. The blame rests squarely at my feet. I had sole charge of him his whole life and what is the result? He lives in a dream-world and spends money like water, while never taking a moment's notice of his responsibilities or duties. I thank God that his father is not here to see this, and then I wonder if his father were still with us, if this would have happened at all. It is not possible for a mere mother to..."

She looked up from her study of the fire.

"Forgive me," she said. "I talk too much. A great fault. I need a husband to tell me when to hold my tongue. I dare say you do not let your wife prattle on."

"My wife is dead," Giles said. "And I am like you – I talk too much."

She turned away from the fire, and came and sat down again by the tea table.

"Oh, I am sorry to hear that," she said. "Children?"

He shook his head.

"I have done nothing as useful as you in that regard," Giles said. "To bring up a boy alone to twenty is no small achievement. And though you may despair of him now, Mrs Maitland, I'm sure that given time, this madness will all be done with," he said, tapping his finger on the pile of bills. "He will look back on this with mortification and wonder what on earth he was doing. Your work and your care will not be wasted. He will come straight again. Be patient and have courage."

She reached out and briefly squeezed his hand, and he noticed she was on the verge of tears, although she smiled. His own heart gave a small lurch.

"Good counsel, sir," she said. "I shall try to heed it."

"And perhaps, when your son does appear, I might talk to him alone?"

"Yes, of course," she said. "And please don't hesitate to put the fear of God into him, Major Vernon. You may be exactly what is needed!"

Chapter Nine

When the butler, Imbray, returned with the news that his Lordship would receive his visitor in the riding school, Mrs Maitland was prepared to take up cudgels at this slight which she at once termed deliberate and provocative.

"He does not know who I am," Giles said, mildly.

"That is beside the point!" she exclaimed. "It is hardly nice behaviour on the part of the master of the house. He ought to have come back at once. Excuse me, Major Vernon."

The riding school was some distance from the house and had been built from the same expensively-dressed stone as the main building and to the same vast scale. Giles began to suspect that Earls of Milburne had as much extravagance as they had nobility in their blood.

The indoor riding school was an impressive space in its own right, but the walls had been hung with colourful banners depicting heraldic animals. In the centre of the manège, wearing a plumed helmet and mounted on a handsome brindle grey stallion, was Lord Milburne himself. He was holding a lance and charging at a tailor's dummy that was dangling from a swinging pole. Giles admired his horsemanship but not his manners, for his Lordship showed no signs of stopping at the arrival of his caller.

Giles, feeling his mother's pain, decided to take matters into his own hands. He strode forward, caught the horse by the bridle and stopped him in his tracks, before Lord Milburne could begin another manoeuvre.

"Sir?" said Lord Milburne, with great annoyance.

"We need to talk, my lord," said Giles. "And I would prefer not to have to stare up at you."

"Who are you?"

"Major Vernon, from the County Constabulary. I need to talk to you about your friend Gosforth. Would you please dismount?" The Earl frowned and seemed disinclined. "It would be far better if you did. This handsome fellow seems tired to me. He needs rubbing down," Giles added, patting the neck of the horse.

This could not be argued with, and Milburne got down and handed the horse to the care of his stable boy. He pulled off his ridiculous helmet and now stood in front of Giles, ruddy-cheeked and heavily perspiring like his poor horse. He seemed young for his nineteen years, and still at that curious stage when manhood had not yet ruined his boyish beauty, nor diminished the petulant, somewhat childish, pout of his lips.

"Did my mother send you?" he said, when the stable boy had gone.

Giles ignored this and said, "I am conducting an investigation. Mr Ampner's ward, Miss Barker, has been found dead in suspicious circumstances and Mr Gosforth has gone missing. I need to talk to him."

"She's d...dead?" Milburne said. "When did she...?"

"She was found dead on Wednesday morning. The morning after the ball at The Falcon. I believe you were there."

"Yes, yes, I was. Oh dear God!" said Milburne. "She's dead?" Giles nodded. "And George is missing?"

"Yes. Can you help me with that?"

"I don't know. I don't know what to say. You said her death was suspicious?"

"Yes."

Milburne nodded and sniffed audibly.

"I can't believe it," he said. "Bel dead." He shook his head again, then wrapped his arms about himself and shivered. "Oh God in Heaven..." He turned away from Giles, his emotion overcoming him. He began to sob and ended by fleeing the ring.

Giles allowed him a few minutes to master himself and then followed.

He found him sitting in a sort of dressing room full of shields, helmets and swords, and various costumes hanging from hooks – in short, he was surrounded by a mess of expensive medievalism.

He started up as Giles came in, wiping his face hastily, and then turning away to attempt to pour a glass of wine. But his hands were shaking.

"Brandy, sir?" he managed to say.

"No, thank you, and I would go steady on that if I were you, my lord," Giles said. "You'd be better with the fire and some sweet tea."

The boy nodded, took only a sip and then set it down again, before staggering over to the fireside. He fell into the armchair and sat with his hands pressed to his face.

"How is this possible?" he managed to say at last, addressing Giles who had sat down opposite him.

"We don't know yet. That is why I am here. It is unlikely that she died of natural causes, I regret to say. I take it from your reaction that you and Miss Barker were involved in some fashion – or that you admired her?"

"No, no," he said. "Well, yes, I did, but not in that way. George, though – George will be – this will break him!"

"Mr Gosforth told you he loved her?"

"Many times. We talked about her – well, we talked about love and which ladies we admired. Bel was George's heart's desire and she his. They were going to be married as soon as it could be contrived. But you said George is missing?"

"Yes. Do you know where he might be?"

"How is he missing?"

"He has not been at home since Miss Barker was found dead. He was there when she was discovered but he has not been seen since. Have you seen him?"

"I have not seen him since Tuesday evening, at the ball."

"And you spoke to him then?"

"Yes, of course. It was the first time I'd seen him since my mother sent him packing."

"You are sure about that?" Giles said.

"Do you doubt my word?" he said.

"You are good friends. I would think you might have wanted to see him as soon as you could and perhaps mollify him. A public gathering which your mother might have attended as well would hardly be the place for that, would it?"

"I may have seen him earlier in the week," Milburne said after a moment.

"You mean you did," Giles said. "Yes?"

"Yes," Milburne conceded.

"Where?" Giles asked.

"There is an inn on the road into Whithorne, just before you get to the west gate into the town. The Black Cat. I saw him there on Monday."

"Have you met with him there often?"

"Yes. It's not much of a place, but the landlord keeps hawks. He has promised to raise one for me."

Giles reached for his notebook and made a note of the name.

"Are there any other places where you know he liked to go? Where he had other friends, perhaps?"

"No, not really. He was like me, new to the district. Ampner and his sister have only been married three years. They are from the Midlands, I believe, but they were living at Bath. That was how they met Mr Ampner."

"And you are quite certain you have not seen him since the evening of the ball?"

"No, no!" said Milburne, with too much emphasis to be entirely credible.

Giles wondered if a distressed Gosforth, full of remorse about what he had done to his sweetheart, had approached his friend for help, without telling him why he needed it. Perhaps Milburne had helped him, but had been uneasy at his friend's condition. His reaction to the news of Miss Barker's death had been extreme. Was it from fear that his friend may have had a hand in her death?

"You are certain of that?" Giles said again, getting up from his chair and leaning over him a little.

"No, sir, I have not seen him since then!" Milburne said in some agitation, jumping up to face him. "Believe me!"

Giles let it go and took a different tack.

"This plan to marry," said Giles. "He had her consent?"

"Oh, yes!"

"You spoke about it being contrived. Did Gosforth confide any particular plan to you, or perhaps ask you if you had any ideas about such things?"

"I can't really say," he said. "I suppose we did talk of it once or twice. We supposed it rather depended on finding a parson who could be trusted, and so forth."

"He did not ever think of asking Mr Ampner for his consent?"

"No, because he knew he would never get it. Not even if Bel had asked him for it – and he would pretty much do anything for her. Except give her the one thing she really wanted." He frowned. "I wish I could tell you where George was, for his sake. I can't fathom why he should be missing. He cannot have anything to do with her death. I am sure of that."

"Unfortunately we do not always know everything about our friends. Sometimes they keep secrets from even those closest to them. Has there ever been anything about George's behaviour that made you uneasy at all? You must have had some doubts about his intention to elope with Miss Barker. That is not a manner in which a gentleman would wish his friend to proceed."

"They had no choice about it!" said Milburne. "Ampner would never have allowed it. And she loved him just as much as he loved her. She told me so herself, sir, on the night of the ball, how happy she was and how she was looking forward to being his wife. When we were waltzing together..." He stopped, evidently distressed by the memory of this.

Giles wondered how this fitted with Mr Earle's account of their conversation. Either one of the men was lying or Miss Barker had been playing complicated games with her various suitors.

"And you have no reason to think she was telling you anything but the truth?" Giles said.

"Are you asking me to doubt a lady's word?" said Milburne. "A dead lady at that?"

"It is offensive, yes, but necessary," Giles said. "So there was nothing about Miss Barker that disturbed you at all? What do you think about her friendship with Miss Rivers? I understand they were close."

"I don't know anything about that! All I can tell you is that Miss Barker was the sweetest creature, and was happy to one day be George's wife! And that George would never harm a hair on her head!"

Giles reckoned this was about as much as he was going to get from him at that point. He suspected it was not the entire truth, but it was some sort of progress.

Leaving the riding school, he was pleased to find that the rain had stopped and even more pleased to see that Mrs Maitland had ventured out again. She was standing in a rather strange attitude, leaning back and squinting up at the façade of the house, her head tilted back. As a result her shawl was about to fall to the ground, so he ran forward, caught it and restored it to her shoulders.

"Oh, thank you!" she said. "I was studying the gutters. I am attempting to identify the source of a leak, but with little success. I hope your conversation with Charles was more constructive."

"It was useful," he said.

"And here is the man himself," said Mrs Maitland. Giles turned and saw Lord Milburne striding along the terrace towards them.

"Major Vernon, I am glad you have not left," he said. "There was something else, I've just remembered it." He glanced at his mother. "If I might have a word alone?"

Mrs Maitland made an ironic curtsey and walked away out of earshot.

"Yes?" Giles said.

"George did say something about how he had been on a drive to Melthorpe with Mrs Ampner and Miss Barker. To look at an old church or something. It seemed the funniest thing to do at this time of year, and I wonder if he was not trying to tell me that, well, perhaps they had gone there to make the match. That they had contrived it."

"I'm glad you remembered that," Giles said. Milburne looked away uneasily. "And you were certain Mrs Ampner was with them?"

"Yes, he was definite about it. George has confided in her, I think."

Giles nodded and from the corner of his eye saw Mrs Maitland turn back towards them. She made an enquiring gesture.

"Is that all?" he said to Milburne.

"Yes, I think so."

"Thank you," he said, and began to walk back towards Mrs Maitland. "I also forgot to tell you something, my lord: I had the honour to serve with your father in the Thirty-third."

"You did?" Milburne said.

"And had the pleasure of your mother's acquaintance as well. You haven't thought of following your father's profession at all? A commission in the Guards, perhaps? Or the Lancers? He would have been pleased by that, and I am sure you would enjoy the life."

Hearing this, Mrs Maitland smiled approvingly, and Giles

found himself delighted by the effect. Rather pointedly, Lord Milburne did not answer, and neither did he smile. It was obviously a sore point.

Chapter Ten

Just as Lord Milburne had described, The Black Cat was not much of a place. It was a low, shabby building, squatting outside the ancient gate to the town like a cat crouching at a scullery door, waiting to be admitted.

It began to rain heavily again as he rode back from Woodville Park, and Giles was glad of the excuse to take shelter. The yard at the back was orderly enough, and a competent boy took charge of his horse and directed him inside.

The interior was cheerful, the tap room clean and warm, and a young, neatly-dressed landlady appeared glad to see him.

"How can I help you, sir?"

"I am looking for Mr Gosforth," Giles said. "I am Major Vernon from the County Constabulary. I believe he comes here sometimes? Have you seen him lately?"

She thought for a moment, then said, "Not for a day or two."

"Can you remember exactly when you last saw him, Mrs – I'm sorry, I didn't catch your name?"

"Patchett, sir," she said. "And about Mr Gosforth, I'm not exactly sure. Well, perhaps it was on Wednesday evening – I didn't speak to him, though; I just saw him sitting there, as he always does."

"So he comes here quite often?"

"Yes. With his Lordship, Lord Milburne, that is," Mrs Patchett added with a touch of pride.

"They come here for the hawking, I understand?"

"Yes, sir, my husband breeds them up and trains them. We have quite a few gentlemen coming here on that account.

My husband takes them out, teaches them the sport. It's a good business for us."

"And you think it was Wednesday evening that Mr Gosforth was here?"

"I think so. I was only downstairs for a little while that night. I wasn't feeling well so I went up to my bed early, and left my husband in charge."

"Was Lord Milburne there?"

"Not that night, I don't think so. I suppose he stayed home because of the rain. That was the day this rain started, wasn't it, on Wednesday? And it's hardly stopped since, has it? Makes my husband jittery. He hates it as much as the birds do."

"Is Mr Patchett about?"

"He will be with the birds. I'll take you to him."

This involved a trip to the bottom of the long, rain-soakcd garden, where a two-storey building apparently served as the hawk house. Mrs Patchett knocked tentatively at the door and called to her husband in a soft voice. At length he opened the door to them, and met Giles' eyes with a wary expression.

"He's a policeman, Ned," said Mrs Patchett. "Let him in, will you? It's bucketing down again."

Patchett stood aside reluctantly and Mrs Patchett went scurrying back to the house.

Giles went inside and found an airy space that had perhaps once been a carriage house. There was a pair of double doors, made with slats to admit fresh air, and a ladder led up to a second storey. Lining the walls were long baize-covered perches for the birds, with canvas screens hanging down from the perch rails. There were a dozen or so birds sitting there: magnificent creatures all of them, of different sizes, colours and species, from a beautiful snowy-plumed owl to an elegant little falcon. In the centre of it all stood Patchett, a priest to his church of birds, in a leather waistcoat, a bright red kerchief about his neck. He stretched out one arm and the little falcon flew to him and alighted on his gloved hand, and he stood there gently caressing the eager bird's head.

"Police?" he said softly. "What is it you want, sir?"

"I am looking for George Gosforth. I believe you know him, Mr Patchett?"

Patchett nodded and raised his hand a touch so that the little falcon flew back to her perch.

"Is he in trouble?" he asked.

"I need to speak to him," Giles said. "When did you last see him?"

"Wouldn't know," he said.

"Your wife mentioned she saw him here on Wednesday."

"She may have done."

"And you didn't?" Giles asked.

Patchett shrugged and turned away, stooping to pick up a white feather from the brick floor.

"Mr Patchett," Giles said. "Did you see him or not?"

"Aye," he said after a moment. He did not meet Giles' eye but rather glanced towards his birds, almost as if he were giving them some signal. Was he priming them to fly at him, Giles wondered, and come to his defence? For he was surely keeping some secret.

"And you spoke to him?"

There was another long silence from Patchett. A brown and cream hawk stirred and turned on its perch, stretching out its magnificent wings and flapping them, as if to warn Giles not to ask any more questions. Patchett gave a nervous glance towards the ladder to the second floor, and rubbed his face.

"Is he in trouble?" Patchett said again.

"He might be," said Giles, deciding that he would go up that ladder. "And you had better tell me if you know where he is, if you wish to stay out of trouble yourself, Mr Patchett."

Patchett grimaced and then pointed upwards towards the ceiling.

Giles climbed up the ladder. As he did, he could hear someone stirring, and as he put his head through the hatch, he saw a white-faced young man looming over him. Giles recognised him from the miniature that Mrs Ampner had shown him.

"Gosforth?" Giles said. The young man retreated back into the shadows as Giles climbed into the attic.

"S..s..sir?" he said.

He looked exhausted and wretched, standing there with his great coat wrapped about him for comfort. A glance revealed that his quarters would not have been comfortable ones for a gently-bred young man: a straw pallet on the floor and no heating.

"I am Major Vernon, from the County Constabulary," Giles said. "I wish to speak to you about Miss Barker's death, Mr Gosforth."

Gosforth nodded, screwing up his face, as if in pain.

"Let's get out of here, shall we?" Giles went on, having an idea that a chair by the fire and a drink would encourage him to unburden himself. The man stank of a guilty conscience.

Inside The Black Cat, Mrs Patchett took them to a snug little parlour where it seemed Mr Patchett's gentleman customers usually sat. She appeared quite shocked at Gosforth's appearance – clearly she had no part in the concealment – and with much head-shaking she went off to fetch brandy, bread and cheese, and hot water.

"Sit down there, won't you?" said Giles to Gosforth, pointing to the chair by the fire.

Gosforth obeyed and stared into the fire sullenly.

Giles sat down opposite and took out his notebook.

"I want you to tell me what happened on Wednesday morning," he said. "How did you learn of Miss Barker's death?"

"There was a scream," he said. "Susan came screaming out of the room to find my sister. That woke me. That was the first I heard of it."

"So you got out of bed?"

"Yes, I went to see what the bother was all about – why Susan was bawling like that."

"And then?"

"I went into her bedroom. I followed my sister in – and my sister was standing there with Bel's hand in hers and saying, 'We need the doctor – go and get Fellowes. Send Jack to get him.' So I ran downstairs and told Jack to go and fetch Fellowes. Then I went back upstairs into her room and my sister was down on her knees by the bed, half in hysterics now, and..." He broke off and looked pointedly away from Giles. "And that was the first time I really saw her, and it was clear that she was – she wasn't there any more. She'd gone. She was cold to the touch."

There was a knock at the door, and Mrs Patchett came in with a tray. Gosforth shrank back into his seat as she set out the food on the table in front of him.

"I'm sorry, Mrs P.," he muttered.

"If you have led my Jerry into trouble..." Mrs Patchett said fiercely, banging down a glass in front of him.

"I – I didn't mean..." Gosforth said, but words deserted him and he stared away as Mrs Patchett left the room. Then when she had gone, he reached for the brandy and drank some of it, with both his hands trembling as they lifted the glass. "I didn't mean any harm," he said, managing to look at Giles now. "I just couldn't. She was gone and..." He took another swig of brandy and began to cough on it. "And everything was dark. Everything," he added, forcing out the words despite his cough. "I had to get away from there."

"You were close, I understand?" Giles said, gently.

"Who told you?"

"Lord Milburne. He suggested to me that you and Bel had married, yes? That is what you both wanted? He thought you might have managed it with your sister's help."

"I loved her," he said. "It wasn't why you think, what everyone will think. I would have done if she hadn't a penny. Please understand that, sir."

"I do; but I need to know a little more. So you were married?"

Gosforth answered by digging into his coat pocket. He produced a gold ring and laid it on the table.

"She couldn't wear it yet, so she gave it to me for safe-keeping," he said.

"She gave it to you? Are you sure?" Giles said. "You did not take it from her room, or from her finger?"

He shook his head slowly.

"She gave it to me after the wedding. After we left the church. You can ask my sister."

"Who has helped you in all this?"

"Yes."

"You both married well, did you not?" Giles said. "A wealthy lawyer and his equally wealthy ward."

"That has nothing to do with this!" exclaimed Gosforth.

"But you don't have money of your own, do you, Mr Gosforth, nor a profession that is likely to make you any?"

"That is irrelevant! I loved her!"

"I am sure. But money has its own attractions. And when a man who has just got himself a fortune takes flight when the source of that fortune dies quite unexpectedly, then sordid questions must be asked. Why did you run away – did you think that Mrs Gosforth's death would raise uncomfortable questions?"

"It was not for the money," he said. "I loved her."

"Whatever you say, Mr Gosforth, but you have pointed the finger of suspicion at yourself by your actions and I am going to need to know exactly why you felt the need to run away and conceal yourself in a hay-loft for three days. Yes?"

Gosforth screwed up his face again and said, "I don't know what I was thinking. I was in such a state of... I could not deal with myself. All I knew was that she had gone." He pressed his hands to his face, attempting to conceal his emotions.

"And you were afraid?" Giles said, softly. "And full of regret, perhaps? Is that why you ran away?"

The young man lowered his hands a little, revealing his tear-soaked eyes. He seemed about to speak, but at that moment the door banged open and a man in a green riding coat strolled into the room.

Giles turned in his chair, and half rose, somewhat annoyed by this interruption. "Excuse me, but this a private meeting!" he said.

"Gosforth, is that you?" said the man. Gosforth had got to his feet at the sight of him. "Perhaps when you have done your business here, you would favour me with your company?"

"Yes, yes, of course, sir," said Gosforth.

The gentleman closed the door behind him. Gosforth seemed to have shrunk into the darkest corner of the room. He had his hands in his overcoat pockets.

"Who was that?" Giles asked.

"Squire Yardley," said Gosforth.

"You're friends?"

"I wouldn't say that," Gosforth said, taking a little flask from his pocket. He fumbled to remove the stopper and then raised it to his lips.

"What have you got there?" Giles said, but Gosforth was already tipping the contents of the flask into his mouth. Giles dashed forward and attempted to relieve him of it, but he resisted, turning away into the corner so that he could finish. Then he flung the empty bottle at the hearth where it smashed and stood defiantly in front of Giles, a smile on his lips.

At the same time Giles smelled the distinct aroma of bitter almonds.

"What was that?" said Giles. "What the devil...?"

Gosforth began to shake and twitch and was soon gasping for breath. Giles grabbed him in the hope of getting him to vomit by putting his fingers down his throat. This was a procedure he knew of only in theory. The reality of attempting it was not easy, especially as Gosforth's gasping and convulsions grew ever stronger. At the same time he was fighting any assistance. There was a terrible manic gleam in his eye that screamed that he meant to die there and then, and that Giles could do nothing to help him.

And then he suddenly collapsed utterly into a dead weight, motionless in Giles' arms. His head fell forward onto his shoulder, and although the boy was not well built, Giles found himself staggering under the unexpected weight. He managed to manoeuvre him towards the settle and put him down, and check for any remaining signs of life, but it was clear enough that there were none. Gosforth was dead.

He stood back and worked for a long moment on his composure. He was shaking with the shock, but he knew he must not be overcome by it.

He scanned the room, and saw the smashed flask lying on the hearth. There was a label about the shattered neck, fixed with ribbon, and the flames were about to consume it. He retrieved it just in time and stood staring at it. Written on it, in the same elaborate hand as the bottles on Miss Barker's dressing table, were the words: 'Endless peace'.

Chapter Eleven

"It's the same concentration of prussic acid that killed Miss Barker," Felix said, finishing his report on the post-mortem of George Gosforth. "Perhaps from the same source, as it was uncommonly high."

"Not readily available, then?" Major Vernon said.

"No."

"So where did he get it?" Major Vernon said, leaving his writing desk and going to the wall where he had pinned his notes. "Or where did she get it? Or perhaps Gosforth obtains it in the first place, and dupes her into drinking it, knowing he will benefit financially. Then loses his nerve when he realises what he has done and goes into hiding. I track him down, and start to interview him, and he decides he just can't face the inevitable, so drinks another dose."

"Murder-suicide," said Felix. "It is plausible. He had access, he had motive and he had means."

"I should have searched him," Major Vernon said. "Why did I not?"

"Because there was no reason for you to think he would have such a thing on his person. It's not commonplace to have a flask of prussic acid of that strength in your overcoat pocket, and even less so to self-murder in such circumstances. He did not present any obvious risk."

"I know, but I still feel I could have predicted something. He was disturbed, and –"

"You could not have predicted it, sir. No one could have predicted that."

"Perhaps," said Major Vernon. He went and sat down again, massaging his temples. "What bothers me is what we still don't know about it. Perhaps it was not an admission of guilt, but something else. It's too neat."

"Such as?" said Felix, sitting down opposite. Major Vernon continued to rub his temples. "Is your head bothering you again, sir?"

"I didn't sleep. It's just because I am tired."

"I should send you home."

"I won't sleep; well, not unless I take something, and I know your feelings about that."

"And I think you agreed with me?" said Felix. Major Vernon had been using laudanum rather too liberally as a cure for insomnia and Felix had been obliged to have words with him about it.

"I do," the Major said, and got up again to put down the blind as if the light in the room bothered him. The room was now distinctly gloomy. "It is not a habit I should get into."

"You could still take a little, if your head is very bad," said Felix, who was torn between advising restraint and wanting to help him. "And you found Mrs Connolly's camomile quite helpful."

"It was, on occasion. Perhaps not this occasion, though." He picked up the little label that had been tied round the neck of the flask and looked at it. "I have to go back tomorrow and find where this stuff came from. 'Eternal Peace' – you know what that sounds likes to me? – a longing for death. There's something so deliberate about it. Maybe Gosforth had been thinking of doing it for days – maybe he needed courage, and that was what happened at The Black Cat – he found it. She had the courage and went first. He was joining her after."

"You mean a compact to self-murder?"

"That's not impossible, is it? I have read of other cases."

"In literature. But in reality?" said Felix. "Surely not."

"Milburne and Gosforth were playing at knights, at chivalry. They were intoxicated by their games. Milburne has run up atrocious debts, encouraged by Gosforth. It was all very elaborate and fanciful. Maybe this is part of that game and Miss Barker was part of it. He kept saying it was not about money. So was it about love? Some wild, fantastical way of being in love. Perhaps death – or 'Eternal Peace', as it says on the bottle – perhaps it is something they aspired to."

"Why would you aspire to death?" said Felix.

"Because you are too young to know what it really means? And it's an escape – a place where they thought they could be happy together, without having to deceive anyone."

Felix thought of the two corpses lying side by side in the morgue at the Police Headquarters.

"Together in death," he said. "Well, they are now. But she was pious. Why would she do that, if she believed it would endanger their souls forever?"

"It isn't hard to play piety either," said Major Vernon. "Plenty of people say one thing and believe another."

"True enough," said Felix.

"It's just a theory, of course," said Major Vernon, "and the simplest explanation, our first one, is on the balance of probability most likely. Money as the driving force. But there is still too much we don't know."

"What was it that Yardley said to him?" Felix said.

Major Vernon consulted his notes.

"He said: 'I would be grateful if you would favour me with your company'."

"And how did he say it?"

"Civilly enough," said Major Vernon. "Nothing you would remark at. But strange, I suppose – given that Gosforth was a nobody in relation to Yardley – that he should say it at all."

"Exactly," said Felix. "So perhaps it was Yardley who put the fear of God into him. What did you make of him?"

Major Vernon considered.

"I was annoyed with him for interrupting, but he seemed harmless enough. Why do you ask?"

"I don't know. I didn't care for him, but it doesn't mean anything. I expect I am clouding this with prejudice."

"But what you say is not so outlandish. Perhaps Yardley did put the fear of God into Gosforth. It did seem to change his mood. Perhaps it was what Yardley represents – the opinion of the town? Obviously they were a little acquainted. Although he does not seem particularly admirable to you, Carswell, he may have had Gosforth's respect. Being taken up by him would matter in a place like Whithorne. Gosforth was clearly someone with social ambitions – hence his friendship with Milburne."

"And Yardley likes the antiquarian trash," said Felix. "Suits of armour and all that medieval nonsense."

"I shall have to talk to him," the Major said.

"I wish you joy of that," said Felix getting up. "Is that all, sir? I should get back. I have a few tests running. And perhaps you should go home and rest. Even if you can't sleep."

"I need to go and dress," the Major said. "I am dining at my sister's."

~

Felix did not leave his laboratory until after seven. Having two post-mortems in hand and testing all the bottles on Miss Barker's dressing table for toxicity had filled his day and he was looking forward to an idle evening, perhaps in Sukey's arms – if she would permit it.

The atmosphere was still cool between them. He had deliberately come home late on the evening of his return to Northminster, and instead of the ecstatic reunion he had dreamed of, he had only exchanged a few words with her, before she had excused herself and gone to bed. She said she was tired. He had taken this as a clear signal that he was not to join her and so had passed the night alone in an agony of anxiety and frustration, wanting nothing better than to creep downstairs and into her warm bed.

How intensely disagreeable this mock-marriage could be. The price they had to pay to be together seemed high.

As he let himself into the house, he heard the sound of piano music. The piano was a new arrival – it had come with Professor Holzknecht and his son. Like them, it was German, and apparently the latest thing in pianos. Certainly it seemed to make far more noise than pianos usually did and today someone was playing an irritatingly jaunty dance tune. As he came into the hall, he saw the door to their sitting room was wide open and the reason for the music was at once clear.

Sukey was dancing with the younger Herr Holzknecht. Felix didn't recognise the dance – it was some kind of vigorous galop that involved a great deal of spinning, turning and hopping, and it was clear that Sukey was thoroughly enjoying it. She was flushed and smiling broadly up at her partner.

"Very, very good, Mrs Connolly," Holzknecht said. "You have it perfectly. Hop, two, three, four..."

"Hop, two, three, four," said Sukey, laughing. "Hop, two, three, four."

Holzknecht spun her again and gave a kind of whoop. He was holding her far too close for Felix's liking, his long arm curled about her waist, the other hand in hers, fingers knotted together.

Felix stood at the threshold, his hat still in his hand, and watched, in a mixture of pleasure and agony. He had never seen her dance before, and the sight of her joyous but graceful abandon was dazzling, but at the same time it was entirely unbearable.

The music stopped at last and they broke apart. Had it gone on a moment longer, he was certain he would have charged forward and broken them apart. Now he watched Holzknecht making an elaborate bow, and whispering over Sukey's hand as she rose from her curtsey.

"Delightful!" said Professor Holzknecht from the piano.

"Rather exhausting, though," said Sukey, fanning herself with her hand.

"Yes, it is a little," said Holzknecht.

Now Sukey saw him at the doorway. He wanted to stretch out his hand to her and claim her. All he managed was a nod of acknowledgement, which she mirrored.

"Good evening, Mr Carswell," she said. "Thank you, gentlemen," she said to the Holzknechts. "That was interesting. I didn't expect to get a dancing lesson today."

"The polka, Mr Carswell," said Holzknecht, snatching the music from the piano and holding it out to Felix. "It is all the rage in Vienna and Paris."

"I'm not really a dancing man," Felix said. Sukey's cheeks were so pink. Was it from exercise or embarrassment?

"Mrs Connolly is an excellent pupil," Holzknecht said. "I hope we will have the pleasure of dancing again, ma'am?"

"I'd better go and see all is well in the kitchen. Dinner at eight as usual, gentlemen."

She walked swiftly past Felix and down the hall. But instead of going to the kitchen she went upstairs.

"Excuse me," Felix said and bolted.

He followed her up the two flights and together they went into his bedroom. She went to the washstand where the usual jug of water was waiting for him.

"This will be stone cold now," she said. "I thought you'd be back earlier."

"I wanted to be. There was a lot to do," Felix said, taking off his coat. He began to loosen his cravat.

"Yes, the Major said you were busy. I'll get you some more."

"This will do," he said, catching her arm as she went towards the door.

"As you like!" she said, wrestling free. "So?"

"So?" he said.

"Why were you looking like daggers just then?"

"Can't you guess? After that?"

"What business of it is yours?"

"Of course it's my business!" he exclaimed, throwing his waistcoat down on the floor and tugging off his shirt.

"You are an eejit," she said, "if you think –"

"He was making love to you."

"He was? I thought he was teaching me the polka."

"And why would he do that?"

"Because he had just got the music. He came back from his work with it. And what was I to do? I couldn't refuse, poor souls that they are."

"Poor souls!" exclaimed Felix. "What on earth makes you think that?"

"Because they're exiles! To be thrown out of your own country and your home because you dared to criticise the government? Doesn't that deserve our pity?"

"Yes, but he was taking advantage. The way he was holding you, looking at you."

"No, he wasn't," she said. "I know a leer and that wasn't one. He's just rather..." she shrugged. "Oh, I don't know! Come on now, don't scowl like that. I'm sorry if I upset you. I didn't think you would care. You needn't care, you know that."

He did not feel entirely convinced by this, and turned away from her and began to wash. In the looking glass he could see she was picking up his discarded clothes and laying them neatly on his bed. The wifely devotion of this made him feel ashamed.

"I know," he managed to say, as he scrubbed himself clean. "I just don't like his manner. He ought not..." He turned back to her, the towel in his hands. "I wish that it could be made clear sometimes –"

"But it can't, can it?" she said, going towards the door. "I'd better see to the dinner."

She was halfway out of the door before he had the wit to

pull her back and into his arms. She struggled for a moment and then responded fiercely in kind, hooking her arms about his neck and kissing him passionately in return.

"Forgive me," Felix said. "I've been in the company of the dead too long today. This case, it's a wretched one. It's made me –"

She pressed her finger to his lips.

"Get yourself dressed and come downstairs. We can have our dinner by the fire in my room. It's a rabbit pie. Your favourite."

~

The excellent rabbit pie dispatched and a jug of beer with it, Felix threw some cushions onto the floor, and stretched himself out on the rug in front of the fire. Sukey lay down beside him, letting him cradle her in his arms.

"The Major's letter," he said. "What exactly is it he wants you to do?"

"He didn't tell you?"

"Not in any detail," Felix said.

"He wants me to get the confidence of a girl – a friend of the dead girl. The idea is that I should help in the house for a few days and see if I can get her to talk to me."

"Do you want to do it?"

"I don't know. I don't know if he's right in thinking I could manage that. It's nice to be asked, but I don't know. It might be difficult."

"And if he couldn't get anything out of her, it will be," Felix said, "when he can get stones to talk."

"How does he do it, then?"

"He has an instinct for the weakest point. Like a hunter can smell prey, he just seems to know where the weakness is. You know what it's like – you must have felt it yourself. And even if you do succeed in lying to him, he makes one feel damned uncomfortable, as if he knows it's a lie and it's only a matter of time before the truth will come tumbling out."

Sukey laughed at that and said, "Then I should be flattered that he thinks I have such powers in me."

"He may be right," said Felix, propping himself up on one elbow and looking down at her. Her features were half in firelight, half in shadow. "You make me uneasy enough."

"I don't mean to," she said.

He brushed aside a lock of hair from her forehead and kissed her on the lips. That she was lying there, pressed against him, looking up at him with such tenderness and allowing him to kiss her, ought to have convinced him. But he never could entirely rid himself of the fear that she would, at any minute, slip from his grasp. He felt like a constantly hungry child who always expected his bread to be taken away.

"Should I do it?" she said, after a moment. "What do you think?"

"Why do you ask?"

"Because you might not want me to. I don't want to make you feel any more uneasy, do I? I know I touched a raw nerve with Mr Holzknecht, and I'm sorry for it."

He sat up and looked into the fire, anxious not to have her eyes on him. This submission was making him deeply ashamed.

He had no right to expect such deference. She had made that clear enough the other day, but now she was bending her neck to him in order not to hurt his pride.

"You must do it if you think it is right," he managed to say.

"Then I won't do it."

"No, that's not what I meant!" he exclaimed. "You may offend me all you like. That side of it doesn't matter – it's neither right nor wrong. I meant, if you think it will help – and if Major Vernon thinks it will, then I should say you must do it! His genius in such matters is not something anyone can ignore."

"But you don't want me to do it?"

"I don't know! Honestly I don't! Even if you were my wife, I should be struggling with it – though perhaps he would never have asked it, if you were. I don't know!"

She got up and went to her writing desk.

"You should read his letter," she said, holding it out to him.

He struggled to his feet, took it from her and scanned it quickly, as the Major's precise, elegant hand allowed him to do.

> This is not strictly speaking woman's work, but it is work only a woman can do, and necessary work, in a good cause. I do not hesitate to ask for your help in this, knowing that because of who you are, it cannot stain you, and that anyone who cares for your interest will see that is the case.

He exhaled heavily.

"I will not do it if you do not wish it," Sukey said.

"You will have to do it," he said, handing back the letter. "One cannot argue with this, can one? We have our orders! What did I say about his instinct for the weakest points? I should have signed on to that whaler!"

"What are you talking about?" said Sukey.

"Instead of coming to Northminster," Felix said, "I almost signed as ship's surgeon on a voyage to Alaska."

"I am glad you didn't!"

"It might have been simpler!"

"You might be dead by now," she said. "That I wouldn't care for."

"You wouldn't have known me to care," he said.

"I should have felt it," she said, taking a step closer to him and taking his hand. She laid it on her breast, pressing her own hand over it. "I would have felt a little crack in my heart, without knowing what it was. I'm sure of it."

"Specious nonsense," Felix said, as lightly as he could, but he was touched beyond measure. "Is it too early to go to bed?"

Chapter Twelve

The last time Giles had called on the Ampners, it had been only an hour or so after Gosforth had killed himself. On that occasion his nerve almost deserted him. He had sat in the carriage outside the house, his head raging, struggling to find the necessary composure to go in and tell them what had happened. He had kept it brief. The news was enough of a shock for them both, and he had made his excuses, anxious to get back to Northminster before the light went.

Now he had to face them again, and his head was still aching.

He found Mrs Ampner sitting huddled by the fire in a little upstairs sitting room, bundled in shawls, her hair falling out of her cap. She presented a shocking sight for one who clearly valued her handsome looks and ability to dress fashionably. She looked up from her study of the fire as Mr Ampner showed him in, and gazed at him for a long moment before her face creased up and she looked away, sobbing.

At the same time, Giles glimpsed in her features those of her brother, and found himself remembering with too much precision the feeling of the boy gasping in his arms, resisting every effort to be saved, so intent on destruction. He swallowed down the nausea that came with it, and tried to master his nerves. The business had sliced into him like a sword. He felt, in some respects, as weak as the sobbing woman in front of him, whose every tear seemed to tell the miserable tale over and over again. There was a part of him that wanted to turn on his heel and leave the room, but somehow he managed to take his place opposite her. He sat for a few minutes in silence, collecting himself, while Mr

Ampner attempted to calm his wife.

"I'm sorry to trouble you again, Mrs Ampner," he said at length.

"Yes, it is a trouble!" she spat out, "and I do not understand it! Why are you here, sir? What more needs to be said?"

"The more we know, the easier this burden will be for you to bear."

"The more we know?" she said. "After what you said, after what you said he did, then – no, I don't want to know. I already know too much!"

"I know this is painful –"

"No, you do not. You do not know. George was like my own child. He was everything to me."

Giles glanced at her ravaged face. He had thought her quite young the first time he had seen her, but perhaps she had been affecting a youthful appearance. Now she seemed to be approaching middle age. Had she just told him a near truth in saying George was like her own child? George was only twenty. Had she made a mistake as a girl, and passed the child off as a baby brother? It was not an uncommon strategy in families, and it would explain her intense attachment to him. How much worse for a mother, especially one who had never been acknowledged, would be the betrayal and desertion implied by suicide?

"I will keep it brief," Giles said. "It will be to the point, but brief. And I must search his room."

She hesitated, giving a great sigh, and then nodded.

"I also must ask if he and Bel were married, ma'am, and if you colluded in that?"

"Who told you that?" she said.

"Is it true?"

"Yes," she said.

"And you had a hand in it?" She glanced at her husband.

"Yes," she said at length.

"Dear Lord," said Ampner. "You did what?"

"It was what they wanted!" she exclaimed. "There would have been a terrible scandal if I had not done something about it. They were – well, you know – and I had to make sure. Better to marry than burn, I thought."

"And how was it arranged?" Giles said.

"I organised a special licence."

"But how could you, without my consent?" said Ampner. "How? When you knew what she meant to me? Married her to that good for nothing, wastrel, fool of a boy!"

Mrs Ampner shrieked in horror at this description and buried her face in her hands, cringing in her corner.

"Who married them?" Giles pressed on. "And where?"

"Mr Haxton. He used to be curate here. Now he is rector of St John's out at Melthorpe. He was glad of the money, and he could see they were in love, and ought to be man and wife. He married young himself!" she added defiantly.

"Oh, how could you?" said Ampner again. "How could you?" He got up and towered over her, looking as if he were about to strike her. But then he turned and left the room in a great hurry, banging the door behind him.

"It was better it was done!" she said to Giles, in the same tone of defiance. "Far better! They were in love."

Giles wondered what sort of romance it might have been that led to such a path of destruction. Why would a happy young bride kill herself?

"On the day I first came here, ma'am," he said, "you were already concerned that George had gone missing."

"Yes, and why should I not have been?" she said.

"Young men are often thoughtless. They come and go as they please, and forget to tell those who care for them what their plans are. Mr Ampner was quite sure that George would be back for dinner, but you were agitated – almost as if you knew why he had taken flight."

"What do you mean?"

"You knew that they were married, and what George stood to inherit now his wife was dead. Men have killed their wives for far less."

"George did not kill her!"

"But you thought he might have done, perhaps?"

She did not answer, but looked down at her hands, which were occupied in wringing her handkerchief.

"No," she said at last. "No. He was not like that. It wasn't for her money he married her."

"Would he have married her if she had been penniless?" Giles said.

"Yes."

"Are you sure? Given he seemed disinclined to work for his living and had expensive tastes and grand friends to impress?"

"The money was not the reason," she said. "It was splendid, of course, that they should have it, but I would not have encouraged them if I didn't know there was real feeling on both sides. George told me how much he felt for her. It was not mercenary, I assure you."

"Did she ever speak of her feelings to you, ma'am?"

"Not directly."

"Did she ever say anything that disturbed you or made you uneasy? That made you feel she was unhappy in some way?"

"No. She seemed happy with the whole arrangement. I heard her make her vows, Major Vernon, and it was affecting."

Giles decided he would not press her further on that point, although he wondered if she was not clinging to a preconceived narrative. It was to her advantage that her brother married well, and she had obviously encouraged the match as much as she could. For her to claim that the secret marriage was to prevent them from falling into sexual sin was somewhat disingenuous. Her words were saying one thing, her manner another. He sensed he had rattled her, and so he would leave her worrying while he searched George's room.

Here he found signs of the same medieval extravagance afflicting Lord Milburne, although on a smaller scale – a banner hanging on the wall, a piece of armour, and a sword. His writing desk was closed but not locked. It contained a ream or so of foolscap covered in scrawled handwriting, and several notebooks, carefully fastened up with herringbone tape and sealed with red wax. A glance through the loose papers revealed that Gosforth seemed to have had literary ambitions. Some of it had been copied out in a fair hand, and elaborately signed: *George, the Knight of Gosforth.*

Giles gathered up the papers and notebooks, dreading working his way through sheets of doggerel in the pursuit of justice. At the back of the desk he found a pile of unpaid bills, accompanied by strongly worded requests for immediate payment from the tradesmen involved. Some were from the same establishments that Lord Milburne had patronised, but it seemed that Gosforth, without acreage and title behind him, was not given the grace of much credit.

Perhaps his debts spurred him towards death, Giles speculated, mentally calculating the money owed. It was a painful amount. Gosforth may have hoped to silence his creditors with news of his marriage, but now his wife was dead, his financial position could have been thrown into ambiguity, causing him to panic and precipitating his suicide.

Had Gosforth, his head in the romantic, medieval clouds, formed a false picture of what he stood to gain by his marriage? If money had been his principal motive and if she had killed herself, leaving him no better off, then desperation may have driven him to self-destruction.

Perhaps there was some truth in Dr Fellowes' cynical remark about the extent of Bel's fortune being greatly exaggerated by Ampner to improve her marriage prospects. Would such a discovery have driven Bel to kill herself, Giles wondered? It would certainly be a harsh blow. And then for her new husband to discover that the prospect on which they had plighted their troths was nothing but an illusion – would that be enough to make him poison himself?

Puzzling over this, he took the opportunity to make another search of Bel's room. There was nothing fresh to strike his eye until he found a tarnished silver spoon, wrapped in a handkerchief and tucked away in a drawer.

It was a strange object, the presence of which he could not at once account for. If this had been a sparsely furnished room in a common lodging house, where a spoon was a treasured possession, it would not have surprised him. Perhaps it had some sentimental value. He put it with the other evidence and went downstairs, wondering when it would be best to tackle Mr and Mrs Ampner again.

He had still to visit the various apothecaries of Whithorne, in the hope of finding where Bel or Gosforth had obtained the prussic acid. He also wanted to buy some laudanum. He had not packed any, attempting to do as Carswell had suggested and do without it, but in the last hour, his headache had come back with raging intensity. He knew he would not be able to read Gosforth's crabby handwriting without a small dose to dampen the pain. So he let the Ampners be for the meantime, and went back into the town.

Whithorne had only two apothecaries. One was a very mean place, and the owner said he never even kept such dangerous stuff as there was no call for it. When Giles asked about toilet preparations and cosmetics with fancy labels and ribbons, the man was nonplussed. His customers would never want such things and so he never stocked them.

Carr's in Market Street was a much more prosperous establishment, boasting brilliant gas lighting which was efficient but hardly what Giles' throbbing head wanted. Mr Carr was adamant that he would not have sold such a thing to anyone without recording it, even though he was quite certain he had not sold any prussic acid to either Gosforth or Miss

Barker. He produced a meticulously-kept poison register and together they determined that he had not sold any prussic acid since June the previous year, and that was to Dr Fellowes himself for a patient.

"There is so little call for such a thing," Mr Carr said. "I only have – well, see you for yourself, sir," he added, taking down the bottle from the shelf. "Scarcely a pint."

"What strength is that?" Giles asked. "The surgeon says that the concentration of the cyanide was very high – something like sixty-five percent."

"Goodness, this is nothing as strong as that," said Mr Carr. "That would be most unusual. This is only ten percent."

Giles nodded and turned his attention to the display of beauty creams and perfumes. However, there was nothing that resembled the extravagant ribbons and labels, nor the fanciful names of the bottles on Bel's dressing table. But the bottles were the same shape.

"Where do you get the bottles for your beauty preparations, Mr Carr?" Giles asked, turning one of the little bottles in his hand.

"Oh, I get them from a man in Northminster – a wholesaler."

"And do you sell the empty bottles on, as well as selling them filled?"

"Yes, certainly. Ladies often buy them for their home-made remedies."

"Mrs Ampner?" Giles asked. "Or perhaps Miss Barker?"

"No, not those ladies. Mrs Ampner always buys my own preparations which she says are better than anything she could make," he said with a touch of pride. "Can I help you with anything else today?"

"I need some laudanum. What is the smallest size you do?"

"This one, sir," said Mr Carr, unlocking a glazed cabinet and taking out a little green flask. "This is a fluid ounce. Forty-five grains of opium, in forty percent pure alcohol, and best West Indian cane sugar to sweeten. I mix my own so you can be certain there is no adulteration."

"That will do," said Giles, digging into his pocket for some change. As he did, the bell jangled and another customer came into the shop.

"Oh, good afternoon, ma'am," said Mr Carr respectfully.

Giles turned a little and saw Mrs Maitland, a basket on her arm. Despite his headache, he could not help smiling.

"Good afternoon, Mr Carr," she said. "And Major Vernon! I am glad to see you," she added.

"Will that be all today, sir?" said Mr Carr, as Giles laid his shillings on the counter.

"Yes," said Giles, taking up the bottle of laudanum and putting it in his pocket. "Thank you." He turned to Mrs Maitland and drawing her aside a little, said quietly, "How is your son? He has heard the news about Gosforth, I take it?"

"He has," she said. "And he is somewhat... I hoped I might see you. I should very much like you to talk to him. We heard that you were there and – oh, I am so sorry that you were; it sounds a most distressing business." She laid her hand on his arm for a moment.

"I need to speak to him," Giles said.

"Perhaps you could come and dine with us tonight?" she said. "Would that be convenient?"

"Perfectly."

"Will you stay the night? It would be no trouble, and since rain is forecast..."

"Then I will, gladly."

"Good, good. We dine, most provincially, at six-thirty," she said, touching his arm again for a moment. "I am so glad to see you. Poor Charles is quite distraught." She shook her head. "Oh, but what dreadful circumstances for us to meet in again!" she added. "How strange all this is." She reached into her basket and took out a list and studied it. "And now, tediously, I must get on with my errands, mustn't I? And I certainly must not keep you from yours."

There was something about the way she said this that suggested she would like to do nothing but talk to him all afternoon, and Giles could readily have fallen in with such a suggestion. It would have been most agreeable to sit with her, drink tea and remember the days of the Thirty-third.

"Quite – I need to go and meet the mail," Giles said, glancing at his watch. "Until this evening, then?"

Chapter Thirteen

"I can't say that I don't need the help," said Mrs Rivers, watching from the doorway as Sukey disappeared into the scullery with a tray full of dirty crockery. "Margaret is ill today, and Louisa is still being so... difficult. And in any other circumstances I would be grateful, but I can't help feeling you have set a spy in my house, sir, just by the nature of your business."

"Of course," Giles said. "That is natural enough. But please be assured that it's not my intention to incriminate your daughter. I simply want her to give us her perspective on events. She may know something important."

"Everyone is saying that she killed herself," said Mrs Rivers. "If that is the case, then I don't quite understand what you think Louisa might know."

"What everyone says is often not the case at all," said Major Vernon. "We have a great many unanswered questions. Mrs Connolly will be gentle and unobtrusive."

"You are very thorough, sir – and very novel," she said. "To use a woman in such a business."

"The dead and those who loved them deserve truth and justice," he said. "And I use what means I must."

At this moment Miss Rivers herself came downstairs and into the kitchen. She was carrying some dirty linen and looked as grey-faced and wrecked as she had the other day. She stood clutching the bundle to her, as if it were precious, eyeing Giles with some suspicion.

"Ah, there you are, Louisa," said Mrs Rivers, taking the linen from her. "Thank you for doing that. You will be glad to know Major Vernon has brought us some help – most providential given that Margaret is ill!"

"I thought," Giles said, "that it might help for you to be relieved from your work for a while. It will give you time to get things straight in your mind."

She did not answer for a long moment and then burst out: "You were there, weren't you, when he...?"

"Mr Gosforth? Yes, regrettably. Where did you hear that?"

"My brother Johnny."

"They have been talking of nothing else at school, I fear," said Mrs Rivers. "Now sit down by the fire, my dear, you look cold."

"I am not," said Miss Rivers, drawing herself up a little, and in that moment, it was possible to see that in a year or two she would become as formidable a beauty as her mother. "I am quite well. And what is this help? We do not need your charity, sir."

"That is for me to decide, Louisa dear," said Mrs Rivers. "And that is not gracious."

"Let me put you at your ease, Miss Rivers; I will go and fetch her," Giles said, and went into the scullery, closing the door behind him.

"Is that she?" said Sukey quietly.

"You will have your work cut out, I'm afraid."

"What here, or there?" she said, indicating the chaotic scullery.

"Do your best. But I know you will. It doesn't need to be said. But she is hostile and suspicious."

"All the more reason to be doing it, then," she said. "She must know something."

"I think so," Giles said.

They went back into the kitchen.

"This is Sukey Connolly, Miss Rivers," said Giles. "She has been in my family's service and has given us great satisfaction."

Sukey made a respectful curtsey, giving Louisa Rivers all her due as the young lady of the house. In her drab brown print dress and check apron, her head plainly-capped and modestly-bonneted, the Mrs Connolly who was the confident proprietor of a handsome lodging house in Northminster was well hidden away.

"I was just wondering, ma'am," she said, turning to Mrs Rivers. "What order you would like the rooms upstairs turned out in? Since it looks as if it will hold dry for a few hours, it's a good chance to get everything aired and put right."

"Oh, just as you see fit," said Mrs Rivers, looking faintly ecstatic at such a show of initiative.

"I will just get on, then, ma'am. Sir," Sukey added with a nod at Giles.

"The boys' room is a disgusting bear pit," said Louisa. "She should start in there."

"Yes, miss, certainly," said Sukey. "Would you show me where, miss, if it's not too much trouble?"

"This way," Louisa said, and took her away upstairs.

~

"What will you call him, ma'am?" said Felix, taking the wriggling, squalling child from Mrs Yardley's fur-blanketed lap.

She was sitting up in her great Gothic bed, with another fur wrap about her shoulders, and her pale, crinkled hair was down and combed out, with a scrap of a lace cap fixed on top of her head. A small crown would have looked better, he thought.

"I haven't decided," she said, smiling as Felix laid the baby down at the end of the bed and began to examine him. "My husband says he must be Briggs, but I think that is an ugly name. What is your Christian name, Mr Carswell?"

Felix glanced up from examining the boy, feeling his tiny

fist gripping his finger.

"Felix," he said.

"Oh, that is a handsome name!" she said. The baby began to scream, not at all liking Felix's examination. "And most appropriate given the circumstances! Felix – yes, I like the sound of that."

"Steady now, little man," Felix said, turning his attention to the baby, rather hoping that she did not appropriate his name. It implied a long-standing sense of obligation, or at least a silver cup at the christening. "He's wonderfully strong, Mrs Yardley. I cannot see anything wrong with him either."

"He is perfect!" she said, stretching out her hands to take him back. "I knew it. And he is feeding very well."

"You are nursing him yourself?"

"I shall do the best for my boy and no one shall judge me for it!" she said, with an unexpected tone of defiance. "After all, it does not matter. I shall not go out in society for at least six months. This little one," she went on, touching his tiny head, "is, after all, the product of two important bloodlines. He must be my first thought. My husband may boast of his lineage and his acres, but I can match them, and this little darling is heir to it all and will be a great man, you may be sure of it! Look at him, Mr Carswell, does he not have the look of greatness about him?"

The birth of a son and heir had clearly given her confidence, and Felix did not like to disagree, but he could hardly read the child's destiny in his features. Fortunately, it seemed to be a rhetorical question and he had no need to answer, for Grace then bustled up to carry off the boy and wrap him up more warmly.

"You shouldn't leave off his bonnet, ma'am," she said.

"Yes, yes, Grace," said Mrs Yardley. "I shall not!" She then added, when Grace and the child had left the room, with a great smile, "She does so enjoy scolding me!"

"You seem in good spirits, ma'am," Felix said, taking her

pulse.

"Yes, I could not be better," she said. "I feel quite giddy."

"And how are you feeling physically? Are you still bleeding?"

"Only a little now."

"And any pain or discomfort?"

"I am still rather stiff, but I believe I am doing very well."

"You do seem to be," he said. "But perhaps I should examine you, just to see that all is as it should be? Would you mind?"

"No, not at all."

"Shall I ring for your maid?"

"There is no need," she said. "I feel quite safe with you, sir. How could I not, when you have done such a great service for me and my boy? Felix!" she said, smiling. "What a happy name!"

Felix got on with the examination as quickly as he could. Fortunately, she was healing well. There were no complications and her bodily strength was returning despite the loss of blood.

He went to wash his hands, while she adjusted her clothes, and then turned back to find her sitting up as formerly, her fur wrap about her shoulders.

"You are doing excellently," he said.

"Good," she said. "However, there is something else, Mr Carswell, something I wish you to convey to my husband," she said. "I would like you to tell him that I am not yet well, at least not well enough for..." She paused for a moment and then said in a whisper, "relations."

"Surely he must understand that already," Felix said. "At least in the short term. Any gentleman would –" He broke off, for she was shaking her head.

"I know I am already completely in your debt, sir," she said, reaching out and taking his hand, "but I would be more than grateful if you could tell him how necessary it is to my health that he desists for at least six months. If not a year?" She squeezed his hand, looking at him imploringly with her large blue eyes. "I'm sure you could contrive some clever reason. He will listen to you."

Felix was not at all sure he would, but how could he not attempt it? It was not pleasant to imagine what she might have suffered at Yardley's hands. What he had seen of the man made him uneasy. To ask a husband to desist from his rights for six months without a compelling medical reason was not entirely ethical, but he did not doubt she had a good reason for asking such a thing of him. He decided that the difficulty of her labour was reason enough not to risk another confinement for some time.

"Of course, ma'am," he said.

She smiled and squeezed his hand again before releasing it again.

At this moment there was a knock at the door and the sound of a screaming child. Grace came in with the baby, accompanied by Miss Yardley.

"Someone is hungry!" said Mrs Yardley, taking the boy into her arms.

"I will take my leave, then," said Felix.

"Will you come and take a dish of tea, Mr Carswell?" asked Miss Yardley. "Or a glass of sherry?"

"Thank you," Felix said. He was glad of the invitation. Before he had carried Sukey off on her mission, Major Vernon had asked him to enquire about Miss Barker's and Miss Rivers' visits to the castle. It was a much more agreeable task to tackle in the short term than speaking to Squire Yardley about his conjugal relations.

Miss Yardley took him into her sitting room, which did not much resemble a lady's private room, but seemed more like an estate office or a counting house, the walls hung with maps and charts, and the bookcases crammed with books on land management and accountancy. A large writing desk showed evidence of hard work in progress, with only a magnificent black and brown striped tiger of a cat to keep her company. With the cat lying at her feet by the fire, eyeing Felix carefully, she dispensed tea, sherry and cake.

"Mrs Yardley has made a remarkable recovery," he said.

"Indeed," she said, handing him the tea. "And we must thank providence you were here to assist her, Mr Carswell."

"You know that the reason I was here in the first place is because we are investigating the death of Miss Barker and now Mr Gosforth?"

"Yes – but it puzzles me. I understood it was self-murder in both cases. What is there to investigate?"

"Major Vernon, who has charge of the case, is not sure that is what happened. And even if it did, he likes to be clear on all points. He is a thorough man. I believe that Miss Barker and her friend Miss Rivers used to come here to see Mrs Yardley, quite often," Felix went on.

"Yes, they were often here. I encouraged them to come. My sister-in-law is still very young – she needed young people around her. She no doubt told you that she had two miscarriages in less than a year."

"And what did you think of them?" Felix said.

"They were both pleasant girls – provincial and, of course, hardly Mrs Yardley's social equals, but they did not presume, which I liked about them. They were pleased to come and we were pleased to have them."

"And you never got any hint of Miss Barker being unhappy, or having some uncomfortable secret?"

"No," she said, with a frown. "Perhaps I was not paying much attention to her. She seemed contented enough. It is a terrible thing that she felt driven to such an act. I hope your Major Vernon does find the cause of it. It will be a comfort to those who loved her, to know."

The door swung open and Briggs Yardley in his velvet gown came sweeping in.

"Ah, you are hiding him in here, sister," he said, seeing Felix.

"Hardly," said Miss Yardley.

"How does my boy?" said Yardley, pulling a chair up to the tea table.

"Very well. And Mrs Yardley," said Felix.

"Good work, good work!" said Yardley and reached out and slapped Felix on the thigh. Felix hoped that this enthusiasm was not at the thought of his resuming relations with Mrs Yardley. How on earth was he to begin that conversation, and when? This was certainly not the moment, he thought, watching as Squire Yardley deliberated over the plate of cakes.

He took one of the iced ones, popped it into his mouth and, still chewing, looked across at Felix, in a manner that Felix found disconcerting. It was not the look of polite enquiry but a challenge, as if they were about to begin a game. A game that Felix felt sure Squire Yardley expected to win. At that moment Felix entirely understood Mrs Yardley's reluctance to resume relations with her husband. The man might have been handsome, in an angular way, but there was something in his manner that induced a feeling of repulsion.

Felix decided there was one matter at least that he could raise.

"I understand from Major Vernon that you were at The Black Cat on the day Mr Gosforth killed himself," he said. Yardley nodded. "It puzzles me – why did you come into the room and try to speak to him?"

"There was nothing puzzling about it," said Yardley, leaning back in his chair, very much at his ease, with a foot resting on his knee. "Merely wishing to know how the poor young fellow was doing. He had lost his love, after all, and in distressing circumstances."

"You knew about that?"

"It was commonly known, I thought – his aspirations for

her hand. But then, who would not aspire to a fortune under your own roof? An easy wooing, and such a beauty!"

"Who told you Mr Gosforth was in the room with Major Vernon?"

"The publican's wife."

"So you knew he was in there with a police officer, and under inquiry?"

"What of it?" said Yardley.

"I am just wondering why you then took it on yourself to go into what was a private meeting."

"It was in a common inn parlour, not a private room. I wanted to see how he was," said Yardley. "And as a Justice of the Peace, I am quite entitled to supervise the business of the police. Indeed it is my duty. And perhaps I should have been a little more vigilant in my duty, Mr Carswell, and not allowed your Major Vernon to push me from the room in such a peremptory manner."

"I very much doubt he did that," said Felix.

"In effect he did. It was not civil."

"In his defence, he did not know who you were, sir."

"Quite," said Miss Yardley. "He would not know you from a common hoodlum, Briggs. If you will frequent such places as The Black Cat in that filthy old shooting coat of yours, you must take the consequences."

Yardley ignored this and occupied himself with the business of choosing which of the little iced cakes he would eat next.

"It's a curious matter, altogether," he said, finally making his choice of a pink one. He relished it, and brushing the crumbs from his beard, went on: "Now I come to think of it, we only have your employer's word for it that the man put the flask to his own lips. No one else saw what went on, after all."

"Briggs," said Miss Yardley, "really –"

"We don't have any objective evidence," Yardley said. "I should not be happy if such a story were brought before me on the bench, I can tell you."

"And why would Major Vernon wish to kill the witness he had been hunting for the last few days?" Felix managed to say after a moment. He had wanted to say something pretty sharp but he realised that was exactly what Yardley wanted from him. He put down his teacup and got up. "Thank you, ma'am. I have taken up too much of your time already."

Chapter Fourteen

"He has a point," Giles said when Carswell had related his conversation with Mr Yardley. They were in the private sitting room at The Falcon. "Oh, and before I forget – I found this in her room, wrapped in a cloth. Why would she keep a common spoon in her drawer? It is probably not of any consequence, but one never knows."

Carswell turned it a few times in his hands, examining particularly the heavily tarnished silver at the end of the handle. He moved over to the oil lamp on the table to look at it better and then pressed it against the flesh of his palm for a minute. He looked down at his palm with satisfaction, and held out his hand to show Giles the mark.

"Does that remind you of anything?" he said.

"No," Giles had to admit.

"Perhaps if I do this," Carswell went on, going to the fire and crouching down in order to thrust the end of the spoon into the heap of burning coals. He left the spoon there, and took off his coat and rolled up his shirt sleeve. Then he pulled out the spoon by the bowl, using the cloth it had been wrapped in, and laid the tarnished, now heated end against his bare skin, grimacing in pain as he did so.

"Lord, but that hurts!" he exclaimed, throwing down the spoon on the hearth. He swore again, waving his arm. "But I think – yes!" he added with triumph, looking down at the mark. "That looks more like it."

"The marks on her thighs," Giles said, coming to his side and looking at the reddened skin. "A heroic demonstration, Mr Carswell. Thank you."

"I should do it again, to be certain," said Carswell. "But I would rather not, at least not now. It was surprisingly painful. And the flesh on her thighs would be much more tender." Giles winced at the thought. "Why would anyone do that to someone?" Carswell went on.

"Or to themselves?" Giles said. "Remember Don Xavier and his cat of nine tails?"

"Self-punishment," said Carswell. "Poor creature to be driven to that. By shame, perhaps?"

"Did you establish whether she was a virgin or not?" said Giles.

"She was probably not. But you say she was married?"

"She may have anticipated the altar. Perhaps he seduced her."

"Gosforth, you mean?"

"She was happy to marry, it seems, though I only have Mrs Ampner's word on that at the moment. I will have to see what the clergyman says. Perhaps it was relief rather than happiness."

Carswell nodded and looked down again at his arm. "That is much clearer now," he said. "And I need a piece of ice."

Giles rang for the servant while Carswell sat down and pressed his lips to his arm. Giles poured him a glass of claret.

"A clandestine marriage, and then an apparent suicide. Perhaps he did murder her," he said, handing Carswell the glass.

"Are you not having one, sir?" Carswell said.

"Not just yet. I have to ride out to Woodville Park. I am bidden to dine with Lord Milburne."

"I shall have to make do with my own company, then."

"My apologies. There are Gosforth's papers if you feel bored. Bad poetry, by the look of it."

Carswell sipped his claret and smiled at it.

"Hence the nice bottle?" he said.

"I thought you might appreciate that. And had I known you were going to burn yourself in the service of justice I would have ordered the '29."

"This will do nicely," said Carswell, getting up from his chair. "Though I wish I could send a glass down to Mrs Connolly."

"If it is any comfort, Carswell, I believe she will be indispensable in this business. It may take a few days, though."

Carswell nodded and drained his glass. He walked over to the table where Giles had left Gosforth's literary output.

"It is a good thing that there is plenty of bad poetry to distract me," he said.

~

Mrs Maitland received Giles in the black and white flagged entrance hall, a room that suffered no loss of splendour for having no furniture.

"This is not a time for celebration," she said, "but I'm so glad to see you."

Although she was wrapped in a large woollen shawl, he noticed that her dress beneath was a quietly festive one, which became her very well.

"I feel a little shabby," he said. "I am only dressed for a hotel dining room."

"You will do nicely, sir," she said. "More than nicely. If a scarecrow or a beggar had wandered in, it would have lifted my mood. I don't know if my son will dress. He may not even appear at dinner although I have done my best to encourage him. I did not scold, mind, I entreated."

"I can't imagine you scolding," Giles said.

"It is the inevitable consequence of motherhood, I'm afraid," she said. "And I, being weak, have perfected it. But on this occasion even I know it would not have served. He is wretched, and I can't bear it – but he won't talk to me. I only want to comfort him, to take his grief away a little, but..." She threw up her hands and sighed. "I am sure you will do him some good, although it will be painful. But first, come and get warm! I have sherry and a fire for you."

They went into her sitting room. The bills and rent rolls had been tidied away, and she had lit many candles and set the wine on a table by the fire, with chairs nearby. He could not fault her hospitality.

Lord Milburne came in a short while later. He had dressed for dinner, in a careless manner, but had apparently omitted to shave, let alone comb his hair. He was civil enough in his greeting, even managing to give his mother a kiss on the cheek, at which she bridled a little.

"I'm not sure you are in a fit state for company after all," said Mrs Maitland quietly.

"And not an hour ago you were insisting I come down and dine."

"That was before you drank a quart of brandy, you –" She broke off and walked away across the room.

"You cannot command me like a child," he said. He gave a stiff nod in Giles' direction, poured himself another glass of brandy and went and stared at the fire.

"I am sorry to see you again in such circumstances, my lord," Giles said. "This business. To lose a friend in such a manner..."

Lord Milburne looked up from the fire and glared at him.

"And worse still, it might have been prevented," Milburne said. "Do you not think?"

"Charles –" began Mrs Maitland, but Milburne put up his hand to silence her.

"You might have stopped him," he said.

"I don't know what you have heard," Giles said, "but it could not have been prevented, not with the best will in the world."

"Are you sure?" said Milburne. "Is your conscience so easy?"

"Not the least, to tell you the truth. I have examined the matter endlessly in my mind."

"You might have guessed that he would –" Lord Milburne began, in an angry mutter.

"And how could I have guessed that?" Giles said. "I had very little knowledge of the man nor of his state of mind. That is why I wanted to speak to him. There was no indication he would do any such thing. I have some experience of these matters; I have had to arrest desperate men in a far more distressed condition than Mr Gosforth appeared to me, and they did not attempt to kill themselves. On occasion they have produced weapons and attempted to use them on me or my men, but they have not turned them on themselves. And I was not apprehending him. I was quite clear with him on that point – I wanted only to talk to him. I took care to put him at his ease."

Lord Milburne continued his study of the fire, his expression remaining impassive. Yet Giles noticed him folding and unfolding his fingers in private agitation.

"You say I might have guessed," Giles went on gently, going a little closer to him. "Is that because you could have guessed? Did you fear that he would do such a thing? Had he ever spoken of doing such a thing to you before?"

Milburne twisted his mouth into a frown and said, "Not precisely, but..."

"Yes?"

"He talked of death – sometimes. We both did. How it would be fine to die for a reason. In battle or combat – to have a reason for the sacrifice."

"To protect a lady's honour?" Giles said.

"Yes, perhaps," said Lord Milburne and walked away and sat down, his head in his hands.

"It disturbed you?"

"A little, sometimes," Milburne admitted. "And sometimes I think he was right – perhaps it would be better to die young and for a good reason rather than lumber on to miserable old age. A death that means something!"

"You cannot say that of Mr Gosforth's death," Mrs Maitland said. "Surely?"

"I don't know!" Milburne shot back at her. "Perhaps it does mean something! I wish I knew! Dear God in Heaven," he said getting to his feet again. "I should never have mentioned The Black Cat! If I had not, then..."

"His death is not on your hands, even though you feel it may be," Giles said. "And anything you can tell me about George's state of mind – no matter how trivial it might seem – will help us to unravel this business. Do you have any idea, for example, where he might have got the prussic acid from? He never spoke to you of such things?"

"No."

"The bottle was labelled 'Eternal Peace'. Does that mean anything to you?"

"No, nothing at all."

"And when you had these conversations about death – did he speak of self-murder then?"

There was a long silence. Lord Milburne drained his glass and went to the decanter to refill it.

"I don't think you should, Charles," Mrs Maitland began, attempting to stop him. He flicked her restraining hand away. "At least answer Major Vernon," she said.

"I can't believe you asked him here!" he exclaimed. "George might be here still – you trapped him, sir, like a damned animal, you trapped him until he had no choice but to –"

"Charles, you will take that back!" exclaimed Mrs Maitland.

"Oh, of course you will defend him!" Milburne said. "No doubt he is an old lover of yours! You are like all women, Mother, fickle and unchaste!"

Mrs Maitland gave a little gasp.

"That is a gross slander, my lord," said Giles. "And you should apologise for it at once."

"I shall not. It is the damned truth! All women are the same!"

"You should apologise," Giles said again, trying to keep the anger he felt from his voice.

"Where did you get such an outrageous idea?" said Mrs Maitland.

"Caffrey told me – he said that all the officers in the Thirty-third were lecherous wastrels, and their wives no better."

"And you believed that?" said Mrs Maitland. "You believed him?"

"He told me that my own father went whoring when you were with child," said Milburne.

"And when did he tell you that?" said Mrs Maitland.

"When you turned him out for no good reason."

"For his endless pilfering!" she exclaimed. "He said that to you? The wretch! Perhaps you remember this fellow, Major Vernon. He was my late husband's servant. I mistakenly kept him in our service only to find he had been cheating me for years! And what a legacy! You were scarcely ten when he left us, Charles – why on earth did you not say something about this then? Why did you not tell me? And do not say you believed that? Please!"

"Of course I believe it! Don't you? Surely you knew?"

Mrs Maitland turned away, as if he had struck her.

Giles could not think what he ought to say. He remembered Caffrey well enough, and also knew, to his shame, that his slander was not so far from the truth. He had seen Maitland often with light women, when he had been occupied the same way. He desperately wanted to offer her some comfort, but the thoughtless lechery of his own past seemed to disqualify him. It would not be comfort, but another insult.

"Why do you think I have no wish to enter that profession?" Milburne went on. "It disgusts me – it's a debasement of all that is honourable and manly." He addressed this last remark rather particularly to Giles, then set down his glass. "I will dine in my room. I cannot stomach this company." He made for the door.

"Charles, for the Lord's sake –" said Mrs Maitland, following him to the door. It was slammed in her face. She stood there for a moment. "Should I go after him?" she said. "I want to go after him."

"I don't think it will serve any good purpose," Giles said, suddenly feeling exhausted. He sat down on the sofa, and looked down at his knotted hands. "About what Caffrey said..." he ventured.

"There is no need to go over that," she said.

"But –"

"I knew it already. How could I not? We women all knew. We were not fools."

She had sat down opposite him and he found it hard to look at her directly. He felt as guilty for his part in it as if it had been an act of infidelity to her. He wondered at this feeling.

"I hate my part in it," he said. "I hate that I was that man. I wish that I had had more discretion."

"I often think," she said, "that the difference between sinners and saints is that the latter never face real temptation. We all have our faults, our weaknesses. We have all done foolish things – God knows I have, and I should never expect anyone to be spotless. How dull the world would be then."

He looked up at her, and their eyes met.

"Very dull," he said.

"I'm sorry my son is such a boor," she said. "His grief has made him unpleasant."

"Something has given him a poor opinion of women, and of fidelity," said Giles. "Yes, Caffrey's remarks have stuck with him, but I think he is nursing a more recent wound. Perhaps about Miss Barker. What has he said to you about her? He was affected when I told him of her death."

"Nothing to make me think he admired her, but then, he does not confide anything important to me. He has not done for years!" she added.

"Or was he angry with her on Gosforth's behalf? Had she been unfaithful to Gosforth?" Giles said.

"You think Gosforth killed her, don't you?"

"It is a strong possibility. Women who are murdered are often killed by a husband or a lover. It is a sad truth. If she *was* murdered, that is."

"Perhaps Charles will be more amenable tomorrow," said Mrs Maitland, rising. "Shall we go and dine?"

Chapter Fifteen

Mrs Maitland had taken care to make sure he was comfortable. It was not the largest nor the grandest bedroom, but on such a cold night who would have wanted grandeur? The fire had been made up and the bed piled with quilts, while on the table a few twigs of berries and leaves had been put into a little silver vase, in lieu of flowers.

Dinner alone with her had been a pleasure, but pleasure of a constrained kind. She had been valiantly at her ease, and he had responded in kind, but he sensed the performance in it. She was worried sick about her son, and nothing could remove her distress. It had flitted about the room like a trapped bird.

He had retired, amused but still bone-tired, his head cracking again. He did not undress but pulled off his boots and lay on the bed, enjoying the warm comfort of the room. As his eyes grew heavy, he imagined he was being cradled in her arms and she was stroking his forehead with a gentle hand – a better treatment than the little flask of laudanum.

He drifted to sleep – he did not know for how long – and woke to cool darkness. The fire was reduced to a pile of glowing ashes and the candle had burnt out. He shivered and dragged himself up, pulling loose his cravat, feeling stiff and depressingly old. At the same time, he realised what had disturbed his sleep: there was a dog yelping in the passageway nearby in a truly piteous fashion, at a pitch that sliced into his still-aching head.

He lit a candle and went to see if he could find the poor creature; it sounded as if it were seriously injured. He had encountered dogs before that were prone to dramatic hyperbole, but the noise was distressing enough to warrant action.

The miserable animal was soon in evidence, lying by a closed door – a brindle pointer that had been denied entry. Giles crouched down and attempted to comfort the wretched thing, who did seem pleased to see him, hopeful no doubt that he would be granted access to his forbidden paradise. Whose room was it, Giles wondered, that was so important to the dog? Perhaps it was that of the former Lord Milburne – surely the room could not be occupied, for no one could have ignored such a performance.

Yet a moment later, he got his wits about him, knocked, and without waiting for a reply went straight in. The door was unlocked.

What he saw at once confirmed the sudden, dark fear that had come over him as he looked down into the pointer's pleading eyes. Animals had instincts beyond those of humans, and this creature was afraid. A moment's glance revealed that it had good reason.

It was a large and splendid bedchamber, very much that of the master of the house, except that the master in question had not yet come of age, and seemed to occupy the place like a shabby tenant. There was a dim, economical fire burning in the grate and one or two candles on the hearth. The room stank of strong spirits.

Milburne sat on the floor by the fire, dressed only in his nightshirt. In front of him was the bowl from the washstand, and there was a flash of steel as he turned an open razor in his hands. The dog padded over to him and attempted to nuzzle him, but Milburne pushed him away and stared up at Giles.

Giles bent down and gently took the razor from him. Mercifully the boy did not resist. Giles closed it and put it in his pocket. Milburne continued to stare up at him, as if stupefied at being delivered from his demons. Then suddenly he began to shake, bent over the bowl and began to vomit.

This went on for some minutes, and Giles busied himself

making up the fire and lighting more candles. He found the boy's dressing gown and draped it around his shoulders. Milburne sat there shivering and with unsteady hands took the glass of water that Giles offered. He took a few sips and began retching again.

Perching on a chair, Giles watched and remembered himself at the same age. He had often drunk to ridiculous excess and then suffered the painful consequences. On one occasion, Milburne's own father had been a witness to his folly. He had not spared him a sardonic lecture, full of amused contempt for idiotic whelps who drank beyond their capacity. At the time he had wanted to punch Major Maitland in the face – an action which would, of course, have been even more unwise than his embracing the punchbowl of the previous night. But in that moment of agonized humiliation it would have given great satisfaction. He expected that Milburne would like to punch him now. His presence there implied a lecture which the boy certainly did not wish to hear.

Yet he had surrendered the razor without protest. That was no small thing. A minute or two later and he might have done the deed, and Giles would have stumbled into a scene that did not bear imagining.

Giles stretched out his hand and snapped his fingers to the dog who obediently came to him. He took the dog's head in his hands and made a great fuss of it. Milburne had stopped retching now and was watching him.

"You have a good friend here," Giles said. "Dog or bitch?"

"Meg," said Milburne and stretched out his own hand to summon her to him. "Come here, girl."

She went and pressed herself against her master.

"You should get into bed and sleep it off," Giles said. "I don't recommend sleeping on the floor in your condition. I've done it myself, and it isn't pleasant. If you put the slop pail handy..."

Milburne groaned and stared at the fire.

"I would have done it," he said after a long moment. "I was going to do it. I swear if you had not..." He shook his head, and said with a sob, "I am a damned coward."

"No, it takes courage to resist such an impulse," said Giles.

"You think there's courage in this?" said Milburne, gesturing. "In living this dirty, meaningless life?"

"Yes. It's harder to face pain than avoid it. Tell me, are you sure George did not tell you where he got the poison?"

"I told you already – no! If I knew, I should have used it myself – and then you would have been able to do nothing about it! You might have found me dead in my bed like Annabella!" He spat out the name.

"You are angry with her," Giles said.

"I hope she is in Hell," said Milburne. "For what she did to George, she deserves to be."

"That's rather different from what you said the other day. You told me she was a sweet creature, in love with your friend. What has changed your opinion?"

"I thought –" Milburne started to say.

"Yes?" Giles said. "Come now. You can't wish a soul to Hell without good reason. What did you really think of her?"

Milburne got to his feet and said, "I should go to bed, just as you advised."

"Just as the conversation does not suit you," Giles said.

"Who do you think you are, to speak to me like this?" Milburne said, drawing himself up and wrapping his dressing gown about him, in an unsuccessful attempt to give himself a little dignity. "To come into my house and... and..."

He staggered a little, and reached for the mantel to steady himself.

"Yes, yes, you may go to bed soon enough," Giles said, "but tell me what she did."

"She tricked him."

"How?"

"She was not – as a man would like his wife to be. She had been – unchaste. Very unchaste," he added.

Giles nodded and said, "And you didn't want me to know this because you felt it gave your friend a good reason to murder his new wife?"

"Yes, I suppose so," Milburne said.

"Did he ever mention anything of that nature to you? He must have been angry."

"He was heartbroken. She was spoilt. She had spoilt herself," he added a touch pompously.

"Has it occurred to you," Giles could not help saying, "that it might not have been voluntary? She may have been seduced – possibly forcibly. There are many unscrupulous men about who will not hesitate to take advantage of a woman if they can. It may have been the greatest of griefs to her, and she could not bring herself to tell your friend, the man she loved."

"She had no business accepting his offer having done that!" Milburne said. "She ought to have declined him. But no, she was so eager for it! Eager to deceive him, the man she claimed to love."

"Do you really expect a women to make such a wretched sacrifice because of a misfortune?" Giles said.

"If a man can remain pure until marriage, then so can a woman! An impure woman, no matter how it happens, has no business marrying a good man like my friend. It was disgusting!"

"Where do you get these ideas?" Giles could not help exclaiming.

"Purity for both sexes before marriage – does that shock you so much, sir?" retorted Milburne. "Fornication for men and women is a great sin, remember. But you are of an age where nothing was held sacred except money and rank!"

"How old are you, Milburne?" said Giles.

"Nineteen," he said.

"And you cannot hold your drink! Your father told me that at the same age, and he did not spare me his scorn. Unlike every other young man and woman of your age, you seem to be able to resist the temptations of the flesh, but you can't resist the temptation of the bottle – nor, for that matter, of reckless spending. I have seen those bills, my lord, and they are not pretty! Those are equal sins and you ought to consider that before you condemn a young woman without knowing the full facts. And perhaps you have been tempted by a woman, tempted to give up your own precious purity, and only just managed to resist. I wonder now, is that the case?"

"I don't know what you mean," said Milburne.

"Is there a woman you desire, whom you would like as your wife, whom you burn for? Do you worry that she is like poor Annabella – spoilt? Is that what makes you into a penny preacher, my lord?"

"She is not spoilt! She could never be!" Milburne said. "She will never be. I will see to it. I will protect her – always!"

"Ah, there you are," said Giles. "That is why you could not do it. Love. Who is she?"

"That's none of your business."

"It might be," Giles said.

There was a long silence. Milburne went and sat on the bed. At length, in a small voice, he said, "Louisa Rivers."

"And you want to marry her?"

"Yes. As soon as I can."

"Marry or burn," Giles could not help remarking. "And is the young lady in agreement?"

Milburne glanced away.

"I am sure she will be," he said after a moment.

"So you haven't declared yourself?"

"Not yet. But soon enough I shall. All the more after all this!" he added with defiance.

"Have you discussed this with your mother?" Giles said.

"Or your trustees? You're not of age yet, after all. They may have –"

"They can say what they like. I will marry her and that will be that."

"If she agrees to it."

Milburne winced and said, "I think she will. I pray she will."

"Then good luck to you!" Giles said, wondering what on earth Mrs Maitland would make of such a match. She was unlikely to be pleased with his giving Milburne even the slightest hint of encouragement. Louisa Rivers was not the heiress the roof of Woodville Park needed. But the boy needed a crutch to get him walking again. A romantic venture might be as good as anything to keep him from putting a knife to his throat. If his suit was successful, of course – but then again, what girl of Miss Rivers' age and situation could resist the prospect of being a countess?

"You will not tell my mother, will you?" Milburne said.

"About Miss Rivers?" Giles said.

"Yes, and about –"

"The razor?"

Milburne nodded.

"Please?" he said.

"She ought to know," said Giles. "She can't help you if she doesn't know."

"I don't need her help," he said. "What can she do to help me when she knows nothing, understands nothing?"

"That's not the case at all –"

"She cannot know!" he exclaimed again. "I insist that you do not tell her. As one gentleman to another, I beg you, do not tell her!"

"I'm not sure I can give you my word on that, Milburne. It is a serious thing, and as your closest kin, she has a right to know that you were in such a state. You will need her help to get beyond this, even though you do not think so. Melancholia and grief – these monsters cannot be defeated alone. Trust me."

"She cannot know," he said again.

"She won't scold you. She will understand."

"She will not. She knows nothing about me."

"She is worried sick about you! She cares for you more than anything in the world. Heavens above, man, you are lucky to have such a woman in your life!" he exclaimed. Suddenly the boy's petulance and wilful ingratitude drained him of all resilience and energy. He wished he could simply leave and go back to bed rather than have to deal with it any more. Yet, for Mrs Maitland's sake, he knew he could not desert the boy.

He took a breath and went on, "Very well, I shall make a deal with you, my lord. About tonight – I will tell her you were ill from drinking and that I helped you. I will not go into details – but only on condition that you will be frank with her – entirely frank, mind – by which I mean you will tell her about Miss Rivers as well, and that you will do this sooner rather than later. If you do not give me your word that you will try to talk to her, and honestly, then I can't give you mine. That is how it must be, I'm afraid."

The boy shook his head.

"It is better she hears it from you than anyone else," Giles went on. "Surely? Will you give me your word, my lord? I will give you mine."

He put his hand out to him and after some hesitation the boy shook on it.

Giles left him to sleep, with faithful Meg lying beside him, and went back to his own room, hoping that the boy would find his courage sooner rather than later. In that moment it struck him that Emma Maitland was the last person in the world to whom he wished to peddle half-truths.

Chapter Sixteen

Felix knew he was no learned critic, but George Gosforth's literary output struck him as execrable. Written in a crabby hand, it was soon clear that the contents were not worth the trouble it took to read them. Neither, Felix thought, were they worth the ink nor the paper they were written on. Gosforth affected a medieval style, using the most obscure and pretentiously quaint language imaginable. It reminded Felix of the rooms at Whithorne Castle, stuffed with Squire Yardley's antiquarian trash.

Surely, he thought, everything was not better simply because it was old. That was a pernicious notion, the sort of idea that stopped people from having their children vaccinated for smallpox. He considered all the barbaric ideas and practices that men of his own profession had believed in with utter sincerity, only to see them overturned entirely by the work of one or two clever men. It made him wonder what ideas he held sacred that would seem ridiculous in a few hundred years hence, or perhaps even sooner. It made him wish he had spent the evening catching up on his medical journals rather than ploughing through Gosforth's twaddle. Worse still, there seemed to be nothing there material to the case. He would have nothing useful for Major Vernon.

He went to bed, and hoped Sukey was comfortable at Mrs Rivers' house. He feared she might have been consigned to some grim attic.

Next morning, as he was shaving, the waiter came in with his breakfast, and announced, "There's a Mrs Connolly here for you, sir."

"Send her up at once," said Felix.

He was so delighted at the thought of seeing her that he went to the landing to greet her, towel in hand. Looking down the staircase, he almost did not recognise her. She was wrapped up in a large drab cloak, and wearing a hideous old bonnet. She had put on these items of depressing ugliness to present a humble, unthreatening appearance to the Rivers family. But then she looked up towards him and nothing could disguise the brightness of her eyes as they met his, nor the roses in her cheeks from the morning air. Even in that vile bonnet she struck him as the most beautiful woman he had ever laid eyes on.

He hurried her into the room and pulled her into his arms, overcome with desire. She allowed him a few kisses and then gently disentangled herself.

"I'm glad you're dressed. I need you to come back with me," she said. "You'd better eat up," she added, gesturing at his breakfast tray.

"Why?" he said, unable to keep the disappointment from his voice. He had been hoping he might lure her into his still-warm bed.

"Louisa Rivers – there is something wrong with her. I think she's – oh, I don't know what's wrong, but there's something. I was sorting the linen and there's a bucket where they put the napkins – you know, the sort of napkins that women use when they have their courses, and when I tipped it out to put with the other washing, they looked all wrong."

"How do you mean?" he asked, sitting down and beginning his plate of ham and eggs. There was a gravity in her manner that could not be ignored and he sensed the urgency of the moment.

"They don't look like they have been used the way they usually are. They've got blood all over them, but it's in the wrong places and it looks different. Oh, it's hard to explain. It just made me wonder. You've been talking so much about bloodstains lately, and the different density and colour – that's what you said, isn't it?" He nodded. "It's as if she has used them on a different sort of wound."

"That sounds strange," Felix said, his mouth full.

"And she's as pale as pale, and weak as a kitten. She's not well, but she's pretending she is. She fainted in her chair last night. I found her slumped in it, passed out. She came round soon enough and then she ordered me out of the room. I am sure she's not well. You have to come and look at her."

"Yes, of course," said Felix. "Just let me finish my coffee."

"And comb your hair," she said, reaching out and attempting to smooth it.

In less than half an hour they were at the little cottage in St John Street.

"I'm sorry to have stepped out, ma'am," Sukey said to Mrs Rivers, who seemed rather surprised to see Sukey coming into the house. "But I thought it best to fetch someone. This is Mr Carswell. He's a surgeon. It's your daughter, ma'am; I believe she's not well."

"What do you mean?" said Mrs Rivers.

"She's not got up yet, has she, ma'am?"

"No."

"I think you should let Mr Carswell see her," Sukey said. "She was faint last night – well, I found her passed out, but she would not let me help her."

"She did look pale," Mrs Rivers said. She turned to Felix. "You are not practising here?"

"No, I work for Major Vernon," said Felix. "May I see her? From what Mrs Connolly has said, she may need assistance."

"Yes, yes, of course. This way."

She led them up a narrow staircase and tapped on the door to the girl's room.

"Louisa?"

There was no answer and Mrs Rivers went into the room.

She at once exclaimed, "Oh, dear Lord!"

Felix followed her at once.

The girl lay there, staring up at them with glassy eyes, with blood-soaked bedclothes twisted up round her. On the floor was a large fragment of glass.

He grabbed her wrist. Her pulse was still in evidence, but worryingly feeble. The amount of blood already shed was alarming. She swooned into unconsciousness as Felix pulled back the bedclothes and pushed up her nightgown to find the source of the haemorrhage.

"Cradle her head," he said to Sukey. "Keep her with us. Use salts – there are some in my bag."

"I have salts," said Mrs Rivers running from the room.

"Come on now," said Sukey, lifting the girl up into her arms, and tapping her cheeks. "Miss Rivers, come now!"

Felix looked down at her belly. It was ripped to shreds, and there was not much flesh to shred. He glanced at the piece of glass on the floor – that had been the object responsible, he was sure of it, and he was certain this was self-inflicted.

"I've got some mending to do here," he said. "I think it's mostly superficial. But I can't see until we have cleaned her up."

The girl's eyes flickered open and she gave a moan.

"It's all right," said Sukey, brushing her hand across the girl's forehead. "Mr Carswell is going to put it all right."

"No, no..." she began and tried to rise from the bed, turning her face away. "No!"

Mrs Rivers came back now with the salts, which when applied, made her cough and splutter. "Leave me alone!" she gasped. "Leave me."

"No, I'm not going to let you die, Louisa," said Felix taking off his coat, "no matter how much you may want to. Mrs Rivers, will you sit where Mrs Connolly is now, and keep your daughter calm? Sukey, I need warm water, a sponge and some muslin dressings. I may have a few in my bag, but you will need to improvise the rest."

Sukey left without another word, closing the door behind her. He heard her speaking to a child on the stairs.

She came back soon enough with the water.

"I've sent the boys to school, and the girls to your neighbour, ma'am," she said, setting down the water.

It was as well she had done so. The work of the next half hour was not pleasant. The girl would not be calm – she writhed and resisted at every touch. She was suffering, it was apparent, under a double burden of physical and mental torment. She wept and screamed and protested, and at times Sukey and Mrs Rivers were both obliged to hold her down so he could finish putting in his stitches. At last it was done, and since the blood loss had been stemmed, at least for the present, he gave her a large dose of laudanum – which again she tried to refuse – and watched with some relief as she drifted into sleep. Mrs Rivers broke down utterly, and Sukey gently took her from the room. Felix covered Louisa with one of the bloodstained blankets.

Sukey came back a little while later with more hot water and a cup of tea for him.

"Did you have a cup yourself?" he said, drinking it gratefully.

"Yes," she said, looking down at Louisa. "Do you think she did that to herself?"

"Definitely. See this?" he said and showed her the burn on his arm. "I did this with a spoon Major Vernon found in Miss Barker's room. I heated it up in the fire. She had burns like this all over her thighs."

"Mortification of the flesh, I suppose," said Sukey, gathering up the bloodstained bedclothes he had thrown onto the floor. She shuddered.

"You saved her life," Felix said, reaching for her hand and squeezing it.

"Oh, I believe that was you," she said.

"She'd have died if you hadn't come to get me."

"Do you think she wanted to die?"

"It's possible," Felix said. "It felt like it, didn't it?" Sukey nodded.

"Will she ever talk to me now?" she said.

"You will find a way," Felix said. "I am sure you can. Major Vernon thinks you can, and he rarely gets these things wrong."

~

"We are both early risers, I see, Major Vernon," Mrs Maitland said, smiling at him as he came into the sunny breakfast parlour. She was seated at the table, the cloth spread in front of her. "The best of the tea and the toast shall be your reward. And we have a pork pie – of my own making; I am not too proud to admit that, these days."

"I wonder you have the time for such feats," he said.

"It is an excuse to see that all is well in the kitchen," she said. "Did you sleep well? I hope you were comfortable."

"Yes, very," he said.

"I wonder if Charles will join us," she said.

"It might be a kindness to send him some coffee and bread and butter," Giles said, sitting down at the table.

"Is that your best remedy for dissipation?" she said.

"I did see him again last night," he said. "And he was rather the worse for wear."

She gave a sigh and stirred the tea pot.

"He is too young to handle spirits, certainly," she said.

"He probably realises that now," Giles said.

"Was he very ill?" she said.

"Somewhat."

"I should have locked them up," she said. "But he is not a child. He must take a little responsibility for himself, but then again, his grief over Gosforth seems to have made him lose what common sense he had." She poured out a cup of tea and offered it to him. "Is that too strong for you?" Giles shook his head. "And thank you for dealing with that. I am not sure I should have been equal to it. I have nursed him through a hundred trifles, of course, but that..." She gave a shrug and offered him the plate containing the raised pie, as yet uncut. "Now you must have some pie, Major. I command you to it!"

"And destroy its perfection?" said Giles. "It's a work of art."

"Cut it and eat it. There is mustard here," she said.

"With pleasure."

He could not help smiling at her eagerness to have him sample her cooking. The pie was excellent and he had no trouble complimenting her on it.

"I'm lucky to have raised pies and leaking gutters to distract me," she said. "If I had only Charles to fret over I would be in a sorry state. I do worry too much about him as it is, probably more than is healthy. I suppose it's because it has been just the two of us for so long. If I had had a husband and other children, then perhaps..."

"You never thought of remarrying?"

"No. I did have an offer or two at one time, but not for many years now, as you may imagine!" she added with a laugh.

"I can't imagine it at all," he said. "I'm surprised there is not a gaggle of admirers at the door this minute, waiting to ask."

"You need to practise your gallantry," she said, refilling his cup. "That did not sound remotely sincere."

"I will try harder."

"Do," she said.

"But you were never tempted by those offers when they came?" he could not resist asking.

"A little. It would have been pleasant to surrender the responsibility of bringing up a child alone, and have a husband to look after me. One of them especially did tempt me, and on reflection I should perhaps have accepted him, even though..." she glanced away. "But if one's feelings are not truly engaged, whatever the worldly advantages might be – my goodness, Major Vernon, you have me being too frank at the breakfast table!" she added, with a nervous laugh.

"I'm sorry. I shouldn't have," he began. "My curiosity got the better of me. You intrigue me."

"Is that you practising your gallantry?" she said.

"No," he said. "You've been honest, so I'm being honest in return."

She looked down into her teacup, and he wondered if he had made her blush. He certainly felt a little warm himself. It was very pleasant to be alone with her like this, in a room filled with bright winter sunshine that seemed to illuminate her complexion to such advantage.

Imbray the butler came in.

"Excuse me, ma'am, but Hicks is downstairs," he began breathlessly. "He's in a right state. Says he was clearing out the culvert in the East Quarter, as you told him to, and that he and the boy have found a lot of bones in there – and God help us, ma'am – he said he thinks they're human."

Chapter Seventeen

"Preliminary thoughts, Mr Carswell?" said Major Vernon.

It was now noon as they stood in the bleak corner of the black field. A bitter wind was coming in vigorously from the east, with an attendant legion of gunmetal-grey clouds which blocked the already low sun entirely from view.

The rain began to fall again as Felix hauled himself out of the culvert and onto the bank. He had been looking for other bones, but with little success, despite wading into the stream. He was now soaked to the knees and although the first cold bite of the water had been disagreeable, being in there for some time was even more so.

"Human, definitely – but only a partial skeleton," he said. "Given the force of the water through here, especially given it never seems to stop raining in this part of the world, some of the smaller bones will have dispersed with the initial disintegration of the corpse. We may not be able to recover them all."

"You've done pretty well as it is," said Major Vernon, looking at the bones as they lay on the bank, spread out on a piece of sacking in the rough outline of a human form.

"We need to get that inside," said Felix, glancing up at the sky. "There is no point continuing here just now."

"No, certainly. And you need to get dry. I have commandeered Lord Milburne's riding school."

"He has a riding school?" said Felix.

"Hung with expensive tapestries, no less," said Major Vernon. "Now, I assume you wish that moved with as little disturbance as possible?"

"Yes, that would be helpful."

"I'll go and see to it. You go and wait in the carriage."

"Gladly," said Felix, wondering how many inches of water he had in his boots and if he had ruined them.

Major Vernon joined him a few minutes later, during which he had already got comprehensively soaked. It was no surprise – the rain was now beating down on the carriage roof.

"This place is surely cursed," said Felix. "Not that I believe in such things, but I might, if I knew no better."

"The bones are in the flat bed wagon, and well covered," Major Vernon said. "It is a ten minute drive, at most."

"It does not matter if they go a little out of order. I was not sure myself at times. I may have put in some animal bones by accident," Felix said. "There was a lot of rubbish in there."

"How long does it take for a body to be reduced to that condition?" Major Vernon asked as the carriage drove off.

"I can't say exactly," said Felix. "It depends when it was put there."

"Which is what I need to know, if at all possible."

"In some ways," Felix said, "a culvert like that is the perfect spot to strip the flesh from the bones. If, for example, it was deposited in the summer heat – if they have such a thing here, that is – then that and insects and so forth would have got the flesh decaying nicely. And then the water from the burn washing it all away and breaking it up periodically. It was a good place to put it, from the point of view of concealment."

"If that is what happened," said Major Vernon. "It may not be a case of concealing a corpse, at least I hope it isn't. It is probably some poor old soul taking shelter, and dying there. Before this autumn, perhaps?" he asked. "Would the body be in a less extreme condition after, say, September?"

"Perhaps," Felix said. "It depends upon a great many things: the weather, the rate of flow of water, the condition of the corpse itself, and whether any wild animals got at it. So I am sorry, but the estimates will be hazy to say the least."

"We shall do the best we can."

"Of course, when I examine the bones in a good light there may be a few more hints. Oh, and I should not say 'it' – it was a woman, given the shape of the pelvis, and she was small in stature."

"That is something," said Major Vernon. "Let us hope we can find a name and some kind soul to bury her properly." He exhaled. "Although it is a complication I could do without. Especially with this business with Miss Rivers. She sounds distressed, to do that to herself."

"Yes," said Felix, who had given Major Vernon the briefest outline of the morning's events when he had met him at the culvert. "I can't form an opinion on that yet, either, except she made a deliberate mess of herself on several occasions and she did not wish to be treated. I shall need to get back to her before too long. She's in good hands with Mrs Connolly, though."

"Indeed," said Major Vernon. "I sent a message to Earle to come here and see the body. He will want to talk to you, and then you can go back to her. Oh, and I'm sure Mrs Maitland will find you some lunch and some dry clothes."

This lady was at the door of the riding school to greet them. Tall and plainly dressed, she did not strike Felix as particularly handsome, but she was energetic and cheerful in a manner that was welcome on such an occasion. She took one look at him and the parlous state of his boots, and came back a few moments later with dry breeches, stockings and a pair of riding boots.

"I think you are about the same size as my son," she said. "There is a fire in there for you to change by."

The boots and breeches were not a bad fit, and Felix did not feel foolish as he went upstairs to a sitting room overlooking the covered manège.

Here was lunch, just as the Major had said there would be: some excellent creamed barley soup and pork pie, served in picnic fashion. Mrs Maitland described the room as 'Lord

Milburne's folly'.

"In other circumstances," she said, indicating the gaudy medieval trappings which lay about the room, "one might almost enjoy this fanciful stuff."

"But you are beyond enjoying it," Major Vernon remarked.

"I am hoping the tradesmen will take most of it back," she said, fingering a velvet wall hanging. "But they will charge for that as well. We shall be out of pocket, whatever." She sat down at the table with them and pushed the cheese plate towards Felix, with a smile. "May I tempt you, Mr Carswell?"

He was just cutting his cheese when he noticed a pencil drawing hanging on the wall behind her – two young ladies drawn in profile: Miss Barker and Miss Rivers. In the light of what had happened that morning he could not help staring at it. Mrs Maitland turned to look at what had caught his eye, as did Major Vernon. The Major rose from the table, unpinned the drawing and laid it in front of their hostess.

"What was your impression of these young women?" he said to her. "I don't know how much you saw of them."

"Scarcely anything, and I'm now wondering why they have pride of place here," she said, picking up the picture and looking at it. "This other young lady – that is Miss Rivers, isn't it? Charles must have drawn this. He used to spend a great deal of time drawing when he was younger, but I thought he had given that up. I wonder when he did this. They were not here, certainly. I would have noticed if we had had young ladies sitting for their portraits."

"Perhaps at Mrs Yardley's?" Felix said. "Miss Yardley told me the girls went there quite often."

"Has your son been going there?" Major Vernon asked.

"Yes, he has, from time to time – and with Gosforth. I thought it was to see the Squire, but perhaps it was to see these young women. A far more attractive proposition." She laid down the paper with a sigh. "Poor, poor girl," she added, stroking her finger across the image of Miss Barker. "And last night you seemed to suggest that it might be Gosforth who killed her?"

"We are not sure of anything yet," Major Vernon said.

"I do not know which is more tragic – murder or self-murder," she said. "And now we have a lost soul washed up from nowhere. Will you be able to find out who it is?"

"We know a little," said Felix. "It is a woman, and of small stature."

"You have not heard anything regarding a missing woman in the neighbourhood?" Giles said. "Perhaps four or more months back? Or longer. Any local stories that you can recall?"

"We have only been here since late August. I cannot think of anything at the moment. A woman, you say?" Major Vernon nodded. "You must talk to Patton. She is the one for information – she is a great taker of tea in all the cottages in the village. They receive me kindly as well, of course, but they do not confide in me, not as they do with Patton. She will have all the rumours and stories, or if not, she will know the best person to supply them for you." She rose from the table. "Shall I get her to come down from the house and talk to you?"

"No, I will come up and speak to her myself, if I may," Major Vernon said. "In an hour or so?"

"Of course. But, now I shall leave you gentlemen to your business. I must go and check on my son's head and temper."

~

After lunch, Carswell went off to begin his examination of the bones while Giles lingered by the fire, making notes and wondering what he should say to John Earle when he arrived. The man had been so certain of Miss Barker's acceptance of him, but his account now seemed curious to Giles in the light of her secret marriage to Gosforth.

Earle arrived, and they stood for a minute or two looking down on the covered manège, where Carswell was diligently arranging the bones on a trestle table. From this vantage the partial skeleton made a suitably sobering sight.

"It's a small woman," Giles said. "That is as much as we know. Can you recall any such person reported missing in the last few years?" Earle shook his head and turned towards the fire.

"You think this is a suspicious death?" Earle said.

"It is an unexplained death," said Giles.

"Will tomorrow be too early to summon an inquest?"

"Perhaps," Giles said. "I have yet to establish even the most basic facts. Perhaps early next week we might review matters?"

"Yes, certainly," said Earle. "And the other cases? How are they progressing?"

"Ah, yes," said Giles, sitting down at the table and gesturing to the empty chair. "I'm glad for a chance to talk to you about that."

"Of course," said Earle.

"Not in your capacity as Coroner," said Giles, "but as a witness. I wonder if I could trouble you again for an account of what happened at the ball that night. What exactly passed between you and Miss Barker, for example." He flicked through the pages of his notebook. "It would be helpful if I could have the sequence of events in more detail." Earle nodded. "You said that you wished to marry her, although you had not discussed the issue with your family."

"Yes, which she perfectly understood, given the circumstances," Earle said.

"By which you mean she assented?"

"With the caveat I had set out, yes," Earle said.

"Quite a caveat," Giles said.

"She understood that my hands were tied," he said. "And

she was anxious only to do what was right."

"Were your hands really tied, Mr Earle?" Giles said, as mildly as he could.

"What do you mean?" said Earle.

"I do understand that you did not wish to proceed without your family's consent. That is only natural and right, but why did you not seek that consent before speaking to Miss Barker? Rather than dangle the possibility of marriage, only to snatch it back?"

"I don't think I follow," said Earle.

"If you were an intemperate young man I could understand it. But you are, what, thirty, Mr Earle, and well in command of yourself. It makes me curious that you chose that way of going about the business. It lacks feeling, to be frank."

"Sir?"

"'You may marry me, Miss Barker, but only if my family like it. Otherwise you must take it on the chin and walk away'. A strange proposal."

"I don't think so, and neither did Miss Barker. Really, Major Vernon, I don't understand your quizzing at all. Miss Barker understood me and was willing to wait. She knew that the situation was not an easy one for me."

"And nothing she said or did that night made you uneasy?"

"Nothing."

Giles leant back in his chair and looked at Earle appraisingly, hoping to unsettle him.

"A great prize then, for you," Giles said, after a moment. "A great beauty and a great fortune. How did you manage it, when there were so many other rivals? Of course, there is a way a man can secure the love of a vulnerable young woman, but I hesitate to ascribe that to you, Mr Earle. It is not the act of a gentleman, certainly."

"What are you implying, sir?" said Earle, drawing himself up a little.

"Annabella Barker was not a virgin. I need to identify her seducer. From my inquiries so far, she may have destroyed herself out of shame and fear of discovery. She would be desperate to regularise her position – and marry the man who had promised her marriage in exchange for her honour."

There was a long silence and Earle said, "I did not touch her."

"I advise you to tell me the truth, Mr Earle," Giles went on.

"How dare you even suggest that I...!" Earle said, leaping up and facing Giles across the table.

"Because it is the truth?" Giles said, mildly. "You will not be the first man to do it, nor the last. She was a charming-looking creature, after all." He pushed the drawing Milburne had done across the table. "Young and innocent, but tempting. You said she was high-spirited. Not to mention exotic."

"I absolutely resent your suggestion, sir," said Earle, grabbing his hat. "And I do not have time to sit and be insulted." With which he left, banging the door behind him, all in all giving Giles the strong impression that he had touched a raw nerve. It was a matter to which he would have to return.

~

"Come and see what you think of this, Major," Felix said, seeing him standing at the doorway. "This is interesting, perhaps."

"Perhaps?" said the Major, coming over to his side.

"I need a second opinion," Felix said, handing him his hand lens and the woman's right ulna bone. "What do you see?"

"What am I supposed to be looking for?"

"Tell me what you see."

"A test," said Major Vernon, with a smile. "Very well. A

rough surface – it looks as if it has been sawn off here, yes?"

"Yes, quite. See this one now," he said, handing Major Vernon another piece of bone, this time the radius.

"The same marking and feel," said Major Vernon, running his finger over the end of the bone. He glanced at the trestle table. "What part of the body are we looking at here?"

"You are holding the radius, and the other is the ulna. The two bones of the lower arm, terminating in the wrist."

"Are you saying that one of the hands has been removed?"

"Quite. One complete hand missing. The right hand."

"It couldn't have just become detached?"

"No. The bones indicate a straight cut. Across here, approximately," he said, pushing up his right sleeve and making a sawing gesture across his forearm.

"An amputation, then," Major Vernon. "Should we be looking for a one-handed woman who has gone missing?"

Felix shook his head.

"This is where it gets interesting," he said. "If you were to amputate the hand of a living subject – and even of a dead subject, for that matter – if you knew what you were doing, you would not do it there. It's an inch too high, at least. You are making horrible work for yourself and a poor job for your patient. You would make the cut here," he said, indicating the wrist joint. "Even the most rustic barber surgeon would know not to cut there."

"Was the hand removed after death?"

"I hope to God it was," Felix said. "Otherwise..." The Major winced, understanding his implication.

"But there is no way to tell from the bones themselves?"

"Not that anyone has observed yet," said Felix. "It is an extremely intriguing question, though. Bone is a tissue, after all, and it does alter its nature post-mortem. But those marks, or rather their placement, suggests that they were inflicted after death. It would be extremely difficult to do such a neat job on a living person – if they were conscious, that is. That is another possibility."

"A most unpleasant one. But it needs to be considered," Major Vernon said, and went over to study the whole skeleton. "Is the hand the only thing that seems to have been removed in this manner?"

"As far as I can tell."

"Have you ever ridden to hounds?" Major Vernon said after a moment.

"No," said Felix, a little astonished by the change of subject.

"When I was ten, I was present at my first kill, and the huntsman sliced off the fore-paw of the fox and smeared the blood on my forehead. A great honour and a rite of passage, of course. It did not stop me vomiting in a ditch five minutes later – fortunately my father did not see me," he said. "Is this akin to that? A hunter taking a trophy at the kill?"

"From a dead woman?" Felix tried to imagine the scene by the culvert: some person unknown hacking off the hand of a dead woman before consigning her body into the darkness beneath the bridge.

"If you had hounded her to her death, perhaps," Major Vernon said. "If you had enjoyed the chase and wanted to commemorate it." Felix wondered at the dark turns the Major was able to take in his mind. "That is the thing about riding to hounds," he went on. "I do enjoy the chase, I freely admit that, but the kill always disgusts me. I have to remind myself of the ravished hen houses and the savagery of the fox. I tell myself it is a sort of execution, and justified, but I am well aware that there is blood lust among some of my fellow huntsmen, that the kill for them is the point of the whole exercise. One cannot help thinking that in some cases that must apply to murderers, as an explanation for their behaviour. There is pleasure in it. A fox kills because he is hungry. A man will kill a fox for the pleasure of it. A man could kill a woman for the pleasure of it, yes?"

"Yes, unfortunately."

"Then perhaps that is what we are dealing with. Why else would you remove the hand, except to remind yourself of the pleasure?"

"But to take the hand away?" Felix said. "That would not be for the faint-hearted."

"Exactly," said Major Vernon. "Someone who does this – they would be inured to the sight of blood and dead bodies."

"But not a medical man," Felix put in. "Too clumsy."

"A slaughterhouse man? A huntsman. An undertaker."

"A taxidermist," threw in Felix. "A veteran of battle."

"Possibly," said Major Vernon. He had laid his hand on the forehead of the skull, almost as if he were giving her absolution. "Someone will have missed her, someone will know something. This will be a great festering secret with someone, I'm sure of it."

"Speaking of festering, how do you hide a human hand, for the Lord's sake?" said Felix. "What do you do with it? You cannot have it mounted like a fox's head and put on display."

"Could it be preserved?" Major Vernon asked. "Do you not have such things in glass jars in pickle?"

"In brandy. But that requires a certain knowledge, and of course the right equipment. A suitable vessel."

"And a cool head," Major Vernon said, consulting his watch. "I have to go and talk to Mrs Maitland's maid. And you need to get back to your patient."

Chapter Eighteen

"She's doing well," Felix said, "given the circumstances."

He had taken Mrs Rivers out of Louisa's room onto the landing in order to speak to her. As he did, he noticed the door to the room opposite was slightly open, and despite the gloom, he thought he glimpsed some familiar-looking bottles on the table inside.

"Oh, thank you," she said.

A man's voice called up the stairs. "Mrs Rivers?"

"Excuse me," Mrs Rivers said, and went downstairs.

His curiosity piqued, Felix took his chance and went into the room. His instincts were rewarded. As well as the bottles on the table there was a large open cupboard full of jars and books. Most significant, however, was a basket of labels, all beautifully painted, with fanciful names just like those on the bottles from Miss Barker's dressing table, and more significantly still, like the label from the little bottle with which George Gosforth had killed himself.

He heard footsteps on the stairs and so, having slipped a handful of them into his pocket, he quickly came back out onto the landing. At the same time Sukey appeared at the door opposite and beckoned him towards her.

"Is she all right?" he murmured, following her into the room.

"No change," she said. "I just had a thought..."

But there was no chance to speak. Mrs Rivers had returned to the landing. Felix noted how she carefully closed the door to her own room before coming back to her daughter's bedside.

"Might a friend see her?" she said to Felix. "Just for a

moment? A good friend of our family."

"Of course," said Felix.

She left and went downstairs again.

"Yes?" he said to Sukey.

"I think we should take her back to Northminster," she said.

"You may have a point," said Felix, thinking of the bottles and labels.

"Could we? Will it be safe to move her?"

"Tomorrow, perhaps, with luck."

"But how will we get Mrs Rivers to agree to it?"

"That might be easier than you think," he said. "I shall have to speak to Major Vernon first. Something has just..."

But he had no opportunity. Mrs Rivers had returned with her visitor: a dark-browed, broad-shouldered gentleman with a definite manner of command about him.

"This is Mr Latimer, Mr Carswell," said Mrs Rivers. He shook Felix's hand fiercely and then looked down at the still-sleeping Louisa with scant tenderness.

"An accident of some sort, then," Latimer said. "I am sure I can rely on your discretion, sir. A young woman's reputation is..."

"Yes?" said Felix.

"This is a delicate matter."

"And one about which we have not established the full circumstances," Felix said.

"But you will be discreet, I am sure."

"Within the limits of what must be done, yes, of course," said Felix. "You seem concerned, sir, if you don't mind me saying."

"She is an innocent child," said Latimer. "And as a friend to this family, her reputation must be my business. In the light of recent occurrences in the town –"

"You mean that her friends have taken their lives?" Felix said.

"I do not wish her branded with the same... Have a little pity, man, for God's sake!" He walked away a few steps.

"Mr Carswell will be as discreet as he is able, sir," Sukey said. "I am sure of it. It's just that in such cases the truth is always better exposed than buried, no matter how painful that may seem."

Felix thought that she said it sweetly and humbly, seeking to calm Latimer, but it made him frown.

"Who is this?" he said with a flick of his hand towards Sukey.

"Mrs Connolly. Major Vernon set her to watch Louisa," said Mrs Rivers. "It is just as well he did!"

"Watch her?" said Latimer, his voice rising. "What does that mean?"

"Perhaps we should continue this downstairs?" Felix said, going to the door and attempting to usher Latimer out. He seemed reluctant for a moment, then pushed past Felix and stomped down the stairs with such force that the wooden frame of the ancient house seemed to tremble. Mrs Rivers went after him.

"He acts as if it's his house," said Sukey in a whisper.

"That's what the Major implied," Felix said, also sotto voce. "That he and Mrs Rivers –"

"Perhaps he's feeling guilty," Sukey said. "About her. About what she did and why. Perhaps he – well, you know..."

Felix looked back at Louisa, sweetly asleep in an opium embrace.

"Mother and daughter?" he said. "Oh, Lord, I hope you're wrong!"

"It would explain a great deal," Sukey said. "Wouldn't it?"

Felix went downstairs, a little astonished at Sukey's reading of the situation, but he had to admit it was plausible, if unpleasant.

Latimer went straight on the attack, as Felix came down into the chilly parlour.

"What precisely is your relationship to this Major Vernon?" he said.

"We are colleagues in the Northern Counties Criminal Investigation Office. Major Vernon is Superintendent of the division and I am the consulting surgeon. We are here to investigate the death of Miss Barker, and now that of Mr Gosforth."

"They are both suicides!" said Latimer. "Surely that is self-evident? What is there that needs to be prodded and poked over at such length, Mr Carswell, with people sent to spy in people's houses without so much as a warrant?"

"I could see no harm in it!" exclaimed Mrs Rivers. "And she saved her life! You were not here. She saved her life!" And then she burst into tears and ran upstairs. Latimer stared after her, as if casting silent curses upon her.

"Surely such things are best left lying, sir?" Latimer went on. "Especially when these tragedies occur among gentle people. There will be enough gossip already among the lesser folk – there is scant enough respect left in this day and age! The world is falling to pieces as it is!"

"I was always taught that respect needs to be earned by exemplary conduct," Felix said.

"What do you mean by that?" Latimer said.

"You say you are a friend to this family," Felix said. "One might read that several ways, Mr Latimer, given your concern for that young woman's reputation."

"You will read it as entirely disinterested, sir," said Latimer after a moment, "if you have any sense about you."

Felix did not feel the threat on his own behalf – he knew he was safe enough from such bullying – but he felt for those unfortunate souls who must live under Latimer's authority. At that moment, Sukey's suggestion seemed eminently plausible.

~

Giles had not gone into the house looking for Lord Milburne, but found him anyway, in the comfort of his mother's little sitting room. Still in his dressing gown, he was stretched out on a sofa with Meg, the loyal pointer, beside him, acting as canine nurse and guardian. A folded cloth covered his eyes, which he lifted gingerly as Giles came into the room.

"I haven't come to hector you," said Giles quietly, seeing him wince at the light. "I was looking for Patton."

"She has gone to get me some broth," Milburne said. "She will be back soon. I don't know if I shall manage to drink it even though she will force me." He straightened himself a little on the sofa and took the cloth from his forehead. "What is all this about a body in the culvert?"

"A partial skeleton of a woman," Giles said. "It's quite a puzzle."

"Poor woman," Milburne said. "My mother is upset – though she does not say it, of course. I'm glad you are here to deal with all this," he added.

"Think nothing of it," Giles said.

"I haven't spoken to her yet about last night," Milburne went on, "but I shall, I promise. I thought this evening; and then tomorrow, I will go and speak to Miss Rivers. Yes?"

"Miss Rivers is not well," Giles said, taking the chair by the fire and wondering how much he should say.

"No?" said Milburne, sitting up abruptly and then wincing at the pain it caused him. "What has happened?"

"My colleague Mr Carswell, who is a surgeon, has been attending her this morning. Quite a serious business, I understand."

"What does that mean?"

Giles took a breath and said, "She appears to be in a state of some mental distress. She seems to have attacked herself with broken glass, wounding herself with it."

Milburne gazed over at him, shaking his head.

"No, no –"

"I am afraid so, my lord. But she is out of danger now. Mr Carswell is an excellent man and she has a good nurse as well."

"But..." Milburne began, and then stopped, shaking his head.

"There is something you might be able to help me with," Giles said. "Something that might help Miss Rivers, in fact."

"Yes, anything," said Milburne. "Anything! May I go and see her?"

"I don't know about that," Giles said. "You would have to speak to Mr Carswell. She may not be ready for visitors."

"Yes, yes, of course. But what can I do? I must do something."

"Last night you told me about Miss Barker's infidelity," Giles said. "Do you have any idea who her lover was?"

"How will that help Louisa?"

"Because she and Miss Barker were so close. They may have shared a great many secrets. Consider – Louisa may have acted out of fear and shame of the discovery of some terrible secret, just as Miss Barker may have done, albeit less successfully, fortunately. It is a brutal fact of our society that we often judge innocent women for the sins that men commit upon them."

Milburne studied his hands and nodded.

"You did say last night," he said after a moment, "that I should not blame Miss Barker. I had not thought – I was so angry on George's behalf that I did not think it could be anything but her fault. But you are right. It might not have been. And if you are telling me that Louisa might too have – then, no, I cannot bear the thought of that, sir. It is too..." He looked across at Giles imploringly. "If it's true, then –"

"It's just a theory. When I am looking for answers I ask a great many questions, and sometimes they are the wrong ones. But Louisa was provoked into her actions by something and I must look for probable cause. Do you have any idea who this man might be?" Milburne shook his head. "Let us unpick the thing a little. How and when did George tell you his suspicions about Miss Barker?"

"It was that Monday at The Black Cat. The day before the ball," said Milburne after a moment.

"And for the sake of clarity," Giles said, taking out his notebook, "did you know about the marriage at that point?" Milburne glanced away. "My lord?"

"Yes, yes, I did. But I swore I would not tell a soul. I gave him my word! And I have told you enough –"

"All right," Giles said. "Just tell me what happened at The Black Cat that day."

"He was miserable. At first he would not tell me why, but then I got it out of him. He and Bel had finally – well, you know what I mean, sir, and he had discovered that she was not – pure."

"And did he say precisely how he came by this idea?" Giles said.

"I believe there are signs – that it's clear enough."

"How many virgins had your friend slept with?" said Giles. "To know with such certainty?"

"None!" exclaimed Milburne. "He had saved himself for his wedding night."

"Then his ideas will have been based entirely on hearsay," said Giles. "And often, in matters of the bedroom, that means nonsense."

"He was certain of it."

"She told him she was not a virgin?"

"No, of course not."

"Then how was he so convinced? What was the sign he meant?"

"He didn't say in particular. He was speaking of his new wife!"

"Whom he was accusing of fornication," Giles pointed out.

"He told me he was certain of it."

"But did he discuss this with her?"

"He did not say that he did. He was asking me what I thought he should do."

"And you said?"

"I don't know. I was so shocked I hardly knew what to say."

"But you believed him in the end?"

"Of course. George wouldn't lie to me! He was miserable."

"It never occurred to you that his inexperience might have misled him?"

"No. He was certain, and since I have no knowledge myself, I thought..."

Giles nodded.

"And he had no suspicions who this other man might be? You didn't discuss that?"

"No," said Milburne. "But I have wondered about it, after we talked. There is someone who..."

"Yes?"

"Earle," said Milburne after a moment. "I think she liked him somewhat. I saw them talking together and wondered. And I know he is not a good man."

"What do you mean by that?"

"It was something I heard Patton saying to my mother. About Mrs Earle always having trouble getting new maids because girls who worked for her were always getting with child. I took that to mean that he was behind it. That's common enough, I believe."

"Unfortunately, yes," said Giles.

At this moment Patton came in with the broth. As she bullied Lord Milburne into drinking it, Giles asked her if she had heard any stories from the villagers about missing women.

"No, sir, I have not," she said. "And I wouldn't believe them anyway – most of them are a dirty, idle lot, truth be told.

They see my mistress' kindness and generosity as a right rather than a blessing and it would not surprise me if they were in the habit of consigning their dead to rot in culverts instead of burying them like Christians."

When he took his leave of Lord Milburne, she followed him from the room, and said, in the same blunt manner, cloaked in only the most superficial deference, "I must ask you something, sir – about my mistress. I have to ask, if you'll forgive me, but what are your intentions?"

It had not been the easiest question to answer in the moment. He had not yet asked himself such a question and he was startled by her saying it, and with so little provocation. He was almost sharp with her for what was, by any standards, an impertinence. Yet, he saw the concern that lay beneath her extraordinary manner and understood her absolute loyalty to her mistress. He knew it would not do to offend her.

The question itself was a disturbing one. It suggested that Mrs Maitland had said or done something to set the woman onto him, like a strange sound or movement would set a guard dog barking in the night. Perhaps it had been the dress she had chosen to wear that night at dinner, or the trouble she had taken to make his room so comfortable. Had Mrs Patton read these signs as deviations from a common standard? She was evidently unsettled by Mrs Maitland's behaviour, and it had made her bold.

"If you'll forgive me, sir," she added, after a moment of silence, and this time there was more sincerity than before, almost a touch of desperation.

Giles nodded, and managed to find some suitable words: "An old acquaintance is something to be cherished, Mrs Patton, and never presumed upon."

"I'm glad we understand each other, sir," she said. She made her curtsey and left him standing in the passageway, wondering what he would say to her mistress when he next saw her. He had not been guarded, it was true.

Minutes later, he found Mrs Maitland in a large drawing room, where what furniture remained was covered in striped dust sheets. She was removing the cover from a marble-topped table, the legs of which were made of writhing gilt mermen.

"The taste of our grandfathers!" she said. "I wonder what we could get for it."

"It hasn't come to that, surely?" he said. "And can you sell that? Isn't that part of the entail?"

"You are probably right," she said. "I shall have to look at the inventory. It is so ugly, though! Would anyone miss it?" She reached out and caressed the bearded chin of one of the mermen. "Forgive me, gentlemen." He could not help smiling.

"They will probably come back into fashion," said Giles.

"Yes, as everything does, in time," she said. "And if I did sell it, I should do it at the wrong moment and lose a potential treasure. Such is my luck."

"You sound like a hardened speculator."

"Fortunately I do not have a penny spare to put into railways or mines, or unfortunately – depending on how your luck runs. I have been given tips by Miss Yardley, and she has the luck of the Devil."

"Miss Yardley?"

"She makes a study of the markets," Mrs Maitland said. "I was rather startled by it, when I first heard her talking so."

"Then it is more than luck," said Giles.

"I suppose so. She has money to play with and the inclination to study company prospectuses and so forth. She says there is luck in it, but that she cultivates her luck."

"I have yet to meet this lady," said Giles. "Nor Mrs Yardley. It sounds a strange family. I have only met Mr Yardley very fleetingly and could form no opinion of him, but Mr Carswell was not impressed."

"He is not impressive. And the way he calls himself the Squire is – well, ludicrous. If anyone is the Squire of

Whithorne it is Miss Yardley. She manages everything – he would have nothing if it were not for her. She even arranged his marriage. Mrs Yardley is worth twice as much as he is, and her trustees would never have allowed the match if Miss Yardley had not been there to reassure them that it would not be squandered."

"She is a queen regnant, then, like you?"

"I am nothing of the sort," she said. "At least not on such a scale. But I suppose the analogy holds; the trouble is that Yardley has never grown out of his childishness, and spends money like water on his antiquarian fancies. This is why I worry about Charles so – I see a man like that, and I worry that my boy –"

"He will not. He has the best inheritance: your common sense."

"I wish I could believe you, but I don't see much sign of it."

"It's like growing asparagus," Giles said. "It takes a while to establish itself. Seven years, I think, to get asparagus ready to harvest."

"Common sense is like growing asparagus?" she said, laughing. "Does it also have a short season?"

"A bad analogy, then," said Giles. "I shall have to think of a better one."

"You had better," she said. "One that does not make the chamber pot unpleasant." She covered her mouth and turned away. "Excuse me," she muttered. "I am rather..." She was blushing now. "As I said, I talk too much."

Her embarrassment at betraying this slight vulgarity was both painful and touching. He reached out and took her hand and pulled her back to face him.

"You are a soldier's wife," he said. "There is nothing to excuse."

She pulled her hand away, shaking her head.

"You make me forget myself," she said.

"I will happily take all the blame," he said. She smiled a crooked smile at that, which made him want to take a step closer to her, but he remembered what he had said to Patton. He would not presume. "I must get back to work, though," he managed to say.

"Yes, yes, of course you must," she said, gathering up the dust cover into her arms. "And so must I."

"Oh, before I go," Giles said, remembering what he was about. "Can you confirm something I heard about Mr Earle? It is probably just gossip."

"Mr Earle?" she said.

"His character with women," Giles said. "Well, more particularly women servants."

"Oh, that," she said with a sigh. "I only have what Patton told me. I did not speak with Mrs Earle about it. Perhaps I should have, since she sent me the girl and gave her a character."

"You took on one of her servants?"

"Yes, briefly. She left us after a month or so."

"Of her own free will?"

"Yes – which was a relief, for it turned out she was with child when she got to us, and then one never quite knows the right thing to do. But she was unwell, and decided to go back to her family after a month or so with us. I hope they were kind to her. I gave her some money and linen for the child, of course. I was at first rather cross with Mrs Earle for passing on the responsibility to me when I had asked her in good faith if she knew any young women looking for positions, but one cannot pick quarrels in such a small place as this."

"And Patton implied that Mr Earle was the father?"

"She did. She told you that?"

"Your son overheard the conversation."

She nodded and went on: "And the other reason I did not confront Mrs Earle about it, is that it's hardly her fault. She must be mortified if it's true that he is so... Frankly, it would be more honourable if he were to go whoring! At least there is an element of –"

"Quite," Giles said quickly, wishing to spare her any embarrassment from her plain speaking, although he found it admirable. "What was the girl's name, and where was she from?"

"Mary Pearne," she said. "I think she came from one of the hamlets a few miles to the east of Whithorne, one quite near the coast. I can't remember the name offhand. It is bleak country out there. I do hope her people were understanding." She gave a great sigh. "I should have made her stay, should I not?"

"If she decided to go, then what could you do? But it's a difficult question at the best of times."

"A few guineas and some baby clothes," she said. "It feels shabby."

"You did all you could – and you've been helpful to her now. I shall need to have a sharp conversation with Mr Earle. He can take responsibility for his pleasures. And I hope that will loosen his tongue on another matter. He was being decidedly coy with me earlier. Thank you!"

She gave a gracious nod and they made their farewells.

"Eadesham," she said, just as he reached the threshold. "That was the name of her village!"

Chapter Nineteen

Felix spread the labels on the table in front of Major Vernon.

"Found in Mrs Rivers' bedroom," he said.

The Major picked one up and examined it. He whistled, and examined another.

"Tell me more."

"Her room is across the landing from her daughter's. I was speaking to her on the landing and she left the door open. She went downstairs and I saw an open press full of bottles – a regular dispensary. Sukey is going to try and have another look if she can."

"How is the girl?"

"Steady enough, all things considered. Physically, that is. Her mental state is uncertain," he said. "When she has recovered a little more strength and there is less need for opiates, then we might try talking to her again. Sukey had an idea that she might take her back to Silver Street."

"That's a good idea. If her mother is concocting and supplying poisons then it's best to get her out of that house."

"You think that is the case?"

"We shall have to see what the lady has to say for herself."

"You may have to beat back that bear Latimer," Felix said. "He was concerned about reputation. Sukey wondered if he hadn't had congress with both the mother and the daughter. And that was the cause of Miss Rivers' distress."

Major Vernon nodded.

"That's a good observation," he said.

"Especially," Felix went on, "if one considers the nature of the wounds that Miss Rivers has inflicted on herself. They were confined to her lower abdomen. I wonder if that means anything."

"What are you thinking?"

"If this self-mutilation is not a form of self-expression, as well as a punishment. Sometimes, when people cannot speak of a thing, when there is too much distress and shame to speak of it, they find another language. If a woman slashes at her belly, the place where a child grows, is she not attacking her womb? I know it sounds most outlandish, but the girl was in such a state."

"And Miss Barker was acting in a similar fashion – to the extent of actual self-murder. I have heard that her 'admirer' Earle is not to be trusted with women servants. I wonder if he was preying on Miss Barker?"

"As Latimer may have preyed on Miss Rivers," Felix said.

"It is a good theory," said Major Vernon. "But I find it puzzling that they should choose these girls. Why? There is a high element of risk in seducing a Miss Rivers or a Miss Barker. These are not housemaids who can be quietly used, and who will stay quiet from fear of losing their places. These are respectable young women whom the wives and mothers of the town asked to tea."

"Isn't that the point?" said Felix. "It's because the other sort of woman is too easy for them. They want variety, novelty, and presumably virginity. I know that some men prize that experience and will actually pay a premium for it – though Lord knows why. I must say I have never understood that!"

"Nor I," said Major Vernon. "But you are right. Perhaps they will pay for their pleasure with the risk. Or does the risk itself add to the pleasure?"

"Perhaps," said Felix. "This town is dreary beyond belief. They are bored."

Silence fell between them for a moment as they considered the implications.

"It is something of a wonder that women will ever have

anything to do with us," Major Vernon said.

~

Mrs Connolly was in the kitchen at St John's Lane, feeding stew and dumplings to the Rivers' children.

"Mrs Rivers is upstairs with her daughter," she said.

Giles followed Carswell up the narrow staircase to the girl's room. They found Mrs Rivers sitting by the bedside, holding her daughter's hand. She looked as if she had been crying. There was a crumpled handkerchief in her lap. One meagre candle was burning.

"If I can just see all is well?" said Carswell, lighting another couple of candles.

She rose and nodded.

"And if I might have a brief word, ma'am?" Giles asked. "In private?"

"Yes, of course," she said, and they went out onto the landing.

"In here?" Giles suggested, indicating the door opposite. "Perhaps?"

She seemed to hesitate a moment and then opened the door. They went into the darkness, and Giles reached for a lucifer and lit the candle stub on the table. As the flame established itself, he saw that the table was quite clear and the cupboard in the corner closed.

"Won't you sit down?" he said, offering her the only chair.

She sat down and looked up at him.

"What is it, sir?" she said.

"Can you tell me about these?" he said, taking the labels from his pocket and putting them on the table before her.

She reached out and straightened one with her finger.

"Where did you get these?" she asked.

"Did you make them?"

"I – yes," she said.

"You write and decorate them?"

"Yes."

"To what purpose?"

"To make money," she said.

"Could you explain a little more about that?"

"I have a few old receipts. Family receipts. For beauty preparations. They are very effective. I make them up and sell them to a woman called Mrs Wilson. She has a bonnet shop in Greyfriars Lane."

"You make them here?"

"Yes."

"What is in these preparations?"

"Oh, nothing much. Almond oil, beeswax, rosewater, lavender oil and so forth. Just simple little creams and ointments."

"With fanciful names?"

"Yes, I suppose they are fanciful. But Mrs Wilson tells me her customers like the names."

"Annabella Barker liked them," Giles said. "She had a great many of your potions on her dressing table."

"Yes, she did," Mrs Rivers said.

"Could you show me where you make these preparations?"

"Yes, of course," she said, getting up and going to the cupboard, and unlocking it with a key she took from her pocket.

"Why do you keep the cupboard locked?" he said.

"Do you not have children, Major Vernon?" she said.

"I don't," he said. "You mean you have to lock it because there are things in there that are dangerous?"

"No," she said. "Nothing I make is dangerous. Of course not. I do not want it disarranged, that is all."

The cupboard door was open now, and as Carswell had

said, it had the look of an apothecary's workbench. One shelf was full of jars and pots with Latin names painted on them, and another contained the various mixing and grinding vessels, as well as measuring tools. On the back of the door several hand-written sheets had been pinned up, apparently for reference.

"Very impressive," he could not help saying, "for a few simple preparations."

"My father was an apothecary," she said. "I inherited some of his tools."

"And his books?" he said, reaching for a volume on the top shelf. It looked well-thumbed.

"Yes. I do not pretend to have studied them, of course. All I have any knowledge of is the creams that I sell to Mrs Wilson – and thank goodness I do, for we should be hungry if I did not. Though you perhaps think it is shameful for me to do it."

"It's enterprising," Giles said. "Tell me, is Mrs Wilson the only person you supply?"

"Yes," she said.

"What about this one?" he said, taking from his pocket the envelope containing the charred 'Eternal peace' label he had retrieved from the hearth at The Black Cat. He took it from the envelope and put it with the others. "The style, as you can see, is identical." She did not answer. "'Eternal Peace'. Is this your handiwork? Pick it up and look at it carefully, will you?"

She obeyed him and then said, "Why is it half-burnt?"

"I snatched it from the fire. It was about the neck of a little bottle – just like these ones here," he said, taking an example from one of the shelves and putting it on the table. "Unfortunately the bottle was smashed, but the contents were quite deadly. A concentrated draught of prussic acid. Would you call that a simple preparation?"

"No," she said. She put the label down on the table again.

Then after a long moment she said, quietly, "That is my handiwork, yes."

"And how did it come to be on a bottle of strong poison? Do you have any explanation for that?"

"Because I made it," she said.

"Why?"

"Money," she said.

"For Mrs Wilson?"

"No."

"Then for whom?"

There was another long pause.

"Annabella," Mrs Rivers said at length. "I made it for Annabella."

Giles sensed the emotion in her voice but he could not feel the sincerity of her words. It seemed too outlandish. He shook his head.

"You don't believe me," she said, rising. "But that is the Gospel truth," she said. "God help me, but I did."

"You know I will have to charge you if you stand by that, ma'am?" Giles said.

"Yes."

"And that I will have to take all this into evidence?"

"Yes," she said.

"So I ask you again, is that really the case?"

"Believe me, sir," she said. "You must, I beg you."

"How much money?" Giles said.

"I'm sorry?"

"How much money did she give you to make the stuff?"

"Oh, I don't know – perhaps ten guineas."

"And you have this money still?"

"Of course not! I had a hundred debts to pay off. I settled various accounts in the town. It was a great relief to do so."

"Sit down Mrs Rivers," said Giles. "And tell me the truth."

"That is the truth. I have told you."

"And you expect me to believe such a fabrication, ma'am? You expect me to believe that, for only ten guineas, you calmly made and supplied a dose of deadly poison to a young woman – no, a girl, who was your own daughter's best friend, in order that she might destroy herself? And not only that, you put a pretty label and a ribbon on the bottle?"

"You must believe it," she exclaimed. There were tears in her eyes now. "You must. Please."

Giles shook his head.

"It's a farrago, ma'am, an utter farrago. Now, I am going to leave you with your conscience and come back tomorrow and then you will tell me the truth, if you have any sense. But first you are going to give me the key to that cupboard, because this is now material evidence, and it will remain locked away until I say so."

She surrendered the key to him, choking back her tears as she did so, and Giles locked the cupboard.

"That is the only key, ma'am?" he said.

"Yes," she said, and then added with a touch of defiance, "what common house cupboard ever came with two keys?"

~

"Will she be able to travel tomorrow?" said Major Vernon coming into Louisa's bedroom.

"It won't be comfortable for her," said Felix. "But she's out of danger, so yes."

"I'll make arrangements, then," he said, glancing about the room. "Are there any painting things in here?" he asked.

"I saw a paintbox in the chest," said Sukey. "Here," she said opening a drawer.

Major Vernon took out the paintbox and examined it.

"It looks well used," he said. "But there isn't much evidence of art work in here, is there? One might expect to see a few sketches pinned up." He went to the lamp on the mantelpiece and started to peer at the palette in the lid of the paintbox, which was still stained with colours. "These colours – we might be able to match them in better light."

"How did it go with Mrs Rivers?" Felix asked.

"She tried to tell me she made the prussic acid," Major Vernon said.

"But you don't believe her?" Sukey said.

"No. She was determined for me to charge her. Practically putting her head into the noose."

"Is she covering for someone?" Felix said.

"My thought entirely. A protective mother, I would say."

"You think she is covering for Louisa?" Sukey said.

"It seems only natural," Giles said. "I think Mrs Rivers has guessed at part of the truth, or observed something that disturbed her profoundly. She is no fool – well, she wasn't until she decided to pretend she had brewed that poison. She knows who did and doesn't want that to come out. She is prepared to sacrifice herself to save her daughter."

Chapter Twenty

"Why am I here?" Louisa Rivers said.

She was sitting up in bed and her dark eyes scoured the room, like a cornered animal.

"To get better," said Sukey. "Now, are you comfortable there, or do you think another pillow will help?"

"You can't keep me here!" she said. "You can't! My mother –"

"Now, please stay calm, Miss Rivers. It's for the best that you're here," Sukey said.

"For whose best?" she said. "Yours?"

"Yours," Sukey said again, calmly but firmly. "Now, do you like chicken soup?"

"I want to go home," she said.

"You can, when you are better," said Sukey. "Now then, how about some of this soup?"

The smell was irresistible and the girl took a spoonful or two, slowly at first, and then her natural appetite got the better of her, and she sat and finished the bowl.

That they had an abundance of chicken soup was due to an unfortunate incident in their absence. Sukey's hen house had been ravished and the fox responsible had slaughtered all the birds. However, he had not removed them all, and enough remained to be salvaged. Martha, Sukey's cook, had laboriously plucked and jointed them, and made a vast quantity of excellent and rich soup, for which Felix might have thanked the enterprising fox, had he not seen Sukey's tears for her brood. The depth of her grief had surprised him a little – indeed she had been surprised herself, she admitted, embarrassed at her feelings. "I'm a fool these days," she said, wiping her eyes. "I can't account for it."

"Perhaps you should try a few guinea fowl instead," Felix had said. "My mother keeps those and they've never been got by the foxes. They are daft things, very amusing."

"Perhaps," she had said, but her tone suggested that he wanted to replace the beloved Swiss Leghorns too promptly.

"Whose house is this?" Louisa asked, laying down her spoon.

"Mine," said Sukey.

"But you're just a servant!" said Louisa.

"I turn my hand to many tricks," said Sukey. "How about some bread and butter pudding? I made this myself."

"What are you, then?" said Louisa.

"I am helping Major Vernon. As is Mr Carswell," Sukey said, indicating Felix in his corner.

"So you are in the police?"

"After a fashion."

"How?" the girl said.

"Luck, as much as anything. And Major Vernon thought I could help with things."

The girl sniffed the bread and butter pudding.

"Nutmeg and cinnamon," Sukey said.

"My brothers love this," Louisa said. "When we have it, which isn't often, I never get more than a bite."

"You shall have as much as you want," said Sukey. "If you like it."

"It is nice," Louisa admitted, her mouth still full.

"It's a cure for a lot of things, bread and butter pudding," Sukey went on. "If I were writing a medical book, I should put in a recipe for it."

"That would be novel," Felix said.

"It would be revolutionary!" said Sukey, and now a wan smile passed across Louisa's grey face. Felix smiled as well, aware of Sukey's quiet genius at work. She would charm the truth out of the girl, that was certain.

At that moment the front door to the house slammed shut with such violence that the whole house shook.

"Can he never close the door like a civilised..." Felix said getting up.

"I am sure the wind just caught it," Sukey said.

"It's intolerable!" Felix said and dashed out of the room. He ran down the stairs and out into the street and saw Georg Holzknecht vanishing around the corner. He wondered if he should give chase, but decided it was undignified and entirely futile, given that the door had just slammed again due to the stiff wind gusting along Silver Street. It was not worth the trouble.

He went back into the house and found Professor Holzknecht staggering about the hall. He was in a state of some distress, doubled up and struggling for breath.

"Herr Doctor..." the Professor began, but speech was beyond him. Felix went at once to assist him, for he was on the verge of falling on his knees.

~

"Have you had such an attack before?" Felix asked later, when the crisis had passed and the old man was installed on the couch in his sitting room.

Professor Holzknecht answered only after a moment. He was still breathless.

"Yes, twice."

"Recently? In the last week, or month?"

"Month," he managed to say.

Felix decided to spare him any more questions for the present and went on with his examination. "You will be glad to hear that I do not think you are in any serious danger, sir," Felix said when he had finished. "You must keep yourself calm, though. Perhaps a little less book work, and a little more exercise? A daily constitutional?"

"Perhaps, yes," Professor Holzknecht said.

"You could walk up to the Precincts, around the Minster and back. That's a pleasant walk." The man nodded. "Or perhaps go and work in the Minster Library?" Felix said. "That's supposed to have a fine collection of books."

"Ach, yes, but not the books I need to consult," said the Professor. "The sort of books I need are not liked by the Church, in general. They disregard the gold I seek – to them it is trifling. And indeed, much of it is not even in the form of books. That is part of my purpose, really. To collect the gold!"

"And what sort of gold might that be?" Felix said.

"Stories," said Professor Holzknecht. "Old, old stories. The sort of tales your nurse told you, Herr Doctor. Those have been my life study. You are a Scotsman, are you not, like the great Sir Valter?" It took Felix a moment to realise he was referring to the author of 'Waverley'.

"Oh, yes."

"You like Sir Valter's tales, I am sure?"

"Yes, very much."

The Professor smiled.

"Sir Valter was a great man. He has made this country appreciate the old tales and ballads – you people understand the importance of these things, because of his genius, yes?"

"I really don't know," said Felix, a little bemused by this. "It's not exactly my line."

"Ach, but it is everybody's 'line', as you say, Herr Doctor. We are made by such stories – they tell the real history of our world and we must catch them and put them down in writing before they are all lost. All the factories and railways and all that is new and so very fast is making them vanish like dew on the grass on a bright morning. Ja?"

"That must be quite a labour," Felix said, and found himself laughing. "Excuse me, I am just remembering my nurse Annie quarrelling with old Jeanie in the kitchen about the ending of some story she had begun to tell. They could not agree which was right. It got quite heated."

"Yes, yes?" said Professor Holzknecht. "What was the tale?"

"That I can't remember," said Felix. "I just remember the quarrel."

"Try and recall it," he said. "It would be a great favour to me if you could."

"I will try," Felix said. The old man put out his hand and touched Felix on the forearm for a moment.

"When I was a young man," he said, "I went about my country trying to find the best storytellers. I would sit and write down their tales. I wish I could do that now, but..." he sighed.

"There is nothing to prevent you doing that again, surely?" Felix said. "If you are careful, you will recover your health. And that would be an incentive to recovery. I am a great believer in that – a good purpose is half the cure."

"It is not my health that prevents me," said the Professor. "I have other responsibilities now. And when I will be home again, I wonder?" He gave a shrug and looked away towards the window.

~

The headquarters of the Northern Counties Investigation and Intelligence Office were by no means impressive. The building was of recent construction, and set at the end of an undistinguished alley. From Felix's point of view the best feature was the large, well-lit basement, its windows overlooking a yard at the back. It had been made for a tailor's workshop, but Felix found it suited him well as a dissection room and laboratory. There was a scullery adjoining with running water, and the lighting was provided by gas: a vast improvement, especially on a gloomy, wintry afternoon such as this one.

The bodies of Mr and Mrs Gosforth had now been removed for burial, but whether they would be buried together, and whether in consecrated ground, seemed difficult questions. Felix was glad it was not his task to answer them. His responsibility was the incomplete skeleton of the woman from the culvert that now lay on his table. What other clues about her identity and her death could such dry bones yield?

"What is it, Frewen?" he called, hearing footsteps coming downstairs. He assumed it was the young constable whom Major Vernon kept as a clerk and door-keeper.

"Not Frewen," said a voice behind him. Felix gave a slight start, and turned to see Lord Rothborough standing in the doorway.

"My lord, I did not know you were –"

"I am passing through, only," Lord Rothborough said. "I am leaving for town again at seven."

"How is Lady Rothborough?"

"I don't know. That's the truth of it. One hears so many opinions. All these eminent men and none of them talk straight. Oh, I'm sorry, I don't mean to criticize your profession, Felix, but..." He exhaled and looked about him, and then at the bones. "You have your usual quiet company, I see."

"Quieter than usual," said Felix. "I am sorry about Lady Rothborough. Was not Sir Joseph going to see her?"

"He did, and it was inconclusive." He rubbed his face.

"You look tired, sir," said Felix.

"Oh, it's nothing," he said, reaching out and patting Felix on the forearm. "The girls I do worry about. Their devotion is beyond that of saints, and it makes them so pale."

"Sir Joseph didn't have any constructive suggestions?"

"Yes, we are to go abroad forthwith – Italy – for the rest of the winter. Florence, in fact, which I am not fond of, to tell you the truth, but she likes it, so that is something, and fortunately Sir Richard Arnforth has a suitable house for us."

"Will business not keep you in London?"

"I have disentangled myself from a great deal, at least for the present."

This was a notable sacrifice. Lord Rothborough lived for the rise and fall of governments, for Blue Books and Royal Commissions, and all his schemes and projects. Whatever it was those eminent physicians had failed to say in plain language, their manner had obviously implied: the situation was so grave that all business must be cast aside.

"I'm sorry," Felix said.

"The post is faster than it was. That's some consolation. I shall expect a Northminster digest, mind!"

"I will do my best," said Felix.

"What's this business, then?" he said, indicating the bones.

"A woman, found in a culvert near Whithorne. On Lord Milburne's land."

"She died some time ago?"

"That's what I am trying to establish. It's a little strange to find human remains in such a place. Major Vernon is still there scouring for missing persons and settling some other matters – a rash of suicides."

Lord Rothborough gave a shudder.

"I never liked that town. It is set all wrong in the country somehow, if you know what I mean."

Felix nodded, and said, "Did you ever have any dealings with Briggs Yardley?"

"I knew his father slightly. A mighty strange fellow. You have come across the son?"

"Yes," said Felix. "I helped to deliver his heir. A rather dangerous birth, all in all."

"Then he will be obliged to us," said Rothborough.

"I doubt it. It's not his way. He's also mighty strange, I

should say."

"One must pity the child, then," said Lord Rothborough. "Though I did know the grand-sire, Mrs Yardley's father, Lord de Warke, before he died. And he was not strange, but it was rather talked about, that marriage. She was his only child and very young when the match was made. A lot of money on that side, not to mention the property, which is not inconsiderable. She might at least have got a title for her trouble. What is she like?"

"Very happy to be the mother of a son," Felix said, feeling rather uncomfortable about not yet having fulfilled her last request to him. He was going back to Whithorne next morning to complete his search of the culvert, and he would rather spend the entire day up to his waist in freezing water than have that conversation with Yardley. But a visit to the castle was unavoidable. He had given her his word.

"I wonder if the old barony could be revived for the little boy," said Lord Rothborough. "It went extinct with de Warke's death, I understand." He came and looked at the bones again. "However will you puzzle this one out?" he said. "Those bones may have been there for years, surely?"

"Yes and no," said Felix. "Major Vernon did establish from the estate records that the culvert was only constructed fifteen years ago. That makes his task a little easier."

"A small mercy," said Lord Rothborough. "Poor woman."

"I am coming to the opinion," Felix said, "that even knowing that the culvert has only been there since 1825, that there might be some other indication that the bones are of recent rather than ancient origin. If one considers old skeletons that are preserved in museums, or exhumed when graveyards are dug over, the surface of the bone bears a certain texture and colouration, which these do not. Just as seasoned and unseasoned wood are different. It is certainly a subject for further study. I was thinking if I took cross sections of both and compared them under the microscope..."

He felt Lord Rothborough's hand on his shoulder, a warm, encouraging squeeze.

"I'd better leave you to it," he said. "I have other errands to run. There are some packages for you upstairs – the long one is for Mrs Connolly. If she doesn't like the colour she can take it back to Fairfax's and change it. But I thought it would suit her complexion." Fairfax's was the most fashionable and expensive lady's outfitter in Northminster.

"That wasn't necessary," Felix said, embarrassed.

"What woman does not like a new dress?" said Lord Rothborough. "Especially with Christmas coming."

As he said this, there was the sound of more steps on the stairs and Frewen came in.

"Mr O'Brien would like a word, sir," he said. "Is it convenient?"

"The famous O'Brien?" said Lord Rothborough. "The proprietor of The Bugle? How interesting. I should very much like to meet him."

"Yes, send him down, Frewen," said Felix, realising he could not avoid this.

O'Brien was Sukey's brother-in-law, and made Felix nervous at the best of times. He felt he was only a few steps away from guessing the true nature of his relationship with Sukey and that when the penny did drop, the consequences would be unpleasant. Now he quailed a little as he heard O'Brien's heavy tread on the stairs, and soon his large frame, augmented further by a bulky overcoat, appeared in the gloomy hall. His expression was lost in the shadows for a moment and in his hand he held what looked like a club.

But a moment later, when he stepped into the bright gaslight, he saw O'Brien was looking his usual, mild, cheerful self, and the club was in fact a roll of papers tied up with tape.

"Good afternoon, Mr Carswell!" he said, taking off his hat. "Sir," he added to Lord Rothborough.

Felix made the introduction and Rothborough shook O'Brien's hand most enthusiastically.

"I was just leaving," said Lord Rothborough. "But I could not pass up the opportunity to meet such a prominent local personage."

"The honour is all mine, my lord," said O'Brien.

"Major Vernon told me that you have plans to add another title to your stable – a serious paper for the middling classes in the county."

"I do, my lord," said O'Brien. "But it has proved a little difficult to get the money together. I can't stretch to it at present."

Rothborough nodded sympathetically.

"You must not give up," he said. "It's a necessary project. And you are not without friends, sir, please remember that. There is a gentleman to whom you should speak at Marshall's Bank – Mr Hope. Be sure to mention I sent you. He manages certain matters for me, and this is a matter I am interested in. He understands my intentions."

O'Brien looked slightly bewildered, as those unused to Lord Rothborough's manner – that of a conjurer pulling rabbits from a hat – were wont to do.

"I would involve myself more personally," Lord Rothborough went on, "but unfortunately I have to go abroad at present. My wife's health..."

"I am sorry to hear that, my lord," said O'Brien.

"Italy," said Rothborough, with a shake of his head. "Where perforce one must live among the faded glories of the past, and not in the future as we do in Northminster!" He looked at his watch. "Mr Hope, Mr O'Brien. That is the name."

"Yes, my lord."

"I must go. I have to see the Bishop. I do not think he will last the winter, to tell you the truth. Ah well, he has a stall in Heaven waiting for him without a doubt, the dear fellow!"

Rothborough shook O'Brien's hand again and then turned to Felix. They made a clumsy embrace, during which Lord Rothborough murmured, "Take care of yourself, my boy. A letter now and then would be a great amusement for us all."

"I will try," Felix said, knowing he was a poor correspondent in Lord Rothborough's eyes. "And Godspeed to you all."

Lord Rothborough kissed his forehead, turned and left without another word, running up the stairs with his customary energy. Felix turned away, feeling an unexpected sense of depression.

"Is the Bishop really that ill?" O'Brien asked.

"That's the first I've heard of it," Felix said.

"And this Mr Hope," O'Brien went on. "You've had some dealings with him, I suppose?"

"I bank at Marshalls," Felix said. "I've never met him though."

O'Brien rubbed his face.

"Does he mean it, when he says things like that?" O'Brien said.

"Yes, generally," said Felix.

"I'm forgetting why I came," O'Brien said. "I had a letter from the Major. He asked me to have these printed up." He handed Felix the roll of papers. "He said you are going back tomorrow so you can take them with you."

Felix unfastened the tape and looked at the papers. They were posters asking for information about any women who had gone missing from the Whithorne area in the last twenty years.

"Is that she?" O'Brien said, indicating the bones.

"Yes," Felix said.

"I'm putting a piece in this week's Bugle," he said. "Major Vernon asked me to see if you had anything else to add."

"No, not so far," said Felix, rolling up the bills again. "I will see he gets these."

"There was something else, since I am here," O'Brien began. There was a hesitant tone in his voice which made Felix feel nervous. "Now, you're not to take this amiss, Mr Carswell, but I thought I'd mention it, since I have the chance. It's just that Mrs O'Brien has been worried about it and I wanted to put her mind at rest."

"Worried about what?" Felix said, as unconcernedly as he could.

"About Sukey," O'Brien said. "She has got this notion in her head that you and she are..."

"Yes?"

"Courting," said O'Brien.

"Courting," said Felix carefully, though his heart was pounding with relief at the innocence of O'Brien's reading of the situation. He had expected something much more cynical. "And if we were?"

"I don't know," said O'Brien. "For my part, I wouldn't have any objections, if your intentions were as they should be, which I am sure they would be – don't mistake me on that – but Bridey, she sees herself as head of her family. She has ideas on the matter, is what I mean to say."

"What sort of ideas might those be?" Felix said.

"So there is something in it?" O'Brien said. "She's been wondering. After all, you spent a lot of time together in the summer, didn't you, and before? And being under the same roof. These things happen, we all know that and I'm not passing judgement, it's just we need to know what's going on. For Sukey's sake, as much as anything. She had such a time with Connolly. Bridget doesn't want her getting hurt. Being led on, or any of that sort of nonsense." Felix was about to object to this, but he did not get a chance. "Now, I know you wouldn't, and I've tried to tell her that, but if you could just give me a hint that could set her mind at rest."

"I don't know what I ought to say," Felix said, with rather more honesty than he intended. He wondered if he should have just issued a flat denial, but O'Brien's manner was too warm, too earnest.

"So are you courting?" O'Brien said. "Yes or no?"

"It's..." Felix began. "I do admire her, yes, very much."

"Ah," said O'Brien, nodding. "That is what we thought."

"But I have not," Felix began as steadily as he could, "spoken of it to her."

This was despicable and Felix was ashamed, but O'Brien was smiling now.

"Of course you haven't!" he said. "Lord in Heaven, it took me more than a year to get the courage up to speak to Bridey," he said, and then added in a more grave tone, "but maybe it isn't just that stopping your tongue. I don't suppose his Lordship there would..." He gestured towards the door as if Lord Rothborough was still there.

"Nor Mrs Connolly's parents, I think," Felix countered.

"No. Though you've deep enough pockets. The old man would like that. He didn't like me. He still doesn't, to tell you the truth. I've never had enough money. But money isn't everything, even to him."

"Would he accept it if I converted?" Felix said. "That is, if she were to accept me," he added.

"You'd convert?" said O'Brien. "You've been thinking of that?"

"A little," said Felix.

O'Brien whistled.

"Isn't your father a clergyman?" he said. Felix nodded. "Then you are serious."

"I told you, I admire her, more than anything," Felix said. "She is –"

O'Brien held up his hand to silence him.

"I will tell Bridey," he said. "This will put her mind at rest."

"I haven't said anything to Mrs Connolly," Felix said, deciding he must shore up his untruth. "You must make that clear."

"But you will, soon enough?" said O'Brien. "Or that German boy will beat you to it. Bridey thinks he is mad for her."

"She does?" said Felix.

"And she thinks Sukey likes him. I'm supposed to go and have a word with him too. Oh saint's above, man, don't look so miserable! I don't think Sukey likes him, whatever my wife may say. I've seen the way she looks at you, and if I were you I should strike while the iron is hot! If you ask me, she's making sheep's eyes at him to encourage you."

Chapter Twenty-one

Felix arrived back at Silver Street with some trepidation. He hoped Sukey had been kept busy with her housekeeping and looking after Louisa. But a picture had formed in his head of her sitting by the fire having an intimate conversation with Holzknecht. He knew he ought not to doubt her, but he felt overtaken by angry mistrust, no matter how hard he tried to be rational or objective about her or her intentions.

He had read of jealousy before and never understood it. He had read a 'A Winter's Tale' and thought the king's sudden descent into envy ridiculous. Othello had succumbed likewise, and he had thought them both improbable monsters. But here he was coming into the hall of his own house, which was not his own house, afraid of his own feelings.

He found her in her sitting room at the writing desk, working at a ledger. She held her hand up to silence him while she completed the column of figures. He was content to stand there for a moment and watch her silently telling the numbers, happy in the realisation that she knew it was him because he was the only person who entered that room without knocking first.

"And seven and six," she said with some satisfaction, and laid down her pencil. "All done," she said and turned smiling to him. "What have you got there?"

"Mysterious objects from Lord Rothborough. This one is for you," he said, tapping the dress length. "From Fairfax's."

"Oh my," she said, getting up and taking it from him. "It's heavy."

"He's gone away to Italy," he said. "Lady Rothborough's doctors have ordered it."

He put the other parcels down and wrapped his arms about her. The dress length slipped to the floor.

"You do love me, don't you?" he said.

"You know I do. What's wrong?" she said, as he pulled her more tightly against him.

"I just had a conversation with your brother-in-law."

"Oh."

"It's all right. They only think we are courting, That's all. Or rather that I love you but haven't told you yet. And your sister thinks you like Holzknecht." He threw the last phrase in as casually as he could, but the words fell out, sounding more angry than he meant to.

"And that's what's upset you," she said, looking up at him. "Yes?"

"Yes," he said, after a moment.

"I thought we had sorted this out," she said.

"Yes, but why would Bridey think that?"

She wriggled out of his arms and stooped to retrieve the fallen parcel.

"Because she thinks I'm not to be trusted," she said. "It's a bad habit of hers." She went to her desk and cut the string on the parcel, and turned back the brown paper to reveal a glowing length of amber-gold silk. "Goodness. How beautiful!"

He came over to her and put his arms about her again, but she resisted.

"Are you sure you don't like him?" he said.

"I will pretend you didn't say that," she said. "I'm going to go and see Louisa. Oh, by the way, I took Professor Holzknecht some tea – he was singing your praises. Poor old fellow, that sounds like a nasty turn he had."

"When did Bridey see you with Holzknecht?" Felix said. "He hasn't given you any more polka lessons, has he?"

She put her hands over her ears.

"I just want to know why she would think that," Felix

went on.

"Because, as I told you, she has never trusted me! She thinks I'm a flirt."

"And why is that?"

"I don't believe you!" she said. "I really don't believe you! How can you even ask me that? After everything?"

With which she left the room, and left him standing there wondering, indeed, why and how he had let such poison escape from his lips.

He sat down by the fire, in the chair he generally used in that room. It had the distinction, even after those few months they had been together, of being his chair, though it could not, of course, ever be spoken of as such. This room, which they used as a sitting room together, necessarily bore no markers of his ever having been there. It was as if he were a ghost in her life, leaving no visible traces.

A moment later he heard the front door open, and Sukey saying, "Oh, good evening, Mr Holzknecht. You're back early today."

"Yes, my employer let me go early."

"That's fortunate – your father hasn't been well. Mr Carswell saw to him, but he'll be glad to see you, I'm sure."

"Oh dear," said Holzknecht. "I will go in at once. But first, I have something for you, Mrs Connolly, if you will permit me? I saw it in the music shop window. A new melody for a waltz. I hope we might have the pleasure...?"

"Thank you," Felix heard her say. "But I can't accept that. It isn't quite right to be thinking of dancing just now, really, sir. Your father..."

There was a little silence and then Holzknecht said, "Yes, yes, of course. Another time, perhaps."

There were footsteps and it fell quiet, and Felix remained for some moments alone in the room, feeling like a fool for doubting her and at the same time, dry-throated with fury at Holzknecht's presumption.

Having mastered his feelings sufficiently, he went upstairs to see Louisa Rivers.

The girl was sitting up in bed, with a shawl wrapped about her. Her dark, thick hair was loose and falling on the white pillows, and her slightly flushed complexion completed the impression of a picturesque invalid. He was pleased to see she had made this much progress. Despite her red cheeks, there was no sign of fever and she was bearing the pain with fortitude and without too much recourse to opiates.

He checked her wounds. They were healing cleanly, with no signs of suppuration. Sukey had cleverly contrived a frame out of a fire guard to keep the coverlets from weighing down on her abdomen, which must have added greatly to her comfort.

"You may not feel it," said Felix, "but you are doing well."

"I wish you would all leave me alone!" she exclaimed, pushing away Felix's hand as he rearranged the covers. "You don't need to bother!"

"I shall bother all I like," said Felix.

She sank back on her pillows, looking pointedly away from him. The picturesque invalid had quite vanished.

"I hate you," she muttered. "I hate you all and this place!"

Felix retreated from the bedside. As he did, Sukey slipped past him and sat down on the chair by the bed. There was a silence for a while and then she asked, in a gentle tone, "So, where would you rather be?"

"Not here!" Louisa said. "Anywhere, anything but here!"

"I can understand that," Sukey went on. "But you might feel that wherever you were. I think you were feeling that even when you were at home."

"What does it matter to you?" she spat out at Sukey.

"Because – and I know you don't believe me – we want to help you. You have been feeling like this for some time and it's been hard to bear, yes?"

"What do you know about that?"

"I'm just guessing, of course," Sukey said, "but I grew up in a little town like Whithorne, and when I was about your age, there was a man, a friend of my parents – a married man. A man everyone thought the world of – very kind, very charitable, very religious, very respectable." She hesitated a moment. "I thought of him when I saw Mr Latimer."

Felix was standing in the far corner of the room, leaning against the wall. There was something in her tone that alarmed him.

"He was the sort of fellow with whom you take care not to be alone in a room," Sukey went on. "One afternoon he – he..." She glanced up at him for a moment and then looked back at Louisa who had turned towards her and was staring. "And afterwards, I felt – oh, I don't know what I felt. Like I wanted the earth to swallow me up. And there was no one I could tell. No one. Not even my sister. Especially not my sister. Now, I don't know about you, of course I don't, but I just remembered how I felt and how..." Her voice broke now and she covered her mouth with her hand and gazed over at him, her eyes bright with tears.

He had thought she was being cynical when she accused Latimer of seducing the girl, but it was evident that the insight came from experience.

Louisa twisted the hem of the sheet in her hands and said quietly, "Truly?"

"Truly," said Sukey, her eyes still on Felix.

He found he must sit down. Awash with a mixture of nausea and anger, there was a part of him that wanted to demand the name from Sukey and at once set off for Ireland with a pistol in his pocket. But he sat there instead, bent forward, as if his stomach ached, his elbows on his knees, his hands locked together, feeling completely powerless.

There was a long silence, and then Louisa said, "Latimer. It was Latimer."

~

"Do you want to talk about it?" he asked.

"Not really," Sukey said.

It was about nine o'clock, and the fire in the grate was dying away. Usually at this hour, in her sitting room, they would have two lamps burning bright and the fire well fed. But tonight was not an ordinary night. They had eaten dinner together as they usually did, but an uncomfortable formality had overtaken them.

She had taken away the dirty plates and returned with the customary pot of tea. Felix had got out his cheroot case, but he had no wish to smoke. He stood watching as she made the tea.

"You'd better go and write to the Major," she said.

"I'll see him tomorrow. Remember?"

"Oh yes, of course you will," she said.

It was unlike her to forget such a detail.

"You're tired," he said.

"Yes."

"I'll go, then," he said, starting for the door.

"Have your cup of tea first," she said, offering it.

"Thank you," he said.

She took her own cup and walked across the room to her usual chair by the fire, but instead of sitting down, she put the cup down on the mantel and stood with one hand on the shelf, her head and shoulders bent. He heard her sigh.

"I'll go and horsewhip him," Felix said. "If you want."

"Not much point," she said. "He's dead. Quite a big affair that funeral was, apparently." Her words dissolved into a sob and her frame jerked as her grief overcame her. Then she threw herself into her chair and began to cry in earnest.

Crouching down by the chair, Felix put his arms about her, and attempted to comfort her, which thankfully she allowed, but it was some minutes before the storm subsided.

"Oh, I feel like such a fool," she said.

"Why?"

"Because it wasn't so bad, and maybe it is one of those things that just happen to girls and that's that. It was just a bit of touching and kissing, and leering, as you'd say, and it didn't last very long and it was just that one time, because after that I was careful, and I shouldn't let it hurt like this. I mean, God only knows what Louisa has been through to want to do that to herself, and here am I, feeling sick with the memory of something I am sure any sensible creature would have –"

"I still want to horsewhip him," Felix said. She straightened and pressed her hand to his cheek, fixing him with her red-rimmed eyes.

"Better save that for Latimer. If he can be persuaded to admit it."

"He would if you questioned him."

"That I would enjoy," she said, and then shook her head. "But he won't. It will be her word against his. It's always the way. Or he'll say that she led him on. That she was a flirt." She twisted up her mouth.

"Is this what Bridey thinks?" Felix ventured.

"Yes. Sort of. I mean, the thing was that he was quite the charmer. Until you were alone with him in a room. How was I to know that laughing at his jokes meant that I was encouraging him?"

"Or dancing the polka," Felix said, sinking back on his heels, feeling the sting of the rebuke.

"She's always thought that I was one for putting myself about. That's why she sent Tom to talk to you."

"He said she thinks you like Holzknecht. That's why I was –"

"I don't, you know I don't!" she said. "When I've thrown my soul to Hell for you!"

"You don't believe that, surely!" he said.

"Sometimes I do," she said. "Sometimes you do too. And don't you dare deny it," she added, prodding an accusatory finger into his shirt front.

"If Hell exists –" Felix began.

"Don't try and be clever," she said. "You know what I mean."

He nodded, and then regretted it. He had not meant to be quite so transparent, but sitting at her feet, it was impossible not to be honest.

He turned away and stared into the fire, which was now dwindling into non-existence. He heard her rise from her chair and start gathering up the cups of tea, which they had not even touched.

"I'd better go to bed," she said. "I have a wretch of a headache coming on again."

"Do you want anything for it?"

"I just want to sleep," she said, and left the room.

Chapter Twenty-two

Mrs Rivers sat in the inspector's office of the old Bridewell at Whithorne, and despite her economical clothing, looked too magnificent for the place. Her demeanour was one of equally magnificent obduracy and it was trying Giles' patience.

They had been talking for an hour or so. He had done her the courtesy of fetching her there that morning, allowing her to make domestic arrangements before leaving and keeping the matter as discreet as he could. He had not made mention of any charges – he was letting the place itself speak of the seriousness of her situation – but he wondered if it was making any impression on her at all.

He sent out for coffee and they drank it in silence. As he tried to form some new strategy to make her more reasonable, he watched her gazing out of the soot-stained window. He wondered if she had turned her head that way to show him exactly how perfect her profile was and distract him. It was a lovely sight, but he would have infinitely preferred to be sitting looking at a silent Emma Maitland, and then reflected she would not be silent so long, and that would be all the pleasure. He felt he could listen to her talk for hours and never tire of it. He felt somewhat ashamed as he realised this, as if Laura herself was reproaching him. *"How you like to hear her talk! You would not care for my talk like that."* He could find no effective argument to defend himself against this. Emma Maitland had inadvertently set a spell over him.

Now Mrs Rivers turned and looked at him again, reminding him of the beautiful birds of prey in Patchett's hawk house. Yet he doubted if she was predatory, for all her glorious hauteur.

He looked down at his notes.

"Can we talk again about the tradesmen's bills you settled, Mrs Rivers? The butcher. Let us go over that again."

"I told you, I gave Harrison ten pounds and seven shillings." She had it by rote. "And threepence."

"You do know how easy it will be to check this, ma'am?" Giles said. "When you give me a figure as precise at that, and the name of the tradesman in question, it does not make it true, no matter how much you wish it were."

"You underestimate the pleasure I've found in paying off such bills," she said.

Giles shook his head.

"You don't wish that it were true because it's unpleasant to be in debt," he said. "You wish it because it's easier to imagine your own guilt – to construct this fancy of yours – than face whatever unpleasant truth it is you are so determined to conceal from me."

"If that is what you wish to believe."

"You do realise that you could hang for this? For making and supplying such a poison to a vulnerable girl knowing exactly what purpose she had in mind – neither judge nor jury will look sympathetically at that, despite your willingness to confess."

She glanced away.

"And even if they do not hang you, you face incarceration for the rest of your life. You will never see your sons grow into men, nor your daughters become wives. And I believe they mean more than life itself to you."

She still said nothing.

"And they are, I think, the answer to this ridiculous attitude of yours, ma'am."

"I am not being ridiculous!" she said, drawing herself up. "I am telling you the truth."

"You are exceeding my patience, and you are making it worse for everyone by this conduct. If you are seeking to protect someone, which I know you are, then you are doing a poor job of it."

"Then what am I to do?" she burst out suddenly. "What?"

"That's better," he said. She looked away as if deeply ashamed, and he decided he would approach gently. "Let us go back to the beginning of this. You have distilling equipment in your house, and the books and the practical knowledge to make simple distillations of plants and so forth, yes?"

"Yes," she said.

"And who in your house shares that knowledge? Johnny?"

"No," she said with a sigh.

"Then who?"

She shook her head, her lips pursed.

"Very well, with whom have you shared your work in making your creams and lotions for Mrs Wilson? Again, the boys are at school and I am sure their handwriting is execrable. But who has a pretty hand, learnt from her mother, and a turn for decorations on labels in watercolour and ink?"

"But, but..." She leapt up from her chair and went to the window. She looked as if she wished to throw herself out of it. Then, in a quiet voice, she said at last, "I do not know why. I can only guess that she did; and if she did, then what will happen to her?"

Giles said, "You are right to say you can only guess. We do not know exactly what happened, only that she may be involved. There is no need, ma'am, to throw yourself on the altar. Nothing is concluded."

"But she does know how. She is good at it!" Mrs Rivers exclaimed, turning to him. "And she said she broke the still in an accident, but believe me it would need to be quite an accident to destroy such a thing. She must have broken it deliberately! Oh God, and now I have said far too much!"

There was a knock on the door. It was one of the

Whithorne constables.

"Mr Carswell has arrived from Northminster, sir," he said.

"I will send him up to you in a minute, ma'am," said Giles, gathering up his notebook. "He can let you know how Louisa is doing."

He left Mrs Rivers with her conscience and found Carswell attempting to get warm at the stove and grimacing over the coffee.

"You've come at a good moment," he said. "Mrs Rivers has just admitted that she thinks Louisa brewed the prussic acid."

"Oh," he said. "As you thought."

"Yes. How is she?"

"Recovering well. But how robust mentally she is, I cannot say. Sukey managed to get her to admit the name of her seducer." He glanced around to make sure they were not overheard. "She says it was Latimer."

"Mrs Connolly has excellent instincts," he said.

"He will probably deny it," said Carswell.

"More than likely, but we may be able to get something to corroborate it. That will help the girl in her defence, at any rate."

"Making and supplying a poison?" Carswell said.

"A clever counsel might argue it. Miss Barker had also been seduced, and wanted to end her life, and so turned to her friend, who having been in the same position was willing to help her. Almost an act of mercy."

"It's you who are being merciful," Carswell said, gulping down the remains of his coffee. "She wasn't showing any sign of admitting anything, at least when I last spoke to her."

"Perhaps Mrs Connolly will get the rest out of her. Now, let us go and talk to Mrs Rivers. I want to see what she has to say about Latimer."

~

"Mr Latimer?" said Mrs Rivers.

"She was quite definite," said Carswell.

"Is it likely, do you think, ma'am, given what you know of him?" Giles said. Mrs Rivers glared at him, as if she resented his implication. He decided he would press on. "There has been some intimacy between you, yes?"

Eventually she spoke: "My daughter is ill – how can you take what she says seriously? She may have a fever, and goodness knows what is going through her mind these days."

"You don't think it is at all a possibility?" said Giles.

"No, no, not at all. He would not, I am certain. He is not that sort of man," she added with an emphatic shake of her head, and Giles hoped her faith in him was justified. That would leave Louisa Rivers guilty of a serious misdirection, but if what her mother had admitted was the truth, she was guilty of far worse than that.

"That will be all today, Mrs Rivers," said Giles, thinking it was best to pursue some other avenues in the immediate future. "You are free to go."

"And when will I be allowed to see my daughter again?" she said.

"As soon as it can be managed," Giles said. "But you understand she is a person of interest to this investigation. Given what you have just told me."

"She is still just a child," she said. "Please remember that."

When Mrs Rivers had left, Giles said, "About this accusation, there is no corroborative evidence, I take it? No helpful witness?"

"There rarely is in such cases," Carswell said with a sigh. "Regrettably. Those commonly supposed signifiers mean nothing, in truth. The presence or lack of the hymen tells us nothing. I suppose the presence of certain diseases might signify it – if he infects her, for example, but who is to say it was not some other man who did the deed?"

"We need to talk to Earle and to Latimer," Giles said.

"I have to go and see Mrs Yardley now," said Carswell. "I will leave that dubious pleasure to you, sir, if I may."

~

Felix was surprised to find Mr Yardley in attendance on his wife when he arrived at the castle. The occasion was the arrival of a new cradle which to Felix's eye was a quite ridiculous object. Suspended on a frame, it resembled a small ornamental boat laid up for the winter. It had a wooden canopy finished with crockets, and the whole was further ornamented with flowing silken curtains, while a gilded pennant topped the whole edifice.

But Mrs Yardley, sitting on her Gothic nursing chair, glowing in pink and gold damask robes, seemed as pleased with it as her husband. She made a charming picture, her crinkled pale hair still down, as she peered over the side at the sleeping infant. The Squire also gazed fondly down, his hand on the side of the cradle, as if about to set it rocking.

"What do you think, sir, what do you think?" he asked Felix.

"Very handsome," said Felix.

"German," said the Squire, caressing the wooden frame. "Had it made in Bamberg. Such craftsmanship. One might take it for an original. In fact, there is a fragment of a cradle of similar design remaining in the Schloss there, but I believe this surpasses it."

"One could put five babies in it," Felix said.

"And note the armorial paintings, here and here. My wife's, and my own."

"Very apt," Felix managed to say, looking down at the occupant. "He looks comfortable. But might I have a look at him? All well with him, do you think, ma'am? Is he feeding as he should?"

"He is feeding well," said Mrs Yardley. "Yes, do take him, Mr Carswell."

Felix reached in and lifted out the child, and walked over to the window to see him in daylight. He stirred from his sleep and gazed up at Felix in such a way that he could not resist smiling down at him.

"Too well," said Yardley. "I have found two good women to take on the business. You cannot advise that my wife continues with such an indelicate task?"

"If you are happy to continue, and there seems to be no difficulty with your milk, then I recommend it, ma'am," Felix said, sitting down with the boy on the window seat. He laid him on the cushion beside him and began to check him over. "He is wonderfully strong already," he added, as the baby grasped his finger. "Everything is looking very promising."

"God be thanked!" said Mrs Yardley. "And I shall continue to feed him." She rose from her chair and came to see what Felix was doing with the baby.

"Do not be hasty, my dear," said Yardley.

"I am not being hasty," she said. "Mr Carswell recommends it. It is practically an order."

"Mr Carswell is not your husband," said Yardley. "His 'orders' are not yours to obey."

"I shall feed him, Yardley, and that is that," said Mrs Yardley.

"My dear –"

Mrs Yardley, her back to her husband, her gaze all on Felix and the baby, put up her hand to silence Yardley. She threw Felix a giddy smile, as if she were well aware of the pleasure and novelty of defiance.

"I have decided," she went on. "And that is final." The

baby now began to howl. "Oh, you are hungry, my sweetheart," she said and picked up the child. She then confidently and modestly latched him onto her breast, as if she were the most practised wet-nurse in the world. She settled herself in the nursing chair, the child still guzzling blissfully.

"Oh, and Mr Carswell also advises," she began, "that we do not resume intimacy for at least six months. Was it not at least six months, sir? For the sake of my health and for any future children I might bear."

Felix tried to be pleased that she had decided to broach this difficult subject herself, but he was not sure that being so to the point was quite the way to deal with a man like her husband. Yet he had to appreciate her courage and find his own.

"What?" exclaimed Yardley. "Sir?"

"It was a difficult labour," Felix managed to say.

Yardley marched over to him.

"That is not the point," said Yardley.

"It is entirely the point!"

"On what authority do you speak?" he said. "You are a police surgeon, sir, not an established accoucheur. Why should I listen to your opinion? You work with cadavers, do you not?"

"I have also been responsible for the health of the constables and their families. Many of the men are married. I have plenty of experience, I assure you, and given the difficulty of Mrs Yardley's labour, I would advise" – he took a breath – "no, strongly advise, that she does not conceive again for at least six months. Another pregnancy too soon might be dangerous. You do not want to leave this child without a mother!"

Yardley scowled, and then getting Felix by the elbow hustled him out of the room, saying, "Let us take this conversation elsewhere, sir." On the landing at the top of the stairs, he said, in quite another tone, "Of course she's a charming creature, Carswell, and you can't help getting a little tender for her. Many men do, and she's a shocking flirt, all in, but I quite forgive her that. After all, she is my wife. But you mustn't let her twist you about her finger, really."

"That is not the case, I assure you," said Felix.

"You aren't married," said Yardley. "And your attendance on her has been assiduous."

"It was neither more nor less than was necessary," said Felix.

"Whatever, you are letting her lead you astray. I quite understand. Of course I might have expected a man of science to be a little more impartial, but with your interesting heritage..." He shrugged. "The hot blood of the Haraalds is quite an established thing, is it not? Blood will speak, even through a polluted line. Sir Roderick Haraald, the Steward of the North, was such a fellow, I believe. There is an account in an old chronicle that – well, I am sure you are familiar with it."

"Mr Yardley," Felix said, with as much firmness as he could manage, "I have no interest at all in your wife and she is not manipulating me. I speak for entirely medical reasons. She has a delicate frame and if she is to bear more children for you, it must be done with consideration for that. You cannot risk intimacy until she is properly recovered. Six months at least, sir. I cannot advise less, and would recommend more."

Shaking his head, Yardley went on: "I believe that some women go stark raving mad after giving birth? Yes? Is that not the case here?"

"Mrs Yardley is not showing any signs of that."

"But she is not being rational."

"She is being a perfect mother," Felix retorted. "She is determined to do her best for your son, and for any future children you might have. That is no small thing. You should be grateful for it. Her mental state is completely unclouded. It is her physical well-being you must think about. To be blunt, you would not put a prize mare to stud so soon, would you?"

"That is blunt!" exclaimed Yardley, and grabbed him by the forearm. "Too blunt! I should throw you down the stairs! But you are not worth the trouble. I will content myself with asking you to leave at once and you should be properly grateful for the mercy of your betters! And you will not come back again! You are dismissed forthwith!"

Chapter Twenty-three

Returning to The Falcon, Felix found Major Vernon in the ballroom where they had first seen Miss Barker's body. He was sitting on the edge of the platform, surveying the room.

"I've been thinking about that ball," he said, seeing Felix. "Let us imagine that something happened that evening to make Miss Barker take the poison she had procured from her friend, Louisa."

"A double dose," said Felix.

"Why did she give her so much?"

"Because she didn't know how strong it was? It had to be a haphazard process, even accounting for the skill she had. A distillation of crushed laurel leaves in spirit – there was no way she would have known how strong it would be – she had no means of testing it. So she gave her the lot, in the hope it would be enough."

"It must have been more than enough. Gosforth died within moments, assuming he was drinking from the same bottle that he found in her hand in her bedroom."

"I should attempt to make some prussic acid in a still of the same size," Felix said, "and see how much I can yield at that strength. The fact that both bodies had exactly the same concentration suggests that the source is the same. But the same bottle – why do you say that?"

"I am just hypothesising. There was so little evidence in Miss Barker's room. Someone had been over it. In fact, two people might have been over it. Firstly Gosforth, making his nocturnal husbandly visit, finds her dead, flask in hand. Does he remove the flask and whatever else he considers incriminating or damaging? Then Mrs Ampner arrives in the morning, with plenty of time to remove and destroy any evidence that does not cast her in a good light. I keep wondering if there were not a note or a diary or some such. Young women confide their secrets to each other, or failing that, to paper."

"If there were, we would be lucky to find it," said Felix.

At this moment, a waiter came in.

"Can I help you, sir?" he said.

"Yes, Ned, you can," said Major Vernon, getting up. "You were at work during the assembly ball on Tuesday last?"

"Yes, sir."

"So, I imagine from my experience of these things, that the dancing happens in here, with the chaperones and the young ladies sitting along the wall, there."

"Yes, sir, that's the usual thing."

"And which room is the card room?"

"That one through there, sir."

"And supper is served where?"

"Back there," Ned said, pointing behind him.

"And is there a room where the men go for a smoke and something stronger to drink? And perhaps for a hand of cards, and to talk business?"

Ned hesitated. "I suppose there might be."

"Might be?"

"I shouldn't really say, sir," said Edward.

"Does someone in particular take this room?"

"There are a few gentlemen who subscribe, sir. I don't know if I should say who."

"Show me the room, will you?"

"Now, sir?"

"Yes, now."

Ned went reluctantly and opened the door to the supper room.

"This way, sir," he said.

They followed him into the supper room, and into the

kitchen passageway beyond. There, tucked away, was a tight little staircase, on the half-landing of which was a door leading to a nicely furnished sitting room.

"This is convenient," said Major Vernon, looking about him at the card tables and velvet benches. "I suppose there is a door to the backyard down near the kitchen?"

"Yes, sir," said Ned.

"I went through it myself to go to the castle," Felix said.

"So if a few gentlemen wished to bring a little entertainment to the ball, other than cigars and spirits, they could easily do so. Yes, Ned?"

"Yes," said Ned. "And they do."

"Girls from the town?" the Major threw in carelessly. "Yes?"

"Light girls, yes, sir, sometimes," said Ned. "Master says we are to turn a blind eye because the gentlemen pay him to do likewise."

"And who are these gentlemen, Ned?" said Major Vernon, sitting down on one of the velvet couches and stroking the cushion. "Who like these comforts?"

"I shouldn't really, sir –" Ned began.

"It won't lose you your place," said Major Vernon. "You need to tell me."

"Are you sure, sir?"

"Yes," Major Vernon said. "Tell me."

Ned took a deep breath and then said, "The Squire, and Mr Earle, and Mr Baines – well, at least before he went away from town for his health. I believe he got the clap."

"And anyone else?" Ned shook his head. "You're sure about that?"

"Those are the only men I've seen in here," said Ned.

"Mr Latimer?"

"Oh no, sir," said Ned. "He likes to dance too well for that. He never leaves the ballroom, nor Mrs Rivers' side for that matter."

"And you are quite sure these were light women going up there?"

"Well, once I saw a couple of them. But on that night, the night you're asking about, sir..." He glanced away.

"Sit down, Ned," said Major Vernon. "Something is troubling you."

"I've said too much already," Ned said, not sitting down.

"Come now," said Major Vernon. "You need to tell me. No harm will come of it."

Ned perched on a chair and said again, "I don't want to lose my place."

"What did you see?"

"Miss Barker."

"Alone?"

He shook his head.

"The Squire was there. I was taking in some wine. She was sitting where you are now, sir, and she was –" He continued in an embarrassed whisper. "Arranging her skirts – well, pulling them down to cover herself. As if – well, you can guess what I thought, sir."

"And how did she seem? How did she look, I mean?"

"I don't know, sir. She was staring away, at the floor. Like, I suppose, she couldn't bear anyone to see her, which is no surprise, if he'd just –"

"Quite," said Major Vernon. "Well, Ned, that is excellent information and you should not worry about telling me anything else you saw. You are certain this was the occasion last week?"

Ned nodded, and then blurted out, "The Squire will kill me if he finds out I've told you. He beat a man senseless out Barsford way. It's common knowledge, but Mr Earle hushed it all up. He hushes it all up for him, being the coroner and that."

"Do you know why he beat the man?"

"It was about some lass. It was her brother."

"You don't know his name?"

Ned shook his head.

When Ned had gone, Felix said, "And Yardley just threatened to throw me downstairs."

"It is time I had a word with him," said Major Vernon, getting up and looking around the room. "What's that?" he said, pointing over Felix's shoulder. Felix turned and saw a tiny scrap of white fabric caught between the closed doors of a corner cabinet.

Major Vernon opened the door, and retrieved the object. He held it up – it was a delicate gauze scarf, that was easy to imagine draped around the bare shoulders of a lady in a ball dress.

"Should be easy to find who this belongs to," said Major Vernon. "It looks expensive, don't you think?"

~

"The Master has gone out, sir," said Squire Yardley's butler.

"And when will he be back?"

"Oh, I don't know, sir."

"This evening?"

"I really can't say, sir."

"Do you know where he went?"

"No, sir."

"Tell Mr Yardley that I called," said Major Vernon. "Here is my card."

"Of course, sir," said the butler.

"Oh, and could you pass this about the servants' hall?" Giles added, taking from his pocket one of the 'Missing Person' bills that O'Brien had printed up for him. "Any information about this would be of great interest. Even the slightest bit of gossip."

"As you wish, sir," said the butler, and was about to turn and go, but Giles beckoned him back.

"How long have you been with the family, Mr...?"

"Henry Proudfoot, sir. Ten years."

"And you are satisfied with your place?"

"Yes, sir, very."

"I'd heard your master can have a temper."

"Not to my knowledge, sir," said Proudfoot. "Is that all, sir? I have my work to get to."

Feeling a little frustrated to let him go, Giles walked back into town, intending to visit Mr Earle. How that conversation ought to go he was not yet certain. He had heard a great many slanders against Earle, but he had no solid evidence. His accusers, coming from the servant classes, were liable to be easily dismissed, especially by a clever lawyer.

He decided he would let that hang a while, and go and see how Carswell was getting on with his second examination of the culvert. It was a bright day, if cold, and he thought the ride out might clarify his thoughts.

A mile or so out of Whithorne, he met a gig coming the other way. Sitting on the high bench driving the pony was Mrs Maitland. She was wearing a scarlet hooded cloak, the fashion of twenty years ago. Giles wondered if he remembered that same garment on her, worn new. He could not be sure, but the image his mind conjured up, false or real, gave him intense pleasure: he saw her as she had been then, sweeping about in its copious folds, demonstrating to all the company its newly acquired perfection.

"This is good luck!" she exclaimed as they drew up to one another. "I was coming to find you. I may have something to help you. Well, perhaps – and now I see you I wonder if I'm not inventing things and shall be wasting your precious time, but I had a most strange encounter, earlier today."

"Tell me. I'm sure you are not. You have too much common sense."

"About this missing woman. Over at Hentfield, a little group of tinkers have just come onto the common and made their camp. They have been doing so for years, but not usually at this time. The curate's wife told me they had come. They are rather wretched at the moment – some of the children have the croup, and there is a poor sickly baby, so I thought I would take what I could to them this morning. Which I did, and was well received, which was a relief because such people do not always take kindly to charity. In fact, I was given tea and allowed to sit by the fire with the grandmother, which I think is a great honour."

"I believe so."

"So I told her about the bones in the culvert and how you thought it was a woman that had gone missing, perhaps last summer or earlier, and had they heard any tales to the effect."

"Thank you," he said.

"How could I not?" she said. "We must find who she is, and what happened, surely?"

He would have reached for her hand and kissed it then, if he did not have his hands on the reins of a hack about whose manners he was a little unsure. And fortunately, she too had her horse to manage.

"What did the lady say?" Giles asked.

"She was shocked to hear it, really shocked, and then said that her son, who wasn't there, had told her a thing he saw last summer, about two men he met on the old road, and he was certain he'd seen a pair of demons and she thought he might have done, because she had a vision of his being in grave danger on the way home. Oh dear, that does sound foolish, doesn't it?"

"He saw two men he thought were demons?"

"Yes, foolish!" she exclaimed. "But it struck me, he might have seen something or somebody. Why would he call two strangers demons? What was it about them to make him say such a thing?"

"In that there might have been something unsettling about their demeanour?" Giles said.

"Yes, quite. Something suspicious."

"It is true," he said, "that people leaving the scene of a crime they have committed often do behave in strange ways."

"That is what I thought. What if these two demons or men or whatever they were had something to do with the body in the culvert? I know that is a ridiculous assertion, but could there not be something in it?"

"There might be," Giles said, "there might not. But given it is the only scrap anyone has yet handed me, Mrs Maitland, we should pick it up and examine it properly. The son was not there this morning?"

"No, but he will be back presently. He had gone to do some day labouring for one of our tenants. The light won't last much longer and he will have to go home for his dinner."

"Then we shall go and talk to him, if you will introduce me. It is always better to have an introduction to these people. They do not talk willingly to people like me. And we will gather up Mr Carswell first, if you do not mind? He can have a look at the children. You and he will smooth my path."

Chapter Twenty-four

Felix had been on the verge of giving up his search of the culvert when Major Vernon rode up, accompanied by Mrs Maitland driving a gig. He was glad to see them. He had ordered the carriage to come and fetch him half an hour hence, but he had got extremely cold and hungry.

In fact, he had been standing and scanning the horizon, dreaming of lying on a sofa by the fire, his head resting on Sukey's lap, his stomach full and a glass of sweet, warming Madeira within easy reach. The wine, dinner, warm fire and the sofa seemed possible, but Sukey's indulgence, less so.

He was a little disconcerted, then, to be told that they were going on an expedition to a gypsy encampment, but consoled himself that they at least would have a good fire going.

"You look as if you have had some success," said Major Vernon.

"Three more human bones. And this – I think it is part of a straw bonnet. Or it may just be rubbish."

He climbed up onto the gig beside Mrs Maitland.

"You wouldn't care to drive, Mr Carswell?" she said.

"No, no, not at all."

"Some young men cannot abide to be driven by an older woman," she said with a smile.

"Only fashionable puppies," said Felix, and then remembering himself, and thinking she was attempting to relieve herself of the duty through tiredness, said, "but of course I shall, if you would like me to, ma'am?"

"No, it is no trouble to me."

"That's a relief. I'm a poor driver."

"You have better things to do," she said, and as they drove off, she began to describe the state of the children in the travellers' camp.

The light was fading fast as they arrived at the common land that edged the hamlet. A heavy crop of bracken covered the approach to the camp, explaining its appeal to the travelling people, for it provided fuel, food and seclusion.

Felix had some experience of the gypsies who regularly came into his father's parish. His father loved nothing better than to sit and converse with the gypsy elders, and get them to teach him their language. Some of this useful knowledge he had passed to Felix, who was able to greet them in their own tongue with the customary: "God bless you!"

Major Vernon glanced at him, evidently impressed.

These folk were sadly not half so at ease as the families that he had been used to seeing in Pitfeldry. Of course, that had been at the height of the summer, when their tents in the heather seemed picturesque and life was easier for them. To be camping in such bleak weather and scrabbling for day labour work was miserable indeed. But Mrs Herne, the matriarch of the little clan, welcomed Mrs Maitland as if she were the Queen herself; and when she was told that he was a doctor, he might have been the Prince of Wales. He was a little surprised, because he knew they had medicines and notions of their own, but a sick baby was a sick baby, and any help would not be turned away. He hoped, as he crouched down and followed the old lady into the tent, that the condition was not a serious one. Mrs Maitland had been anxious and that made him nervous.

The reality was depressing. As his eyes adjusted to the dim lights he could see that the child, some six months old, was not thriving, but neither was her mother, Mrs Herne's daughter-in-law. She looked dangerously thin and exhausted. The comforts Mrs Maitland had brought that morning had ameliorated things a little. The child was carefully wrapped in new flannel, and as warm as could be expected; the rich broth had helped the mother, but the tramping life obviously did not suit her. It was her first child and Felix feared it would be her last if she continued to live in such rough conditions. There was nothing in the way of medicine he could do to help her. What she needed was to be indoors.

He finished his examination. The other children, the offspring of the eldest Herne son, Jasper and his wife, were not in so alarming a state, and he was able to reassure their mother that their sickliness would pass.

Emerging from the tent, he drew Mrs Maitland aside for a moment and said, quietly, "Have you an empty cottage where they might lodge for the winter? I don't give much hope for mother or child unless they get into sturdier lodgings. I should pay their rent if necessary," he added, thinking of the kindness and respect with which such people had treated his father.

"I was thinking that myself," she said. "There is a place in the park, a sort of glorified tea-house. It is very secluded, and it might suit them. I can easily find work in the house for the women, so that no one will feel offended."

"You must take care to tell them that they are free to go at any point," Felix said. "They hate the thought of settling properly, but it isn't uncommon for them to go into lodgings to get through the winter, if they can manage it." She nodded, and went to discuss the matter with Mrs Herne.

As she did, the Herne sons returned from their work, looking a little wary at the sight of the visitors, but a rattle of words in Romany from the mother put all right.

Felix, Major Vernon and Mrs Maitland were invited to join everyone by the fire, which was now set up into a mighty blaze to bring the blackened pot of pease pudding to the boil. Felix was pleased to see that the ailing mother came out with the baby in her arms and settled down by her clearly adoring husband, while he ate his dinner. In fact, they tenderly shared the same bowl.

"True love," observed Mrs Herne to Mrs Maitland. "My sons have had good fortune with their brides, yes?"

"It's a handsome family indeed, ma'am," said Mrs Maitland. "You must be proud."

Jasper Herne laid down his bowl – he had made short work of his dinner – and said, "Mother says you wanted to know about my seeing those demons."

"We would be grateful," said Major Vernon. "We have the bones of a woman, without the name of a family to bury her. We think someone has done great violence to her."

Jasper rubbed his face.

"It were a strange thing. My mother –"

"I felt it," Mrs Herne put in. "I felt it that night – you were looking evil in the face, and then you came back and told me what you saw." She blessed herself and shuddered.

"What exactly was it you saw, Mr Herne?" Major Vernon asked.

"There was two of them. It was dusk time, but in the summer, so later than now, and I'd been helping with harvest at Farmer Gentle's – you know him, ma'am," he added, acknowledging Mrs Maitland. She nodded.

"Is that the farmer you were working for today?" Major Vernon said.

"Yes, and so we were camped here, as ever, and I was walking back a little later than Ben here because I'd stayed to talk about a sick horse with Farmer Gentle. He reckons my opinion worth something and I was glad to give it. So I walked back alone, on the field road yonder, from the far field – they call it the North Two-acre – and I saw them. And I thought, who is that? For mostly you know all the fellows about in a place, but these were strangers, and they weren't dressed like gentlemen but they weren't dressed ordinary. And they were laughing. Not like mortals. That's what I thought, and they stopped and laughed as I walked towards them."

"Can you remember what they were wearing?" Major

Vernon said.

"One of them had a long, white coat on, and a straw stove-pipe – well, he wasn't wearing it, he was carrying it, swinging it as he walked. And the other, he had an old-fashioned riding coat with brass buttons on it, I am sure of that, and looked dirty."

"And how old were they?"

"The white-coated fellow, he was young, and tall and fair. The other, I can't say, to be honest." He screwed his eyes shut, evidently trying to remember. "Maybe a bit thin on top?"

Major Vernon nodded.

"Clean shaven, bearded? Anything of that nature?" he asked.

"He had a beard, the one in the riding coat," said Jasper.

"And they were laughing?"

"Like they were drunk, but then not. That was a queer thing and it's what made me think: that's a pair of devils that had been up to no good."

"And you didn't speak to them?"

"No, I know better than to speak to the Devil," he said. "And I am sure these two were at the Devil's work. Sure as sure."

"You never saw them again when you camped here?" Major Vernon asked after a moment. Felix could tell he was weighing the likely use of this strange evidence. Jasper shook his head. "Thank you, Mr Herne," he added.

"Might it be of use?" Mrs Maitland enquired.

"It may well be," said Major Vernon. "We have so little at present. And might I ask you others, have you heard any talk of a woman going missing in this district? Perhaps someone running away from home? That sort of tale?"

There was a silence and then Mrs Jasper said to her mother-in-law, "Didn't one of the daughters run off from that place up yonder? You know, that house with the black shutters and the thorn hedge. Far side of the chapel."

"That's right," said Mrs Herne. "Ran off with a soldier."

"No, a foreigner," said Mrs Jasper. "That was it."

"Maybe so," Mrs Herne said. "And who'd be surprised at it? He's a sour man, and his wife the same. Never a kind word to spare for anyone."

"Do you mean Ash Farm?" said Mrs Maitland. "Mr and Mrs Taylor?"

"Aye, that's the one, ma'am," said Mrs Jasper.

"Yes, certainly, he is sour," said Mrs Maitland. "That was quite my impression."

"I shall have to pay him a call," said Major Vernon. He got to his feet. "Thank you all very much."

He stretched out his hands to Mrs Maitland to help her from the ground, which assistance she took. At the same time, old Mrs Herne had risen, and was glancing between them, her eyes twinkling. She put her hand over their joined hands for a moment, as if blessing them, and then turned to Mrs Maitland and said, with a wink and in a whisper, "That's a good man you have, lady, and he'll bring you good fortune." Mrs Maitland turned her face away into the shadows and Felix could not tell her expression. The Major looked bemused, but not displeased.

~

The clock struck ten, and Giles found himself alone with Mrs Maitland, sitting opposite her at the tea table by the fire in her sitting room. This was not by any deliberate contrivance on his part. Carswell and Lord Milburne had gone to bed only a little while before, and he supposed he should also make his excuses and say good night. Yet the moment had a sort of enchantment to it and he did not want to stir from his place.

She too sat still and quiet now, her darning abandoned in her lap. It had long since been put down, for the conversation had been a lively one, in which she had taken the leading part. Carswell had been talking about the German professor and his collection of folk tales, a project about which Mrs Maitland expressed great enthusiasm.

"I have always loved old stories," she had said. "I always thought they had such truths in them, like the parables in the Gospels." Then she turned to recalling the ghost stories of her old nurse. This was enough to make even Lord Milburne stir from his sullen silence and smile briefly, for it seemed she had told them to him when he was a child. He admitted that they were still the most terrifying things he had ever heard.

"Then you should write them down, ma'am," Carswell had said. "And publish them. Yes, Major?"

Giles had nodded at that, imagining the pleasure of taking such a volume in his hands, guessing it might capture the piquancy of her character between its boards. How he might enjoy her, without self-reproach, in such a form!

"I should ruin them if I wrote them down," she said. "I have no literary talents."

"You would do it very well, Mama," said Lord Milburne, getting up and going to kiss her. "Excuse me, I must go to bed."

Carswell left soon after him, and they were alone.

"I never expected such a compliment from Charles," she said, breaking the silence. "I thought he would hate such an idea. He is not as advanced in his ideas as Mr Carswell."

"He liked the stories," said Giles. "Who does not love a good story?"

"A man with no soul," said Mrs Maitland with a smile. She leaned back in her chair and said, "It's a relief to me he said that. He has been so difficult, so distant – that's the first kindness I have had from him for weeks. Thank you."

"For what?"

"You must have said something to the point to him."

"I don't know about that," said Giles, trying to work out

if Milburne had actually done what he promised and talked to her about his despair and his ambitions for Louisa Rivers' hand. "I told him he ought to confide in you and I'm not sure he has."

"No," she said, her smile fading. "He has not. About what? Was there something in particular?"

"I made a little deal with him. He must speak with you about it, and I will not speak to you about it. Forgive me!"

She glanced away.

"I suppose that was all you could do," she said.

"He gave me his word. He probably has not found his courage yet," Giles said. "I will have another word with him tomorrow."

"He will be angry if he knows you have told me this much," she said. "Of course, I am the last to be told anything!"

"I told him that you should be the first to know, always. I was clear about it."

"You were too merciful," she said, "with your little deal. And now he has made you keep secrets! How disagreeable."

"I didn't expect him to be so dilatory," Giles said. "It's true. I thought by the next time I saw you that he would have talked to you. I'm sorry. I misjudged him."

"Oh, it doesn't matter," she said, throwing her darning into the basket at her feet and getting up. "It's all ridiculous! I must simply accept that he's a grown man and I am becoming irrelevant. He may pay me silly compliments and I can feed on the scraps, but he is a lost cause! A wasted effort!"

"No, not at all. He only thinks that he is a grown man," he said, rising also. "The truth is he needs you as much as ever. He just needs to find his courage. He will find it. You will prevail, just through your example. He will see how fortunate he is to have you."

She sighed.

"But I have no patience," she said. "I have used it all up. I want to go to his room now and scream at him. How is that admirable?"

"But you are not doing that. You are here, and –"

"And unburdening myself to you, which is just as bad, and for which I apologise," she said. "I have presumed on you."

"It doesn't feel like that," he said. "It feels..." He restrained himself from stepping a little closer to her. "Perhaps I am the presumptuous one."

He was aware of her looking at him with a careful gaze, the sort of gaze that makes a man's blood quicken.

"No, not at all," she said. "I like that you are here, very much, although it is unsettling. Unexpectedly so." She stretched out her hand towards him for a moment and then pulled it back.

"Yes," he said. "And I..." He broke off, reached for her hand, and held it in his. "This is a strange business." She nodded and looked away. "I think you understand that I'm not yet in the position to be..." Again the words failed him: what was this? Was he courting, wooing or paying his addresses? He only knew that any approach he made to her would be with the most serious of intentions. "My late wife..." She nodded, but it did not stop her putting her other hand over his and squeezing it for a moment.

"Of course," she said, breaking from him. "It's rather late. I must go to bed. Patton will scold me."

"Patton is more likely to scold me," Giles said.

"Oh no, she will not," she said. "She is already your slave!"

Chapter Twenty-five

Ash Tree Farm lay in a spot that would make any inhabitant despondent and sour, Felix thought, as they drove up to it in the grey light of the next morning.

"I shouldn't be surprised if all of the children had not run off," he remarked, as they crossed a muddy yard to the front door, "and the mother too," he added, for they seemed to wait an interminable time for the door to be opened to them.

When it did, it was only by a chink, and a woman, in suspicious tones, asked, "Yes, what is it?"

"Mrs Taylor?" Major Vernon said. "May we come in? I am Major Vernon from the County Constabulary."

"What's your business?"

"A delicate one," Major Vernon said, gently pushing the door, "that would be better talked of inside, ma'am."

Reluctantly she let them come in and they went through to a large, old-fashioned and not at all cheery farm kitchen. There was no one else there and Felix wondered if his idea about all the children being runaways had been correct.

"So?" she said, leaning against her kitchen table, her arms folded. She was a tall, gaunt woman with a look of great physical strength about her.

"Are all your children still at home, ma'am?" Giles said.

"My sons, yes," she said. "They are out with their father."

"And your daughters?"

"I don't have any daughters," she said, scratching her ear.

Major Vernon let the statement hang in the air, which meant he felt she was lying.

"I'd heard you did have a girl, Mrs Taylor," he said after a moment.

"What is it to you if I did?" she said.

"We are trying to establish if any women have gone missing from this area in the last couple of years," said Major Vernon, taking O'Brien's bill from his pocket and laying it on the table.

"So?" she said.

"I was told that you had a daughter and that she left home."

"So?" she said again.

"We have discovered the skeleton of a young woman in a culvert on Lord Milburne's estate, not far from here."

Felix saw a flicker of distress cross her previously impassive face. It was not an established fact that the woman was a young one, but he could happily allow this inaccuracy to pass. She was rattled, certainly.

"What has that to do with me?" she said.

"Very possibly nothing. Tell me about your daughter, please, Mrs Taylor."

"There is nothing to tell," she said.

Major Vernon wandered over to the dresser and opened the large wooden box that sat among the pots and jugs. He lifted out a solid volume that could only be the family Bible and held it up to her.

"You have no right –" she began, but it was too late. He had flicked open the title page which was dense with names, as was the custom.

"Three boys – yes, I see, Mrs Taylor. Nathaniel, George and Jacob. And one name crossed out."

Now she snatched the book from him and held it close to her.

"Mary, I think?" Major Vernon said. "Your mother's name, of course."

There was a long silence. Felix saw her glancing down at the bill on the table.

"She's in London," she said at last. "She went to London.

She's in London." She closed her eyes as she said that for the last time, almost as if she were repeating a prayer.

"Why don't you sit down, ma'am?" said Major Vernon.

She did as she was bid, still holding the Bible close against her.

"You've never had any letter or any kind of communication from her, I suppose?" said Major Vernon. "Perhaps she wrote to one of your boys."

"She wouldn't dare!" she exclaimed. "Mr Taylor, when he put her out, he told her she wasn't to write – ever! And quite right too. She brought shame on us all."

"Was she with child?" Mrs Taylor nodded. "And the father?"

"She wouldn't say," she said, and added with a sigh, "not that we didn't try to get it out of her."

"How far gone with the child was she, when she left?" Felix asked.

"Four or five month," said the woman.

"And when did she leave home?" Major Vernon asked.

"At harvest time."

"And was your daughter at home before that? She did not go away from home to work?"

"She worked in Whithorne – at the big inn, in the kitchens."

"The Falcon?"

Mrs Taylor nodded. "She would go off. She would never stay at home and do her duty. She was always a wicked, restless girl. I suppose that's where she met him."

"And she said nothing about him?"

"She said he would take care of her. That it didn't matter what we thought. She gave my husband some tongue that night, I can tell you. It's a wonder that he didn't..."

"Yes?"

"He didn't lay a finger on her!" she exclaimed, jumping up. "Oh, I know what you are thinking. But he didn't! Swear on the Bible! He'd have had every right to, the way she spoke to him, but he didn't. And afterwards, I've never seen him so cast down. It fair broke his heart."

"And when was this, Mrs Taylor? When was it you last saw her? Had the harvest just begun or was it later than that?"

"It was about two weeks into August, I suppose. She came home for a holiday, but then we saw the state of her – and the next day she went. There was a terrible row, all that night, and in the morning she upped and went."

"She took her things with her?"

"All she took was a silly band box with a bonnet and a few bits in it. She said he was going to take care of everything."

"So she was going to meet him, do you think?"

"Maybe. I suppose that is sort of what she said."

"And how was she dressed?"

"In a pink sprig gown. Very proud of that she was. He gave it to her, she said."

"So she left most of her possessions behind here?"

"I suppose," said Mrs Taylor.

"Do you still have them? Might we see them?"

She shrugged, and said, "As you like."

They followed her up two flights of a narrow staircase to a slot of a room, tucked under the eaves. As the door opened, the engravings and fashion-plates the girl had pinned to the walls rustled and flapped. The room seemed to have been little disturbed since its last occupant had left. Her abandoned clothes and linen remained on the foot rail of the bed, as if she were about to return at any moment and tidy them. Perhaps Mrs Taylor hoped she would.

She left them to their search.

"Middle of August," said Major Vernon, squatting down and looking under the bed. "Can a body be reduced to the bone in such a space of time?"

"Yes, in those conditions, it is possible."

"Did you notice how quick she was to say there was no violence involved?"

"Yes."

"In these cases, unfortunately," Major Vernon went on, still peering under the bed, "it's often the father, the brother or the lover. Now, what is that?"

Felix crouched down and looked under the bed.

"That paper?"

"Yes. Let's move the bed."

They pulled the bed from the wall, and Major Vernon reached in and retrieved it.

"That fancy edging caught my eye. Maybe it is nothing, but..."

It was a folded card, with a pierced border, with a ribbon threaded through it. On the front was a garish-coloured engraving of turtle doves. He opened the card. Inside, predictably enough, was a printed verse.

"From her mysterious lover, perhaps?" said Major Vernon.

"Shame he didn't sign it," said Felix. "But I suppose that is the point."

Major Vernon tucked it into his pocket. "You haven't found anything in your search of the culvert that suggests the remains of an unborn child?"

"No," said Felix. "Even at five months, one might have expected to see something – a skull at least. And how was Mrs Taylor so confident it was four or five months? She would have been going by the word of her daughter, and she would most likely have lied about it until she couldn't conceal it any more. So the pregnancy could have been much further along than that. First-time mothers often don't show a great deal, even up to the moment of delivery. There are plenty of cases one can cite, the mother herself being too ignorant to realise that she was even with child."

"So this is a dead end?" said Major Vernon, glancing

around him again.

"Unless one lets one's imagination run riot," Felix said.

"Yes?" said Major Vernon. "What are you thinking?"

"If you can amputate a hand after death, you might be able to take an unborn child from the womb. Someone that cool-headed, and that way inclined – hard though that might be to imagine, of course." Yet even as he said it, he found he could all too easily imagine it, and there was a face to go with the deed, the same face that had peered so eagerly down on Miss Barker's remains. "Didn't Jasper Herne say that one of the men he saw that night was wearing an old riding coat?"

Major Vernon was looking in his notebook.

"Yes, indeed."

"Once, when I was at the castle," Felix went on, "Miss Yardley upbraided the Squire for wearing a disgusting old riding coat – the coat you saw him in at The Black Cat. And we already know he's an animal when it comes to women, from what Ned at The Falcon said, and his wife even..."

"Yes?"

"She asked me to tell him that it was dangerous for her health for them to resume marital relations for at least six months."

"Is that why he threw you out of the house?" said the Major.

"Yes," said Felix.

"You haven't thought a great deal of him from the moment you met him."

"That doesn't make him a murderer," said Felix, "as you are about to tell me, no doubt. But he unsettled me. There is something so – oh, I can't quite describe it – when he invaded my post-mortem. You put it well yourself, sir, when you said he was the sort of man who enjoys a public execution."

Major Vernon nodded.

"Mary Taylor worked in the kitchens at The Falcon," said the Major. "She could easily have met Yardley there. We don't know how often that little parlour was used, after all. Perhaps not just on ball nights. And this girl was young, like Miss Barker, and presumably pretty, and easily impressed. Strung along with trifles, and then disposed of when she became pregnant."

"Something like that."

"There are a lot of difficulties in this theory, of course," said Major Vernon, going to the window. "Mary Taylor leaves one morning, in the middle of harvest time, when the fields are full of people, or the roads are full of people walking to work in the fields. Does anyone see her walking along the lane with her bonnet box and her pink sprigged gown? Surely they would remember her? She would, I presume, go down the hill, towards the village. If her mother is telling the truth about her departure, that is. She left without her possessions. That is a significant point. Surely these things," he gestured about him, "trifles though they are, were not trifles to her. Why would she leave them?"

"You think the father –"

"A sour man, Mrs Maitland said. His wife explicitly said there was no violence in her putting out. Perhaps she did not see it. It might have taken place late at night – a violent argument, perhaps somewhere else on the farm. She dies, perhaps from a beating, perhaps by some accident during the argument. Father and sons dispose of the body and tell the mother that Mary has left of her own free will."

"But the amputated hand?" said Felix.

Major Vernon nodded. "That does not fit with such a story," he said. "And we do not know if Mary Taylor is not quite happily living in London with her lover and her child."

"That will be like looking for a needle in a haystack," said Felix.

"I will talk to Mr Taylor. If he is responsible, he might be sick of the secret by now. But first, while we have the gig, we should survey the area a little. There are only so many ways a girl on foot could go."

They left the farm, with the Major telling Mrs Taylor that they would be back to speak to her husband and sons. He did it in such a fashion – quietly, but with a steely authority – that Felix imagined that the woman would soon be on her knees praying to God for mercy.

They drove down the hill to the village, which was not a large one. There were a few low cottages and an unimpressive inn, at which Major Vernon drew up.

"Odds on I will be disappointed," he said, as he jumped down from the gig, "but they may have a map."

The innkeeper came out of the kitchen door, eager to assist.

"Who is your landlord, Mr Keane?" Major Vernon asked, when they were inside. "Lord Milburne or Squire Yardley?"

"The Squire, sir," said Mr Keane. "His land runs all the way from here to Whithorne. His man comes here to take the rents."

"So you have a map of the area?"

"Yes, sir, we do. This way."

"Excellent. And some coffee, if you have some?"

Mr Keane showed them into a room that seemed to be kept only for the purpose of conducting estate business. It had a baize-covered table, an inkstand, and a chair for the agent, but none for the tenants. There was also a large map on the wall.

"You can see where the two estates abut each other here," said Major Vernon, standing in front of it. "There is Ash Farm, and here we are. And there is the culvert, on Lord Milburne's side, above Grange Farm." He measured the distance with his fingers from Ash Farm to the culvert. "About three quarters of a mile, as the crow flies."

"A long way to carry a body," said Felix.

"A slight fifteen-year-old girl," said Major Vernon. "And a strong farming man, perhaps with assistance. But you have a point. It is a long way to carry it and not be seen."

Mr Keane returned with the coffee.

"Does Squire Yardley ever come here in person?" Major Vernon asked. Keane shook his head.

"I've never laid eyes on him, sir," he added. "Don't have much trade with the gentry, to be honest."

"What do you know about Mary Taylor going missing?" said Felix.

"Only what the gossip says, sir," said Keane. "Her father put her out, and she went to London."

"Would you know her if you saw her?" Major Vernon asked.

"Yes, she was a pretty thing."

"Do you remember the last time you saw her?"

The man thought for a moment.

"Perhaps at church at Easter. She was home then, I think. My boys and the missus were gawping at her fancy bonnet. The whole village was, to be honest. I suppose that's when the talk started that she'd lost her way."

"And you didn't see her at harvest-tide?" The man shook his head.

He left, and Felix took a tentative sip of his coffee. It tasted both weak and burnt.

"I can see why no one comes here," he said.

"Better than nothing," Major Vernon, drinking his own down and then wincing. "But I see what you mean." He turned back to the map. "So maybe she had a tryst elsewhere. If she did leave of her own free will. There is a field path up from the farm here, going towards this building. And here is the road back down to the village. Very convenient."

Major Vernon went to the door and called back Mr Keane.

"Yes, sir?"

"This property," he said, showing him the spot on the map. "Can you tell me who lives there?"

"Nobody," said Mr Keane.

"But it belongs to the Squire?"

"Yes, but it's half-falling down. I don't know why he doesn't put it in order," said Mr Keane.

"Thank you."

Mr Keane left and Major Vernon was measuring again with his fingers, this time to the culvert.

"It's possible," he murmured. "Much closer."

"But why?" exclaimed Felix, wondering that Major Vernon was taking his macabre theory so seriously. He did not like to think that there could actually be any truth in it.

"You should trust your instincts, Carswell," said the Major, pouring himself another cup of the dreadful coffee. "Do you not want some more? We have a tramp ahead of us."

Felix declined his offer.

~

It was not such an arduous journey along the road from the village to the deserted house that Major Vernon had identified on the map. In fact, it was pleasant enough, with a wintry, midday sun making a gallant attempt to accompany them up what passed for a hill in such flat country.

The house itself was not readily visible from the road. But a stone with a few roughly carved letters on it, placed at the bend, suggested where it might be and they followed a track along some quarter of a mile until it came into sight.

The house sat in a shallow dip in the landscape, making Felix feel it must be damp and without any pleasant prospect. This no doubt explained its lack of a tenant. A high thorn hedge surrounded the place, and the hand-gate needed a good shove to get it open due to a mixture of rust and bramble suckers.

"No one has been here very recently," said Major

Vernon, kicking away a tangle of brambles in the path.

Felix looked up at the grey stone face of the house. There was creeper over half the windows and others were shuttered.

"Not the most charming place for a tryst," he said. "Perhaps it looked better in August."

"She may have suggested it," Major Vernon said. "She knew the village, after all."

He turned the front door handle, but it seemed the door was locked.

"Might there be a key lying about?" he said.

"As if we would be so lucky," Felix said.

"People are often both careless, and predictable," said Major Vernon, who was already looking in the undergrowth by the front step, turning up loose stones. "You see," he said, bringing out a key.

"Why even bother to lock the door if..." Felix began, but as Major Vernon unlocked the door and pushed it open, he found himself silenced. Through the open door he caught sight of a woman's boot lying on its side, on the black and red tiled hall floor.

Seeing it too, Major Vernon said, "That could mean nothing."

"Or everything," said Felix.

Major Vernon went into the hall and picked it up.

"Sturdy and re-patched," he said. "The boot of a woman who works for a living, who knows she will be on foot. And why would she abandon it?"

"Because her lover gave her a new pair?" Felix said. "And they drove off in a carriage and pair? But..." He crouched down, and reached for his hand lens. As his eyes adjusted to the gloomy hall, he began to see what looked like stains on the floor.

"Do you need more light?" said Major Vernon.

"Yes," said Felix, wondering if his eyes were not playing tricks on him and if the marks were not shadows. But as the

Major lit a candle stub and held it nearby, he could see he was not deceived.

"Do you see it? That long trail of brown coming from there – and then the spots, there." On his hands and knees now, he followed the stains until he got to the back door. He glanced back. "And it starts –"

"Over here," said Major Vernon, by another door. "The kitchen I presume," he said pushing it open. "Dear God," he said softly. "Carswell..."

There was something about the Major's manner that made him reluctant to look.

"What the devil..." he found himself saying as he joined Major Vernon at the threshold. There was a mess of bloody sheets lying on the floor, while thrown onto the chair was a heap of women's clothes: body linen, stockings, stays, a bonnet, and a pink dress. Beside them was the other boot.

Major Vernon was looking through them.

"Not stained, but ripped," he said, holding up the remains of a shift.

Felix picked up one of the sheets. It had two corners knotted together.

"I think this might have been used as an apron," he said, looking down at the spattering.

"And can you say that that is human blood? I know you have been doing some studies."

"Not conclusively yet, but we might be able to say that this is all blood from the same source – matching one stain with another."

"Any laundry marks on it?" said Major Vernon, turning his attention to the other sheets. "Here's another apron."

"Two of them," said Felix. "Two devils."

"There's a crest. And this is best quality linen."

"I've seen that crest before," Felix said, his throat drying. "It was on Mrs Yardley's bed sheets."

Major Vernon nodded.

"What in the Lord's name went on here?" Felix exclaimed. "This much blood spatter – it suggests that the injuries were not post-mortem. That they stripped her while she was still alive and..."

Major Vernon did not answer, and they stood in silence for some moments. The pictures formed by the objects in the room and what they already knew came unbidden to Felix, and he felt his heart choke with anger and pity for the poor child and what she may have suffered. She was fifteen, her mother had said.

"It is so brazenly wicked," said Major Vernon, at length. "So confident. To leave all this here. Anyone could have found this at any time. And to take her across the fields and leave her in that culvert." He reached into his coat and took out his pocket diary. "When was the full moon, I wonder? If it were done at night, there was a chance they might not have been seen."

"He thinks he is untouchable," said Felix.

"He shall soon find he is not," said the Major. "Nor this other fellow."

"I wonder what else they have left lying around," Felix said, crossing the room to what he assumed was the scullery door. A passage opened from it, leading to a scullery and all the usual stores. He opened the first door, and detected at once a familiar smell: that of the dissection room.

"The candle, sir – might I?" he said, returning to the room.

"What is it?"

Felix could not speak. Instead he held up the candle, and let the sight speak for itself.

For there on the slate shelves where a careful housewife had once kept her stores, there was a glass jar containing a right hand, and next to it another, containing an unborn child.

Chapter Twenty-six

"Mr Carswell!" said Miss Yardley. "A great pleasure to see you. We had hoped you might call again and disregard my brother's foolish bluster. And Major Vernon – a great honour, sir, to know you at last."

Miss Yardley was a fine old type of maiden lady, in her mulberry-coloured silk and lace, and she received them with such kindness that Giles wished he had not come with such savage news in his pocket.

"We were hoping to see your brother, ma'am," he said. "Do you know when he will return?"

"No," she said. "But sooner or later he will be back. You are more than welcome to wait until he does," she said. "In fact, you must dine with me. I had resigned myself to a solitary dinner, and now –"

"I am not sure in the circumstances that we ought to impose, ma'am," Giles said.

"That sounds grave."

"I'm afraid that is the case."

"Then more to the point that you eat a decent dinner. You both look in need of one," she said.

"We are not dressed..."

She waved her hand to dismiss the notion.

"I appreciate your scruples, sir," she said. "But I entirely overlook that deficiency for the pleasure of your conversation. And I have a debt to repay to Mr Carswell, which one dinner, ad hoc as it must be, cannot begin to repay, but one must try," she added with a smile at Carswell, crossing the room to ring for a servant. "Hot water and towels, I think?"

Giles consented to her plan, though feeling it was a little

weak of him. But he was tired, cold and hungry, and he needed to fortify himself for the next stage of the business which would not be at all pleasant. He had a night in prospect in the charmless circumstances of the Whithorne Bridewell, attempting to get Yardley to confess.

"We must ask her about missing sheets," he said, when he was alone with Carswell in the bedroom to which the servant had shown them.

"She has a low opinion of him already," said Carswell, pulling off his shirt and going to the washstand. "Mrs Yardley obviously told her what happened this morning. I would imagine that both of them know a great deal without realising it, if you get my meaning."

"Yes," said Giles. "But the truth of it will still be a great insult to them, as a family. They may turn on us and seal their lips. That's common enough."

"Then you must charm all the secrets out of her over dinner," said Carswell.

"I shall do my best," said Giles, picking up one of the towels from the washstand and studying the elaborate embroidered crest. Unlike the white embroidery on the bed sheets, this was in red and black, but the pattern was otherwise identical. "What must be done, must be done. We can only hope that he does come back tonight. I must have a word with his man."

"She seemed confident that he would. Oh, thank you," Carswell said, as Giles, acting the part of manservant, handed him the towel to dry himself.

"I have asked Sergeant Haines and two of his men to come here at nine, with the carriage. We ought to be able to get him away without too much fuss."

As they went down to dinner, Giles asked the footman to find his master's valet, and waited in the hall to speak to him, sending Carswell into the dining room.

"About your master – did he give you any indication he

would be back tonight or not?"

"I wouldn't know, sir," said the valet. "He doesn't really tell me such stuff. He is either here or he is not, so to speak, sir."

"So sometimes he doesn't come back?" Giles said. "He is away all night, and longer?"

"Sometimes, yes, sir," said the valet.

"He never asks you to pack a bag for him?"

"No, he just takes himself off for a night or two, or more."

"And you never see what sort of humour he is in when he takes himself off, as you put it?"

"No, sir."

"Thank you, that will be all," Giles said, and went to the dining room, hoping that he had not lost sight of his quarry so early in the hunt.

He sat down uneasily, wondering now if the old lady's hospitality had not been calculated. If Yardley had gone off that morning and was not likely to be back that night, a fact well understood by the household, then to blithely assure them that he would be back and insist they ate dinner, was interesting to say the least. But he smiled at his hostess and drank his soup, and considered the best way to approach the subject.

The soup plates cleared, he said, "Your brother is out on estate business, I presume?"

"Most unlikely," said Miss Yardley. "He takes little interest in that, unfortunately."

"But he will be back tonight, you think?"

There was a tiny pause and then she answered, "I imagine so."

"So he is often away at night?"

She gave a sigh.

"Sometimes he is. Sometimes not. Oh dear, now you have me as a teller of untruths, sir," she said.

"No, ma'am. You had a reasonable expectation of his returning," Giles said.

"Not entirely. And I should have said so at once," she said. "Forgive me. I was concerned the moment I saw you. The gravity of your manner, Major Vernon – no, your mere presence here..." She made a little gesture of surrender.

"It does not matter," Giles said. "But perhaps you could tell us where he might have gone. His regular haunts?"

She glanced away, pursing her lips.

"I know this is unpleasant," he went on. "But can you tell us anything more?"

"We – that is, Mrs Yardley and I – suppose he has a woman somewhere. Which is just as well. He is..." She turned to Carswell. "Perhaps there is an acceptable medical term for a man who has strong passions in relation to the other sex? An unnaturally large appetite."

"Not exactly, ma'am," said Carswell. "But it is a good description."

"That is his nature," she said. "I have seen it grow in him from a boy. I am his senior by nearly twenty years, you see. When my late father remarried, I was sixteen. A year after we had buried my own dear mother. My father naturally was concerned to continue the family name."

"That cannot have been easy for you, ma'am," Carswell said.

"A name such as ours is no trifle," she said. "And my stepmother was a sweet woman who unfortunately soon followed my own mother into our vault. She died giving me a little sister, who also died. That was the great sadness for me. And I was left de facto a parent to Briggs, for my father was overcome with his grief, and who else was there to direct the household and the nursemaids, indeed manage the estate?"

"And these passions in your brother..." Giles began, but Miss Yardley now rose from the table. They rose also.

"I knew this day would come," she said. "What has he

done? What is it you want with him, sir?"

"I wish to speak to him about the death of Mary Taylor."

She nodded, supporting herself with her chair back.

"Of course. Of course," she said after a moment. "I cannot detain you any more. The truth will be out. It must be out. God forgive me!"

"What truth is that, ma'am?" Giles asked.

"The truth of what he is," she said. "When he was ten years old, I had a fine cat, who gave birth to a litter of kittens. I intended to keep them, but I came down one morning to find they had all been stolen from their mother – and she was wretched with it. And I found Briggs out in the garden with a knife and those poor innocent creatures, butchering them without a qualm. At ten years old! And knowing my feelings for them. He laughed at my grief and told me that they should have been drowned sooner or later, and that this way we could make a muff from the skins. Of course I shook him and tore a strip off him – I would have done worse. But I took him to my father to be punished, and he was whipped for it, but it made not the slightest difference. He had enjoyed himself too much. The punishment meant nothing to him. My tears meant nothing to him. And I knew then he was not like the rest of us, and that one day..." She gripped the back of the chair, and shook her head. "I believe that day has come," she said. "Go and find him!"

~

Later that evening, Giles set to work in the Bridewell at Whithorne, armed with maps of the district and all the resources he could muster at such short notice. He had sent a sergeant and two constables to wait at the castle, and others to visit all the public houses.

"And we will go and talk to Earle," he said.

"Does he fit Herne's description of the other man?" Carswell said.

"I was thinking about that, given that he seems to be somewhat complicit already. And he frequented The Falcon."

Earle was having tea with his mother and sister in the drawing room.

"Rather late to be calling, gentlemen," he said.

"My apologies," said Giles. "But the business is rather urgent. If we might have a word alone, Mr Earle?"

"Yes, yes, of course," he said, and showed them into his study.

"I presume you are calling on me in my capacity as coroner –" he began.

"No, sir," said Giles. "I want to return to the matter we were discussing the other day at Lord Milburne's. About Miss Barker."

"I have said all I wish to say to you about that."

"Yes, of course. But I have had some interesting new information on that matter, Mr Earle. Perhaps we should sit down?"

"You have been listening to gossip," said Earle.

"It may be gossip," Giles said. "It may not be. I never dismiss anything I hear so lightly. In the rubbish there are often scraps of gold. I was talking to one of the inn servants at The Falcon, you see, a fellow called Ned, who was kind enough to show me a sitting room upstairs, tucked away, but with easy access to the ballroom."

"So," said Earle. "What of it?"

"He told me that you and Mr Yardley were in the habit of using the room for amorous recreation. That he had seen Mr Yardley and Miss Barker there on the night of that last assembly, clearly having just finished the act of congress."

"Servant's gossip," Earle said, sharply. "Why do you give such stuff credence, sir?"

"Because my experience tells me when a man is lying and

when he is not," Giles said. "And you, sir, have been lying to me."

"That I resent!"

"Then tell me differently, Mr Earle. Make a case for yourself that I find remotely credible. But be warned, I have heard what kind of man you are and what your tastes are. Your mother and sister will know already. They cannot be blind to pregnant servants and they will tell me the truth, you may be sure of it. They still have the honesty that you seem to have put aside for the pursuit of your pleasures."

There was a long silence, and Earle sat down, composing his speech.

"They were not unwilling," he said at length. "They were eager enough to be there."

"They?"

"Bel and the Rivers girl. And Bel, I thought..." he gave a great sigh. "I thought we had an understanding. I never thought that – there was no reason for her to destroy herself! I would have married her, as the Lord is my witness, and she knew that! What a fool she was to do that – and Christ knows, what a fool I was to think it was anything but that, and to bring you here!"

"You say they were eager?" said Carswell.

"Yes," said Earle. "All women are, at heart. They say they don't like it, but they are as bad as us fellows, if not worse."

"So there were several occasions when this took place?" said Giles.

"Two or three at most. And I promised her marriage, sir, remember that."

"And was it only Miss Barker with whom you had congress?"

There was a little silence.

"Miss Rivers as well?" Giles prompted.

"As I said – they were not unwilling."

"How did this business begin, Mr Earle? Presumably

these young ladies were in a state of innocence at some point before you and Yardley set to debauching them."

"They were not virgins," said Mr Earle. "I had no hand in that."

"But Yardley did?"

There was a silence, then Earle said, "I am sure they were quite happy to give him that. He had a way with them."

"That did not amount to coercion?" put in Carswell, incredulously.

"There was no coercion. Absolutely none. Good God, what sort of man do you think I am?"

"A man of thirty who preys on a fifteen-year-old girl of his own class is a –" began Carswell.

"We will let Mr Earle's conscience speak to him, Mr Carswell," said Giles, feeling that Carswell's temper was about to get the better of him.

"If he has one," said Carswell.

"Oh, I do believe he has one. Miss Barker's death is a heavy weight, sir, is it not?"

"I would have married her," repeated Earle.

"Tell me about your friendship with Mr Yardley. This business with the young ladies – presumably there were other adventures, prior to this one?"

"There may have been," said Earle.

"But those were common girls – not so interesting, perhaps," said Giles. "Not so piquant. There's no fruit more sweet than that which is forbidden."

"Yes, I suppose so, if you put it like that. And as I have said, I was prepared to marry the girl."

"A great sacrifice, I'm sure," said Giles, "considering how wealthy she was."

"That has nothing to do with it."

"You did not propose to Miss Rivers," he pointed out.

"She was nothing more than a child."

"Whom you tupped just the same?"

"I would not have laid a finger on either of them if I had thought they did not want the attention. But the fact they were there in the first place – they were eager, sir, I tell you, eager and willing."

"Does the name Mary Taylor mean anything to you, Mr Earle?" said Giles.

Earle shook his head.

"She was a kitchen-maid at The Falcon," he said. "A girl of fifteen or so. Very pretty. You don't remember her upstairs in that sitting room, as an amusement, perhaps last winter? Supplied by Yardley, of course."

Earle shook his head.

"Yardley is away from home. I understand from Miss Yardley that he often goes away for days at a time without telling a soul. Perhaps he told you where he goes, since you seem to be in close association."

"I really wouldn't know," said Earle, with a shrug.

"Are you sure?"

"Of course."

"And you have told us too much already," said Giles. "He won't be pleased with you."

"I don't know what you mean," said Earle.

"Come now, a man like Yardley would not admit you to such a dangerous enterprise without being sure you could keep quiet. Which you cannot, it seems. He is not going to be amused if he finds out about this. I suspect that loyalty is important to him. However, the more you tell us, the better for you, Earle, because I want you to understand that Yardley's day is over. He is a dead man. Time to change your allegiances."

Earle went and sat down, his head in his hands. He was breathing hard.

"I believe," he began slowly, "though I cannot give you any evidence for this, that he goes to Northminster. He has some property there. But he goes incognito. That is all I can tell you. I swear it."

~

"Do you believe him?" Carswell said as they walked back to the Bridewell.

"I don't know," said Giles. "But it is at least a glimmer of a direction we can follow. Though not to the exclusion of others. It is certainly a place where he could lose himself and wallow in vice for a few days, despite all our efforts. And it will be easy enough to discover where his property is."

"Would he be so stupid as to stay there?" said Carswell.

"He was stupid enough to think that no one would look in the farmhouse. Perhaps he believes himself invincible and has been getting away with monstrous behaviour for some time."

"I can believe it. And as for those poor girls," Carswell said, "I do not believe they were consenting for a moment. That is why she gave Latimer's name – she was too afraid to tell us the real culprit. Yes?"

"Very likely."

"Mrs Connolly made the observation," continued Carswell, "that in such cases the victim is always blamed."

"That's unfortunately often the case."

"I can easily believe that Yardley bullied them into supplying sexual favours, threatening to expose them as whores if they did not continue to comply. Perhaps he was sweet and charming, and then..."

"You think he raped them?" Giles said.

"What about during those tea parties with Mrs Yardley? Could he not have lured them off into another room, for a while? He's strong enough, and wily. I understand that this is how these things happen."

"Oh, yes?" Giles said, glancing at him.

"It was something Mrs Connolly said," said Carswell after a moment. "She –"

"A painfully gained insight," Giles said, feeling angry to think what she might have suffered. "Well, at least we can put a stop to this animal."

"And the other man, the man in the white duster coat?" said Carswell. "Not Earle?"

"No, I don't think so. That's another puzzle for us, but that may not be a bad thing. It is a source of weakness for an enemy when he does not act alone. It may be the key to unlock a great deal more when we find him."

Chapter Twenty-seven

Felix arrived back in Northminster on the first mail coach from Whithorne, acting as a postman himself, with a sheaf of reports to be delivered to Captain Lazenby and various other officers at the Constabulary. Major Vernon was remaining in Whithorne for the rest of the day in order to quiz the household at the castle, and discover if he could find the names of any other known associates.

Having taken his post to The Unicorn, Felix walked back to Silver Street. It was the Saturday market in Northminster, a small affair covering only a few streets, and nothing like the larger market on Thursday which was a great event. But this one was notable for the variety of things sold, including cheese, and in a corner by the old market hall, there was a small poultry market.

Felix noticed an old woman sitting with a pen of guinea fowl, the birds which his mother set such store by and which had amused him in his childhood. Seeing them now, and thinking to please Sukey and restock her hen house, he went and picked out two likely creatures: one silver-grey, the other a pale buff.

"Those are the best ones," the woman said, as he handed over his money. "You have an eye for them, sir. Not everyone likes a glinner."

"Too good for the pot, that's the trouble," he said, watching as she packed them into a basket.

"You're right, sir," she said. "Companions, they are. I hope your lady likes them."

"I hope so too," said Felix, and he set off with his peace offerings making their distinctive chirps.

Margaret was sweeping the hall when he came in.

"Where is Mrs Connolly?" he asked.

"What have you got there, sir?" she asked, indicating the now noisy crate under his arm.

"Guinea fowl," said Felix.

"She's in the kitchen, sir."

He went along the passageway and saw her through the open door. She was standing by the kitchen table, frowning over the open cookery book in her hand, while Martha the cook stood behind her at the range, stirring a pot.

"Good morning, Mr Carswell," Sukey said. "I didn't think you would be back today."

"We have had a development," he said, "and..." He pointed at the crate.

She put down the book and came out into the passageway. There were servants observing them on both sides. There was no way of greeting her the way he wished.

"I wonder if you have room for some more lodgers," he said. "I know there are vacancies in the hen house."

"Let's go into the garden," she murmured, and went towards the back door. He followed her.

"Guinea fowl," he said, holding out the basket to her, when the door was safely shut and they were alone.

"What?" she said, not taking the basket.

"Guinea fowl. Much better than chickens. Able to scare a fox off."

"Really?"

"Really. And these are beauties – come, let me show you."

He started off down the path to the hen house.

"Glinners, the old lady called them," he said. "How is Miss Rivers?"

"Much better."

He put down the basket and took out the silver bird.

"Good. What do you think of her?" he said, holding up

the bird.

"Oh, she's strange," said Sukey. "But very pretty."

"I thought you would see it," he said. "And they don't grub up the plants. So my mother says."

Sukey had taken the other bird from the crate and was admiring it, a broad smile on her face, which filled him with relief. To see her happy and at ease was, he realised, all he had wanted. She glanced at him, still smiling, and shook her head.

"What?"

"You," she said.

"I'm sorry," he said. "You do like them, though?"

"Yes, yes, I love them! Thank you!" she said, popping the bird into the run and watching it trot away. "Here, put the other in," she added.

"You cannot eat them, of course," said Felix. "Well, you can, but I defy you to do it. And the eggs are small."

"So not very sensible, then."

"There is more to life than that," said Felix, as the silver bird rushed around exploring her new domain. "That one is such a character."

"Oh, I must tell you," Sukey said, as they stood watching the birds. "Miss Rivers had a visitor."

"Who? When was this?"

"Lord Milburne, yesterday afternoon. She was asleep, so I sent him away and told him to come back today. Was that the right thing to do?"

"He did ask me where she was," said Felix. "Yes, absolutely."

"He seems a nice enough fellow."

"The Major and his mother are old friends," said Felix.

"Really?"

"Really," said Felix, thinking of Mrs Herne giving them her blessing. He reached for Sukey's hand, and she permitted it.

"Your headache went away?" he said.

"Yes," she said, but took her hand away. "I must get back to work," she said. "Though I could stand here for hours looking at these ladies."

"You will have to find some names for them."

"That's always a mistake. What if that fox comes back?"

"Foxes are scared of them. In Africa they scare away lions, you know."

"I don't believe that for one minute. And I won't give them names, just in case. I can only stand so much heartbreak." With which she went back into the house.

He went back inside a few minutes later, having made sure the coop was secure and its new occupants quite comfortable.

He went up to Miss Rivers' room, and found her in a stable condition. Agnes, one of Sukey's maids, was sitting with her, knitting diligently in the lamplight.

"You've eaten well, I see," he said, noting the tray of empty plates which Agnes took away with her when he dismissed her.

"Suppose so," she said, assuming her usual sulky expression with him.

"May I have a look at the wounds?" he said, drawing back the covers. "I shan't be long."

"If you must."

He did so, and was pleased to see that they were healing satisfactorily.

"When will I be able to go home?" she said, when he was done.

"That depends," he said. "Major Vernon will want to talk to you, and you probably know that things cannot go smoothly with you, given that it seems –"

"Yes?" she said, with some hostility.

"The best way you can help yourself is by being absolutely honest. About everything. That is my advice."

"I don't know what you are talking about," she said.

"For what it's worth," Felix said, "I was impressed. Practical chemistry isn't the easiest branch of the sciences to master, and you managed quite a feat. The distillate percentage was remarkable. How did you do it? Triple distillation, yes? You must have been meticulous."

"What if I was?" she said, looking at him warily, yet he could see that her vanity had been piqued a little.

"I am just saying that it was a nice piece of work. Professor Baxter, who taught me at Edinburgh, would have commended that to the class."

"Girls are not allowed to take chemistry classes," she said.

"No, and perhaps they should be," he said.

"In cloud cuckoo land," she said, and he felt her bitterness – it was as strong as the prussic acid she had brewed. In her world, girls were repeatedly assaulted and bullied into silence instead of given books and lectures and a useful purpose in life. Bullied, he realised, into brewing destructive poisons which they gave to their friends to end their sufferings and bullied into tearing their own flesh up with broken glass.

"Still," he said, "there are books. One can learn a lot from the right books. You clearly did. I'll get you some of mine. It will help you pass the time." He got up and went towards the door.

"Until you hang me," she said.

"What?" he said, turning back to her.

"Well, surely that's what you want?" she said. "To hang me? For giving the poison to Bel? Isn't that what Major Vernon wants? Assisting in self-murder – it's a capital offence, I understand."

"You don't just read chemistry books, do you?" he said, sitting down. "And, no, we don't generally hang fifteen-year-old girls in this country."

"They might make an exception for me," she said, pulling herself up a little. "To make a proper example of me."

"You will have a defence counsel and he will make such a case that it will not come to that. No matter how much you might want it."

She looked across at him furiously.

"But what else am I to do?" she said. "What else has this world got for me? I would rather die! And at least I shall be famous for brewing poison. No, I shall be notorious."

"You might marry," he said, at which she scowled.

"Marriage!" she said. "No, I would rather hang."

"Lord Milburne called yesterday, asking after you, I'm told."

"How shallow do you think I am, sir?" she said.

"You don't like him?" he said.

"Have you met him?" she said.

"Yes, briefly," he said.

"Did you like him?"

"He seemed..." Felix searched for the word. "Inoffensive enough. And –"

"And handsome and with a title? It is what every girl is supposed to want, isn't it?"

"All right, not Milburne," said Felix, getting up again. "But some fellow may come along and you might revise your opinion of the whole business. Someone not at all like Lord Milburne. In the meantime, you are going to distract yourself with a solid course of reading, Miss Rivers. That is your best defence against these destructive thoughts, and you are intelligent enough to know you are wounding yourself with such attitudes." She did not answer. "Botany, chemistry and physical science? Yes?" he said. "And I'll quiz you on them. That should focus your mind."

"And if I refuse?"

"That's entirely your business," he said. "But I don't think you are that stupid."

~

"Well done," said Giles, after he had read through the account of the conversation that Carswell had had with Miss Rivers. "That is a straightforward admission of guilt. But what we do with it, at this point, is another matter."

"Exactly," said Carswell. "If we catch Yardley, and get him to admit to the rape of Miss Rivers and Miss Barker, her defence will look much stronger. If she can be persuaded to take counsel's advice and admit she is a victim."

"You seem to have a high opinion of her intelligence. Self-preservation will have to come into play, once she realises she has a life worth preserving," Giles said, laying down the paper.

It was early evening and Giles had come back to Northminster. It was pleasant to be in his own sitting room in Silver Street with a pot of coffee made exactly to his liking. He poured out another cup, thankful for Sukey Connolly's genius at such things.

"Any new leads?" said Carswell. "No sightings?"

"What we have so far is this," Giles said. "Yardley left Whithorne Castle on horseback yesterday morning, shortly after you last saw him, but his destination is unknown and he didn't take any luggage. He did visit his banker in Whithorne five days ago, on the nineteenth, and withdrew twenty-five pounds in small coin. So he's solvent, and he may have other resources. He owns quite a lot of property in Northminster, but they are all good addresses, and according to the rent roll, they are all let. But we shall check them all as a matter of course. His horse is perhaps our most useful lead. It is a young thoroughbred called Prince, a chestnut with a white blaze, sixteen and a half hands, and worth upwards of one hundred and fifty guineas. Somewhat temperamental, the groom at the castle told me."

"So he could have been thrown and be dead in a ditch," said Carswell. "That would be convenient."

"Yes, very. However, his head groom reckons Yardley is a skilled horseman. He is also assiduous, not to say extravagant, in the care of his horses. I saw that for myself on my visit to the stables. He is not going to entrust such an expensive animal to just anyone. So, the livery stables will be our first point of attack. If we can find the horse, we raise our chances of finding him. Oh, and there is a Yardley monogram on the saddle – the letters 'Y' and 'W' entwined, as we saw on the sheets."

"Well, that is certainly memorable," said Carswell.

"The other thing we know is that he has a definite taste for very young women," Giles went on, "an area of the vice-trade which, despite all our best efforts, seems to persist in Northminster. It may be one of the reasons he comes here."

"He could be propping up that business to some extent," said Carswell, "given he has money."

"Quite. So with luck he will be known here, by someone in the trade. Not that they will want to tell us that, given their livelihood may depend on it. However, Holt may be able to help us. I have had him looking into this problem for me, prior to this business. He has been developing sources of information."

Carswell looked a little surprised at this.

"He's on the books of the office?" he said.

"Very discreetly," said Giles. "None of the men we have at the moment have his talent for this kind of work, though one or two of them may learn it in time. Holt has. He's back from his holiday today, fortunately. I am meeting him later. We are going to make a tour of some of the less salubrious districts."

"Do you think you should, sir?" said Carswell, going to the window and looking out at the rain. "It looks as if it will be a foul night."

"I have brought the Whithorne weather with me, haven't I?"

"It might be best for you to take stock for an evening and get some rest. And what difference will an evening make, in all truth? He does not know we are after him yet."

"Unless Earle has warned him."

"You think that possible?"

"Yes," said Giles. "Anyway, I have put a watch on his office and his house, just to see there is no attempt at flight. And if you can continue your good work with Miss Rivers, and get her to admit to his name, then we have grounds for arrest."

"That might take a day or two," said Carswell.

There was a tap at the door. It was Sukey Connolly.

"The Professor is in a bad way again," she said. "Will you come down? I took in his tea, and he was rolling around on the floor in agony."

They left without another word, and Giles followed in case he could be of any assistance, which was just as well, for he was needed to help lift the old gentleman onto the chaise under the window. He was in a very sorry, distressed state, describing his condition – in a voice hoarse with pain – as like being stabbed by a hundred daggers. Carswell gave him something for the pain and suggested he retire for the night.

"It is the same as before," he said. "An acute gastric acid attack. This type of condition is a little out of my present area," he said. "You might send for Dr Pooley in the morning. He has quite a practice in this sort of thing. In fact, I will call on him tonight and tell him to come tomorrow, if you like."

"That would be very kind, thank you," the old man gasped. "You are all so very kind."

"Where is your son?" asked Giles. "Perhaps we should get him for you?"

"Still at his work, I think. He has taken to it very well."

"What does he do?"

"He is in the counting house at Mr Hardie's manufactory.

Mr Hardie is a distant cousin of my late wife. She was from Northminster. He has been very kind to us, and I hope Georg is repaying him a little with his labours."

"I'm sure he is," said Sukey, who was gathering up the teacups. "So no dinner for you tonight, sir, I'm afraid."

"It is this lady's excellent cooking," the Professor said. "That is what we must blame!"

"I think that is a compliment," said Sukey with a smile, going to the door. "I'll get the fire made up in your bedroom, sir, and the bed warmed. It will be more comfortable for you then."

"Would you like me to send your son home?" said Giles. "I shall be going that way shortly."

"You are very kind," said the Professor. He was struggling to sit up. "And Mrs Connolly, what a good woman! I am amazed she is not a wife, or shortly to be one, especially in this houseful of likely bachelors. Yes, Herr Doctor? Some of us more likely than others, I think, Herr Major?" he added with a conspiratorial chuckle. "I am feeling much better now. It will not be necessary to fetch Georg. In fact, it is better perhaps that you do not."

"But you will still go to bed and rest, sir?" said Carswell.

"Ja, ja. I promise that. But tell me, Herr Doctor, did you remember that tale? The one that your nurse quarrelled with the cook about? Although that sounds like a tale in itself, do you not think?" Giles found himself smiling at that.

"I cannot, I'm sorry," said Carswell.

"Oh well, another fish lost from my net. Perhaps you, Herr Major, have a tale for me? Where is your home?"

"Northumberland. Near Alnwick."

"Near the Scottish border, I believe?"

"Not so very far."

"Then you will have some excellent tales. That is a good country for them. What sort of family are you from, if you do not mind me asking?"

"Nothing very remarkable," said Giles. "But we have been there a long time, if that means anything."

"For stories, yes. In the same house?"

"Yes."

The Professor glanced around him. "I must get my notebook ready."

"You are going to bed, sir," said Carswell. "Remember?"

"And I must go to work," said Giles. "But when you are feeling better, you ought to talk to my sister, Professor. She probably remembers them better than I do. And there is another lady, Mrs Maitland, who has ghost stories from her nurse. We were talking of them the other night, were we not, Mr Carswell?"

"Yes, but they will have to wait until you are rested, and certainly until Dr Pooley has seen you," said Carswell.

"Ach, yes, of course, of course," said the Professor, staggering to his feet. "You are very right. But I worry that I shall never get them all, and there is so much still to be done." He gestured across the room, which was littered with scholarly detritus. "So much..."

When they were alone together again, Carswell said, "With any luck Pooley will send the pair of them off to Stanegate to take the waters."

"Surely he will have to stay and work?" said Giles.

"Not if I lay it on thickly enough with Pooley," said Carswell. "The son will be a necessary part of the recovery."

"Has he offended you?" Giles said.

"Yes," said Carswell. "In regard to Mrs Connolly."

"Surely –"

"Ask Mr and Mrs O'Brien," said Carswell. "They seem to be quite convinced by his attentions. And Mrs O'Brien thinks that Sukey –"

"That is nonsense," said Giles, "and you know it."

"I think I do," said Carswell. "But how can one ever be certain?"

"That's a bad habit," said Giles, shocked that Carswell could even entertain such an idea. "To be uncertain in such matters. It has to be an article of faith."

"You sound like my father," said Carswell.

"But it should not enter your head. Especially in such a case. Mrs Connolly is –"

"Even when the evidence suggests otherwise?"

"She is not a person to be doubted," Giles said. "She is your wife, Carswell."

"But she is not."

"In all but name, she is," said Giles. "What you have between you is a marriage, you are bound together now, and no good will come if you allow such foolish thoughts to enter into your head. I would have thought you would have more sense. To doubt the character of such a woman as Sukey? What the devil are you thinking?"

He had not meant to express himself so strongly but there was something about Carswell's petty quibbling that infuriated him. He could not imagine, had he been the lucky recipient of Sukey's affections, that he would ever have doubted them.

"You didn't see them together," said Carswell. "He was teaching her the damned polka, and she was..." He went to the door. "I'm going to see Pooley," he added, and left, banging the door behind him.

Chapter Twenty-eight

"After you'd gone home, sir," said Holt, coming in the next morning with Giles' clothes, "I did have a bit of luck. Remember what I was saying about the woman they call Mrs Hill? Got myself an introduction. Or at least an address. Whether she will speak to me or not, I don't know. But it's a house up in Bull Lane – you know, behind the Rag Market. Somewhere called Bridle Yard. Not heard that name before, I have to say."

"I've heard the name plenty of times," said Giles, putting down his razor and going to the large plan of the city that hung on his bedroom wall. "But I have never found it on any map. It is an alias. I suspect it might be this one, Martins Lane, in reality, but I have never been able to prove it."

Holt came and stood beside him.

"They told me it was to the left of the Green Dragon. Which is about there, isn't it, sir?" he said. "Martins Lane is as likely as anywhere."

"That would be interesting if it is the case. Well done, Mr Holt, an excellent bit of work. You were right to send me home."

"One fellow is easier to trust than two, sir, with all respect," Holt said. "In this line, at least."

"A good maxim," said Giles, returning to the looking glass and his half-shaven face. "So you will attempt to talk to her?"

"If I can, sir," said Holt. "Now, which cravat today, sir? The black figure or the navy?"

~

When Giles arrived at the office, he discovered Mrs Maitland waiting for him. She was sitting on one of the benches in the hall with a small portmanteau on the floor by her feet. She had the look of someone who had run away from home.

"You did give me your card," she said, rising to meet him.

"Certainly," he said, a little surprised at her direct manner.

"Charles has gone missing," she said. "I didn't know what else to do."

"Let's go into my office," he said, taking up her bag.

She nodded and followed him upstairs.

His two clerks in the outer room leapt to their feet as they came in. Both had papers and information to press on him, but he waved them away and steered Mrs Maitland through to his office.

He closed the door and saw her glance about. Unlike his rooms at The Unicorn which had had a certain picturesque charm about them, his room here was small and strictly utilitarian.

"He's here in Northminster," Giles said. "At least, he was yesterday."

"He was?"

"He called at my house yesterday and the day before. I did not see him, but Mrs Connolly, my landlady, did. He came to see Miss Rivers. He did not talk to you or leave you any sort of communication?"

"No! He simply left, having bribed Imbray to stay silent about it, which makes me extremely angry. To bring a servant into a family quarrel! I shall have to think of giving him notice now."

"I see," said Giles. "So he did not confide in you at all?"

"No!" she said. "He certainly did not. And why you thought that he might –"

"My apologies," he said.

"So where is he now?"

"Still here, I think. He has a reason to remain."

"Which is?"

"That is for him to tell you," said Giles.

"Why are you protecting him?"

"I gave him my word."

"Yes, yes, of course you did," she said. "That wretched conversation. Your gentlemen's agreement."

"I don't like to break my word. The circumstance was a delicate one."

"What on earth was it that passed between you?" she said. "You must tell me!"

"I don't think I may," he said. "He must do that."

"Have you any notion how infuriating this is?" she said.

"Yes, and I apologise for my part in it. Look, let me talk to him again. Let us see what can be done," he said. "You can be sure he is no danger. He's here and that is as much as can be managed."

"Where is he staying?" she said.

"That I don't know. He may have mentioned it to Mrs Connolly."

"Then I will go and talk to her," she said, going to the door. "After all, I cannot take up any more of your time. Your clerks looked eager for your ear."

"I will send someone to find him," said Giles, blocking her way. "It will be easy enough." Certainly he supposed it would be easier to find Lord Milburne than Yardley. "Yes?"

She hesitated for a moment, and then collecting herself, said, "Yes, yes, I suppose you are right. And in all likelihood he has gone to the same hotel we stayed at when we came here before to see the lawyers."

"The Mitre or The Blue Boar, perhaps?" Giles said.

"The Mitre," she said. "And why did I not go straight there and ask? You must think me quite the fool now, Major

Vernon, wasting your time."

"You were worried."

"I was angry," she said. "A far more dangerous condition."

"You have every right to be angry with him," Giles said.

"But it does not mean I should indulge myself," she said.

"Do you want me to rebuke you for it?" he could not help saying.

"That would imply an intimacy that we have not quite..." she said, and gave a nervous laugh. "Or have I charged down a fence or two, coming here, unbidden and asking you to deal with my difficulties when previously I should not have dreamt of asking anyone for help?" Her voice wavered as she finished this speech, and she turned away. "Perhaps you should rebuke me for other things – though the Lord knows there will be quite a list!"

He could not resist taking her hand. Her discomfort moved him intensely.

"You told me yourself that you believed that the difference between sinners and saints is that the latter never face real temptation. Remember? As a sinner myself, I found that consoling."

She twisted her hand so it was about his, and squeezed his fingers for a moment before releasing herself.

"I will go and find him for myself," she said. "And you will not send one of your men for him. You have more serious business to deal with than this, at present."

"Might I suggest something?" Giles said. "That you hold your fire a little, and let him alone for now?"

"There may be some advantage in that," she said. "I do need to compose myself."

"Quite," he said. "Now, I have some business this morning on the far side of town, and that will take me in the way of a lady I should very much like you to meet."

"Yes?"

"My sister, Mrs Fforde."

"Your sister?" she said.

"She lives in the Minster Precincts. Her husband is the Canon Treasurer. I think you will like each other, and her house is a better place to wait for your recalcitrant boy. He can come and find you. I will have Mrs Connolly send him there if he comes calling again."

"Will she not mind being imposed upon?" said Mrs Maitland.

"She will not," said Giles. "In fact..." He stopped, for she had given his arm a brief, light touch.

"Are you sure?" she said.

"She will be glad to know you. And, she will have to know you soon enough."

"You think so?" she said, in a manner that attempted to be arch, but she could not disguise the tremor in her voice.

"She will like you," he said. "I am sure of it."

"She may think..." she said. "After all, I have nothing."

"I have nothing either," he said. "And she is used to my wilfulness."

She shook her head and began to laugh. He could not help laughing as well, and they stood there for a moment in a state of foolish hysteria, until they were interrupted by a brisk knock at the door.

"I shall have to deal with them," he said. "Give me ten minutes."

~

Half an hour later found them walking through the Minster Precincts in the direction of his sister's residence, the Treasurer's House. Giles was pointing out the famous array of carved saints and apostles that decorated the west entrance to the Minster, as a polite host was bound to do, and Mrs

Maitland, the equally polite guest, stopped and looked up at them.

"And that, I think, is St John – the Evangelist, not the Baptist."

"Yes, I see him – how well they have lasted all these centuries," she said. "Not a broken nose among them!" She gave a sigh. "Really, I do not think I should impose myself."

"It will not be an imposition," Giles said. "And it's too late now – that's my brother-in-law coming out of the door."

Lambert Fforde was not alone. Accompanying him was a taller, slighter younger man, also in clerical dress, who strongly resembled him. Giles now remembered that Edward Fforde, Lambert's younger brother and a rising man at Oxford, was visiting. They spotted Giles with Mrs Maitland and at once came over to them.

"Giles, how good to see you!" said Lambert, shaking his hand. "I thought you had been carried away on business for some time."

"I was carried back, fortunately," Giles said. "Mrs Maitland, may I present my brother-in-law, Canon Fforde, and his brother, Dr Fforde? Gentlemen, this is Mrs Maitland. We were on our way to call on you, as a matter of fact."

"Excellent!" said Lambert. "Then come and drink tea with us, Mrs Maitland. We always have it at this hour. You will be more than welcome – as is any friend of my brother-in-law."

"Thank you," said Mrs Maitland. "Excuse me, sir, for asking such a direct question – is it Fforde, spelled with a double F?"

"Yes, it is," said Lambert.

"And, please forgive me, if I'm mistaken, but perhaps one of you gentlemen is the author of a history of the wars in France in the Middle Ages?"

"That would be me," said Edward Fforde with a bow. "Have you read, it ma'am?"

"Only a little of it at present, I must confess, but my son knows it chapter and verse, so to speak. I gave it to him last Christmas. He did read out some passages on the Maid of Orleans to me – very memorable."

Edward Fforde looked suitably embarrassed and pleased.

"Your son has excellent taste," said Lambert, smiling.

"Surely the taste was mine for choosing the book?" said Mrs Maitland, and Giles laughed. He caught Lambert's eye, and his expression was distinctly quizzical as well as amused.

They went in, and Sally met them with her usual warmth. That she was alive to the novelty of his appearing with Mrs Maitland was not hard to read, but she did everything to put her at her ease. In truth there was not much difficulty to be surmounted, whatever Mrs Maitland's fears might have been. To have praised Edward's work without having been prompted made her a heroine in all their eyes.

~

"Remember you are coming to dinner tonight, Giles," said Sally, accompanying him to the door when he took his leave. He had had to force himself out of his chair, unwilling to leave the comfortable conversation that had broken out over the tea table. "And Mr Carswell?"

"He accepted?"

"Yes, for once. We are honoured. I am not sure what it is that keeps him away so much these days. Oh well," she said, with a shrug. "And I shall ask Mrs Maitland and Lord Milburne as well, yes?"

"Only if you care to."

"I will do whatever you like," she said. "So shall I?"

"Yes. He will enjoy talking to Edward. It will be good for him."

"And it will be good for you," she said, laying her hand

on his shoulder, "to have dinner with someone you clearly admire."

"I didn't mean to be so transparent," he said after a moment. "It is not that –"

"I am imagining a coup de foudre," she said, "that has struck you both."

"Then it is a sort of folly and it ought to pass. And perhaps ought not to be encouraged, given that –"

"Time has nothing to do with these matters," said Sally. "And she is such a delightful person! One can see that in a matter of minutes. There is no shadow in her character."

"Yes," he said, simply. "Yes, indeed. But I am – well, Sal, you know what I am, of all people."

"You are a good man and you deserve a good wife," she said. "Now go and do your work, and I will look after her for you, just as you wish."

With which she dismissed him.

Giles crossed the Precincts, feeling that by the time he got back it would be a settled matter. Perhaps taking her to Sally had been a mistake.

In other circumstances he would have been ridiculously happy at such a prospect. But he wondered if he were actually suited to marriage any more, and if it was fair to ask any woman to share his strange life. His prospects were not glittering ones. Death and life were divided by such a narrow passage. Perhaps it was not wise to risk one's heart so precipitately when uncertainty lay at every corner.

Yet her heart, he felt, was already laid out for him, like a specimen on Mr Carswell's dissecting slab, ready for him to butcher as he pleased. He did not know if he could be trusted with such a charge, and wondered if he ought not withdraw before any more damage was done. But perhaps this had happened already. She had told him that she had resisted pragmatic offers of marriage. She only wanted marriage when her affections were truly engaged, and it seemed he had engaged them, and profoundly so, even in such a short space of time. To walk away now would be too cruel, and yet...

Perhaps I am mistaken, he thought; perhaps she is only amusing herself.

He turned his attention to his work, as he walked down a narrow lane from the far side of the Precincts, and hastened his steps through the curious hinterland that this quarter of the city presented. One of the new railway lines ran through it, as well as a broad stretch of canal. It was not urban but neither was it rural, and the buildings were a mixture of the ancient and the starkly modern. Dirty cottages huddled together, overshadowed by formless workshops, thrown up to accommodate businesses that were growing fast.

The gates of a large timber yard signalled he had reached his destination: the property of George Bickley. Although he had set a couple of men enquiring at the various livery establishments of the town for Yardley's expensive horse, it had occurred to him that Bickley might have some information about Yardley himself. He was well known as a dealer in quality horses and it was more than possible that the two men had crossed paths. Yardley might even have arranged to stable his horse with him.

Bickley was an interesting character, to say the least. He lived an existence on the fringes of legality, pursuing many lines of business that seemed to be more lucrative than they should be. Giles suspected him of a great deal of criminal activity, but could never prove anything. He was clever and slippery. He never allowed anything to stick to him. He also had a reputation as the best horse doctor in the district, though Giles would never have trusted one of his own animals to him, feeling an example would be made of it. There existed a perfect state of mistrust between them.

Giles had not had any direct dealings with Bickley for some time, and certainly not since he had set up the Bureau. But he had sent a man undercover as a day labourer in the yard for a while, and had begun to form a better picture of his enemy. It was still a very imperfect picture, however.

"Yes?" asked the man set to watch the gate.

Giles held out his card.

"I'd like to speak to Mr Bickley."

The man went off without another word and returned a few minutes later.

"You're in luck," he said, and signalled to Giles to follow him.

Giles was pleasantly surprised to be led to the stables, from where Bickley ran his horse trading and doctoring operation. The stables were immaculate and the horses in the stalls were all objects of great beauty and power. But an initial glance did not reveal Yardley's chestnut.

Bickley was in his shirt sleeves, crouched down and vigorously massaging the flank of a stunning grey stallion. Nearby one of his men stood holding his coat, as if that was all he ever did.

"Major Vernon, what can I do for you?" Bickley's manner was perfectly civil, and Giles felt encouraged.

"I wish I could say I was here to buy a horse," he said. "This is quite impressive, to say the least."

"They don't pay you enough, Major Vernon," said Bickley, continuing to massage the grey. "A man in your position ought to be able to afford the best. Doesn't look good for the city."

"What's the trouble with this fellow?" Giles said, indicating the grey.

"A touch of arthritis," said Bickley. "Mayhap his hunting days will be over. I'm hoping not, for he's a grand ride. But he'll still go to stud. I could let you have one of his foals in due course. All broken and ready for you. You could put some money down and pay me the rest when you can. I'd have no trouble with your credit, I think."

"I still couldn't afford it," said Giles. "But thank you."

Bickley straightened, turned to the stable lad and handed him the cloth.

"Keep rubbing in the mixture," he said. "At least another quarter hour. And then I'll come and look at him again."

The attendant held out his coat and Bickley insinuated himself into it, for it was tight-fitting in the latest fashion, and it had been cut to show the man's formidable physique. Bickley had been a noted-prize fighter in his youth and kept the tautness of muscle, even though his hair was now thin and grey. He adjusted his cravat and said, "So what can I do for you, Major Vernon?"

"Have you had any dealings with a man called Briggs Yardley? He's got an expensive taste in horses. I wondered if he might have bought from you."

"Briggs Yardley?" repeated Bickley. "Well, that's an interesting question."

"Then you know him?"

Bickley pursed his lips and said, "Let's go into my office."

The room did not resemble an office, and was dominated by a round table with seats for eight – the perfect spot for a game of cards. As Bickley offered him a chair, Giles wondered who had last occupied the seat and how much they had lost.

"Tell me about Yardley," he said, hoping that he would get a good hand of cards.

"Tell me why you want to know," said Bickley, pouring two brandies. He put one in front of Giles. Giles pushed it away with a shake of his head. Bickley took it up again with a shrug and began to drink it himself. "What is he to you, Major?"

"A problem," said Giles. "I sense he is that to you also, sir."

"You may be right," said Bickley, sitting down opposite him. "Cigar? – no, you won't, will you?"

"My apologies."

"Caution is never to be apologised for," said Bickley.

"Yardley – you want him?"

"Yes."

"For what? Something serious, I'll be bound."

"What makes you say that?" said Giles.

"You only deal with murder and the like now, I'd heard."

"Seems to be so," said Giles, not at all wishing to disabuse him of this impression.

"So you want him for murder?"

"Yes, and rape."

Bicker knotted his fingers and leant his elbows on the table.

"And if I oblige you, Major Vernon," he said, "what can I expect?"

"The satisfaction of doing your duty," said Giles. Bickley smiled with a distinct lack of humour. "These are serious charges," Giles went on. "The man is dangerous. He needs to be dealt with."

"I can't disagree with you there," said Bickley. "After what he did to me, he deserves to feel it."

"So what was that?" Giles said.

"Not so fast," said Bickley. "You cannot come to this table empty-handed, sir."

"If you know something I can use, Mr Bickley, I advise that you tell me, for your own sake. Concealing evidence in such a case is not advisable."

"A threat is not a favour, sir," said Bickley. "I want a favour."

"You sound like a child asking for a sugar plum," Giles said with all the flippancy he could manage. "And I shall not give you one. For your own good."

Fortunately the man laughed at it. "All right, I shall help you, but you will do something for me, Major Vernon," he said, getting up from his seat. "You will not set any more of your men labouring in my yard. I won't have any more of that."

"I have no idea what you are talking about," said Giles. "As if I would stoop to such practices."

Bickley laughed and said, "Just mind you don't do it again. My business is my business and if you want my help, you swallow that. I don't care if you won't drink my brandy, but I want you to swallow that."

Giles shrugged and said, "Very well. I shall promise to never again do something I have never done." As he spoke he determined it would be done again, and this time with more finesse and circumspection. "Will that do, sir?"

"It will have to," said Bickley, sitting down again and beginning on the second glass of brandy. "And you are in luck, sir, in the quarry you have marked, because he has offended me. I shall be glad to see you hang him."

Chapter Twenty-nine

"I don't want to go," Felix said. "I shall send my apologies."

"Of course you must go," said Sukey, "when you said you would."

"I should stay here. The Professor –"

"If there is any change, I will send Holt up to get you. Why don't you wear your new waistcoat?" Sukey said, going to the press. "It's about time it had an outing."

"I have no idea why I bought that," said Felix, as she held it up. The plum and gold silk seemed in that moment much too fancy and feminine.

"It suits you," she said.

He shook his head. "Major Vernon will despise me," he said.

She shrugged and put it on herself, over her dark dress. She fastened it up and went to the glass to look at herself.

"I like it," she said. "Yes?"

"Yes," said Felix. "Much better on you. In fact..." He went towards her, stirred by imagining her dressed entirely in men's clothes. Standing behind her, he put his hands on her waist and bent to kiss the nape of her neck, knowing how hard she found it to resist such an advance.

"I don't want to go out," he said, punctuating his words with kisses, "because I want to stay here with you."

"Sometimes you have to put duty before pleasure," she said, but she had relaxed in his embrace, and leant against him. He began to unbutton the waistcoat.

"I would be happy to go if I could take you with me," he said. "It is so unjust."

"The world is full of greater injustices, I should say," said

Sukey.

"If we were married, they'd have to receive you," he said.

"No, they wouldn't. They wouldn't even ask you then. Nobody would. We would have to take a passage to New Zealand and probably even there... Oh, why are you even talking about this?"

"Because – because – well, you know why."

She quickly disentangled herself.

"You need to get dressed." She finished unfastening his waistcoat and tossed it onto his bed, leaving the room without another word.

Felix sat down on the bed, feeling a most unpleasant mixture of thwarted desire and fury. He was angry at her, but more angry at himself for mentioning marriage. Whenever he did, it never ended well, but he never seemed to learn his lesson.

He hauled himself into his evening clothes, feeling increasingly truculent as he did so. By the time he went downstairs, he was on the verge of writing to excuse himself, especially when he saw that Major Vernon was talking to young Holzknecht in the hall. At least there was no sign of Sukey, but as he approached, he saw through the open door that she was in the sitting room with the Professor.

"He seems a great deal better," Major Vernon said.

"Dr Pooley was most reassuring," said Holzknecht. "Thank you, sir, for your recommendation," he added, turning to Felix and giving him a little bow. "And my father is much calmer now."

"We must go," said Major Vernon, consulting his watch.

Felix had no wish to leave, especially since Holzknecht went into the sitting room after the Major moved towards the front door.

"Mr Carswell?" the Major prompted.

"We will be early," said Felix, who was searching for a pretext to extract Sukey from the room, and failing to find one.

"I need to talk to you first," said Major Vernon. "If you would?"

Felix followed him out into the street, and with great determination decided he would attempt breezy indifference. He reached for his cheroot case and found instead that his fingers were clumsy with agitation as he tried to extract one, and ended up by dropping the case. The contents spilled out onto the pavement. At least that gave him the excuse to swear a little, as he retrieved them.

"You have nothing to worry about," Major Vernon said, as he stooped in the gutter. "You know that."

"I'm not worried," Felix said, not at all consoled by his apparent transparency.

"Of course, not," said Major Vernon mildly. "Do you want a light?"

For the Major, who was no friend to smoking, to make such a concession was equally humiliating.

"Thank you, but that won't be necessary. In fact, you'll be pleased to know they are all spoilt," said Felix, putting the muddy case back into his overcoat pocket. "So what was it you wanted to talk to me about?"

"Yardley. I have had some good information. I went to see Bickley."

"That's the horse doctor fellow – the one you think is managing some sort of vast criminal enterprise?"

"I'm more sure of that than ever, especially after my visit there today, and he will have to be dealt with soon enough. But, in the meantime, we shall let him be – for it won't be easy to topple that edifice, I am sure of it. First we must get Yardley."

"Whom you thought might have had some dealings with him?"

"Given his taste for expensive horses, yes. I was right. Better still, Yardley offended Bickley, and Bickley is not a man to offend. He was glad to let me take the trouble of hanging him."

"Offended him?"

"Attempted to cheat him in some fashion. I'm surprised Yardley's not dead already, to be frank."

"Do you think Bickley would go so far?"

"I don't know. His manner suggests he is ruthless – and I imagine he is not afraid to take violent action to maintain his position. But in the short term, it's interesting for what it tells us about Yardley. It confirms what we suspected – that he likes to engage in risky behaviour."

"In crossing swords with Bickley?"

"Yes, and those who take risks always make mistakes, and make themselves visible. Anyway, Bickley gave me some interesting information about what Yardley has been getting up to."

"Such as?"

"Whoring, dog-fighting, ratting, betting. Nothing so surprising there. He's clearly thoroughly dissolute. Obviously Bickley was a little vague on names – but he told me to look at the area about Bridle Lane, which is interesting, because Bridle Lane, as Holt and I have recently established, is possibly a criminal alias for Martins Lane, behind Bull Lane. So that is something we can begin with."

"And you trust Bickley's information?"

"Not entirely," said Giles. "But I don't think he's playing with me. He doesn't have any reason to protect Yardley."

"I'm surprised you are still prepared to go out to dinner," Carswell said, "and not plunging into Bull Lane at once."

"A man has to eat," said Major Vernon.

When they arrived at the Treasurer's House, Canon Fforde met them in the hall and took them into his library. There they found Lord Milburne agitated and pacing the room.

"You got my message, then?" Major Vernon said.

"Yes," said Milburne.

"Have you seen your mother?" said Major Vernon.

"His Lordship has only just arrived," said Canon Fforde.

"I wanted to speak to you, sir, before..." Milburne broke off. "If you please?"

"Of course," said Major Vernon.

"Let us go up and join the others, Mr Carswell," said Canon Fforde. "Yes?"

Felix went upstairs with Canon Fforde and into the drawing room where he received an enthusiastic greeting from Celia Fforde.

"Mr Carswell," she said, taking both his hands. He could not help smiling at it. "We have got a pair of white rats. Will you come and look at them?"

~

When they were alone, Milburne burst out, "I am not sure I like your way of arranging things, Major Vernon!"

"Forgive me," Giles said. "It is a little ad hoc, but with both of you appearing on my doorstep I had to improvise."

"Your brother-in-law is very civil, of course," Milburne said, remembering his manners after a moment.

"Yes, and you will like his brother. He wrote –"

"Yes," Milburne said. "So I hear. In other circumstances I should be delighted."

"Then talk to your mother, my lord, and clear the air. She is as miserable as you."

"And you have said nothing to her?"

"No. I gave you my word. And she understands that. So shall I go and fetch her?"

"There will be no point!" said Milburne, throwing up his hands. "In all honesty I cannot see the point of anything. She hates me, Miss Rivers hates me – she will not see me. It really would have been better if you had let me cut my throat, Major Vernon, don't you think?" He threw himself into one of the armchairs and pressed his hands to his face. "Ever since George told me about Bel, and what she had done," he said, "ever since then, everything has been so wretched. I thought I had friends and now I have none. She will not see me! That housekeeper of yours said so! Oh God, how I wish I were dead!"

Giles sat down opposite him and wondered how he ought to proceed. He did not want to belittle the young man's despair, but he did not think he should allow him to wallow in it. So he held his tongue. Fortunately his steady silence seemed to have some effect, allowing Milburne to gather his reason and regain his composure. At last the young man looked up and said, "Do you really think my mother will understand?"

"I believe so," Giles said. "From what I see, you are quite alike. Passionate and strong-willed. And she cares so much for you, and she will forgive you anything in the end, if you are straight with her. That is all she wants from you – honesty."

Milburne looked keenly at him, for a long space. In the firelight his features lost their boyish cast. Then he rubbed his face and sighed.

"You are probably right," he said.

"Might I offer you some other advice? You don't need to take it – you have heard quite enough from me, I imagine," said Giles, "but this is worth saying: get yourself a profession – the church, the law, politics – anything that interests you. Something that you will have to work for and that will take you into the world."

"You don't suggest the army this time, I see," Milburne said.

"What you said had some truth in it," Giles said, getting up from his chair.

"So when shall I talk to her?" said Milburne, rising also. "I promise I shall do so, this time, sir," he added, a little sheepishly.

"Perhaps after dinner? A good meal will put you both in a kinder frame of mind, and my sister keeps an excellent table. In fact, just the sight of you will put her mind at rest. And of course there is Dr Fforde eager to be told how remarkable his book is. You will be very welcome!"

"It is remarkable. You must read it."

"I will, when..." Giles stopped, thinking of Yardley and the task ahead of him. "When I have my next leave, though Heaven knows when that will be. Now, shall we go upstairs, my lord?"

~

When the white rats, Hebe and Dorcas, had been admired, encouraged to do tricks and then put away, and Celia herself had gone to bed, Felix returned to the drawing room. As he sat there with Canon and Mrs Fforde, Mrs Maitland and Dr Fforde, he was aware he was adding very little to the party. He could not shake his annoyance at the impossibility of Sukey ever being admitted there to sit beside him. How was it that their world, this particular world, usually so civil and generous and charitable, should be so utterly inflexible on this most important point? She was not their inferior, only different.

The worst of it was that she seemed to agree with them, and was quite willing to accept the status quo. That he could not begin to understand.

Perhaps, he thought, their mutual ineligibility, which she so liked to point out, was in truth a convenient excuse. Maybe she did not want to marry him because she did not truly love him. This alarming idea slithered into his head just as Major Vernon and Lord Milburne came into the drawing room.

Naturally there was a burst of greetings and the necessary introductions were made. There was even a tender passage between Mrs Maitland and Lord Milburne who embraced quite as if they had not seen each other for many months rather than two nights.

They went into dinner, and Felix tried to distract himself with Canon Fforde's excellent wine, but he found he had no heart for even that, nor much appetite for the food. He wanted to go back to Sukey and fold her in his arms, desperate for the reassurance of her, the feel of her warm skin against his, the touch of her fingers in his hair. Yet at the same time he was tormented that it was all some kind of diabolical illusion, that it meant nothing and that she meant nothing by it.

Edward Fforde was going on at some length, having found an adoring audience in Mrs Maitland and Lord Milburne. Felix had no opinions about Joan of Arc, let alone the Kings of France and their endless wars.

"And she really wore a suit of armour?" Mrs Maitland was asking.

"Yes, the Dauphin had it made for her, by one of the finest armourers in France. It is a shame it did not survive," Dr Fforde said.

"I read that part of it did," said Milburne. "The right glove, at least."

"I fear that was a forgery, knocked up to gull some eager antiquarian. Or if not a forgery, certainly not having any connection with the Maid," said Dr Fforde.

"That's the sort of thing I can imagine Squire Yardley buying," remarked Felix.

"Yes, quite," said Mrs Maitland. "Have you any acquaintance with the Yardley family, Dr Fforde? They are neighbours of ours at Whithorne. He is quite the medievalist, as Mr Carswell says, but I suspect of the entirely spurious type."

"He is a great deal more than that, unfortunately," said Major Vernon.

"Oh yes?" said Mrs Fforde, with a frown. "That sounds

ominous."

"It will be for him, God willing," said Major Vernon. He turned to Dr Fforde. "Tell me a little more about Joan's alleged armour. Where did you hear about that?"

"It was from a correspondent of mine in Paris," said Dr Fforde. "Father Le Montagne. He is a Dominican and a splendid scholar."

"Did someone buy it?" Major Vernon asked.

"I believe they did, and then took it to some authority for verification. They then discovered it was not all that it seemed. A most unfortunate business."

"Certainly." Major Vernon glanced across the table at Felix, while at the same time tracing patterns on the white damask cloth with his forefinger. "But that could be of some use to us, yes, in drawing him out?"

"Are you thinking of constructing a lure?" said Felix.

"Not perhaps Joan of Arc's armour," said Major Vernon, "but some interesting trifle, rather rare, that piques his curiosity. Yes?"

"Mr Yardley's curiosity, I take it, Major?" put in Mrs Maitland.

"Yes."

"What do you think he has done?" said Canon Fforde.

"He is a murderer, certainly, and more."

"Dear Lord," murmured Mrs Fforde.

"The poor girl in the culvert?" said Mrs Maitland.

"Mary Taylor," said Major Vernon. "Yes."

There was a silence, and then Lord Milburne said, "There is something, sir, that might help you. Do you remember, Mother, when we called there first, he showed them to us – that collection of old manuscripts?"

"Oh yes, I remember," said Mrs Maitland. "Too well. He would not stop talking about them. You were most polite and enthusiastic and I was finding it quite hard to be. Fortunately I was rescued by Miss Yardley."

"They were interesting," said Lord Milburne. "And he told me that he wanted a copy of the Chronicle of St Remy. Which is of course very rare."

"Perhaps you have one in your library, Dr Fforde?" said Major Vernon.

"I wish I did," said Dr Fforde. "Neither Salvator's nor even the Bodleian has such a treasure."

"But perhaps you have come across something akin to that?" Major Vernon said. "A few pages, an incomplete version. Something that we can begin a rumour about."

"Yes, I see. Well, I suppose that might be possible."

"It only needs to sound plausible. It does not have to exist. It is just a means of bringing him out into the open."

"Very cunning," said Mrs Maitland with a smile.

"But a little dubious," said Dr Fforde. "Forgive me for saying so, but if such a rumour were begun, even with such an object in mind, it might reflect rather ill on my reputation if a bogus item were linked with my name."

"We can keep your name out of it," said Major Vernon. "All I want from you is a confection."

"That is not something anyone has ever asked of me before," said Dr Fforde, "I must say."

"That's the difference between Oxford and Northminster," said Canon Fforde, raising his glass to his brother. "I am asked for confections all the time, Ned."

This attempt at humour failed completely. Dr Fforde remained stone-faced.

"I don't think that anyone should scruple at such means, Dr Fforde," Mrs Maitland said, "if you don't mind me being so bold? We must do all we can to assist the course of justice, and this man Yardley – well, to kill an innocent girl, and leave her body in a culvert to rot away – it is beyond monstrous!"

"And the details –" Felix said.

"We can spare this company the exact details," said Major Vernon, cutting in. "Dr Fforde, I do appreciate that this may seem unusual, but the situation is an unusual one. I am anxious to put a stop to this man's activities. He is very dangerous. I hope you can consider assisting us."

Edward Fforde sipped his wine and seemed to be considering the point.

Then Lord Milburne said, "It is just like Gaspard de Huringen luring out the grey beast, in the Chronicle of the Green Rood, is it not?"

Dr Fforde, clearly surprised, said to Milburne, "You have read that?"

"Oh yes," said Milburne. "I tried to make a verse translation of it, but I didn't have much success."

"Why are you not up at the University?" said Dr Fforde.

"A good question," said Canon Fforde.

"That is all my fault, I fear," said Mrs Maitland. "Our prospects have been so difficult for such a long time that my son's education has not been all it should have been. Oxford always seemed quite an impossibility until..." She stopped, looking truly mortified.

"No, Mama, it is not your fault," said Lord Milburne. "It was too expensive. And then when I got the title and the estate..." He shrugged.

"Would you like to go to Oxford?" said Major Vernon.

"It must be Oxford," said Canon Fforde, "and Salvator's, or you shall never dine here again, my lord."

Lord Milburne looked bewildered at that.

"I am sorry, sir?"

"Excuse my levity," said Canon Fforde. "No, you must choose for yourself, Lord Milburne. Choose the Other Place if you must, and we will write all the letters you need, whatever you decide, yes, Ned?"

"Yes, certainly, but I do think you have the temperament of an Oxford man."

"And a Salvator's man," said Canon Fforde. "But you may have family connections that incline you otherwise."

"Could it be managed?" said Lord Milburne. "What about the estate?"

"We shall get some better advice. That is well overdue," said Mrs Maitland. "Do not let the thought of that trouble you. This is more important."

On this triumphant note, the ladies left the dining room. The cloth was cleared, the port brought out and Dr Fforde set to interrogating Milburne, in a manner that made Felix remember the horror of viva examinations in his weaker subjects at Edinburgh. However, Milburne was surprisingly sure of his ground, given it was an unexpected attack.

"I think Ned already has him lined up as a future fellow and ally in all senior common room disputes," said Canon Fforde. "You won't have another?" he added, when Major Vernon refused a second glass of port.

"Regrettably, we have work to do, don't we, Carswell?" he said, as Felix picked up the decanter. Undeterred, Felix took another glass. If Major Vernon was planning a grim exploration of the less salubrious parts of Northminster, he would not go with him without some fortification.

Chapter Thirty

"We have to conclude that Bickley's information, if well-intentioned, was vague," said Major Vernon. "At least in the first instance."

"Well-intentioned?" said Felix. "Surely nothing about the man is that?"

"Yes, perhaps that isn't quite the right expression for it," said Major Vernon, reaching for another piece of toast, and buttering it.

Felix yawned – he had not had a great deal of sleep. For the last two nights they had been scouring the town late at night for signs of Yardley, a process that had proved both sordid and futile. Returning last night in the small hours, he had longed to climb into bed with Sukey, but had exercised what self-control he had left and gone up to his own room. Here, he found that the hot water bottle she had ordered to be placed there was now tepid, and no substitute at all for the warmth of her body against his.

Now, sitting at breakfast with Major Vernon, he felt he would like to crawl back to bed, or at least loaf the day away by Sukey's fireside, perhaps reading a novel to her while she did the mending. In his fancy, this scenario would necessarily evolve into idle conversation and kisses, and then perhaps something else.

Major Vernon gestured towards the coffee pot.

"It's a poor substitute for sleep," Felix said, refilling his cup.

"Here's to better luck in future," said the Major, draining his own coffee cup. "And painful though it might seem, it is a beginning in a process of elimination. Also we have the rudiments of our lure in hand."

"If Dr Fforde has not had second thoughts."

"We shall goad him into it," he said, and got up from the table. "I wonder how Miss Rivers is this morning."

"You want to talk to her?"

"You should continue with it. You seem to have her trust. Try mentioning Yardley if you think the moment allows it. See what she has to say about him."

"I will try," said Felix.

Major Vernon was putting on his overcoat when there was a knock at the door and Sukey came in, a tray in her hand, to clear away the breakfast things.

"I hope we did not disturb you coming back so late," Major Vernon said.

"No, I didn't hear a thing. And thank you for locking up, sir," she said, gathering up the dirty plates and avoiding – Felix felt – looking directly at him, although he still sat at the table, finishing his coffee. "Will you want dinner tonight?"

"Probably not," said the Major, drawing on his gloves. "But I shall let you know by noon, if I do."

"I'll put something cold by for you, whatever," she said, "Mr Carswell?" she added, glancing at Felix.

"I don't know," he said.

"I was just in with the Professor," she said. "He's looking grim this morning. Should we get Dr Pooley back, or will you look at him?"

"I am going that way. I can call at Pooley's," said Major Vernon. "Has young Mr Holzknecht gone out already?"

"Yes," Sukey said.

"I will go and look at him," Felix said. "There is no need to get Pooley just yet."

"As you like," said Major Vernon, and taking up his hat made his farewells, leaving them alone together.

Sukey would have followed him with the tray, but Felix blocked the way, taking the tray from her and putting it down on the table.

"I need to get on," she said. "And so do you."

"Five minutes," said Felix, closing the door. She nodded. "What's wrong?"

"Nothing," she said.

"There is something," he said. "You look..."

"It's nothing."

He attempted to take her hand and she resisted. Instead she walked across the room, her arms wrapped about her.

"Is it because of the other night?" he said. "Because I talked about marriage?" She shook her head. "Then what is it? I didn't come in last night because it was so late, I didn't want to disturb you. I'm sorry, should I have? I wanted to."

"It's nothing," she said. "That doesn't matter." She came and leant against him suddenly, her arms about his neck, her head pressed against his chest. She sighed as he wrapped his arms around her. "I'm all right."

"If you are sure," he said, feeling her clasp him a little tighter. "You will tell me, if there is something?"

"Yes," she said, but it seemed to him that she did not sound certain she would. The pleasure of having her so close was quite spoilt by the fear that she was suffering, and would not tell him of it.

"Promise?" he said.

"Promise," she said, and pulled herself away. "Now I have to go, and so do you. I have to see to those cheeky birds of yours, on top of everything."

"Yours now," Felix said.

"Only if they take the trouble and lay for me," she said. "Otherwise I shall put them in the pot."

"You will not," he said and tried to be encouraged by this show of levity. Yet he could not quite believe in it. "Oh, for the Lord's sake," he exclaimed, "what is it? You can tell me anything, you know that."

"Nothing, I told you!" she said. "Can't you just take my

word for it?"

"I would, if I could believe it, but I can't. Something has happened. What? Was it something I did?"

"No, no," she said. "Please, Felix, I don't want to talk about this any more. I've far too much to do, as do you. Now, will you go and look at the poor Professor, before he dies in his bed!"

~

Hardie's ribbon mill was not strictly in the direction that Giles had intended to go that morning, but finding he had a little time in hand, he made a detour and went in search of young Holzknecht.

He went up to the manufactory offices and found a dozen clerks on their stools, while below, the looms in the giant weaving sheds were ploughing inexorably on, making miles and miles of ribbon. It was one of those establishments where the looms never ceased, and only the hands changed at night.

The entrance to the offices had a large window overlooking one of the weaving sheds, and he gazed down on the curious world beneath while his card was taken in by one of the clerks. He had a good view. It was as brilliantly lit as a theatre. The hands were predominately female and they struck him as too young, despite the recent restrictions in law. What sort of life for such creatures was this, he wondered. Until recently, they would have been country dwellers, spinning wool on their distaffs and weeding the crops. Now they were crawling beneath the warps to pick up loose threads, or bent over the great tide of threads to correct a mistake or adjust the tension, always in danger from a flying shuttle.

They were no doubt tired, bored and ill-paid. A life of immoral ease would be tempting, he reflected, as women had always been tempted, sometimes to their cost but sometimes to their advantage. It was a question of what one was prepared to risk to feed oneself adequately – the question that any labourer, male or female, had to face daily. If men like Hardie paid their female hands a little better, might there be less of a plague of whores in some of the districts of Northminster? The question came to him as he watched a girl frantically winding threads on a shuttle, her overseer glaring at her. But Hardie no doubt would say he paid the going rate, and that there were plenty of hands asking for jobs at his door each morning.

He began to speculate whether Yardley liked to come to Northminster not because it was full of whores, but because it was full of girls who were not yet whores: girls who could be tempted to supplement their meagre wages, or even simply bribed with food and drink to surrender their innocence to him.

"Major Vernon, how may I help you?" Mr Hardie said, coming out of his office to greet him.

"I did not mean to disturb you, sir," said Giles. "I was looking for Georg Holzknecht. I believe he works here."

"Yes, he does," said Hardie. "But he isn't here at present. His father is not well. The Professor was married to a distant cousin of mine. Georg seemed concerned. It seemed unkind to chain him to his stool in such circumstances."

"Yes, of course," said Giles.

"And is that all?" said Mr Hardie.

"Yes," said Giles. "He will be at his lodgings, then?"

"Yes. In Martinsgate, I believe."

"Of course," said Giles, suppressing his surprise. Was Hardie mistaken, or had he been given a false address for some reason? "I shall try there. I am sorry to hear about the Professor."

"A famous scholar, I understand," said Hardie, nodding. Then he hesitated a moment, and said, "And what was it you wanted with young Georg, sir, might I ask? It was not police business, was it?"

"Has something been troubling you about him?" Giles asked.

"It is probably nothing," said Hardie. "And he is kin, albeit distant, and I should not, but... perhaps we might step into my office for a moment?"

Giles assented and followed him through the large general office and into a little cubby-hole of a room at the far end. Hardie did not waste money on show, it was obvious.

"I have discovered a few discrepancies in the books of late," he said. "And a payment from a customer has gone astray. It was a customer that Georg is supposed to deal with. I hate to think that he may be responsible, but I cannot find another explanation. When Fred handed in your card, I wondered if this was the reason. It was a cheque, you see, that went astray. It has been cashed. My customer has told me that much, but I can find no sign of the money."

"And you think this is connected to Holzknecht?"

"Yes. Most of the other men have worked here for years, and I can vouch for them. And they are not clever enough, if you know what I mean. Georg is clever. He is like a machine with numbers. That is why I took him on, that and the family connection. I was trying to help him and his father, but I rather fear..."

"I shall make some enquiries," said Giles, taking out his notebook. "How much was the payment?"

"Twenty-four pounds, six shillings and ninepence. From Mr Arthur Parsons in Stafford. He has a warehouse – a good customer. It was a cheque drawn on the Northern Provincial Bank, made out to Hardie and Co, as usual."

"You are quite sure about that?" Giles said. "You didn't see the cheque before it disappeared?"

"No, but Mr Parsons is scrupulous. His cheques are always properly made out."

"And how long has Holzknecht worked for you?"

"Since September."

"Thank you," said Giles. "I'll see what I can find out."

There was a knock on the door and a man came in, holding a spool of broad ribbon woven in a pattern of oak leaves.

"Just thought you'd like to see this, Mr Hardie," he said, holding out a length. "The new design. Comes out nice, don't you think, sir?"

Hardie took the ribbon and examined it.

"Colours are excellent," he said. "That's a good result. See this, Major Vernon, this is Northminster beating the Frenchies at their own game. I dare say you'd know a lady who'd like this for her bonnet?"

"Certainly," said Giles, thinking of Mrs Maitland, and how pleasant it would be to have the excuse to call upon her with a length of it.

"Take it," said Hardie. "With my compliments."

Giles shook his head and left.

~

Felix found Louisa Rivers deep in his own well-thumbed copy of Hutchinson's 'Principles of Chemistry'.

"Do you think a woman might become a doctor?" she said.

"Who knows?" said Felix.

"You don't think it would be wrong?"

"Not if she passed all the necessary examinations," he said. "And many female patients might prefer it. Especially when it comes to childbearing, and so forth."

"That is what I thought," she said.

"But whether she would be allowed to sit the examinations," Felix said, "is another matter. Perhaps one day."

"When I am dead and buried," said Louisa Rivers, laying down the book, and sighing. "I should like to try to do something like that. I would like to be the person who tried, at least, but..." She looked away, her voice choking up with emotion. "But I suppose that is impossible now. I have to..." And then she broke down completely, and began to cry in earnest, picking up the chemistry book again and flinging it down on the bed. "They are going to hang me, aren't they?" she burst out. "Aren't they? Oh God above, if He exists..."

Felix tried to calm her as best he could, but her wretchedness was not easily dismissed.

"Your best chance is to tell us everything," he said, when she was a little calmer. "Everything. We need to know why you did this thing. Make me understand it, if you can. There must have been a reason why you made the stuff, yes?"

She dried her tears on her sleeve and sank back on the pillows.

"Yes," she said.

"So tell me the man's name."

"You are sure it is a man," she said.

"Yes, and not Latimer, I think?"

"Perhaps."

"Don't be afraid," he said. "We are going to get him. He's going to the gallows, and not you, I'm sure of it."

"And what power do you have in these matters?" she said.

"Evidence. Very good evidence. And that is the foundation of everything."

"So he can be got?"

"Yes, certainly. And with your help it will be even easier."

"It's like a nightmare," she said, after a long pause. "I don't like to think about it. I try not to. What happened... I think so often I could have prevented it, somehow, that it was our fault for not being more careful." She looked at him with imploring eyes, her face still beautiful despite her distress.

"It was not your fault," he said.

"What do you know?" she said.

"It was not your fault. You did not consent."

"He will say –"

"We will prove otherwise."

"How?" She said this with a bluntness that for a moment silenced him.

"Tell me what happened," he said. "Tell me his name."

"You know his name," she said. "Surely?"

"We have an idea. Mr Earle has told us a great deal," he added, and saw her flinch at the mention of that name. "Don't worry, he will certainly be punished for his part in this."

"You will truly believe me if I tell you?" she said.

"Yes."

"But against his word and Mr Earle?" He noted how she forced out the name.

"Yes. They have every reason to lie and you have every reason to be honest. Your desperate actions speak of the distress you and Miss Barker were caused. You have nothing to lose and everything to gain."

"What did Earle tell you?" she said after considering his words for a while.

"I want your account of it first."

"You will not believe me. I know it," she said, twisting up the edge of her sheet in her fingers. "Sometimes, I don't even believe it myself. I don't want to believe it, I suppose. Then I could say it was a nightmare or some such, couldn't I?" She screwed up her face for a moment, took a deep breath and said, "It *was* Squire Yardley."

Felix nodded, and asked, "Where?"

"At his house. Bel and I were there having tea with Mrs Yardley, as we had done quite a few times I suppose."

"Just you and Miss Barker?"

"Yes, on that occasion."

"And can you say when this was?" Felix said.

"Oh yes, I remember well. It was September the third," she said. "And it was unusual in that my mother usually came with us, but for some reason she did not. And often Lord Milburne and Mr Gosforth and Miss Yardley were there, but that day it was just the three of us, which was pleasant enough, and then he came in, which was nothing strange, as he often did when Mrs Yardley was at home. He liked the iced cakes – he would gobble them up," she said with a shudder. "It was so disgusting. The crumbs in his beard."

"I've seen him do that," said Felix.

"Apart from that, he was quite amusing. He did some clever tricks with a pack of cards and told lots of silly stories. Mrs Yardley seemed quite pleased with him and he was affectionate with her. After a while, she got tired, so she went away to rest, and we were supposed to leave, but instead, Mr Yardley asked us to come and see the toys he had got from Germany for the baby. So we went downstairs to his library. There didn't seem any harm in it. He was not being – well, you know."

"Yes, I think so."

"He was anxious about them – the toys, I mean. He so wanted Mrs Yardley to like them. He was almost worried she would not. So we went into the library and it turned out the toys were not there, but in a sitting room off the library, and of course, we followed him in, not thinking anything of it. Of course, one is always told not to be alone with a man in case of... but there were two of us. We both thought that there couldn't be any harm in that. A married man who wanted to show us the toys he had bought for his unborn baby? In his own house?"

She began twisting the sheet again.

"I think my mother, if she had been there, she would have said: yes, go. He didn't seem..." Felix nodded, thinking of Sukey's story. "I didn't like him much, that's true enough, I thought he was a bit silly, and I hated the way he ate those cakes, but I didn't think he was going to..."

"So you went into this little sitting room?"

"Yes, and he closed the door, saying he didn't want the servants wandering in, because they would be tempted to steal the toys if they knew they were there. And he gave us each a glass of wine – it was very sweet and I could tell it was quite strong, so I decided I wouldn't drink much of it. And he had dishes of sweets all about room, and he kept insisting we had some, as if we were little children or something. It was quite funny. I kept glancing at Bel and I could tell she found it funny as well, to have him fussing round like that, feeding us sweets and showing us these ridiculous toys, none of which you would have given to a baby. It was very hard not to burst out laughing. There was a clockwork one with a rabbit that popped out of a lettuce. It was the most silly thing I have ever seen, and so funny, and we could not help ourselves, and soon we were laughing fit to burst. And then suddenly he was on the sofa in between us, and tickling Bel, so she was laughing more and more, and could not help herself, and then, just like that he was all over her, kissing her and mauling her, and she started to protest, and he slapped his hand over her mouth, and told her to shut up or she'd live to regret it."

She stopped and covered her face with her hands. He saw her take a few deep breaths to steady herself.

"I did try to stop him," she said. "I tried and tried. I was beating him on the back with my fists, but he didn't seem to care. He just kept on at her, and so I thought I would make a bolt for it and get some help, but just as I got to the door, he grabbed me and pushed me down on the floor and his breeches were open and his thing was out and Bel was crying on the sofa, and I lay there, and he was on top of me, I couldn't move. I just couldn't move and he – oh God!"

She was shaking violently now and her breathing was irregular and painful. She began to retch, and Felix grabbed a basin from the washstand. She was howling with misery at the same time. He sat perched on the bed beside her, supporting her as best he could, alarmed at the intensity of her distress, wondering if he had pressed too hard for this revelation. Her body was still fragile from her wounds, and her convulsions of grief were violent and exhausting. And as he held her, he wondered why she had not contrived to give the poison she had made to Yardley. It would have been a better use of the wretched stuff.

Chapter Thirty-one

After a morning spent at his desk, much to the satisfaction of his chief clerk, Giles went back to Silver Street. Meeting Sukey in the hall, he asked, "You don't happen to know if Holzknecht came back yet?"

"Why do you want to speak to him?" said Sukey.

"I looked him up at work but it seems he has used his father's illness as an excuse to take a holiday," said Giles.

"He can stay out as long as he likes," Sukey said and turned away down the hall.

"Yes?" Giles said, following her down the passage to the kitchen door. "Has he offended you?"

"No," she said. "What makes you say that? Did Mr Carswell –"

"Your tone was rather heartfelt," he said.

"He gets under everyone's feet, that's all. He's better away," she said. "Oh, and I have a message from Mr Carswell for you. He's been called away to the Infirmary to assist Mr Harper. He's left some notes on your desk. About Miss Rivers..." She sighed.

"Yes?"

"It's in the notes. She told him everything. It's not pretty – it was Yardley, it seems." She sighed again and shook her head. "I was just sitting with her."

"How is she?"

"Calm enough, but how do you ever get over such a thing? I can see why Miss Barker killed herself, to be honest. I hope you find him, and soon, Major – he deserves all the torments of Hell and worse!"

"I will do my best," he said.

"Do you want some lunch? I know you don't set much store by it, but there's barley soup. All these invalids in the house..."

"That would be excellent. In about twenty minutes? I want to speak to the Professor first."

"Of course. And I'll make you a pot of coffee, just the way you like it. You are going to need it."

She went into the kitchen and he went to the Professor's door and knocked gently.

"Yes?" came the reply.

"It's Major Vernon, sir," Giles said. "Might I have a word?"

"Of course, of course!"

The old man, in his snuff-coloured dressing gown, his nightcap on his head, was sitting at the table with his back to the fire. In front of him and in no discernible order were piles and piles of paper.

"Not resting today, then, sir?" Giles said.

"I am, in truth," said the Professor. "I am only moving papers from one pile to another. There is no purpose in it. You may tell Mr Carswell and Dr Pooley that."

"I shall," said Giles.

"Please, do sit down."

Giles took the chair on the other side of the table and said, "Your son is out running errands for you?"

The old man crumpled his brow for a moment.

"No, he is at his work."

"Oh, I understood that he was on leave, because of your health."

"He told you that?" said the Professor.

"Mr Hardie told me," said Giles.

"You know Mr Hardie?"

"Only slightly. He is related to your late wife, I think?"

"Yes. A good man. He helped us when no one else would. We were in some difficulty. He has been good to

Georg."

"I went to speak to your son at the mill this morning. I thought I had better give him a report of your health, but he wasn't there. Mr Hardie said he had given him leave from work."

"How kind of Mr Hardie," said the Professor after a moment.

"But Georg has not been home this morning?" Giles said.

"No."

"When I spoke to Mr Hardie this morning he touched on a slightly disturbing matter concerning Georg," Giles said. "The proceeds from a cheque appear to have gone astray. I was hoping I might speak to him about it." The old man glanced away. "It is probably just a misunderstanding, but I have to look into the matter."

"Yes, yes, of course you must," said the Professor. "But I cannot help you in finding Georg. If he is not at work, then..." he shrugged. "I suppose he will be back for his dinner?"

"I will speak to him later, then," said Giles getting up. "And as I said, it is probably just a misunderstanding." He glanced about the room, and noticed an elaborate pipe rack containing an array of fancy pipes. There were also two brown tobacco jars. "Are those yours, sir?" he asked.

"No, I do not indulge. That is a young man's vice. My son is fond of his pipe, though I tell him it is a poison! But do the young ever listen? I think not."

Giles nodded and took his leave.

~

Sukey had been right about his need for coffee. Carswell's report of Louisa Rivers' testimony was harrowing. Yardley had, it seemed, used the threat of exposure to reduce both girls to a state of concubinage, and had raped them on many occasions. It left him angry with himself at having failed to locate Yardley. He could not form a coherent strategy to find him, and turned his mind to the simpler matter of the purloined cheque. It had occurred to him where Holzknecht may have disposed of it, given his taste for tobacco.

Naturally there were many tobacconist's shops in Northminster – smoking was a universal vice. However, there was only one where the owner had recently been transported for forging signatures on bills of exchange, namely Gale's in Healygate.

Giles made his way to Healygate, a narrow, twisting street of antique construction. It was busy, for people were drawn there by the many small shops selling a large variety of goods for little money. All of them were brightly tricked out to attract customers, and the shopkeepers were neither shy nor discreet. Some of them even stood at their doors and called out their latest bargains. It had the feel of a market.

Gale's shop was signalled by the customary Red Indian statue at the door. In this case it was a particularly large one and appeared to have been recently repainted in the most gaudy colours. Judging by this, and the bright gas lights inside, the shop seemed to be thriving despite the notoriety of its now absent proprietor. Giles had heard that Mrs Gale had taken over the management of the establishment and he suspected she had also taken over the forgery business. He had not met the lady in person, but he was sure that she was not the fashionably-dressed young woman minding the shop. She was resting her elbows on the counter, leafing through an illustrated magazine showing the latest modes. She looked up at Giles as he came in, with more than a touch of suspicion.

He wandered over to a display of fancy pipes, some of which he had already seen in Holzknecht's rack.

"How much is this one?" he said, pointing to a bearded Jack Tar.

"Shilling," she said.

"Are they popular?" he said.

"Suppose so," she said.

"Have you had a young man in here, a German, buying these?"

"German?" she said, straightening.

"Young and good-looking. About my height, fair hair, slightly curled, and a moustache? Very striking." She considered the point. He went on, "Does anyone like that come in here to get his tobacco?"

"May do," she said, with a practised evasiveness that made him wonder if this might be Miss Gale. This idea was confirmed a moment later by the entry from the back of the shop of a handsome middle-aged woman, who from her manner and sumptuous dress had to be Mrs Gale herself. There was a marked resemblance between the two women. However, her manner was a great deal more accommodating.

"Sir, good morning to you! May I help you?" she said. "Cigars, I should say, sir, from the look of you, and choice ones, yes? If so, you are in luck. I have only today had a delivery of some fine Havana oscuros. Quite the rarest, sweetest tobacco, from an estate –"

"He's asking about a German," said the girl, with an emphasis that suggested she meant a particular German.

"Oh, is that so, sir?"

"I do have the right place, ma'am?" Giles said. "My friend Herr – well, you know his name as well as I do, he told me he found you most attentive. Not just on the matter of his pipe tobacco, which he is particular about, but –"

"This is a tobacconists, sir," she said. "Plain and simple."

"Then perhaps I am mistaken," he said. "Perhaps I mistook his directions. I am speaking to Mrs Gale?"

"Yes," she said. "But –"

"I am new to Northminster," Giles went on. "I find the tradesmen here are suspicious and won't take anything but ready cash. The word of a gentleman seems to be worth nothing here. So I am in need of some tin and I believe you may be able to help me."

"I'm not sure what you mean, sir," she said.

He leant forwards and said, "I have a cheque for one hundred. What can you give me for it? I would be obliged, ma'am, if you could assist me. You may be assured of my complete discretion."

She pursed her lips, thinking for a moment.

"We should be able to help, yes. Perhaps you would care to step this way for a minute, sir?"

He followed her into the back of the shop, which was fitted out as a snug little parlour, complete with a pair of spaniels dozing in the best armchair. There were also engravings of spaniels on the walls, china spaniels on the mantel, a spaniel in Berlin wool work on the fire screen and several copies of Harrops Annual of Sporting Dogs lying about the room.

"What charming little beasts, ma'am," he said, bending over and petting them. "Quite magnificent!"

"Thank you, sir," she said. "I do think they are rather pretty." He suspected she was more fond of them than her daughter or her absent husband.

"They must be related to the Rothborough Cavalier spaniels, surely?" he said. "May I?" he added, venturing to pick one up.

"Oh, as you like, sir. I can see that you have a way with dogs," she said, as the dog in his arms responded to a good fussing.

"No, she is just well-mannered and well-managed. My compliments, ma'am." He held the bitch out and looked her over. "Her points are really just as fine as my lord's dogs."

"You know Lord Rothborough, sir?" she said.

"I do," Giles said.

"I don't like to flatter myself, but I have always thought there is a touch of those lines in these two. I was fortunate to get them." She scooped up the other dog and kissed her on the nose. "I am hoping to breed them soon."

"Have you a sire in mind?"

"Yes, but I am not quite sure about it."

"I wonder if I could help you," Giles said. "If you could help me? My lord owes me a favour."

"He does?" she said.

"I should be happy to expend it on your service, ma'am," he added. "In such a good cause."

"Perhaps you'd like a glass of wine, sir?" she said. "And we can discuss terms? And a cigar? Compliments of the house, of course. You are a cigar man, I think?"

He put up his hands to refuse.

"No, no, I cannot impose any longer, regretfully, ma'am. You have been too kind already," he said, catching her hand and kissing it. She looked a little surprised by this, but not displeased. "I know that you will help me in my difficulty, which is all I need to know at present. I shall come back later, if I may, and we can settle properly. And perhaps talk a little more about spaniels? Nothing could be more delightful."

"Of course," she said, and then added, with a flutter of cap ribbons, "only if you promise you will come back, sir? Oh, but you haven't told me your name?"

"Long, ma'am – Colonel Henry Long."

Her hand was on his arm for a moment.

"Delighted to know you, sir," she said.

A rather easy conquest, he thought as he left the shop, and wondered what Emma Maitland would have said about his impersonation.

Chapter Thirty-two

"I'm glad you were able to come," said Mr Harper. "That was a neat manoeuvre."

"Time will tell if it has worked," said Felix, not entirely satisfied with what he had achieved.

"I have read about it, of course, and thought it an excellent plan, but I was still at the theoretical stage with it. Very glad to see it performed."

"It's only the third time I've done it," said Felix.

"Didn't look like it," said Mr Harper.

Felix was relieved, and a little flattered. It had been a risk, but it had to be taken, in his opinion. He had made the suggestion to Mr Harper, hardly expecting to be taken up on it. Instead Harper had nodded, and said, "That is my opinion also. But perhaps you would like to do it?" And so he had.

Harper was an experienced surgeon, who had recently taken over as Chief Surgical Officer at the newly expanded Northminster Infirmary. A native of Bristol, he spoke with a gentle burr that lulled his patients into a state of trusting calm. Felix had attended one or two of his operations previously and had been impressed at his skill and knowledge. On this occasion the patient had been run over by a cart, causing an open compound fracture that required the bold and novel strategy of suturing the broken bones with silver wire.

"I was talking about you with Captain Lazenby at dinner the other night," said Harper. "He said you had saved a man's leg in similar circumstances. I thought a second opinion might be useful today and I was fortunate to be able to get you. You seem to spend more time with the dead than the living."

"That does seem to be the case."

"There is plenty of work here, should you want it," said Harper. "In fact, there are at least four cases I would like you to have a look at. There is a distinct shortage of surgical talent in this town. I must find who I can to help me. It's important work."

"Yes, of course," said Felix, thinking of his quiet laboratory and his investigations and experiments. It was a different world from the Infirmary where difficult decisions had to be made in a moment. He had found it exhausting and was in need of a glass or two of brandy, in addition to the strong sweet tea that Harper had supplied.

"A Christian must use his talents wherever he can," Harper went on, mildly enough, but behind him on his office wall hung an engraving of St Paul on the road to Damascus. His evangelical sympathies were well known.

Felix drained his teacup and considered it for a moment. A year or two ago, he would not have hesitated. Harper was an impressive figure and he felt he could learn a great deal from him. There had been moments during the course of the operation when he had felt himself to be dangerously out of practice, but at the same time, he had relished the challenge of it. Bloodstains and incomplete skeletons, of course, provided puzzles of a different sort: more cerebral, less visceral. Which kind he preferred, was a difficult question to answer.

"I shall leave that thought with you," said Harper as Felix got up from his chair. "I have no doubt that you will be guided as you should. I'm a great admirer of your father's sermons," he went on. "It would be a privilege to hear him preach them. They are most distinctive. I seem to hear his voice when I read them –" He stopped, a little embarrassed by his own enthusiasm. "Excuse me."

"He'd be amazed to know anyone had read them," said Felix. "He scourged himself for the vanity of publishing, especially when no one seemed interested."

"They are read," said Harper. "And much appreciated.

You must tell him."

"I shall," said Felix.

"And it was he who guided you into our profession?"

"I was told that I ought to be useful in life," said Felix.

He was used to being taunted for his connection to Lord Rothborough. Harper took him at face value as the son of a clergyman who had published a book he admired. It was rather a novelty.

Walking back from the Infirmary to Silver Street, he stopped at The Black Bull, deciding he wanted a brandy and hot water to steady his nerves. The atmosphere of the ancient inn, quiet and congenial and where the landlady knew him, was soothing, and he sat by the fire and took three glasses of brandy before he made his way home.

It was a little after four o'clock when he opened the front door, and saw Sukey limping through the gloomy hall towards him.

"What happened?" he said, running forward and catching hold of her.

"I tripped and twisted my ankle," she said.

"Let me look at it."

"No, it's nothing. You know how clumsy I am. It happens all the time."

"Please, let me look at it."

He steered her into her sitting room and then towards the armchair where she sat down reluctantly. He pulled up the footstool and lifted her foot onto his lap. He saw her wince as he gently ran his fingers over the joint.

"It really isn't anything," she said, attempting to get up. "Really," she added.

"Stay where you are," he said. "It's obviously very tender." He took off her shoe and then pushed up her skirts in order to loosen her garter.

On past occasions, they had sat like this and he had taken off her shoes and stockings and rubbed her feet after a long day. It had been a playful exercise, not to say a stimulating one. She had been happy to lean back in the chair and allow further explorations. Today she sat bolt upright and frowned as he pulled loose the knot that fixed her garter. Then when his fingers touched her bare skin, she flinched and pushed him away.

"Not now," she said. "I've too much to do."

"You are not doing anything," he said, and pulled off her stocking regardless.

"Felix!" she exclaimed with annoyance, reaching forward and snatching the stocking from his hand. "Didn't you hear me?"

"You must be in agony," he said. "The swelling on this is quite impressive. How did you manage it?"

"It's just a little twist."

"And I'm the Emperor of China," Felix said. "This needs to be elevated with a poultice. Are your wrists all right?"

"What?"

"Your wrists. You must have fallen on them."

"I think so."

"Let me see," he said. "What is this?"

"What?"

"That contusion," he said. "How did that happen?"

"I must have knocked it."

"That's impossible. It looks as if someone has been holding you by the wrist. I can see the fingermarks."

"You're tired and a bit tipsy," she said, pulling her hand away and tucking it under her other arm. "And the light in here isn't –"

"What happened?" he said, snatching her hand back.

"Nothing, I told you! Will you stop fussing?"

"I'm not fussing. You're in a shocking state." She scowled at him and he said, in a milder tone, "Will you at least let me put a poultice on that ankle and rest for a while?"

"Oh, as you like."

"You'll bitterly regret it if you don't."

She thought for a moment and said, "If you turn up the lamp and pass me my work basket."

These attended to, he went to the kitchen to make up a poultice, more than a little puzzled and on the edge of annoyance at her behaviour. He could not believe her stubbornness. What was she about?

He came back, applied the poultice and bound up her foot. She was calmly at her mending now, and seemed not to mind the attention.

"Is that better?"

"Yes," she said. "Yes, it is."

He plucked a half-knitted sock from her work basket and put it over her bandaged foot. The heel had just been turned and the needles stuck out of it, making a sort of spiked anklet. She laughed and shook her head.

"There, that should tether you, ma'am."

"You make me sound like a wilful old cow."

"Your words, not mine," he said, reaching for her hand and kissing it. At the same time, with the lamp brought near, he could see the contusions on her wrist more clearly. The impression of grasping fingers was disturbingly clear.

"What happened?" he said. "Who did this to you? What happened?"

"Does it matter?" she said. "It doesn't hurt."

"Someone had you by the wrist. Who?"

"I don't think it matters," she said.

"You don't want to tell me," he said. "Why not?"

"Why don't you read me another chapter of Kenilworth? If you're not too tired. What did they want with you at the Infirmary?"

"Don't try to change the subject," he said.

"I have to, if you speak to me like that," she said, sharply. "How much brandy did you have at The Black Bull? More than usual, by the smell of it."

The amount in question had not seemed excessive at the time, indeed a necessity, but now he felt needled by her question, as if he had come home swaggeringly drunk. He was sure he was not in such a state, whatever she said.

"None of your business," he said, and at once regretted it. He had meant to say it lightly, with a touch of good humour, but he realised it had sounded petulant.

"And so we both have our secrets," she said, and glanced away, biting her lip.

"What do you mean?" he said, getting up.

"I didn't mean anything," she said. "Really. Why don't you sit down, and read to me? It's been ages since..." Her voice died away. "Felix?" she said quietly a moment later. "Won't you?"

He stood there still, in front of her, and became aware that he had cast her in his shadow, and that she had shrunk back a little in her chair.

"What happened?" he said again, aware he was being relentless but at the same time unable to stop himself. She hesitated a long while and said, "I will tell you if you promise me something."

"Yes?"

"Promise me you won't go daft on me."

"Oh, for the Lord's sake, Sukey, what happened?"

"I need to know that you will not –"

"Will not what?"

"Lose your temper."

"And why would I..." He broke off. "Was it Holzknecht? Did he do this to you? Yes?"

"Promise me –"

He shook his head.

"He attacked you?"

"No, no, nothing like that."

"Nothing like that?"

"He just –"

"Just? I can't believe –"

"It was nothing. I didn't want to tell you because I knew you would take it all wrong. And I was right!"

"What happened?" he said again.

"He just tried to kiss me."

"He just tried to kiss you?" Felix repeated.

"Yes, and it was nothing! And of course, I wasn't having that. He was a bit enthusiastic, but I was the match of him, you can be sure. He won't try it again."

"But now you have a sprained ankle, and a bruised wrist. Did you fall trying to get free of him?"

"Something like that," she said after a moment.

"I will –" he said, starting towards the door.

"You will not! Felix, you will sit down and believe me, that it was nothing! Please! Promise me you won't be daft and –"

"Is it daft to want to give the brute a good thrashing?"

"Yes!" she exclaimed. "It was nothing. You have to believe me!"

"How can I? When you have told me that women never tell the real truth about these things? How the devil am I supposed to take your telling me it was nothing, when I can see with my own eyes it was not!"

"Oh, for the love of God!" she exclaimed.

"When you conceal rape out of shame!" he went on.

"It was not that! He just tried to kiss me."

"What kind of a kiss leaves your wrist with marks on it like that? And makes you sprain your ankle trying to escape it? He attacked you – don't deny that! And in fact, the more you deny it, the more I must believe it!"

"Oh, believe all you like!" she said exclaimed. "I don't care, I really don't! Make a proper fool of yourself! Do what you like! Kill the fellow if it makes you feel better."

"Don't tempt me," he said, and left the room.

~

"With respect, sir," Lord Milburne said, "would it not be better to make a little more noise about the connection to Margaret of Angouleme? That will be the thing that draws him in, surely?"

"Yes, yes, I quite see your point, and it has many merits," said Dr Fforde, "but we must at first be sure that our fabrication is built on a sure foundation of possibility. If this man has any pretensions to scholarship, he will want to satisfy himself on all the points. We do not want him to rumble us too early – if that is the word, Major?"

"Yes, and it's a good point, my lord," Giles said, "but yours was too. We want dazzle and substance."

"This underworld language is fascinating," Dr Fforde went on. "If one was inclined to make a study of it, I'm sure it would be rewarding."

"We are already compiling a sort of lexicon," said Giles.

"I should be interested to see that," said Dr Fforde. "Now, where were we?" he said, taking up his pen.

Milburne consulted his notes and said, "Connection with the library of the Monastery of St Gordian, and the Abbé de Valsorges."

Giles walked over to the window, reminded suddenly of the evenings of his childhood. His father and brother had been fervent fly fishermen, and were adept at creating the most alluring and beautiful flies out of silk. In the evenings, the candles were lit and placed on the round table in the drawing room for the purpose of this fine work, rather than for the benefit of any woman who might want to sew. It was usually his mother or sisters who read aloud, while his father and brother bent over their coloured floss and feathers, constructing their tiny masterpieces to dazzle and tempt the fish onto the hooks. Lord Milburne and Edward Fforde now bent over their work in the same way. The lure was well in hand and the excitement of the chase had clearly caught them both.

Through the window, rather charmingly, he could see Mrs Maitland and Celia taking a turn about the garden in the last of the afternoon light. They were having an animated conversation and seemed like old friends already.

After some minutes, Edward Fforde got up from the table and left the room, in search of a book. Lord Milburne came and joined him at the window.

"How is Miss Rivers this morning?" he asked.

"Much better, I understand," said Giles. "Physically, that is. But she is in some mental distress."

"Do you think I should call? My mother –"

"You have discussed this with her?"

"The other night. I laid it all out. All."

"And?"

"You were right, sir, she was not angry. In fact, it was very good, but I feel..."

"What did your mother suggest, if I might ask?"

"She said she would not stand in my way if my feelings were genuinely engaged. That she only wanted my happiness."

"Of course."

"The thing is – about Miss Rivers. I do not know what I truly feel. I thought I was quite clear but now – oh, it feels so disloyal, especially when she has been in such distress, and to walk away would be dishonourable of me, surely?"

"No, given you never told her your feelings. You did not?"

"No, but I felt them. I would have done anything for her, and to abandon her now, because I do not feel so strongly... I do not like myself for doing it. I know she does not want to see me, but I wish I could somehow make it clear to her that she still has a friend."

"If perhaps not a lover?" said Giles.

"Yes, quite. My mother was right to tell me to talk to you. Can men and women simply be friends, do you think?"

"I hope so. And you are being a good friend to Miss Rivers in doing this for me. She has suffered because of Yardley, and catching Yardley is the most important thing."

Milburne nodded.

"Do you think this will work?" he said.

"I don't know. But it is an approach. The problem is that he is wily. I wish I had your first-hand knowledge of him."

"From what has been said, I wish I did not," said Milburne.

"Did he ever say anything to you that might be of use to us? Taking you into his confidence about anything, perhaps? I imagine he would treat you with some respect."

"Yes, he did," said Milburne, "but it did not feel comfortable. It was... George used to say that he was a talking gargoyle – but he was making light of it."

Giles went and sat down, making an effort to remember every detail of the evening of George's death: how Yardley had come into the room, and how his presence had seemed to terrify George.

"Do you think George had any knowledge of Yardley's activities?" he said. "He never hinted to you anything of the kind?"

"I don't know. I was lying awake this morning thinking about that. That there was something he did not tell me. I wish to God he had – he might still be alive now!"

"Was this on the last time you saw him?" Giles said. "That night of the ball?"

Milburne nodded.

"My thought is," Milburne said, after a moment, "that Yardley knew about his marriage to Bel. That George confided in him rather than me. Because I should have told him not to do it and I suppose Yardley told him he should. Does that make sense?"

"Yes," said Giles. "And thus he feared exposure from Yardley as Bel's murderer?"

Milburne gave a shudder and sat down at the table again. He picked up one of the pages of notes.

"Will this work, sir?" he said. "Truly? I will happily go and search every cellar in Northminster until I find him. George and Bel deserve that much!"

"Fight fire with fire," said Giles, getting up and taking the page of notes from him. "That is the only way with someone like Yardley."

~

As he was leaving, Celia and Mrs Maitland came in from the garden.

"Can't you stay for a cup of tea, Uncle Giles?" said Celia, grabbing his hand. "I shall make it for you. I am getting good at it."

He kissed her forehead and shook his head, although he was tempted.

"Another time, I promise."

He was aware of Mrs Maitland's quiet gaze upon him and her smile. He would readily have kissed her forehead as well, wanting suddenly to feel the warmth of her skin on his lips.

"Promise!" said Celia, departing and leaving him alone with Mrs Maitland, almost as if it had been prearranged.

"You're a great favourite," said Mrs Maitland.

"It's perfectly mutual," said Giles.

"Have you just seen Charles?" He nodded. "The conversation we had the other night – I can't begin to thank you, Major Vernon. It was..."

She threw up her hands in surrender and in a moment, she had stepped up to him and kissed him on the cheek. It was the slightest gesture – no more than that of a kiss of greeting to a distant cousin, perhaps, but it made her turn away in embarrassment when it was done, and he felt himself colouring.

"It was nothing," he said, and felt moved to take her hand.

"You saved his life."

He shook his head. "Your pointer, if anything, did that."

"She is a dear old thing," she said, and detached her hand. "And much though I, like Miss Celia, would like you to stay and drink tea, I believe you have work to do."

"Unfortunately," he said.

"Another time then," she said, and suddenly she kissed him again, this time on the other cheek. "And please be careful."

"Why do you say that?" There was something in her tone that suggested more than polite concern.

"I had a wretched dream about..." She checked herself. "I am talking nonsense. Excuse me," with which she briskly left him.

He stood there for a moment collecting himself, wondering at her words and her actions. That he had apparently entered her dreams was both gratifying and disturbing. He imagined her waking in the night, distressed, and alone. It was too easy for him then to picture himself comforting her, taking her shaking form into his arms, and lying beside her until she slept again. He wanted to feel her pressed against him, to sense her fear subsiding into peace.

Chapter Thirty-three

"Is that you, Fe– oh, excuse me, Major."

Mrs Connolly had come out into the hall at the sound of Giles opening the door. In fact, she had come hobbling towards him, wincing as she did.

"What on earth happened to you?"

"I twisted my ankle. Have you seen Mr Carswell?"

"No. Shall I go and look for him?"

"I don't know!" she exclaimed, and then grimaced with pain and reached out to the wall to steady herself. "I need to sit down."

"Certainly you do," he said, and lifted her into his arms and carried her the small distance back into her sitting room. "This chair?"

"Yes, thank you," she said. "Oh dear Lord, what a business!" She was half laughing, half in tears, as she put her foot back on the stool.

"What happened?" he said, turning up the lamp.

"There was something between them. I don't know what. An argument, a fight even. Shouting, and then the doors slamming. I wanted to go out and try and stop it but I tried to get up, and this wretched..."

"Between who? Carswell and...?"

"Holzknecht!" she exclaimed and then winced again.

"Did you have some laudanum?" he said.

"No," she said.

"I can't believe he left you here in this state."

"Oh, I can!" Sukey said. "I said things. He said things."

"And there was a fight of some kind between him and Holzknecht?"

"Yes. I knew I shouldn't have told him. I was stupid to tell him. I knew he wouldn't be able to deal with it like a sensible person. I knew he would..." She sobbed for a few moments. "And now it's all – oh, excuse me." She swallowed back her tears with some difficulty.

"What exactly happened, if I may ask, to provoke all this?"

"Holzknecht tried it on."

"Do you mean he tried to –?" Giles said.

"It was just a stupid bit of goosing, that's all. You know the sort of thing. All right, he was pretty determined, and he was very free with his hands, but it wasn't anything I couldn't deal with. I was just stupid enough to trip myself up."

"And your wrist?" Giles said.

"I bruise easily," she said, with a shrug that seemed to Giles to be anything but careless.

"I can see why Mr Carswell was concerned."

"Yes, but you're not going to go and horsewhip him are you? Are you?"

Giles considered for a moment. He could quite understand Carswell's anger, and he felt his own annoyance growing in the face of Sukey's distress. Now she went on, "Maybe you would if we were.. well, you know what I mean, Major. When this sort of thing happens, why does it always turn a woman's fellow into a raging wild animal, no matter how much of a gentleman he claims to be? James was the same. Another man just had to look at me. Perhaps it's just the men I get involved with," she added. "Perhaps it's me. And he'd been drinking."

"Carswell, you mean?"

"Yes. And he can't hold his drink; you know that as well as I do. Oh, why did I tell him, why?"

"Because you were upset and you had a right to expect him to comfort you," Giles said.

"No," she said. "It was because I was stupid. I should

have known better. I brought out the devil in him, I did. Just like I always did with James. And maybe I shouldn't have been so nice to him, to Holzknecht. Maybe it was all my fault."

"No," he said, firmly, but gently. "This is not your fault. And Carswell could have managed a little self-restraint, by the sound of it. He should have considered your feelings and wishes first."

She gave a bitter laugh.

"That's the worst of it," she said. "I was so angry I told him he could do what he liked. Murder the devil if he liked!"

There was at this moment an urgent rapping on the door.

"Ma'am, ma'am!"

"Yes, Agnes, come in," said Mrs Connolly. "What is it?"

Agnes flung the door open and rushed in, saying, "There's something on fire in the garden, ma'am!"

"Stay here," Giles said, for Sukey was attempting to rise from her chair. "Please, I beg you."

She sank back, and he went with Agnes to the garden door, which was wide open. The pair of guinea fowl came running into the house, making extraordinary noises of alarm and distress. He wondered how they had got out, as he ran down the garden path towards the blazing hen house.

It struck him forcibly how quickly and evenly the flames were consuming the structure, and that the gate to the coop was wide open, which had allowed the glinners to escape. Had someone set the fire? Was that a tang of lamp oil he could smell as he got closer?

Anne the kitchen maid and Martha the cook were drawing water from the well and attempting to put out the blaze.

"Anne, go and raise the alarm in the street," Giles said, taking the bucket from her.

"There's someone in there, sir!" screeched Martha. It was then that Giles saw what she saw: two figures in the heart of the fire. "It's the old man and his lad! Oh Lord above, sir, can you get at them?"

The fire was so fierce and consistent, he did not know in truth if he could, or if it was wise to even attempt it, but like Martha, he could see that within the wooden shelter, there were two figures, one prone on the ground, the other crouching over. He reckoned if he dashed in, he might be able to pull the crouching figure, which he thought was the old Professor, out to safety. But he could not risk more than a few moments there.

He plunged in, his breath held, and strode through the coop and into the shelter, grabbing the old man by the shoulders and hauling him back with him. He was a dead weight and the few yards distance to safety seemed like a few miles. He found he was choking and spluttering for breath, and was glad to see Carswell advancing to assist him.

"Pulse is there, but only just," Carswell said, crouching down and taking the Professor into his arms.

"I'll go back," Giles said, although he found he was gasping for breath.

"I don't advise it," said Carswell. "Look!"

Giles glanced back. The hen house roof was collapsing, burying the body within it.

"He's gone," said Carswell. Then he reached again for the pulse of the old man in his arms and felt it. He shook his head. "They both have."

Chapter Thirty-four

On the Major's instructions, both father and son had been brought to lie in Felix's dissection room in the basement.

Felix turned up the gas to supplement the raw early morning light, and tried to be objective. It was not easy.

Less than ten hours ago, he had dragged young Holzknecht out of the Professor's room, and into the street. Here, they had proceeded to scrap, in a most unheroic fashion, at least on Felix's part. His opponent proved handy with his fists, and recovered himself quickly while Felix's initial burst of strength deserted him utterly. He found himself on the receiving end of a rather merciless attack and had struggled to stay on his feet as he got a thorough pounding. But then, as if Providence had changed her fickle mind, a cobble mired in horse excrement sent Holzknecht sprawling onto the ground, and allowed Felix to avenge himself in the form of several hearty kicks.

Joyous though this moment had been, good sense whispered in his ear and he had decided to leave while he could. He therefore beat a swift retreat to The Black Bull before Holzknecht could do any more damage. He did not know, as he sat in a private sitting room at the inn, examining his bruises and drinking brandy, if his honour was satisfied or even if justice had been done. All he knew was that he had a suspected broken rib, a torn coat and little chance of any sympathy from the woman he wanted it from most of all. The landlady and the maidservant, seeing his bloody nose, were all kindness and fuss, but he sent them away. He had sat and cried like a child, longing for her to come to him in his distress, and knowing at the same time that she would not.

At length, he had made his way back to Silver Street and found the place in uproar, and the alarm raised. He had seen Major Vernon drag the Professor from the hen house and the prone form of Holzknecht being buried by the collapsing roof. Sukey, he had only glimpsed – she had limped to the door of her sitting room and Major Vernon had at once sent her back to rest, and she had gone, obediently, closing the door behind her. He might have gone to her then, but he was needed with Holt and the Major to extinguish the fire.

When this had been done, what remained was the puzzle that now confronted him at five in the morning, as he stood in his laboratory with the cadavers on the table before him.

There were footsteps on the stair outside and Frewen came in with a tray of coffee and some freshly baked baps. Major Vernon arrived a moment later.

"I thought we might need some sustenance," the Major said, pouring out the coffee.

"Thank you," said Felix, tearing into the bread, which was indeed welcome.

"We have a lot of work ahead of us," said Major Vernon, circling the two benches, surveying the corpses, coffee cup in hand. He paused in front of the younger Holzknecht. "So?"

Felix finished his mouthful, considering what to say.

"The first thing," he said, "will be to determine the cause of death in the case of Holzknecht the younger. The knife in his chest may be post or pre-mortem. It is so neatly placed that I am inclined to think he must have been unconscious when it went in, but there is a lot of blood staining, which suggested his heart was still beating, but not as much as one might expect, which suggests he was dying as it was done. Smoke inhalation from a blaze of that intensity could reduce him to unconsciousness in a matter of minutes, and then..."

Major Vernon nodded.

"But why it was done?" Felix said.

"More importantly, by whom?" Major Vernon said. "It

may help you to know that the entire stock of lamp oil for the house had been poured onto the hen house, and it looks as if the straw had been brushed to the sides to intensify the blaze."

"Someone turned the place into a pyre," Felix said. "One of the Holzknechts?"

"The Professor?" Major Vernon said. "Anne did see him going out into the garden. She assumed he had gone down to the privy. This was at seven-thirty, about an hour after your brawl, which was at half six, I understand."

"I suppose so," said Felix. "I came back from the Infirmary at a little before six. And it was not a brawl."

"It wasn't?"

"I had good reason!"

"Perhaps," said Major Vernon.

"And what would you have done if –"

"Your anger was justifiable, but not your actions," said Major Vernon. "It would have been better to cool your heels and think of a more sensible way to deal with the situation, don't you think? Rather than distressing Mrs Connolly further. She ought to have been your first concern. Not your own slighted sense of honour."

His tone was mild, but there was a chill in it.

"That is all very well for you to say," Felix managed to say. "And it was not my slighted sense of honour! He mauled her and he deserved to be horsewhipped for it! Her distress was what made me..." He stopped, silenced by the inert form of Georg Holzknecht on the table in front of him, the dagger in his chest. Be careful what you wish for, he thought. "I suppose it was about half six when I left," he said.

"Young Holzknecht rang for Anne at half six," Major Vernon said. "He wanted hot water and for her to brush his coat. Then she took them their dinner at a quarter to seven and at seven thirty she saw the Professor go out to the privy."

"And by eight thirty the place is on fire, he's lying dead with a dagger in his chest and the old man is on the verge of death," Felix said.

"I got back at a quarter past eight. I remember looking at my watch as I came into the hall," Major Vernon said. "And I was sitting with Mrs Connolly in her sitting room until Agnes raised the alarm. During that time we did not hear any footsteps in the hall or the garden door banging shut."

"Holzknecht always banged doors," said Felix.

"Unless he was careful, and did not wish to be heard going out," said Major Vernon. "Perhaps if he thought he was going into the garden to meet someone."

"Well, he was – his father, it seems," Felix said.

"Perhaps his father told him otherwise," Major Vernon went on. "Perhaps his father told him to go and speak to Mrs Connolly, who might have gone out to see to her guinea fowl. Perhaps he told him he ought to go and apologise to her. No doubt your anger with him did not go unmarked. The whole house heard you shouting at him."

"And then he sets the hen house on fire with his own son inside? And stabs him, so that the smoke kills him? Why?"

"That's the mystery," said Major Vernon.

"And stays there with him," said Felix, "until he destroys himself? No, no one would do that. That cannot be the case, surely?"

"It is only a theory."

"It makes no sense to me," said Felix.

"Perhaps you will discover something to contradict it. Or else confirm it. That dagger certainly belonged to the Professor – it was his letter opener. I noticed it on his desk when I spoke to him about the stolen cheque."

"Holzknecht stole a cheque?"

"Possibly – from his employer. Loose-handed and light-fingered."

Felix frowned, and poured himself some coffee.

"How is Mrs Connolly?" he asked, after a moment.

"Asleep, I hope."

"What exactly did she say to you, when you talked?"

"That is for you to discuss with her."

"If she ever consents to speak to me again!" Felix said.

"She will," Major Vernon said. "Women are naturally merciful creatures."

"What did she say to you?"

"She would not like me to repeat it," he said.

This discretion hinted at something so serious that Felix felt wretched.

"Sometimes," he said, "I wish I was free of her – no, free of having to feel so much for her! If I felt nothing, if it was merely for my own comfort and convenience, as some other men arrange these things, then..." He broke off and turned away, ashamed he had said so much. "I had better get on with this," he said.

"You had," Major Vernon said, and left.

~

Giles went up to his office and spent a couple of hours writing reports, organising orders and trying to make some sense of the business he had just witnessed at Silver Street. The sequence of events was as baffling as the results had been shocking. He had seen no signs in the old man of such extreme behaviour, but that he was the chief architect and enactor of it all seemed an inescapable fact. Perhaps once they had combed their rooms for evidence some answers would emerge.

He finished his notes and set off to The Unicorn to brief Captain Lazenby. But as he turned out of the little court and into the street, he had a sudden memory which made him decide to head instead to the Minster Precincts.

He found Lambert, his brother and Mrs Maitland at the breakfast table.

"Forgive my intruding," he said.

"It could never be an intrusion," said Lambert. "Sit ye down. Coffee?"

"Yes, thank you," he said, sitting down opposite Mrs Maitland. He was rewarded with a smile and an offer of a plate of bread and butter. "It was Sally I was after particularly. I have a question for her."

"She will be back in a moment. You look, if you don't mind me saying, as if you have been up all night," said Lambert.

"I have," said Giles, rubbing his chin, which was now thick with stubble. "Forgive my appearance."

"Has something happened?" asked Mrs Maitland.

"Yes, something rather..." He broke off, not wanting to bring such bad news. "Remember the old German professor I was telling you about? The collector of stories?"

"Yes, of course," she said. "What was his name? You never said – or you did and I have forgotten."

"Holzknecht," he said. "No, I did not tell you his name."

"Goodness," she said. "I did wonder if it might be him when you told me! But I could not imagine how such a famous scholar came to be in Northminster."

"Was he not exiled by the Elector of Augsburg?" said Edward Fforde. "There was something of a purge, I understand. The Elector is an absolutist. I did not know Holzknecht was here. Goodness indeed, Mrs Maitland! I must pay my respects."

"I'm afraid it is too late for that," said Giles. "He died last night."

"God grant him rest," said Edward Fforde. "And what a great loss. His work was quite unparalleled in his field. Tell me, ma'am," he said, turning to Mrs Maitland, "how did you come to know his work? I didn't think it was translated into English yet."

"I don't think it is. I read it in German, dictionary to

hand. I have a great love for these old tales, and a copy of his collection came into my hands by chance. Oh, but it is so sad," she said, looking across at Giles. "Such a sweet character, I'm sure. One could tell by the writing. Well, as far as I can judge, for my German is not as accomplished as it might be."

"I am sure it must be very accomplished," said Edward Fforde.

"I hope he did not suffer much," Mrs Maitland said.

"I wish I could say that he did not," Giles said. "I am always the bearer of bad news, Lamb, am I not?"

"Yes, Giles, you are," said Sally, coming into the room behind him.

"He has a question for you, my dear," said Lambert.

Giles rose and turned to her.

"This is going to sound strange," he said, "but bear with me. Do you remember Meggie Houseland, the woman who came in sometimes to mend when we were children?"

"Yes, a little."

"How she would come and sit by the nursery fire with Nance and she would tell those strange stories while they did their sewing? And they would send us away if we tried to listen, but we stayed behind the settle back to hear them?"

"Yes," she said.

"Do you remember the story of the man who found his son was a devil? I can only remember part of it. How he went to talk to the wise woman in the woods to ask her what to do."

"The devil and his father," said Mrs Maitland. "That's in Holzknecht's book of tales. *Der Teufel und zein Vater.*"

"It is?" said Giles. "How does it end? Do you remember?"

"Yes, because it is striking and sad," Mrs Maitland said. "He goes to the wise woman and confides in her his fear that his son is a devil and that everything he has done to make him take to virtue has failed. He is afraid of the harm his son will do to the world and asks what he can to do to stop him. She tells him she must trick him first. 'How can I do that?' the man asks. 'How can any man trick a devil?' 'Offer him an innocent heart,' the old woman says."

"Oh yes," said Sally. "That's it! That is what a devil wants. I remember that, yes, and it was Meggie Houseland."

"It must be the same story. And to think you heard it in Northumberland!" said Mrs Maitland.

"But how does it end?" Giles said.

"He offers his son an innocent heart," Mrs Maitland went on, "the pretty maid he admires above all others and who has, of course, resisted him, seeing him for what he is. The father tells the son that she has changed her mind and will be waiting for him in a little house in the forest. Of course it is a trap, but for once the devil-son does not see it. He is blinded by his desire for her. So he goes to the forest, and when he is in the little house, the father sets it all on fire, and then when the son is overcome with smoke, he puts a dagger in his heart, killing him twice. For that was the old woman's other piece of advice: to kill the devil you must strike twice. And thus the devil is killed by his father, but it is too late and the fire kills the man too."

Giles reached for his coffee cup and found his hands were shaking. The cup rattled in the saucer.

"Giles, are you all right?" said Sally.

He was for a long moment quite lost for words. Then, carefully he said, "And this tale is in Holzknecht's book?"

"Yes," said Mrs Maitland.

"And that is certainly the story that Meggie told," said Sally.

"Yes, I remember it all now," he said. "But why on earth should..."

"What has happened, Giles?" said Lambert.

"Last night," said Giles, "the Professor lured his son into Mrs Connolly's hen house, set it on fire and stabbed him in the chest. And then he died in the flames himself. Well, not quite

– I dragged him out of there, and then he died."

There was a moment of shocked silence.

"You dragged him from the fire?" Sally said.

"Good Lord," murmured Lambert.

Mrs Maitland rose from her place, and left the room, almost overturning her chair in her haste.

Giles could not resist following her, and found her in the hall. But as she became aware of his presence she put out her hand, her fingers outstretched, to prevent him advancing any further on him.

"Excuse me," she said.

"Emma, please, what is it?"

Her Christian name fell from his lips, her distress prompting him to this intimacy.

"I told you the other day that I had a wretched dream about you. You disappeared, and I felt you were in terrible danger, and then I woke in terror, so sure it was true! And now you say –"

"I was only in there for a moment. There was no real danger."

She nodded, drew herself up a little and said, with a careful smile, "I'm glad that my powers of clairvoyance are so poor. You must laugh at them, Major Vernon, if you will? If you wish to spare me distress."

"Certainly," he said. "How foolish you are, ma'am – yes?"

"Yes, very, thank you," she said.

"I need your help," he said. "I have several trunk-loads of German manuscripts that need to be examined if we are to get to the bottom of this mystery. Could you make yourself useful there, do you think? Would it be an imposition?"

"No, not at all."

At this moment Lord Milburne came downstairs. He looked pleased to see Giles.

"I have remembered something," he said, "about the Squire. He did mention the name of a man he bought some things from in Northminster – some scraps of illumination, cut from old books. Lovely things, but an utter desecration to take them from the books, so one must wonder about the fellow's probity. You probably know him – his name is Moss. I do not know if he has a shop, but Yardley said that he lived in Whitefriars Street."

"I do not, my lord, and that is useful."

"It just struck me as I was shaving. And thinking about our lure. Dr Fforde and I have done a great deal more on that, since we saw you yesterday, sir. I think you will be pleased with it, and I wondered if Mr Moss might be someone to talk to about it. Yes?"

"You have good instincts, my lord," said Giles. "Yes, we will pay him a visit. You and I."

"Really, may I?"

"Yes. I must make what use of you I can, until Salvator's and Dr Fforde claim your loyalties forever."

Chapter Thirty-five

Establishing where in Whitefriars Street Mr Moss lived took rather longer than Lord Milburne anticipated, and Giles felt he had an excited young puppy out on the leash for the first time. Milburne was impatient to be on with the adventure, and certainly not ready for the often dull realities of criminal investigation.

Whitefriars Street was not especially notable for criminal activity, but it was a busy thoroughfare: a mixture of shops, workshops and crowded dwelling houses. It was a good place to go unnoticed.

Mr Moss had rooms on the fourth floor, and the stairs grew darker the higher they climbed. Rather surprisingly, a small girl of about five years old, dressed in a cherry-red silk dress and a frilled apron, opened the door to them, and a flood of light filled the landing.

A moment later, a grey-faced, haggard man appeared.

"Mr Moss?" Giles asked.

"Go and play, sweetheart, Papa has to talk to these gentlemen," he said, and gently pushed the little girl back into the room.

"I've no one to mind her, since her mother's gone," he said and began to cough.

"May we come in?"

Moss could not speak for coughing, but indicated that they could, and they followed him into the room, which was light and airy due to the large window that filled one wall. A bookbinder's bench stretched along its length.

Moss sat down, and at length his cough subsided.

"Yes, gentlemen?" he managed to say. "Are you wanting

some work done?"

"I wanted information about someone you have worked for: Mr Briggs Yardley." Moss frowned. "What can you tell us about him?"

"Why do you need to know about him, sir, if you don't mind me asking?" Moss said carefully.

"I'm a police officer," said Giles.

Moss sighed and said, "Well, he's a gentleman with a particular desire for particular things."

"Indeed. And you have done business with him?"

"On occasion, yes."

Moss sat knotting his fingers together, his chest rising and falling alarmingly. Then he reached out and took up one of his bookbinding tools and turned it in his hand.

"There used to be enough money in just the binding work," he said. "But people don't care about getting a proper binding these days, they just want the book. My father used to bind books for all the gentry, and they wanted it done properly, but now..."

"Did you do something other than bind books for Mr Yardley?" Giles said.

"At first I did. He was kind enough to bring me some fine old books to repair. A lovely job, I must say..." He began to cough again.

"Have you seen him recently?" said Giles.

"Yes," said Moss. "He was here the day before yesterday. He had got a set of prints he wanted binding up. I haven't begun it yet. To tell you the truth, I haven't had the strength to, though it will be bread on the table. And the prints are of a nasty sort. I don't want to do anything with them until I know my girl is safe asleep."

He pointed to a large portfolio propped up against the wall.

"May I?" Giles said. Moss nodded and Giles went and opened the portfolio.

"Martyrdoms of the saints," said Moss. "So-called."

The images were certainly disturbing, showing a relish for torture couched in the guise of devotion.

"Nasty stuff indeed," said Giles, closing the portfolio. "And will he come back to collect the work?"

"Yes, but I don't know when. I had better get on with them."

"Do you know where he is staying?"

"He did not say, sir. He comes and goes."

"He had never mentioned an address to you in town?"

"Once he did – last year he had me send something to a shop in Healygate. Gale's."

"You are certain of that? Gale's the tobacconist?"

"Quite."

The man began to cough again and the conversation necessarily stalled.

Was this simply a coincidence or suggestive of something deeply unpleasant: a connection between Holzknecht and Yardley? His mind went back to Jasper Hearn's description of the devils on the high road – one in the old shooting coat, the other tall and fair in a light-coloured frock coat, carrying a straw top hat.

At last his coughing fit abated and Giles asked, "So, as well as bookbinding for Mr Yardley, Mr Moss, you have had other business dealings? Yes?"

Moss twisted up his mouth and looked away.

"Things have been so hard," said Moss after a moment. "I shouldn't have done it otherwise. It was ready money when all is said and done, and that is hard to refuse, sir. I had a friend who acquired –"

"Acquired?" Giles said.

"I don't know where he got 'em!" Moss said. "I didn't ask."

"I see," said Giles. "So you had your doubts about their origins?"

"Maybe," said Moss.

"And these things were?"

"Old books. Illuminated. Very choice. Beautiful old work – the sort of stuff you can sell for good money if you know the right people."

"And Briggs Yardley was the right sort of person?"

"I didn't like to do it," Moss said. "Cutting up a book like that – it's like killing something. But I needed the money, and I knew Yardley would pay three times over just for the little paintings, and I could pay my friend, and leave some to pay my bills. A lovely Our Lady with the child Jesus there was, and some scenes of the harvest."

"And your friend is in Northminster? The person who 'acquired' these books?"

"I haven't seen him since my wife died," Moss said. "He's a Dutchman. Went back to Rotterdam."

"Very convenient," said Giles.

"God's honest truth, sir!" exclaimed Moss. "I have nothing more to lose, have I?"

He glanced to the side. The little girl was now standing in the doorway to the room, watching them with solemn eyes, her thumb in her mouth. He gestured for her to go back into the room, which she did at length.

"I can't fool myself," he said, when she had gone. "It's only a matter of time. My lungs are failing me... and then who will look after her?"

"If you help us, Mr Moss," Giles said, "we could perhaps see that arrangements were made for her."

"You will take care of her?"

Giles nodded.

"If you help us a little more," he said. "Next time Yardley is here, I shall expect to know about it at once, and furthermore I want you to tell him that you have heard that some interesting and valuable documents have become available – perhaps your friend in Rotterdam has been to visit."

"I could, sir, I suppose. I should need some more details."

"We have all the details." Giles indicated to Milburne to take out his papers.

"A complete provenance," said Lord Milburne, handing it over. "And description."

Moss read over the first page or two.

"He will like the look of that, yes," he said with a sigh. "I shall do my best, sir; I suppose I can do no other."

He dropped the papers to the floor. He looked utterly exhausted.

"I may send Mr Carswell to have a look at him," said Giles as they went downstairs. "I fear he is in danger of not staying the course."

"And the poor little girl?"

"There is a charity school for girls attached to the Minster – the Grey Maids' Hospital. My sister has a hand in its management. I think we could find a place for her there."

"An orphanage?" said Milburne, with some repulsion.

"It's not like the workhouse," Giles said. "It's a kind place and the girls get a good education."

~

Felix worked on the post-mortems until a little after two when hunger, exhaustion and his lingering hangover, not to mention his bruises, got the better of him.

He covered the bodies, scrubbed his hands, locked the door, and headed towards the chop house on the corner of the street. It was not the most salubrious place, but it had the virtue of anonymity.

He knew he ought to go back to Silver Street and make peace with Sukey, but he did not know how to begin. He wanted only to hear her forgive him and press her hand to his forehead and give him hot broth and comfort, but he knew that these things would come only if he said the right things and behaved with the correct degree of contrition. He felt the latter strongly enough, but he had no idea how he was supposed to convey it to her convincingly.

So instead he found a seat in a dark corner, and ordered a bottle of porter and two mutton chops. He took the edge from his appetite with the bread and butter that was placed on the table, as if for free, but always charged for and excessively so, for the bread was stale and the butter not fresh. But Felix scarcely cared. He ate mechanically.

After some minutes the waiter appeared with the chops, the porter and a jug of claret.

"I didn't order that," Felix said, as the waiter put the wine on the table.

"Your friend did, sir," the waiter said, and then Felix saw that Briggs Yardley was looming up behind him. He stared and blinked as if it were a vision thrown up by tiredness and his own disorderly mind, but he seemed quite solid.

"Please take it away," he managed to say, at the same time knowing it was not what needed to be said. He should have quietly told the waiter to fetch a constable and lock the door to the shop so that Yardley could not get away.

"As you like, sir," said the waiter and went away. As he did, and before Felix had a chance to call him back, Yardley was standing at the table.

"No fancy for claret today, Carswell?" he said.

"No, thank you, sir. It was kind, but I've no stomach for it," Felix said, repulsed by this closeness.

"No offence taken," said Yardley. "It was a mere token, to express my thanks, once again, for the safe delivery of my boy."

"Quite unnecessary, sir," said Felix, pushing away his scarcely touched plate of meat.

He decided he would make a swift departure and go to find some assistance for himself. In the meantime, it was important that he was able to leave Yardley with the impression that he did not know he was the object of an intensive police search. He got to his feet and said, "If you will excuse me, sir, I have a pressing appointment."

"You do?" said Yardley, and reached out, clamping Felix's hand to the table with surprisingly strong fingers. Felix attempted and failed to pull his hand away. He found himself remembering Louisa Rivers' account of being overpowered by him. "And leave all your meat?" said Yardley. "What kind of appointment can that be?"

"I have no appetite, as I said," said Felix, again trying to disentangle himself, but finding that he could not.

"Sit down, Mr Carswell."

"I do not think –"

"I believe a certain lady would prefer it if you stayed and talked to me."

"What?"

"The pretty Irish widow. Your pretty Irish widow. Such a charming creature. I was quite bowled over when I finally made her acquaintance. I can see why you have made her your mistress, Mr Carswell. You have exquisite taste."

"Excuse me, sir, but –" Again he tried to get out, but Yardley had him by the shoulder and shoved him down onto the bench.

"Now, now, let us not be coy, Mr Carswell," he said. "She's your mistress. And perhaps she serves your colleague, the famous Major too – I don't know, but she certainly warms your bed. Yes?"

"That is none of your business," said Felix, and attempted to push him away.

"It is, since she is now my guest, and I hope more."

"Your guest?"

"She was glad to come away with me."

In his mind Felix could only see the bloodstained debris in that remote farmhouse, the girl's boot lying on the hall floor.

"Where is she?" he said, attempting to rise again. "What have you –"

"All in good time," said Yardley and pushed him down on the bench again and kept him there, a leaden hand on his shoulder. "Why don't you drink your claret and eat your meat? Then we shall go and see her, and talk over the business."

"What the devil have you done with her?" Felix said.

"She is my guest," said Yardley. "And quite safe! My, my, sir, what do you take me for?"

"I know what you are," Felix said. "I know what you have done and you will hang for it. All the police in the city are looking for you. You will not get away with this!"

"Oh well, they may be looking," said Yardley. "But they are not going to find me. I am quite certain of that. So sit still," he added, with a violent shove that sent Felix crashing into the corner, "and eat your meat. Then I may let you see your sweetheart."

"You will take me to her directly?" Felix said.

"Yes. If you do not try and cause a fuss, I may allow that."

At which point he reached into his coat and produced a several-chambered pistol and shoved it into Felix's ribcage. Felix had no doubt that it was primed and loaded.

Felix did as he was told. In the moment he could not form any other plan. The gun was hard against him.

He attempted to eat his mutton chops but his mouth was so dry that it felt like he eating scraps of wool. He could scarcely swallow.

Yardley urged the wine on him. He wondered if he would choke or vomit. He was not sure what caused him greater unease: the pointed pistol or Yardley's eyes fixed upon him as he sliced up his chop. Once or twice Yardley reached out with his bony fingers and stole a morsel of the mutton. He popped it into his mouth and relished it with disgusting noises.

"Sir, I cannot..." Felix said after some laborious minutes of this, which felt in truth like hours. "Please may we go and see Mrs Connolly?"

"Your tone is improved," said Yardley. Felix felt he might retch up what he had just eaten. He had hated the necessity of pleading but it was all he could think to do. "A little more befitting your station. Ah, but she has the better of you, has she not? You are her slave. That is never advisable, Carswell. A woman should be your slave, and not the other way around. But I can understand it. She is bewitching."

"If you have so much as laid –"

"If I have, what?" said Yardley. "Mind your manners, Carswell. Do you want to see her or not?" Felix nodded. "Have another glass of wine."

The claret was of such poor quality that it would turn a man to temperance, but Felix drank the vinegary stuff, conscious that he was making a lamentable mess of this whole business. The Major, no doubt, would have had Yardley cuffed and begging for mercy by now. Every strategy he considered seemed ridiculously foolhardy and liable to put him further from the most important consideration: getting Sukey to safety.

"That will do," said Yardley. "Now, settle your bill like a gentleman."

"What?"

"I'm not paying," said Yardley, giving the gun a painful thrust into Felix's ribs. Felix dug into his pockets and produced a handful of coins, far more than the cost of the food, but he flung them on the table none the less.

"Now, let us go and drink tea with Mrs Connolly," said Yardley, standing up and shoving the gun again into Felix's chest. "I shall not hesitate to shoot you if you fail to behave yourself, Mr Carswell," he added. "I do hope you understand that."

Chapter Thirty-six

"Where is Mrs Connolly, Anne?" said Giles when he returned to Silver Street with Mrs Maitland.

"I don't know, sir – she went out, a couple of hours ago now."

"Did she tell you when she would be back?"

The servant shook her head.

"No, sir," said Anne.

At this moment Holt came in with a large bucket of coal.

"Mr Holt, have you seen Mrs Connolly?" Giles said.

"No," said Holt with a frown.

"Perhaps you would go down to Mr O'Brien's and see if she is there?"

"Of course, sir," said Holt, turning towards the stairs. "I'll just get the fire up in your room, sir."

"No need for that. If you could lay a fire in the Professor's sitting room instead. This lady will be working in there. Mrs Maitland, this is Edward Holt, my man. Holt, this is Mrs Maitland. Her late husband was Lieutenant Colonel Maitland, with whom I had the honour to serve."

"Very glad to know you, ma'am," said Holt, and opened the door to the Professor's room to them.

Mrs Maitland stood looking about her while Holt and Giles lit the lamps.

"I expect rather more papers than you anticipated," he said. "That is the difficulty with police work."

"It is so sad," she said, taking up a paper and studying it, "to see all this work abandoned. To think he felt driven to such an act."

Giles glanced around, aware that someone had come to

stand in the open doorway. It was Louisa Rivers, wrapped up in a shawl and clutching a book.

"Should you be out of bed, Miss Rivers?"

"I was looking for Mr Carswell," she said.

"He's not here, Miss," said Holt from the fireplace, clanking the tongs and coals.

"Good afternoon, Miss Rivers," Mrs Maitland said.

"Ma'am," said Louisa.

"I hope you are a little better," Mrs Maitland said.

"I am much better, thank you," she said, drawing herself up a little. "Though I should pretend to be an invalid as long as I can, I dare say. Then you cannot charge me."

"I have no intention of charging you with anything at the moment," Giles said.

"When will Mr Carswell be back? I have a question for him." Louisa tapped the book she was holding.

"Oh yes, of course, he is coaching you," said Giles. "He thinks you are a prodigy. You might be able to help us now, since you are feeling better. Tell me, do have any knowledge of German?"

"I do," she said. "I got through Schreiber's Grammar last winter. I have a little understanding."

Mrs Maitland said something in German and the girl responded promptly.

"Very good," said Mrs Maitland. "You could certainly help us."

"This is to do with what happened last night – the fire?" Louisa said.

"Yes. We are trying to establish why on earth the Professor should do such a thing," said Giles.

"So, these German gentlemen – it was Professor Holzknecht and his son?" Louisa said, picking up one of the papers from the table.

"Yes."

"Anne told me so, but I was not quite sure she had the

name right," Louisa said. "You do know they were at Whithorne? Last summer. It was before you came, Mrs Maitland."

"What?" said Giles.

"The old man gave me a copy of his tales to practice my German," said Louisa. "He gave one to Bel too, though she couldn't speak a word of it."

"He was in Whithorne? Where?" said Giles.

"At the Vicarage. Mr and Mrs Foyle were lionising him. It was quite funny but he was interesting and it was kind of him to give his books."

"Were the Professor and his son staying at the Vicarage?"

"No, they were living in a little house in Bull Street. Then they left. I don't know why. Didn't you know?"

"No," said Giles.

"It is horrible, then," said Louisa, pulling her shawl round her. "That it was him."

"And the son, did you have anything to do with him?"

"No," said Louisa.

"And you never heard anyone mention what brought them there?"

"No," she said.

"Did you know if they associated with Mr Yardley?" The girl shook her head.

"Well, that is very interesting, Miss Rivers. Thank you," Giles said, then looked through the open door to the adjoining bedroom. "Forget the papers for a moment. I'm looking for a straw top hat and a light-coloured frock coat. Could you...? I need to go and talk to someone urgently."

"Yes, yes, of course," said Mrs Maitland. "We are quite capable of finding those, are we not, Miss Rivers?"

~

With the pistol pressed hard into his ribs, and a firm hand on his collar, Yardley proceeded to force Felix into a covered gig. Felix contemplated for a moment hurling himself into the street, but in a moment Yardley was on the seat beside him and had the gun in his face.

"Put your hands out!"

Felix did so, feeling he had little choice.

"Now, just a small precaution," Yardley said, and clapped one half of a handcuff on him, and then fastened the other to the rail of the gig so he could not escape. "Never worn those before, I dare say. If you were a gentleman I might trust you without such precautions, but since half of you is such poor stock... A French whore, I understand? I've had a few of those," Yardley went on, picking up the reins and cracking his whip. "Deuced expensive, though. Why pay through the nose when you can get a pretty bit of English flesh for nothing? Not to mention Irish flesh."

Had he? Felix thought, nausea rising in his throat. Was Sukey even still alive? Had he...

"I hope that you did not do this to Mrs Connolly," Felix managed to say.

"Of course not," said Yardley. "I spun her a tale instead. I know how fond she is of her sister. She came willingly. It was easy. Women are so gullible, don't you think? Possibly she was attracted to me. Perhaps she is looking for a new arrangement, though it looked as if she was comfortable. A nice set-up all round, paid for by your illustrious sire, no doubt."

Although his spirit was in active revolt at this barbaric treatment, Felix knew he must hold himself in check, stay silent and save his energy and wits for whatever battle lay ahead. So he sat there, feeling the weight of the iron on his wrist, and tried to ignore Yardley's poisonous chatter. It was not easy.

He peered out, trying to work out where he was being taken. They were driving fast – Yardley did not spare the poor pony his whip – and taking a circuitous route of which Felix could make no sense. The quantity of rain falling was prodigious and masked any familiar landmarks in grey sheets of cascading water. The streets were deserted, and if Felix had wanted to cry out and get some help, there was no one to hear. It was as if Yardley, with diabolic powers, had hidden the ordinary Northminster away. It felt more like a nightmare than reality, and Felix prayed he might wake up and find himself dozing in Sukey's sitting room and her laughing at him for snoring.

At length they turned into a narrow lane that was terminated with a pair of half-open gates. They passed through them into what appeared to be an overgrown garden of some kind, but a garden on quite a grand scale. He glimpsed a row of crumbling statues dripping with ivy and brambles, and he sensed, despite the ingress of undergrowth and seeded trees, that there were carefully constructed rambles, made long ago to amuse ladies in hoops and men in tricorns. Certainly the path they went along, the brambles slapping at the side of the gig, twisted and turned in a fashion that was not the least bit straightforward, and he was quite surprised when it terminated abruptly in a commonplace stable yard.

Yardley jumped down and went to see to the horse. Given how badly he had just treated it, Felix was surprised to see how tenderly he took it out of the harness and led it away. He took the chance to attempt to loosen the cuff on his hand from the gig rail, but with no success, and wondered where he would go if he did, in those few moments, manage to get free. How long would it take to get back through the undergrowth?

At the same time he became aware of a most miserable sound emanating from the direction of the stables: a low animal howl of profound distress, the like of which he had never heard before. It touched him with a cold fear that seemed to set his limbs rigid. What creature could make such a noise?

Yardley reappeared.

"Oh, are you still there?" he said, leaning into the gig and releasing the cuff from the rail. "I thought you would be trying to make a bolt for it. But maybe you don't have that sort of fire in you. What a disappointment. You are nothing but a milksop. I should have taken your master instead."

"My master?"

"Vernon. A more worthy opponent than you," Yardley said, grabbing his hand and fastening the other cuff to Felix's wrist. "More of a challenge. I like a challenge of course, and it would be such a pleasure to lay such a one low. But perhaps he will come calling and then we will see who has more steel in his soul. In the meantime I shall have to make what amusement I can with you, Carswell. Out you get! Mrs Connolly will be wondering where you have got to."

With which he flicked the gig whip across Felix's face with some force.

Getting out of the gig with his hands fixed was not easy and ended in his sprawling in a great puddle, which caused Yardley much amusement, and he cracked the whip again across Felix's shoulders as he struggled to stand upright.

Felix would have lunged at him then and there, such was his mounting fury, but Yardley had produced the gun again.

"Let's go inside, shall we?" he said.

They went into the business area of what seemed to be a substantial house and then up the backstairs. They reached the landing, and Yardley pressed the pistol to his temple and forced him to walk along a passageway. Still with the gun to Felix's head, he took a key from his pocket and unlocked the door in front of them. He pushed it open a chink, and called out, "Now, Madam Vixen, if you were thinking of trying anything, I should tell you I have your lover here, with a gun to his head, so think before you act. I'm not a fool, you know!"

With which he kicked the door violently open. Felix heard

Sukey cry out. He realised she had been waiting behind the door to attempt an escape and he had probably just slammed the door into her face.

"In you go," Yardley said. "She'll be glad to see you, I dare say. A lover's reunion. Very touching," he added, and shoved Felix through the open door.

The room was dark and Felix could see nothing, but he could hear Sukey breathing hard. Then Yardley lit a lucifer and he saw her, standing with her back to the wall, her hands pressed flat against it. She was a little distance from the door which had swung wide open. She did not smile and there was no relief in her eyes. He held up his chained hands by way of explanation, and she gave a tiny nod of acknowledgement, before turning her attention to Yardley who was now lighting the candles on the mantelpiece.

As the candles were lit, he saw that they were in a large room with two shuttered windows. It was scantily furnished, but the walls were hung with pier glasses and sconces, the whole encrusted with elaborate plasterwork in the Chinese grotesque style, fashionable a hundred years ago. There was a canopy bed in the centre of the room made in the same fashion, but lacking all its hangings: it was a skeleton bed, with a sack of straw for a mattress.

Yardley lit four candles and then stood rubbing his hands, looking at the reflection in the glass above the mantelpiece.

He turned and made a courtly mocking bow.

"I'm so glad you both managed to come. I was feeling very dull. Since I have lost my dear companion in such irritating circumstances... well, something had to be done."

"Your companion?" said Felix.

Yardley did not answer but walked over to Sukey and put out his hand to her. She declined to take it, and he grabbed it instead and pulled her towards him.

"You know who I'm talking about, don't you?" he said to her. "You had him at your beck and call. I tried to tell him you were not worth the trouble, but would he listen?" He reached out and stroked Sukey's cheek, and she flinched. "No, but Georg would have his notions." He gave a great sigh. "And now the poor fellow has gone and I do not know where I shall find as good a friend."

"You and Holzknecht!" Felix said. "So it was him at the farm with you."

"Did you see our work?" said Yardley.

Felix grimaced. Yardley now had his hands on Sukey's shoulders and had pinned her against the wall.

"You were very unkind to my friend," he said to her. "Very unkind. I hope you are sorry for it. I suppose he didn't have enough money for you. After all, you have negotiated yourself a good position, considering Mr Carswell is only Lord Rothborough's bastard. His Lordship must be quite taken with you. Did you negotiate directly with his Lordship, ma'am? Is that the secret of all this?" Yardley laughed. "But then the *on dit* is that the noble Marquess is a fool when it comes to Mr Carswell. But perhaps you should consider your future. He was making love to my wife, you know. I had to throw him out of my house. No, stay where you are, sir!" he said, as Felix moved to intervene. "Or I will shoot her!"

With that he produced the pistol and held it to Sukey's chest.

"I might well do so, anyway," he said, looking at Sukey. "I have to say I don't really want her, though I should have no difficulty having her. I should be more interested in seeing you attempt to save her life. How does one get the bullets out, and so forth? I have always wanted to see a first-rate surgeon at work, and I do hear that of you, Mr Carswell, that you are accomplished at that, at least. And then if you don't save her, you can show me how to do a post-mortem – and this time you will let me assist you. You owe me that much, sir, you must admit it."

Felix could see Sukey's eyes were closed. Was she praying

for deliverance?

He found that he was too, but had no idea what form that might take.

Then he saw her put out her hand and lay it over Yardley's, where he was gripping the pistol. He wanted to cry out to stop her taking such a risk, but some instinct told him to hold his tongue.

"You might say you don't want me, sir," she said, in a soft, sweet voice. "But you know, I might want you. I like a bold man." Then she trailed her finger along the muzzle. "I am sure it might be interesting. And an honour."

Yardley glanced over his shoulder, and grinned at Felix.

"Interesting, yes, certainly it might be," he said, "wouldn't it be, Carswell?" He began to laugh. "Oh yes, ma'am, interesting."

"It would be good for him," Sukey went on. "Instructive."

"Oh, you are quite something, madam, are you not?" Yardley said, and stroked her cheek. Sukey smiled, her lips parted. "What a splendid idea."

There was a part of his disordered brain that was almost convinced by this piece of play-acting. Felix knew it was acting, but her tone cut through him like a knife. It hurt him more than anything Yardley had yet said or done. He stared down at his helpless hands and heard again in the distance the horrible roar of pain that he had heard earlier coming from the stable. He wondered if it was his tortured imagination conjuring it up, for it was exactly the noise he would have made to express his misery at that moment.

However, Yardley seemed to hear it too, and was distracted from the prospect of Sukey's charms. He went to the window frowning, and then in another moment left the room entirely, locking the door behind him.

"What the devil is that noise?" Felix said.

"I don't care," said Sukey, coming over to him, her gait

still clumsy from her earlier injury. "Oh God, will you look at your face..."

"What?"

"You're bleeding," she said. He went to the pier glass between the windows and saw that Yardley's horsewhip had left an impressive weal across his cheek. She began to dab it with her handkerchief.

"What you just suggested..." he began.

"Yes?"

"Were you in earnest?"

"Any other ideas?" she said, matter of factly. "What else can we do? It's his weakest point. We know that. And nothing disarms a man like a woman's attention."

"But –"

"If that's what it takes, then so be it. And you can give him a good whack on the head when he's at it."

"Unless he anticipates that," said Felix. "There is no way out of here, is there?"

"I have been thinking about that," Sukey said. "And now we have a bit of light. Look at this – the lath and plaster in that corner is half-gone with damp. I was pulling away a bit of it when I heard you coming up, but I couldn't really see what I was doing. If we both worked at it, we might be able to get into the room next door. It's just a partition wall."

He stared at her, lost in admiration at her suggestion. She was already crouched down in the corner, attempting to prise loose a lump of plaster. He could do little to help her with his hand, so he began to kick at the rotten wood that was already exposed, imagining with each blow that it was Yardley's head.

Chapter Thirty-seven

"I wondered when you'd show your face again, sir!" exclaimed Mrs Gale as Giles walked into the shop. "Or if you'd have the nerve!"

"I'm sorry, ma'am?" Giles began, as she bustled forward from behind the counter to confront him.

"You said you knew him – the German scoundrel!"

"Mr Holzknecht?" Giles said.

"Aye, him!" she said and gave Giles a poke in the chest. "And any friend of his is not welcome here, even if you are a high and mighty Colonel. If you are even that. I told my friend Mr Bickley about you, and he said, well –"

"What did Mr Bickley say?"

"That you sounded an unlikely fellow, and I think he is right. He usually is."

"Unlikely?"

"Untrustworthy," said Mrs Gale. "And given you came in here using that filthy Holzknecht as your calling card, I'm inclined to believe him. So, away with you. I shan't be helping you, sir, not for all your talk about Lord Rothborough's spaniels!" With which she made an emphatic gesture towards the door.

"Ma'am, I am very sorry Holzknecht has offended you – he has only ever been the slightest acquaintance of mine. Perhaps, though, I might be able to help you find some redress? What has he done?"

She looked at him long and hard.

"Mr Bickley told me not to trust you," she said.

"And I would advise you not to trust Mr Bickley," said Giles.

"Who are you?" she said.

"I'm surprised at Mr Bickley being so discreet," said Giles. "I am a police officer, Mrs Gale. Now please tell me how Holzknecht has offended you."

She hesitated a moment and said, "What's it to you? Are you after him?"

"Very much so. And his associate, whom I believe you also know."

Mrs Gale nodded.

"Mr Bickley did mention..." she began. Then she darted forward, turned the shop door sign to 'Closed' and fastened the bolt. "We'll go into the back and talk."

He followed her into the back of the shop where Miss Gale was sitting in the spaniels' favourite chair, staring moodily at the fire. She looked as if she had been crying, and when she saw her mother in the doorway she gave her a furious look.

"What now?" she said.

"This little trollop," said Mrs Gale, folding her arms, "was all prepared to elope with Holzknecht. If it hadn't been for the creak on the stair, she'd have been off out and away goodness knows where. Left in the gutter, I dare say! It's as much as you deserve."

"We're going to get married!" said Miss Gale. "How many times do I have to tell you that, Ma? Georg has it all arranged. Don't you think you can stop it! Mr Yardley is going to help us set up house."

"A likely tale," said Mrs Gale.

"I'm afraid I have bad news for you, Miss Gale," said Giles sitting down opposite. "Georg Holzknecht is dead. And we need to know everything you can tell us about his association with Yardley."

"Dead?" said Miss Gale. "No..."

"Oh, my Lord," said Mrs Gale.

"You're lying," said Miss Gale, shaking her head.

"No, he died in a fire in Silver Street in the early hours of this morning. With his father."

The girl began to sob bitterly, and her mother at once forgot all her anger and went to comfort her.

"How?" the girl said.

"We aren't sure yet. Could you tell me what you know about Mr Yardley?"

"Other than he's been my ma's lodger?"

"When was he last here?"

"He hasn't stayed here this year," said Mrs Gale. "I wasn't having him again. All that coming back at any hour of the day or night, and in such a state. And his nasty books and pictures." She gave a little shudder. "I only had him here because I needed the ready. I don't usually have lodgers, especially ones my dogs don't like."

"But he has been here recently?"

"Yes," she said with a sigh. "He brought that wretch Holzknecht here, and he spent a lot of money too, so I didn't like to be too unkind to him. I was afraid he was going to ask me if he could stay again, but he only wanted to have a few things sent here. He said he had a place of his own now but it wasn't ready."

"He's bought the Resort, Ma, I told you that," put in Miss Gale. "And he's going to have it fixed up nicely, and put Georg in as tenant, except that..." She began to cry again. "Except now he's dead!" She struggled up from her chair and fled towards the door.

"I know this is no comfort, Miss Gale, but you will find out soon enough that Holzknecht was not at all what he appeared to be. He was a dangerous, violent man and your mother's fears for your safety were well-founded."

"What?" exclaimed Mrs Gale.

"We have evidence that Yardley and Holzknecht together tortured and then murdered a girl out at Whithorne last summer. She was induced to leave her family by Holzknecht promising her marriage."

"No, no, no!" said Miss Gale. "No, you're wrong. Why are you saying this?"

"Tortured!" said Mrs Gale, almost at the same moment. "Dear Lord."

"What is the Resort, Miss Gale?" Giles said.

"It's to the north of Walmersgate," said Mrs Gale. "You know it, sir, I'm sure – that awful run-down place hard by the big manufactory that just went up. Funny sort of place to buy and fix up, if you ask me, but that's Mr high-and-mighty Yardley for you!" She gave a shudder. "Murder, you say? Well, that doesn't surprise me one bit!"

Giles frowned, annoyed he could not at once place it.

"By Walmersgate?" he queried.

"Yes," Mrs Gale went on. "It has great big walls all round it, and set back from the road, the gates are. Used to be a sort of pleasure garden – when my mother was a girl she said it was quite the thing, with wild animals and dancing and what not. When I was a girl they said it was haunted."

"Oh, I know it," said Giles, seeing it in his mind now. It was a bleak spot for a pleasure ground.

"I thought it belonged to Mr Bickley," Mrs Gale said. "He told me he was planning to build houses on it."

"No, he lost it at cards to Mr Yardley," said Miss Gale. "Mr Bickley thought he was cheating, but Georg said it was simply that Bickley is a fool compared with Mr Yardley."

"Oh, I see," said Mrs Gale. "Well, that explains it, why he was asking for Yardley that time. Seems he is as bad as I thought and a fool to cheat Mr Bickley, certainly. The dogs always know, sir, they always know," she went on with a sigh. "Look at them now. They love you, Colonel or whatever you are." They had both settled at Giles' feet.

"Major Vernon," Giles said, getting up, but not before caressing each dog's heads lavishly. They really were most attractive creatures, and he wondered if he should get another dog. "They certainly know more than we imagine," he added, thinking of faithful Meg's noisy vigil at Lord Milburne's door.

"I don't believe a word of it!" said Miss Gale. "I don't! I can't!"

"No, dearie, of course you can't now," said Mrs Gale, going to her and comforting her. "But it seems you've had a lucky escape."

~

Resisting the temptation to go at once and visit the Resort without reinforcements, Giles made his way back to Silver Street. It was not a pleasant walk. The rain showed no sign of letting up and the streets were becoming difficult to negotiate due to the deep muddy puddles that were forming on the surface. What drainage there was in the city appeared not to be working.

Northminster had not flooded badly for some years, but given the growth of the population and of the various new mills and manufactories, there was always the risk that the delicate equilibrium between the river and the city could be upset. A few more hours of unrelenting rain and there was the severe danger of an inundation.

Returning, he was gladdened by the sight of Mrs Maitland sitting at the Professor's desk, a cheerful fire behind her. She looked up from her reading and saw him standing at the threshold.

"The rain has not let up, I see," she said. "You look somewhat sodden."

"It is worthy of Whithorne," he said, unfastening his macintosh cape and draping it across the newel post at the foot of the stair.

"I am praying that Whithorne is spared," she said, as he came into the room. "Our poor roof could not bear it."

"I hope this roof holds out," said Giles, "and half the city bridges."

"I think we have found what you wanted," she said. Laid on the chaise, where the Professor used to lie, was a light-coloured frock coat and a straw top hat. "The coat seems stained in the lining," she said.

Giles picked it up and examined it.

"Mr Carswell may be able to do something with this. Thank you."

She gave a little shrug.

"I sent Miss Rivers to rest – she uncovered what we think may be Georg's diaries and she was keen to get on with it, but she went pale as a sheet and almost fainted, poor child. She's an interesting young woman. My son has good taste, and she has good sense to resist the onslaught. In other circumstances, I might even be happy that he was in love with her. But that is neither here nor there. However, this is," she said, holding out a pasteboard-covered journal.

He flicked through it. The pages revealed dense blocks of tiny script, interleaved with drawings that ranged from detailed studies from life to obscene and violent caricatures.

"You were right to send Miss Rivers to bed," said Giles.

"No, some of that is not fit for the eyes of a young woman," Mrs Maitland said, "no matter how intelligent."

"And I am sorry to pull you into this mire," he said.

"You must use what resources you have in battle," said Mrs Maitland.

"Do you happen to know if Mrs Connolly came home?" he said.

"No, she has not," said Mrs Maitland. "Your man Holt – what an excellent fellow he is – he did not find her at her sister's and asked me to tell you that he is looking about for her elsewhere. He went to the Roman church, and to Mr O'Brien's print shop as well. He took the trouble to make me comfortable, and then went out again." Giles did not answer at once, and she added, "That worries you?"

"Yes," he said after a moment. "It is not like her."

She nodded, and got up from her place.

"From what I gather," she said, "she had many good reasons to return to the house within an hour or two at most. She told Anne, for example, that that afternoon they would be checking over the linen, and given she seems to be a most perfect housekeeper, that is not the sort of appointment she would miss."

"Did Holt say he had spoken to Mr Carswell, or been to the office? She may be with him." She shook her head. "That is the most likely explanation."

"It is?"

He hesitated for a moment. "They have been living as man and wife."

"Oh, I see," she said, after a pause of her own. "Of course. Oh dear."

Was she shocked to find him living in such a household and tolerating such an arrangement? She certainly seemed a little uncomfortable, and he wondered if this information had clouded her view of him. That was perhaps a good thing – but he felt a strong urge to explain it all to her, and defend himself. He hated that she might think less of him, that his lustre had been diminished. He realised he had been taking great pleasure in her unconditional admiration – it was the wealthy relative of the pleasure he had taken in the fawning spaniels at Mrs Gale's.

However, to command that power over a woman was not good for a man, no matter how delightful it might be. It was better that she know his faults and adjust her opinion accordingly. It was better, on balance, that she thought nothing much of him.

"I am going to take these to Mr Carswell," he said gathering up the frock coat and the hat. "And if I may, I shall take you back to my sister's. I cannot have you labouring so long at this wretched stuff."

"I am perfectly content to do it. It needs to be done, after all. This passage I have been working on here – it is such a puzzle. It was written four nights ago, or at least that is what the date says, and there is drawing of a bear, and he keeps talking about a bear garden. Is there such a thing here?"

"There used to be," said Giles.

"This is the bear," she said, laying the book open on the table. "The hungry bear, he calls it." She tapped her finger on the open page.

"Does it say anything about the name of the bear garden? Or where it is?" said Giles.

"I had just got to this bit," she said, going back and taking up her notes. "Excuse me, this is a very literal rendering – it says something like: cut work, and went to the bear garden. The bear is very amusing. We throw him a – I am not sure what that is – a cut of meat, or some such – and he howls for more, and more, but we shall keep him short until his dinner has come. She was easy to convince. Y –" She paused and looked at him. "'Y' being Squire Yardley, do we think?"

"Yes, I believe so," Giles said.

"Miss Rivers found a letter from him. I'm sorry, I should have mentioned it at once." She darted across the room and took it up. "There is a familiarity of tone in it which suggests an association between them." She handed it to Giles.

It was addressed to the lodgings in Martinsgate that Mr Hardie had mentioned.

"This is excellent work," he said. "Thank you."

"Miss Rivers found it. It was well-hidden. She seems to have an instinct for where something might be concealed."

"She might well do," Giles said, and sighed. "She is far too quick-witted for her own good. What else do your notes say?"

"This is where it begins to puzzle me," she said. "It says 'Miss G was easy to convince'. Do you know who that is?"

"I think it must be Miss Gale," said Giles.

Mrs Maitland frowned. "Then it becomes rather unpleasant: 'Y says that we will toss for the pleasure of taking her maidenhood, but I do not care about it much, amusing though it might be. My heart cares only for one woman now, but she continues to run from me, like the hare from the hunter. But I believe she wants me to catch her. I can see it in her eyes. She is making me dance to her tune, and I know that I should not allow her to make such a fool of me, I will be the fool for her, as long as it takes, and then I will be her master forever. It will be worth the game to have her forever.'"

"And does he give any indication who this other woman is?" Giles said, his heart sinking as a distinct possibility came to his mind. "Does he give her name anywhere?"

"Susann."

"And is that the German form of Susanna?"

"Yes."

"That is Mrs Connolly's Christian name. Holzknecht had been pestering her. Well, more than that."

"Is this her, then?" said Mrs Maitland, pulling out another drawing from the paper. It was a portrait of Mrs Connolly. Giles nodded.

"I need to find Carswell," he said. "One can only hope that they are together."

"But you think not?"

"I do not like to come to any sinister conclusions until I have some solid evidence, but she has been away from home too long."

"You have a little evidence," said Mrs Maitland, "given the state of Holzknecht's feelings for Mrs Connolly. That came over clearly. He was utterly obsessed with conquering her."

"Yes," said Giles.

"Perhaps he told Yardley – given they seem to have been exchanging confidences."

"Given that they have already acted together before,"

Giles said, looking down at the stained lining of the coat. "And once Holzknecht is dead, what is left for Yardley but revenge against those who hurt him? And Holzknecht's death will have hurt him. The father is dead, and who is left to take his revenge on?"

"Mrs Connolly, who spurned his friend," she said. "Yes, go and see Mr Carswell, at once."

"I will take you back now as well, before a flood cuts the town in half."

They walked quickly down to the Northern Office and found the place deserted, except for Giles' chief clerk, Williams. He stated that Mr Carswell had left at a little after two and had not returned, and Mrs Connolly had not been seen. Furthermore, all the other constables had been requisitioned by Captain Lazenby to assist with reinforcing the flood defences and rescuing those stranded. The river had almost broken its banks up at Whiteladies Meadows, and the western quarter of the town was in imminent danger. There was a note asking him to report at once to The Unicorn for further instructions.

While he was speaking to Williams, Mrs Maitland studied the large map on the wall of his office.

"Where might this bear garden be?" she said.

"I believe it is this property here," he said, pointing out the area north of Walmersgate. "The Resort."

She nodded. "The bear – they said they were starving the bear. Keeping it short, until –"

"His dinner comes," Giles said.

"Is it like Mr Carswell to leave his work?" she said.

"He may have been called to some emergency at the Infirmary. He has had some cases in hand there." He turned to Williams and asked about it.

"No, sir, that can't be it," said Williams. "There was a message from them, asking for him. Two in fact. Oh, and Mr Holt came in and asked after him."

Giles took from the locked drawer in his cupboard a pair of pistols, a flask of powder and a pouch of bullets.

Mrs Maitland observed him making these preparations without any show of alarm. Her calm demeanour was impressive.

They walked in silence up the steep hill to the Minster Precincts. They were not alone. Many people of the poorer sort had decided to take refuge in the Minster, a traditional right of the city folk in extremis. They were labouring up towards Stephensgate, burdened with what possessions they could carry. Everyone looked drenched and miserable.

"I am sure my brother-in-law will have all the braziers burning in the Minster by now," Giles remarked.

At this moment a uniformed man on horseback came riding up. It was Captain Lazenby.

Giles called out to him, "Sir! I am sorry I have not been to see you earlier. I only recently got your message. I have been pursuing something else. Where do you need me?"

"Down at Whiteladies. I need a reliable observer and someone to take charge. I am sure the bridge there will go in the next hour or so and I cannot leave here. The water is backing up at Hall Street as well. It is looking serious," said Lazenby, dismounting and thrusting the reins of the horse into Giles' hand. "Take her, and tell me what you think. Send one of the constables back with your report. I have set up another headquarters at the Golden Lion Tavern."

"Of course, sir."

"God willing the structure will hold," said Lazenby, "but I am not at all convinced." He turned and began to make his way briskly back along the street, against the tide of people.

Giles turned to Mrs Maitland.

"You will be able to get back yourself, I hope? It is only a little distance from here. I have my orders, you see."

"Certainly you have," she said, taking the reins of the horse from him so that he could mount. "So you must go.

And I shall go and make myself useful, if I can, up yonder." He mounted up. "And I am sure that is all that your friends are doing," she went on, steadying the horse as he settled into the saddle. "Making themselves useful somewhere."

"Yes, quite so," he said, and reached out and caught her hand and squeezed it. "Good luck!"

"Good luck to you too!" she said, and turned and left him without another word. A few yards ahead he saw her stop to assist a woman with a struggling child.

Chapter Thirty-Eight

At a little after three in the morning, the rain stopped, and mercifully the bridges of Northminster were spared. However, the river had burst its banks at intervals and the great flood meadows to the south of the city were completely submerged. Some of the low-lying streets around the wharves had collected a foot or more of standing water. There were some unfortunates forced out of their houses but the warehouses at the wharves seemed to have taken the brunt of the damage.

Captain Lazenby's management of the situation had proved eminently sensible, and Giles could not fault his successor's handling of the resources available.

"An impressive piece of work," he said, as they met in the temporary headquarters Lazenby had established on the top floor of one of the warehouses.

"I hope you did not mind my issuing you orders," Lazenby said, as they stood drinking scalding coffee in front of a brazier bright with coke.

"Of course not," said Giles.

"I'm always conscious that you have laid such a sure foundation for me, Major Vernon," said Lazenby. "I've only begun to take things a step or two further and that would not have been possible without your work. Never more so than over the last twenty-four hours. You don't regret not being involved on an operational level any more?"

"I have operations of my own to keep me perfectly content," Giles said. "Speaking of which, I am conscious I owe you a report or two regarding my investigations. We have established a significant link between the dead Germans and Yardley, and a possible address for the latter in Northminster."

"That's good to hear. What do you need in the way of men?"

"I will let you know. I want to do an assessment first. I also have a lure in place to tempt him into the open. If that works, it will make matters much easier."

"Let me know what you need, and when, Major," said Lazenby. "From what you told me the other day, the man is a public menace, and the sooner he is dealt with the better. In fact, if I might take the liberty of issuing another order? Go back home and get some sleep. You will need your wits about you to deal with him, I suspect. Everything is under control here now."

What Lazenby said could not be argued with. To seize an hour or two of restorative sleep would be sensible, and there was the added benefit of seeing that all was well at Silver Street. As he made his way there, he hoped that he would find Sukey and Carswell safe by their fireside.

But as he unlocked the door, and an exhausted looking Holt staggered into the hall, he found his optimism vanishing.

"No sign of them?" he asked.

"No, sir. And not for lack of trying. What's the state of the river, sir? It didn't look promising when I was out an hour or so ago."

"Better now the rain has stopped," Giles said. "Wharf Street and St Martin's got a good soaking, but nothing worse than that, thank God."

Holt nodded.

"Shall I get you some breakfast, sir?"

"No, I am going to bed for a couple of hours, and you should too. There is nothing else we can do at this stage."

"Right you are, sir. I shall be glad of some kip, to tell you the truth."

The idea might have been a good one in principle, but Giles found it impossible to settle. After an hour or so, he dressed again and then made a careful study of the large plan of Northminster that hung on his sitting room wall. He could no longer delay his fears.

It was a little before six when he left the house and made his way up to Walmersgate. Here he found himself standing in a muddy lane just beyond the city walls, facing an eight-foot boundary wall. This was topped with formidable spikes, presumably to deter those who may have thought of entering the pleasure gardens without paying.

It was his plan to walk around the boundaries of the property and see how many entrances there were. From his study of the map, he had estimated the property extended to at least seven acres, which in its present heavily wooded and abandoned state would represent, to a certain kind of Northminster mind, a prime opportunity to make money. He could see why Bickley would have been so annoyed at losing such a parcel of land to Yardley.

He began his progress and came across two gates, made in elaborate wrought iron, but now entirely grown over with rampant ivy. Peering through them he saw what once might have been broad walks, completely covered in brambles and thorns.

He carried on for some minutes, keeping the wall on his left, and found a plain set of gates left wide open. This surprised him. Why was Yardley so careless in defending this citadel? Did he think that the reputation of the place would deter all but the most foolish visitor? Or, perhaps not he, nor anything of any significance, was there.

As he stood and tried to make sense of what he saw, holding up his lantern and marvelling a little at the relentless conquests that nature could make on unmanaged land, he became aware of a low, deeply disturbing sound, the origin of which he could not at once pinpoint. It sounded like a creature in profound distress. Was that an animal being tortured? The hungry bear – the phrase came into his mind, and he reached for his pistol, thinking of the realism of the sketch in

Holzknecht's journal.

There had recently been an atrocity involving a bear at a pleasure ground in Leeds, where the bear had escaped from his pit and killed both the owner and his wife before being shot. It had been written about at some length in the newspapers, and Giles wondered if Yardley had read it and taken pleasure in the story.

Had he acquired a bear and let it roam in his abandoned wilderness? It was a wilderness from which the beast could easily escape and cause who knew what kind of chaos.

Giles weighed his options, then put out his lantern. There was just enough light to find his way along the lane. He had no wish to draw attention to himself. Before he went in, he transferred his other pistol to his overcoat pocket for more easy access, and wished at the same time he had his favourite fowling piece to hand. That was surely a better weapon for hunting a bear.

He made a tentative progress along the path, noting as he did that there were deep marks in the mud, suggesting that a horse and vehicle had been along it recently. The path had been constructed to wind and twist, presumably to increase the element of surprise and delight of the original visitors to the gardens. Now the complexity had a distinctly sinister feel to it, perfectly suited to the character of Yardley.

He turned a sharp bend and came to a little crossing of paths, and looked around him, attempting to read the muddy track and determine which way to proceed. The animal cry had ceased for the moment. Yet, as he turned, he thought he saw in the shadows some movement suggestive of another presence and he heard the cracking of twigs underfoot, and the squeak of wet vegetation.

He peered into the undergrowth. Was that a flash of a red cloak he had seen? Surely not – it must be his mind playing tricks from lack of sleep.

He hastened on, as quietly as he could, and then heard

another swish of sodden branches. Then a woman's cry of surprise rang out.

"Oh, ma'am, did I startle you?" a man's voice said. Yardley, Giles thought, crouching down in the bushes. He went on: "In fact, you rather startled me! What an interesting encounter! To find you here, of all places!"

"Yes, Squire, it is," she said.

That *was* Emma Maitland. What the devil was she doing there? Giles wanted to get a clearer view, but he had no wish to advertise his presence. He began to inch his way forward as quietly he could, practically on his hands and knees.

"To what do I owe this considerable pleasure, Mrs Maitland?" Yardley said.

"I heard a curious sound, from the lane," Mrs Maitland said, rather as if she stood in a drawing room and this was an ordinary social call. Her bravado was both impressive and terrifying. "A most distressing sound, to tell you the truth. I thought I might be of some assistance."

She had heard the bear, of course, as he had.

"A distressing sound?" said Yardley. "How curious."

"I thought it might be a bear," she said.

"A bear! Goodness, why would you think that? What a fancy you have!"

"Not really," she said. "I had heard there might be a bear hereabouts. I thought it sounded dangerous, especially as the gates were unlocked. It was very easy for me to get in here, sir, so it might be as easy for a bear to get out, don't you think?"

"But a bear, ma'am, really?"

"I am sure there is one," she said.

Giles could now see the hem of her red cloak, but where exactly Yardley stood he could not be sure. He could, however, make out a little clearing edged by a low wall. Was that perhaps a bear pit?

Then, as if on cue, the animal began its piteous song again.

"And that noise, sir?" Mrs Maitland said.

"I see you have found me out, ma'am!" said Yardley. "That is indeed a bear, my bear. Would you like to see him? He is just here, quite safely lodged in his pit."

Now Giles could see Yardley. He had his hand outstretched.

"He's a most magnificent specimen, ma'am," Yardley went on. "Do come and see. Would you like to feed him, perhaps?"

"I don't think I would," she said.

"No, of course you wouldn't, but I regret to say you will have no choice about it," Yardley said, moving towards her. He began to laugh as he did. "It is quite fortuitous that you have appeared, Mrs Maitland. He is very hungry and you will make him an excellent bonne bouche!" Then suddenly he made a swift movement and produced a pistol, which he aimed squarely at her.

Giles sprang out of his hiding place, intending that the element of surprise would allow him to tackle Yardley and disarm him. But Yardley was too fast for that. He spun round and aimed the gun at Giles. He responded with his own weapon, and attempted to fire, but as he squeezed on the trigger, he realised that the rain had dampened the powder rendering his pistol useless. He reached for the other, but Yardley had his measure. He advanced on him, thrusting the pistol into his face.

"Hands up, sir!" he said, and Giles, feeling the cold metal of the muzzle touch on his forehead, had no choice but to comply.

"Oh, this is most interesting," said Yardley. "Shall I shoot him, ma'am? Would you like to see that?" Mrs Maitland did not answer. "Ma'am?" Yardley said.

There was a loud bang, which Giles knew to be a pistol shot. He assumed that Yardley had shot him but for some strange reason he could not yet feel the bullet.

He saw Yardley stagger back, his hand clapped to the side of his face. It took Giles a moment to understand that it was Yardley who had been shot. He glanced to his side and saw that Mrs Maitland was standing with her arm outstretched, a small travelling pistol in her hand.

Yardley exclaimed in fury and turned towards his assailant, now aiming his pistol towards her. Giles lunged at her to push her out of the range of fire, and another shot rang out. Giles hit the ground, a white-hot searing pain passing through his thigh and then his whole leg. He struggled to right himself but could not. He managed at last to drag his other pistol from his overcoat, but the gun slithered from his fingers. He closed his eyes, for the pain had become unbearable.

The bear was howling again, no doubt roused by the sound of the shots.

"Well, ma'am," he heard Yardley say, in a strangulated voice. "You may have winged me, but that shan't stop me feeding my bear. I have two bullets left, you know, and you have none."

Giles made one last effort to reach his gun. He was floundering in a muddy puddle, while Yardley, blood cascading from his open wound, now had hold of Emma, the gun at her temple. He attempted to manhandle her towards the edge of the pit but she was putting up a fierce show of resistance, and he was weakening. At the same time Giles hauled himself across the ground towards them. He grabbed hold of one of Yardley's ankles, and got kicked in the face for his trouble, but it was enough to allow Mrs Maitland to get free. Instead of taking flight, she gave him a violent shove and Yardley toppled backwards into the pit, bellowing as he did.

Only then, peering over the side of the pit, did Giles see the beast. Its mangy fur was matted with blood from a liberal application of the whip and its eyes were mad with hunger. It reared up, its claws extended, and attacked Yardley with a ferocity that was sickening to witness.

Mrs Maitland snatched up Giles' pistol and took aim. This time the powder did not fail. She shot the bear square in the head and it collapsed on top of Yardley, trapping him. He shrieked and fell silent.

~

"Did you hear that?" Sukey said.

"Gunshot," said Felix.

They were standing in the courtyard behind the house in the cold, dank morning air. They were covered with plaster dust and looked, he suspected, like a pair of ghosts.

It had taken hours to make a hole large enough to crawl through, and they had battered, bleeding hands to show for it. When at last they had finished, Sukey had slithered through first, with great efficiency, like an adder through wet grass. But it had been far harder for Felix with his cuffed hands. The effort had been ridiculous. He had felt like an old man as he lay sprawled on the floor of the adjoining room, attempting to catch his breath and find some strength.

They had allowed themselves as much time as they dared to recover, lying in each others' arms on the bare boards and feeling extraordinarily thankful that Yardley had not yet interrupted them. Felix's theory was that he had been in company with his punchbowl and had drunk himself into a stupor.

But even stupors did not last for ever, and they had got to their feet and crept out of the room and then downstairs, finding their way as best they could in the gloom. The back door to the yard made a noise to wake the dead, and they pressed themselves against the wall and into the shadows, feeling sure that at any minute they would be discovered.

It was at this moment they heard another pistol shot.

"Over there," Felix said, and began to run along one of

the paths opening from the court. In a matter of moments he found himself stumbling to a halt, about to fall over the man and woman who were crouching on the ground. It was Major Vernon and Mrs Maitland.

~

"I want to see him hang," Major Vernon said, as Felix inspected his wound. "Go and see what you can do."

"Yardley can wait," Felix said. "And you must save your breath. By the look of it, it is just a flesh wound, but as there is not much flesh on you these days, sir, it might be a little dangerous. Do you have your skeleton keys on you?"

"In my waistcoat pocket."

Sukey drew out the keys. Propped up against her and with shaking hands, Major Vernon managed to unpick the lock that secured the cuffs. Felix's hands were free again to make a proper examination of the Major's wound.

"As far as I can see it just grazed you, sir," he said. "But we will strap it up."

"If anyone has a pocket knife," said Mrs Maitland, "I can provide a bandage."

"There is one in my coat," said Major Vernon. Sukey passed it to Mrs Maitland, who calmly proceeded to rip a five inch strip from one of her petticoats.

"It is the least I can do," she said.

"What were you doing here?" Major Vernon asked through gritted teeth as Felix fastened a tourniquet. "Did Yardley entice you by some means or other?"

"This can wait," said Felix. "Silence now, sir, if you please."

"I will go and find help," Mrs Maitland said, and went running off, her red cloak streaming behind her.

Chapter Thirty-nine

Giles woke from an opium-induced sleep in a narrow bed. The room was comfortably warm, with a good fire going. It was just as well, for the rain and wind had begun again, rattling at the lattice window that was set high in the wall.

He became aware that Carswell and Captain Lazenby were there, talking quietly in the corner by the fire, and then more aware of the burning pain in his right thigh.

He tried to sit up but he could not, and his general weakness caused him to exclaim in frustration.

In a moment, Carswell was at the bedside arranging pillows and assisting him.

"How long have I been out?" Giles asked, now recalling being carried on a hurdle out of the Resort.

"A few hours – it's a little after one," said Lazenby. "Very glad to see you with us again, Major."

"You had better go," Giles managed to say. "My fate is hardly as significant as the bridges. How long has it been raining like that?"

"It just started up again," said Lazenby, taking up his hat. "And you are right, Major. You are in good hands here. I hope your mending will be speedy!"

"So do I," Giles managed to say, grimacing as another wave of intense pain passed through him.

"Keep me informed of his progress, Mr Carswell," said Lazenby as he left.

"Where are we?" Giles said.

"The Moon and Sixpence Tavern," said Carswell. "It was the nearest decent place."

"And Yardley?"

Carswell shook his head.

"Damnation," Giles could not help saying.

"He would have enjoyed being on trial too much," said Carswell. "He would probably have conducted his own defence and made a mockery of it all."

"You may be right," said Giles, closing his eyes against the pain. "Am I permitted any more laudanum?"

"Yes," said Carswell. "And you should eat if you can. I believe Mrs Maitland has that in hand."

Giles saw her red cloak hanging on the hook on the back of the door.

"What was she doing there?" Giles said. Carswell gave a shrug and pulled back the covers to examine the dressing. "What were any of you doing there, for that matter? I know I am foggy with laudanum but I want to make sense of it."

"He told Sukey her sister been taken ill, and prevailed on her to come and help her. And as for me, well, he got me at gunpoint. I didn't have any choice. Yes, I know it is pretty raw just now, sir," Carswell went on, having lifted the dressing and caused Giles to exclaim fiercely. "But it is just a flesh wound, thank God. If you rest properly and are sensible you will be back to full strength soon enough."

The door opened and Emma Maitland came in, carrying a tray. She had put on an apron patterned with faded checks, and in her plain, dark dress, could have been mistaken for the landlady of an establishment such as The Moon and Sixpence rather than the chatelaine of Woodville Park. But perhaps that was due to the careworn expression on her face and the bowing of her shoulders from fatigue.

"I have some good thick soup, Mr Carswell, which I think you should have as well as our patient," she said, and Giles wondered if he heard a note of forced cheer in her voice. "There is a message for you from the Infirmary. Mr Harper –"

"Then I will have some and go," said Carswell, taking the bowl she offered him and standing by the fire to eat it. "Mrs

Maitland knows exactly what needs to be done. Four grains in some brandy, every three hours, yes, ma'am?" She nodded.

Carswell made quick work of his soup, and shortly afterwards left.

"I wish I had his appetite," said Giles, who had managed only a few spoonfuls. "I must find it again."

"Certainly you must," she said.

He stirred his spoon about for a moment and took another mouthful. He watched her cross the room and stand at the table with her back to him. From the sound of it she was rearranging the dishes on the tray.

"Why were you there?" he asked. "I know he prevailed on Mrs Connolly, and threatened Carswell, but I cannot quite see how – he cannot have known of your connection to any of it."

There was a pause and then she said, still with her back to him, "It was nothing to do with him. I was there because – because I chose to be."

"I'm sorry?" he said.

She turned and came to the bedside.

"It was the sound of the bear," she said. "That awful moaning. I swear I would never have crossed the threshold if I had not heard it."

"The threshold of the Resort, you mean?" he said. She nodded. "But what were you doing there in the first place? You were at my brother-in-law's, surely?"

"Yes, yes, I was," she said, glancing away from him. "But I could not sleep. It struck me that I must go there. I know it was foolish but –"

"You went there of your own free will?" he said.

"I was concerned. I was stirred up. What I had read in Holzknecht's journals was so alarming. I was worried for you."

"But what on earth were you thinking?"

"That I wanted to help. That I could help you."

"In what possible way could you have helped, ma'am? Throwing yourself into danger like that?" The mixture of pain and exhaustion had made him speak far more plainly and strongly than he should. He saw her flinch and regretted it. Yet at the same time he could not at once put down his outrage at her stupidity. That was not too strong a word for it. "He might have killed you! He nearly did!" he exclaimed. "What were you thinking, for the Lord's sake? I had you down as person of good sense!" he said. "A woman one might rely upon, not some feather-brained fool!"

Now she turned away and he saw her swallowing down her tears.

"You should try and finish your soup," she said in a strangled voice, walking away to the table. He would in fact happily have hurled the wretched bowl across the room, especially as he was forced to watch her sit down on a wretched little three-legged stool. Or rather she collapsed onto it, as if she had been punched by him. Her tears overcame her and she sat sobbing, with her hands pressed to her face.

He leant back on his pillows, riding a wave of pain, both physical and emotional, the cooling soup bowl still in his exhausted hands. He knew she was punishing him with those tears, forcing him to see her misery, making him regret everything he had said. Another sort of woman would have run from the room, but she sat there, brazen in her wretchedness, allowing him to feel it all, and more.

"Do you think," she said, at length, having apparently mastered herself, "that I have not regretted every moment of it for myself? I do not need you to point out my errors, sir," she finished. She drew herself up to her usual elegance, the bow from her shoulders now quite gone, and returned to the bedside, taking the bowl of soup from him without another word.

He stared up at her and their eyes met. She sighed and shook her head.

"You seem, sir," she said, "to unlock a seam of stupidity in me that I didn't know I possessed. Or rather that I have deliberately locked up and attempted to forget. But we are all capable of goodness knows what in unusual circumstances. I have thoroughly lost my head, and that's the cold plain truth of it – just as I did before."

She walked away with the bowl, her back to him.

"Before?" he found himself saying. "What do you mean?"

"I didn't only admire your hair, Major Vernon," she said. "I was a foolish girl, remember, and what do foolish girls do when in the company of sympathetic, charming, kind young men?"

"But you were married," he said. "Happily married. Surely?"

"So you thought," she said, her back still to him.

"And I did not..." He paused. "Did I?"

She turned back to him, shaking her head.

"No. No, you did nothing wrong. It was all my fancy, my foolishness. My feather-brain. And I will pay again as dearly for my honesty as I did before."

"What do you mean?"

"I was foolish enough to tell my husband. I never learn, do I? I see the same bewildered disgust in your face, now. God forbid a woman ever raises the subject of her affections unprovoked! She should rather seal up her lips for ever!" He searched for words to respond to this, but she went on. "And now I have lost you, just as I lost him. If I ever had you, of course. I am only softening my fall with the hope that you may have felt something, however slight."

He rubbed his face with his hands, feeling his head throbbing now.

"This is too much now," he said. "Forgive me, but..."

"Of course it is," she said. "I shall give you some laudanum and leave you in peace. I can do that much for you. The landlady here, Mrs Prince, is a kind woman. I will give her all the necessary instructions, and of course Mr Carswell will be back before you know it. Then I shall go and take my leave of your charming sister."

She handed him the little glass of tincture mixed with brandy. He was moved to catch her hand, but she pulled it away with a brisk shake of her head.

"C'est fini," she said.

~

Felix found Sukey in her favourite chair by the fire in her little sitting room at Silver Street. She glanced up as he came in and then bent her head back over her work. For a moment he hesitated at the threshold, enjoying the sight of her, and at the same time nervous of breaking the silence.

"You should give yourself more light when you are doing such close work," he said at last, coming in and turning up the lamp.

"I was trying to save oil," Sukey said. "We are still a little short."

"You shouldn't be up at all," he said.

"I am resting," she said. "Look! Just as you told me." She pointed to her foot which was resting on a stool. "And it doesn't hurt much now."

After they had got Major Vernon to The Moon and Sixpence, Sukey's damaged ankle had given way again, and he had sent her home.

"May I have a look?" he said, pulling up a chair close to her.

"If your hands are warm," she said, and he could not help smiling. It sounded like her old playfulness. He reached out and pressed his palm to her cheek.

"Is that warm enough?" he said.

She pulled his hand away.

"Get on with it, will you?" she said.

So, as before, he pushed up her skirt, and loosened her

garter before rolling down her stocking. He did it as gently as he could, and as he took her foot in his hand and touched the swollen joint with his fingertips, she winced.

"Not that much better," he said examining it. The swelling was still prominent and livid. "We need to get this up a little higher, and another poultice." He reached for a cushion and raised it up. "I'll go and make something up. Before then, you will just have to make do with this." He bent and kissed the reddened flesh. "There is no evidence that it will do any good, of course," he added and kissed it again, "but it is worth the experiment. Yes?"

He glanced up at her, trying to read her expression, but at that moment the door opened.

"Excuse me!" Felix exclaimed. He was, he thought, the only person allowed to enter her sitting room without knocking and he highly resented this invasion. His words did not stop the intruder, however.

"What is he doing in here?" said Mrs O'Brien, sweeping into the room. "Sukey?"

"He was looking at my ankle," Sukey said.

"Oh, are you now?" she said to Felix. She went and pulled Sukey's skirts back down over her bare leg. "That isn't at all how it looks to me."

"I was just going to make up a fresh poultice," Felix said. "I didn't know you were here, ma'am," he added.

"Clearly you didn't. Major Vernon's man came and told me that I was needed. I didn't hear you coming back, sir. Do you make a habit of coming into my sister's private room?"

"I came in to examine her ankle," Felix said. "As you can see, she's had a nasty sprain, and –"

"What I can see is what I have suspected all along," Mrs O'Brien said. "Oh, saints in Heaven, Sukey, how could you allow yourself to do this? Haven't you any self-respect at all?"

"I don't know what you are talking about," said Sukey.

"Did you think I wouldn't guess?" said Mrs O'Brien. "Do

you think I am such a fool? Well, perhaps I am, for giving you the benefit of the doubt for so long, but from the moment you took this house, I have been wondering, and praying it wasn't so, that it couldn't be that my own sister would be so wicked! But it seems you are."

"Ma'am –" Felix began.

"Don't you ma'am me, you dirty rogue," Mrs O'Brien said, waving her finger at him. "Don't you dare open your filthy mouth!"

"When I spoke to your husband –" Felix went on, as steadily as he could.

"You told him a fat packet of lies!" she cut in. "All that talk about marriage, when I know that someone like you would never marry someone like Sukey. Never."

"I would marry her, ma'am," Felix said. "I have asked her a hundred times. She won't have me, and that's the honest truth!"

"What?" Mrs O'Brien turned to Sukey. "You chose this? You chose to be his mistress when you could have got him as a husband?"

Sukey did not answer for a moment, and then, pulling herself out of the chair and putting the weight on her good ankle, said quietly, "Marriage would have been misery for both of us."

"And this is better?" said Mrs O'Brien, grabbing her by the shoulders and shaking her. "To be living in sin? To be fornicating? Have you lost your reason, Sukey? Don't you care about your immortal soul?"

"I didn't care to put myself in bondage again!" Sukey said, pushing her sister away. "You wouldn't know about that, Bridey. Your husband is a good man, not a... You don't know what it is like to be a slave! Why should I ever submit to that again?"

"You're more brazen than I thought," she said.

"I don't know why you are so surprised," Sukey said.

"You've never had a very high opinion of me."

"But you could have married him, Sukey!" Mrs O'Brien exclaimed. "You could still, yes?"

"Yes," Felix said.

"There's no reason to be talking about bondage and slavery, you stupid girl," Mrs O'Brien said, in tears now. "He'll take you, and no one need be any the wiser about all this. You can save yourself still." She stretched out her hand to Sukey. "Otherwise, what can I do but never speak to you again? I can't let the children near you and – oh Sukey, just be sensible for five minutes, and sit down and think straight for once! Please?"

There was a silence. Sukey sat down again, and folded her hands in her lap.

"You're right," she said after a moment. "I can't go on as I am. I can't. I can't marry you though, Felix. It wouldn't work."

"We will make it work," he said, going towards her.

"No," she said. "Everything that has happened tells me it won't. We are better ending it now. I'll go home, Bridey. Mother and Father want me back now he's not so well. I can make myself useful there."

Chapter Forty

"It's such a pity you could not come to the christening, Mr Carswell," said Mrs Yardley.

Little Felix Yardley lay sleeping in his Gothic cradle while his mother gazed lovingly at him. Ostensibly she was wearing mourning, but it was like no mourning Felix had ever seen: her black silk might have been in the requisite dull weave, and her cap ribbons crêpe, but she had not stinted on her black lace. Felix was no expert but it looked extremely expensive.

"Did he behave himself?" asked Lord Rothborough, looking down into the cradle.

"Yes, he did," said Mrs Yardley.

"He is certainly a handsome lad," Lord Rothborough said, touching the boy's forehead with his forefinger.

"He suits his name, does he not, my lord?" said Mrs Yardley, smiling across at Felix, in a way that made him uneasy. He felt that the only way this situation might be considered bearable would be if he still had Sukey to discuss it with later.

I should be the one in mourning, he thought, failing to smile back. I have lost everything, and you, ma'am, have got everything.

He turned away and went to the other side of the room, where Miss Yardley was sitting at the tea table. Behind her was a great fireplace, the mantel of which was dripping with evergreens, ribbons and red berries. The castle had been decorated with the same lavishness with which Mrs Yardley had applied the lace. He was glad to see that much of Yardley's collection had also been removed. Gone were the stuffed animals, the gruesome paintings, the weapons and the instruments of torture. Had they lit a great celebratory bonfire in the courtyard? It would have been tempting.

"Come and sit down, Mr Carswell," said Miss Yardley, "and have a glass of wine. You look pale and cold, I must say. It is all this business – it has knocked the life out of you. Lord Rothborough, you should send him to Italy for his health. He has lost weight, I am sure of it."

"We were thinking of going to Italy," said Mrs Yardley. "Would it be safe to take little Felix, do you think, Mr Carswell?"

"I can't think why not," said Felix, accepting a glass of sherry. "He seems in perfect health."

"It is certainly doing my wife a great deal of good," Lord Rothborough said. "I would not have come back if I did not think she was improving daily. I shall be going back just after Christmas, of course."

"Is there much society in Florence, then, after New Year?" Mrs Yardley asked.

"A great deal. I'm sure you would find many friends there," said Lord Rothborough. "The Hamiltons, I think you know, and Mr and Mrs Gilisland?"

"Oh yes," said Mrs Yardley, smiling. "They were great friends of my father's. I didn't know they were there still. I have directed my letter wrongly. How annoying. Do you know if they intend to remain there long?"

"Indefinitely, as far as I know," said Lord Rothborough.

"I knew I was right to think of Florence," said Mrs Yardley. "I had a dream about it, that I was there. Now we shall go, Amelia; I am decided."

"Very well," said Miss Yardley, and added, "and we cannot persuade you, Mr Carswell?"

"I have my work," Felix said.

"I have had so many curious dreams lately," Mrs Yardley went on. "It is as if I have not had a dream for years. Perhaps I was too frightened to dream or had never been sleeping properly, but now..." She made a delicate gesture with her hands, that shook her lace ruffles.

"Only pleasant ones, I hope," said Lord Rothborough.

"Oh yes," she smiled. Miss Yardley nodded. Then Mrs Yardley shot out her hand and laid it on Felix's. "I still cannot believe how everything is changed. That we can think of going to Italy! I never thought I would be able to leave this house, and if it had not been for you, sir, and Major Vernon, then who knows how long this misery might have gone on!" And she squeezed his hand and her eyes filled with grateful tears.

"It is Mrs Maitland to whom you really owe the most," he said, gently taking back his hand. "She was the one who shot the wretched beast."

"Ah yes, indeed," said Miss Yardley. "It hardly surprised me to hear she was a fine shot."

"But," said Mrs Yardley snatching back his hand, "you and Major Vernon found him out. You saved us all and gave me my beautiful boy."

~

"She's a charming young woman," said Lord Rothborough when they were driving away in his carriage. "But I suppose that is wasted on you at the moment."

"Somewhat," Felix said.

"It will pass," Lord Rothborough said.

"Oh, will it?"

"Eventually, yes."

Felix pressed his hands to his face.

"How could she be so cold?" he said. "That is what I can't make any sense of. As if there was nothing between us. As if we had never –"

"Oh, I don't think it is so cold. She will be wretched too."

"I hope so! And since she has consigned herself to a

miserable penance, it's likely enough. But why, for the love of God?"

There was a pause and Lord Rothborough said, "You probably won't thank me for this, but I have made the usual arrangements for her. It gives her a little independence should she need it."

"The usual arrangements?"

"Yes, the custom is that those intimately connected with the family should be recognised for their service. It's not a fortune, but as I said, it provides independence. I would not want her to suffer unduly, and neither would you, I think, in the long term."

"She won't want that," Felix managed to say.

"Then, it will quietly accrue and perhaps one day she will need it," he said. "It can't go amiss."

"When nothing I seemed to give her was good enough? When all I seemed to do was make her unhappy? Why would she want anything to do with that?"

"It is a custom I like to keep," said Lord Rothborough, airily. "And she is a sensible woman when all is said and done."

"You agree with her?" said Felix.

"I did not say that," said Lord Rothborough.

"To say she is sensible when –"

"She has your interests at heart, as well as her own," he said. "She –" he hesitated. "She did write to me. It was a poignant letter, I must say, and you should console yourself as best you can, put aside your fury, and look to the future."

"May I read it?"

"No," said Lord Rothborough. "She was clear on that point and I agree with her. I burnt it."

"What did she say?"

"That will not help you, Felix. Yes, you are wretched with it now, and angry, but God knows, we all have disappointments in love, and we survive them. If we are wise, we learn from them."

"I do not have the stomach for homilies, thank you very much, sir!"

"No, of course not," said Lord Rothborough. "And I am quite used to you only listening to about a tenth of what I say, but I shall not stop my tongue because of that. One day, who knows, you may find yourself speaking to your own son like this, and you will remember what it was to be young and broken-hearted, just as I do, and try, out of affection, to put some kind of salve on the wound. However inept that might seem."

"Most unlikely," said Felix. "That would involve trusting a woman with my feelings, and if a woman I thought so much better than all others can still treat me with such contempt, then I am better off without one!"

~

Mrs Edward Latimer, lately Mrs Rivers, was now possessed of a drawing room and all the elegant objects that went with it. The silver candlesticks that had been the only ornament of her frugal house in St John Street, however, were not in evidence.

Her beauty was not diminished by the luxury of her surroundings. Rather she seemed perfectly placed, at last, as did her younger daughters who no longer played with wooden spoons on the kitchen floor, but had the command of a new property of their own: a large doll's house.

Louisa sat near them on a low stool, turned towards the game but not involved in it. In her lap she held the doll dressed in red silk that Bel had given to her sisters. Although she appeared much restored in terms of health and looks – her clothes smart new ones, and her wild hair carefully tamed and arranged – she did not seem to wear her new-found prosperity at all comfortably. She looked both haunted and hunted, and her smile of acknowledgement when Giles had come in was brief and barely polite. Then, when he had gone to shake hands with her, she had seemed to flinch, almost as if he had hit her.

"I thought Mr Carswell was coming with you," said Mrs Latimer.

"He will be here shortly," said Giles. "As will Mr Porter and Mr Wakefield. I have already had a preliminary meeting with them. It should not take long."

Now Louisa got up from her place and went to the window.

"She is nervous," said Mrs Latimer, softly. "She is still not sleeping. I was hoping to consult with Mr Carswell about that, if there is time. She talks of him constantly."

"He got her confidence."

She nodded.

"It has been hard for her to understand – all this," Mrs Latimer went on, making a little gesture to indicate her new-found state. "But with time, she will know it is for the best."

"It was a little surprising," Giles could not help saying. "And your son and Master Latimer?"

"They have declared a truce," she said. "For my sake and Louisa's, for which I am deeply grateful. It was an effort for them but it shows they both have reserves of character, do you not think?"

"Yes," said Giles. "I hope it holds."

"It will, you may be sure of that," said Mrs Latimer. "My husband and I are both determined," she added with a touch of steel, which suggested a sort of martial law had been imposed on the boys.

Giles had been surprised by Latimer's determination to marry Mrs Rivers. Her power over him must have been considerable, and his feelings profoundly engaged. He had struck Giles as a pragmatic, worldly man who would think long and hard before marrying a woman in such a complicated situation, with a host of troublesome dependants. He wondered what Emma Maitland would say of the case. Her piquant opinion on it would have been worth hearing and in that moment, he wished that he might go to her after this business and sit and talk it all through with her. However, that final passage between them and her subsequent emphatic withdrawal had made it quite clear that it would not be possible. There were of course many good and sensible reasons why he should accept her actions, but they did nothing to remove the desire to see her again, which at times was acute.

"Here is Mr Carswell," Louisa said from the window, "and the others."

"We had better go downstairs, then," said Mrs Rivers.

"Must I?" Louisa said to Giles. "Must I really? Cannot I write a letter or something for them?"

"It is better that you face them. They feel that justice must be served with this. Remember what you might be facing, Miss Rivers. This is merciful of them."

She closed her eyes for a moment, and nodded. Then she kissed the doll on the forehead and put it down on the stool.

~

"And in your opinion there was no way that a poison of this strength could have been created unwittingly, Mr Carswell?" asked Mr Wakefield, one of the magistrates.

The Latimers' dining room had been pressed into service as a temporary magistrates' court, with green baize spread on the long table, and the three Justices sitting, cabinet-room fashion, with their backs to the fire.

"No, it required skill and determination," said Felix.

Louisa was sitting at the far end of the room, her head bowed.

"But I would add," he went on, "that since Miss Rivers became my patient, I was able to see that she did not act out of mischief or malice in brewing the prussic acid."

"It is not mischievous or malicious to brew such a concoction with the express intent of extinguishing a fellow human's life?" said Wakefield.

"Not if you consider Miss Rivers' distressed state of mind. Miss Rivers was acting to help her friend. They had both been raped on several occasions by the late Yardley and John Earle –"

"That is only your opinion, Mr Carswell. Mr Earle denies any wrong-doing. He is adamant that there was consent," Mr Wakefield said.

"But he has resigned as Coroner and fled the country," said Felix, "which says a great deal, does it not?"

"You will have to excuse me a moment, Mr Carswell," said Mr Porter. "I am new to the facts of this case. I fail to understand how Miss Rivers could, in a state of – as you put it – extreme distress, behave so calmly and rationally. Those things seem to be entirely contradictory to me."

It was supposed to be a settled thing, a mere formality. He had not expected such a thorough examination.

"She is an intelligent young woman," Felix said. "We all deal with the buffets of fortune in our different ways. Miss Rivers, having suffered multiple rapes, chose to help her friend by giving her a merciful death. It was an act of compassion." Porter frowned. "Literature is full of cases where women who have been violated, destroy themselves out of shame. Miss Barker – I am sorry, Mrs Gosforth – did that very thing, and asked her friend to assist her."

"That a thing is glorified in literature does not make it justifiable, Mr Carswell."

"No, but it says a great deal about how we regard women who have had to undergo such trials. We prefer them dead and silent from shame. We think them spoilt, though the fault is not theirs. Miss Rivers and Mrs Gosforth were used like the commonest whores – indeed worse, because not a penny was put on the table at the end. Earle and the late Yardley raped them both, on more than one occasion. That we are sitting here quibbling over the rights and wrongs of Miss Rivers' behaviour strikes me as outrageous when John Earle has been allowed to escape the country without being charged!"

"We are not here to consider that matter," said Wakefield.

"Then why *are* we here?" said Felix, growing impatient. "To pillory a young woman who will never do anything outside the law again and who is perfectly aware that she made a grave mistake? Miss Rivers has a conscience, gentlemen, I have seen that for myself. I see no such evidence in the case of John Earle."

"You are passionate, Mr Carswell," said Wakefield. "I think we ought to hear from the young woman herself. Come here, Miss Rivers."

She came slowly across the room and stood next to Felix. He could see she was shaking.

"You have a gallant champion, Miss," said Mr Porter. "I hope you are grateful."

"I am," she said.

"Will you take the oath?"

"Yes."

She did so, and Mr Porter offered her a chair. She refused it, and continued standing by Felix.

"So, Miss Rivers, do you have something to say to the court?"

"I do, sir. I admit that I made a poisonous distillation of cherry laurel and supplied it to my friend Annabella Gosforth, so that she could destroy herself."

"Which she duly did."

"Yes, sir. And I wish I had not. I wish I had advised her to some other course, but I could not think of anything. We were..." Now her voice broke. "She was in so much pain. We both were. I know it was wrong, but..." She took a step forward and steadied herself on the table, with the outstretched fingertips of one hand. "Imagine she was your daughter, please, gentlemen, imagine if you knew what had been done to her, again and again, and that she did not even dare tell her husband, in case he thought her responsible..." There was a little silence while she gathered her strength again. "Yes, my poison killed her, but she was half dead already, and Yardley and Earle are to blame for that." Then with a burst of vehemence, she added, "And as for me, you may do what you like. I am half dead as well!"

Silence fell in the room again. The magistrates glanced at each other. Mr Porter, the chair said, "We shall withdraw and deliberate."

With which they filed out of the room.

"Well done," murmured Felix.

"I said too much," she said. She was breathing hard.

"No, no, not at all," he said.

"I told you they would hang me," she said and went back to her seat. Felix, in his turn, went to stand by Major Vernon, who was glancing through his notebook.

"I cannot think why they need to deliberate," said Felix. "I thought it was all agreed."

"Apparently not," said Major Vernon. "I hope good sense prevails with them. And Miss Rivers was impressive."

"Do you think you will be able to get something to stick to Earle?" Felix said.

"It will be a shocking injustice if we do not," said Major Vernon. "But it was good to get his name aired in court."

The door opened and the magistrates came back in. Miss Rivers was summoned back to stand in front of them, and Felix found himself twitching with anxiety on her behalf.

At last Mr Porter spoke: "This has not been an easy matter to decide upon. We do not like to dismiss such serious charges but in the light of somewhat exceptional circumstances, the tender age of the accused, and her clear show of contrition, we have decided that Louisa Rivers be bound over to keep the peace and no further action be taken."

Epilogue

Sitting by the fire at The Falcon Hotel, Felix gazed into the depths of his empty wine glass. He had drunk it down like water.

"Compliments of the management," said Major Vernon.

"For getting rid of their landlord?" Felix said.

"Apparently," said Major Vernon. He sipped his wine and made an appreciative noise.

"It becomes more and more like one of the Professor's tales," said Felix.

"I am surprised they did not ring the church bells for us, for saving the town from a demon," said Major Vernon.

"One hardly expects to run across one, even in this line of work. The complete absence of conscience – when conscience is what makes us human, after all."

"It's not so uncommon," said Major Vernon, with a sigh. "When one starts to look at the literature. There was a case in Southern France some thirty years ago – it's well documented. A man who had killed five girls after brutally raping them. He had absolutely no qualms about it. When he was caught, he told the investigative magistrate that it had been just like trapping rabbits for the pot. He was hungry and so he acted. He did not consider the women as anything but his prey. The doctors declared him to be suffering from moral insanity, but I do not like that term. To call it insanity is to cover such actions with a cloak of disguise. The man in France was rational and deliberate, just as Yardley was."

"What is required," Felix said, getting up and refilling his glass, "is a system to identify such types before they can do any real damage."

"A phrenologist would say that he could read such tendencies in the shape of the head. In fact, I had a letter from one asking if he could measure Yardley's skull. I did not pass it on to you, knowing your feeling on that subject."

"Thank you," said Felix. "Though it might have been amusing to write a thorough rebuttal."

"You probably would not have changed the man's mind," Major Vernon pointed out.

"True," said Felix. "I don't seem to have adequate powers of persuasion."

"You were persuasive this afternoon."

"I only said what needed to be said. If they had not bound her over, then..." He took a long drink of wine. "Thank God they did. It would be unbearable otherwise."

"Quite," Major Vernon said. "Her life will be difficult enough. She has too quick a mind for such a narrow place as this."

"I should ask Mrs and Miss Yardley to take her with them to Italy," Felix said. "They would do that for me. I am quite in favour there."

"I don't advise it," Major Vernon said. "Although it might be excellent for Miss Rivers, I don't think Mrs Yardley, if she has a tendre for you, would be pleased at having to take your protégée under her wing, when the girl is so handsome and clever."

"Oh Lord, I suppose not," Felix said.

"And I think you have extended your patronage quite far enough where Miss Rivers is concerned. She is best left alone, Carswell. No more chemistry books, certainly."

"Did you think I was making love to her?" said Felix. "She's a child."

"She is not any more – she's a vulnerable woman who has been through a dreadful trial. Of course, you were not making love to her, but she may not see it that way. You need to take care."

Felix took another glass of wine and flung himself into his chair. The Major had a point. There had been an earnestness in Miss Rivers' level gaze that equalled Mrs Yardley's fluttering eyelashes. How it was that he could be admired by women who meant nothing to him, and yet the woman he wanted above all others cast him aside?

"You haven't had a letter from Ireland, I suppose?" he ventured to ask. "Lord Rothborough had one, and burnt it, and told me..." He stopped, and then saw Major Vernon reaching into his coat.

"I shouldn't really let you see this," he said. "It is probably not what was intended."

He held it out. For a moment Felix hesitated to take it. He wished he had not asked for it now. He felt that the sight of her handwriting alone would be unbearable. But then temptation overcame him.

The letter was brief, polite in tone and mostly informative. But the final paragraph read, in her neat, round hand:

> Re Mr C. He has probably scorched your ear on the subject of my cruelty and cold heart. Do not trouble yourself to defend me – I have no defence, only the pain of knowing what could never be.

He read it several times and then handed it back to Major Vernon.

"Thank you," he said. He found himself surprised at how he was able to bear it. He had even derived some vague comfort from it, almost as if she had come into the room, kissed him on the forehead and then left again. He stared at the fire feeling the same pain of which she had written, but knowing at the same time that it had grown a shade or two duller.

He glanced at Major Vernon, who was also making a study of the fire, the letter still in his hand.

"Tell me, what did you think of Mrs Maitland?" he said, breaking the silence.

"Sir?" queried Felix, wondering for a moment if the Major was dreaming aloud.

"It strikes me I give you far too much unprovoked advice on such matters," Major Vernon went on. "And on what authority? I am as in the dark as you are."

"Do you admire her?" Felix said.

"I wish it were that simple. It does not feel as it has with other women. Not with my wife or..." He rubbed his hand across his face. "If I could label it admiration or affection or mere attraction then it might be a great deal easier. I could file it away and continue as I am. But she is..." He paused. "Not to be ignored. Tell me what you made of her."

Felix considered for a moment.

"Energetic, sensible, good-humoured, a good manager, a good nurse, very amusing. Oh, and an excellent shot."

"Yes," said Major Vernon, and smiled briefly. "A very good shot."

"Intelligent and well-read," Felix added. "A good mother, too, and I suppose one would say, she would make a good wife, now one thinks about it."

"Do you think marriage is even compatible with this profession of ours?" Major Vernon said. "Given what happened to my wife? And what happened with Mrs Connolly, and then Mrs Maitland – although she admitted she was reckless."

"Thank God she was!" said Felix. "We should have been lost without her. You did not chide her for that, sir, I hope." Major Vernon did not answer. "Is that why she went away? I must say I was quite surprised to find her gone when I got back to The Moon and Sixpence."

"I did. I suppose I shouldn't have, but dear God, it was foolish of her!"

"If you did, then you need not worry about her acting so

rashly again," Felix said. "She will not dare."

Major Vernon got up and walked across the room, drew back the curtain and stared out into the frosty night.

"Am I such a tyrant?" he said.

"No, I only meant that you have a way of putting things so that sensible folk take heed."

"Very tactful. I was a brute. And now..." He gave a shrug and pulled back the curtain. "Is there any of the wine left?"

"Yes," Felix said, refilling his glass and taking it over to him. "Here. And you asked me what I thought of her; well, she and you seem to be cut from the same cloth. And perhaps, in time...?"

Major Vernon took the wine but did not answer. He was looking out into the street.

"It's started snowing," he said at length. "We shall have cold work of it tomorrow."

~

The burial of Mary Taylor and her unborn child took place the next day at noon, in the churchyard of the parish church that had witnessed her baptism and confirmation. The snow had continued to fall and settle overnight, and Felix and Major Vernon had some difficulty getting there, but were in time for the final committal.

An ancient pair of yews, dressed in unaccustomed white, formed the backdrop to the black-clad figures of the Taylor family and their neighbours around the open grave. The snow eased off a little as if out of respect, just as the clergyman read the final prayers.

There was silence after that, as the mourners moved away, their footsteps muffled in the snow. Mr and Mrs Taylor remained alone there, looking down into the grave.

Farmer Taylor was openly weeping, perhaps for the

reconciliation which could never come, while Mrs Taylor had her arms about him, as if she meant to hold him up. She looked across and saw them.

Felix remembered her standing in the kitchen, denying the very existence of her child. Now she beckoned them over.

"Thank you for bringing her back to us," she said, in a voice dry from crying. "And the baby."

"Yes," muttered Mr Taylor, drying his tears as best as he could. "Yes. But it's a wicked shame those evil buggers couldn't have gone to the gallows."

"God will judge them, Sam, and that will be that," said Mrs Taylor. "And they cannot harm another poor soul now, thank the Lord." She gave a shudder and turned away from the grave, and began to make her way back through the snow, with Taylor following after.

The snow came on again more thickly, and Felix and Major Vernon also made haste to get to the shelter of the carriage. As they passed through the Lych Gate, they were surprised to find Mrs Herne standing in the corner, wearing a bright red cloak.

"My boy was right about them being devils," she said.

"He certainly was," said Major Vernon. "Is that cloak not –?"

"Your lady's fine cloak, yes, sir," said Mrs Herne. "She gave it to me before she set off to Oxford with her lad. A great kindness, after so many others."

"Not *my* lady, alas," said Major Vernon.

"Hold your faith, sir," she said, laying her hand on his arm. "It's marked in the stars that you and she will be man and wife. Trust me."

"No cheerful prophecies for me," said Felix, when they were in the carriage again.

"I'm inclined to be sceptical about that one," said Major Vernon, reaching into his pocket and taking out a sheaf of papers.

"What are those?"

"Intelligence reports – mutinous navvies." Giles handed Felix some of the papers. "I'd appreciate your thoughts."

It was a matter about which he knew nothing, but he welcomed the chance to push aside gloomy thoughts. As the carriage made its tentative progress, the pure light reflected by the snow sharpened the words on the page. They sat in silence, absorbed in their reading. What the future might hold was as hidden as the features of the snow-covered landscape, and Felix resigned himself to the necessity of uncertainty. There was comfort, at least, in work and friendship.

~ THE END ~

Dramatis Personae

Northminster

Major Giles Vernon: Chief Superintendent of the Northern Investigation Office

Felix Carswell: consultant surgeon to the Northern Office

Sukey Connolly: landlady of the house in Silver Street where Giles and Felix live

Herr Professor Holzknecht: an exiled German scholar, famous for his collection of fairy tales, also a lodger in Silver Street

George Holzknecht: Professor Holzknecht's son

Tom O'Brien: proprietor of The Bugle

Bridget O'Brien: Tom O'Brien's wife and Sukey's sister

Whithorne Castle

Briggs Yardley: landed gentleman and the owner of Whithorne Castle, known as Squire Yardley

Mrs Yardley: Squire Yardley's wife, a wealthy heiress in her own right

Miss Amelia Yardley: elder sister of Squire Yardley

Whithorne

Dr Fellowes: a physician

John Earle: a solicitor and the coroner

Mr Ampner: a prosperous and respectable attorney

Mrs Ampner: Mr Ampner's wife

Mr George Gosforth: Mrs Ampner's younger brother

Miss Annabella Barker: an alleged heiress and Mr Ampner's ward

Mrs Rivers: a beautiful but impoverished young widow

Louisa Rivers: Mrs Rivers' daughter

John Rivers: Mrs Rivers' eldest son

Mr Patchett: keeper of The Black Cat Tavern

Edward Latimer: a wealthy local banker

Woodville Park

Charles, Lord Milburne: unexpected heir to the title and property

Mrs Emma Maitland: his mother, widow of Major Maitland and old acquaintance of Major Vernon

Mrs Patton: Mrs Maitland's maid

Mrs Herne: a gypsy

About the Author

Harriet Smart was born and brought up in Birmingham. She attended the University of St Andrews, where she read History of Art, and married a fellow student. She now lives with her husband in an eighteenth-century house in Northumberland.

Harriet has an M.A. in screenwriting. She has published twenty novels as well as helping to design the creative writing software Writer's Café and the e-book editor software Jutoh.

She has been writing the Northminster Mysteries since 2010.

You can follow Harriet at www.harrietsmart.com and BookBub.

Printed in Great Britain
by Amazon

36800612R10233